"My dear Sarianna, of course you will be mine." He grasped her shoulders suddenly and turned her against the nearest tree so that she could not move past him.

"I see," she said coolly. "And do you mean to tie me to the tree until I submit?"

"Oh no," Cade murmured, "I mean to capture your lips and prove you are capable of the kind of feeling that will lead you to my bed," and he lowered his head meaningfully, slanting his mouth across hers, waiting for her to deny him and sure that she wouldn't.

"This is hardly proper," she managed to say with some asperity.

"We don't have time to be proper, Sarianna," he said roughly. His mouth hovered over hers for a long, breathtaking moment before he crushed her lips beneath his, seeking to imprint her with his urgency and his ever growing desire.

Possession was everything, and he possessed her now as she came to him willingly, seeking his kiss with a hunger that was growing greater than his own, making her yearn for the very thing she thought she would never have—someone who would love and desire her as she was for all she was. . . .

ROMANCE REIGNS
WITH ZEBRA BOOKS!

SILVER ROSE   (2275, $3.95)
by Penelope Neri

Fleeing her lecherous boss, Silver Dupres disguised herself as a boy and joined an expedition to chart the wild Colorado River. But with one glance at Jesse Wilder, the explorers' rugged, towering scout, Silver knew she'd have to abandon her protective masquerade or else be consumed by her raging unfulfilled desire!

STARLIT ECSTASY   (2134, $3.95)
by Phoebe Conn

Cold-hearted heiress Alicia Caldwell swore that Rafael Ramirez, San Francisco's most successful attorney, would never win her money . . . or her love. But before she could refuse him, she was shamelessly clasped against Rafael's muscular chest and hungrily matching his relentless ardor!

LOVING LIES   (2034, $3.95)
by Penelope Neri

When she agreed to wed Joel McCaleb, Seraphina wanted nothing more than to gain her best friend's inheritance. But then she saw the virile stranger . . . and the green-eyed beauty knew she'd never be able to escape the rapture of his kiss and the sweet agony of his caress.

EMERALD FIRE   (1963, $3.95)
by Phoebe Conn

When his brother died for loving gorgeous Bianca Antonelli, Evan Sinclair swore to find the killer by seducing the tempress who lured him to his death. But once the blond witch willingly surrendered all he sought, Evan's lust for revenge gave way to the desire for unrestrained rapture.

SEA JEWEL   (1888, $3.95)
by Penelope Neri

Hot-tempered Alaric had long planned the humiliation of Freya, the daughter of the most hated foe. He'd make the wench from across the ocean his lowly bedchamber slave—but he never suspected she would become the mistress of his heart, his treasured SEA JEWEL.

Available wherever paperbacks are sold, or order direct from the Publisher. Send cover price plus 50¢ per copy for mailing and handling to Zebra Books, Dept. 2665, 475 Park Avenue South, New York, N.Y. 10016. Residents of New York, New Jersey and Pennsylvania must include sales tax. DO NOT SEND CASH.

Shameless Ecstasy

THEA DEVINE

ZEBRA BOOKS
KENSINGTON PUBLISHING CORP.

ZEBRA BOOKS

are published by

Kensington Publishing Corp.
475 Park Avenue South
New York, NY 10016

Copyright © 1989 by Thea Devine

All rights reserved. No part of this book may be reproduced
in any form or by any means without the prior written
consent of the Publisher, excepting brief quotes used in
reviews.

First printing: May, 1989

Printed in the United States of America

With much love, for my parents, Murray and Claire Cohn, who had the wisdom and foresight to buy me my first typewriter.

And unending appreciation to my wonderful John—I owe you for this one.

1

"*Sarianna!*"

Jeralee Wayte paused and then made a moue of impatience when this imperious summons was not immediately answered. She dropped the filmy curtain over the French window out of which she had been looking at the long, empty front driveway, and turned abruptly toward the hallway door to find one of the housemaids had silently entered at her call.

"Alzine! Where is Miss Sarianna? I need her up here immediately."

"Yas'm," Alzina said and glided toward the doorway. "She done gone to confer with Mr. Rex, I expect; you want me to pull her away from dat?"

"I do," Jeralee said unequivocally, dismissing Alzine and turning her attention back to the window. She could see no clouds of dust yet, but the steamer must have arrived; the guests had to be on their way. She felt a thrill of excitement as she hugged her wrapper closer to her body. She had to see who had come—if *he* were coming—and then she could get dressed and sweep down the stairs to make her entrance. Where *was* Sarianna?

Her exasperation heightened as she heard their driver's horn. The carriage was coming, and Sarianna had not appeared. But heavens— there had been two carriages, maybe three, and several saddle horses. And two boatloads of neighbors and friends. He might not—

"My dear Jeralee, *why* are you exposing yourself in that window?" Sarianna's voice inquired gently behind her.

She whirled, and there was Sarianna, all cool and dressed, ready for a party in her usual no nonsense way, her oval face composed, her

7

golden hair a mop of unruly curls that could not be contained in a ladylike net snood, which even now was hanging down the back of her serviceable blue silk dress.

Well, she had no time to teach Sarianna the niceties; that was for Mama anyway. She drew back the curtain and flung open the French doors. "Hurry."

"For what?"

"You have to stand out on the balcony and tell me who is arriving."

"I?" Sarianna asked with just a touch of mockery in her tone.

Jeralee looked at her warily. She always had the feeling that Sarianna was laughing at her. There was always just the faintest amused twist to her firm lips, the merest tone in her voice that told Jeralee that Sarianna knew exactly what she was about and wasn't fooling anyone. Jeralee hated it, but she needed Sarianna just at this moment.

"Yes, *you*. I can't be standing there, looking as if I'm *waiting*," Jeralee said irritably.

"And *I* can?"

"But you're not waiting for anyone," Jeralee pointed out; she knew she did not need to finish the sentence: *Because no one ever comes to see you*, was implicit in her provoking tone of voice, and she saw by the flashing blue light in Sarianna's eyes that her pointed gibe was taken exactly as she had meant it.

"And you are?" Sarianna questioned, edging over to the window.

"That man Mama met in Savannah she said she used to know. He is the most dangerous animal I have ever seen—from afar that is—and Mama said he is deliciously rich; she found out all about it before she invited him. I told you all this . . . please, Sarianna—tell me if you see anyone like that. He's got dark hair—black—he's tall, and he looks . . . rough."

"Vesta's instincts about gentlemen do run true," Sarianna murmured, not a little curious herself to see who had gotten the very self-absorbed Jeralee into such a pelter. And if she were taking care of this little need of Jeralee's, she did not need to be downstairs catering to Vesta or her father. Six of one, she thought moodily as she stepped onto the balcony, but on the whole, she would rather watch the guests arrive, even if she knew the guest list by heart. Vesta's mysterious invitee was another matter, and Vesta had been annoyingly coy about his identity.

"Let's see—the Grays and Rudleys are just emerging from the carriage; it doesn't look as if any rough gentleman has accompanied them. I doubt if they would have gotten in the same carriage with him at any rate. Oh, and Eula is with them, and Victoria. Peter and William. This is ridiculous, Jeralee."

"Yes, but he said he'd come. He said he was coming anyway, so Mama had no choice but to invite him since everyone else is coming," Jeralee said, peering over Sarianna's shoulder, using Sarianna's body to conceal her own.

"You're talking in riddles," Sarianna snapped, shielding her eyes to see in the distance. Another horn sounded, and the second carriage heaved into view. "Besides, a *rough* man might not like to be confined in a carriage with all those perfumed ladies and gentlemen."

"I only caught a glimpse of him," Jeralee said defensively. "But Mama was right glad to see him, and he had the broadest shoulders."

"Pure nonsense," Sarianna said, "as if shoulders make him eligible. And what did my father say to all this?"

"Rex said Mama could invite anyone she liked."

"I bet he did," Sarianna muttered beneath her breath. "Ah—here come the Langfords; Emory Bardell is with them—Emory? Now really, Jeralee, he couldn't remotely be said to have broad shoulders. . . ."

"Ooo—is Gaff with them?"

"He's probably riding; Gaff couldn't fit his length into one of these carriages. Yes—I see him; you know he does have rather a distinct seat."

"Trust you to notice a man's bottom," Jeralee sniped.

"Spoken like a proper gentlewoman who doesn't like horses," Sarianna shot back. "What if your *rough* stranger comes from the vast west and is accustomed to *sleeping* on them?"

"Oh, hush, what do you know about what men do or where they sleep? For heaven's sake, Sarianna . . . someone else is coming—"

"Samuel Summers," Sarianna said flatly.

"Damn; he will probably ask Mama if he can address me still another time. That man is so desperate for a second wife he would even propose to *you*, Sarianna."

Sarianna stiffened, and Jeralee pretended to—or really did not notice. She slid her curious chocolatey gaze around Sarianna and went so far as to move out from behind the cover of Sarianna's body.

"Look at him. Flabby as a fish. Fifty if he is a day."

"And what was my father, pray, when he asked Vesta to marry him?"

"Oh, but Rex . . . really, Sarianna, there's no comparison. Rex is so elegant, so refined in his manners. Samuel may have ancestors, but he has no deportment whatsoever."

"He is a kind man," Sarianna said, her face softening in sympathy for Samuel Summers' cruel and casual dismissal by Jeralee. Jeralee could do worse, she thought. Maybe Jeralee needed a kind, lax, wealthy older man who wouldn't take a firm hand to her, and would let her spend his money as she would. Lord knew her own father could not control her. "And he has pots of money. *Three* plantations, Jeralee. And nothing to do with the money but plow it right back into seed and fertilizer. You had better rethink your position on him, I really think so."

She was amused as she felt Jeralee's body shift, almost as if Jeralee were considering what she had said, that the bottom line figures might make an unenticing man that much more appealing. She could even predict what Jeralee was thinking: All that money and no one to spend it on. And what if he decided he wanted Sarianna, and Sarianna married him, then he died. Sarianna would have all that wealth to herself, and then Sarianna would be courted and petted and even Rex wouldn't mind that she hadn't been the son he desperately wanted. No one would even care about her funny left-handedness because she would be her own mistress then. And Sarianna would have everything that Jeralee wanted—money and independence.

"You might be right," Jeralee said thoughtfully. "But—oh! Look! That's *him*, I *know* that's him. He's riding. I knew he would ride. Quick, Sarianna—isn't he fantastic?"

"How can I tell?" Sarianna murmured, against the quivering excitement of Jeralee's words. She lifted her hand over her eyes once again to study the figure on the cantering stallion. He sat ramrod straight, moving elegantly with a horse he had never ridden before. He was dressed plainly, and she could not see his features from that distance, only that his dark hair seemed to be unfashionably long, and that he wore no hat. Beside him, another man rode, also someone she did not know, but this one was not comfortable on horses. A city man, she thought, curious. Someone Rex would not have invited to his home.

10

"Oh, God," Jeralee moaned. "Don't let him see me!"

"Don't be ridiculous. I'm the only one anyone can see, and we all know no one wants to see me," Sarianna snapped with intense bitterness in her voice. The pair drew closer, and she wondered angrily what indeed they did or could see from that level on the long moss-overhung drive. There was a point at which the house would just come into view, the columned portico rising impressively over the dentil molded doorway; the little balcony overhead on which she now stood set in the shadow of the roof's overhang would just become visible, its white balustrade hardly noticeable against the pristine white of the house.

But she, gowned in blue, her golden hair in furious disarray *as usual,* she might be eminently noticeable against the dark recesses of the room behind her.

She crossed her arms militantly in front of her. And what if they noticed her? All she needed to do was protect Jeralee's unholy curiosity while allowing her the moment of triumph she craved that the man her mother had as good as begged for her had indeed shown up.

Well fine; she, Sarianna, did not need any of that folderol. She made her own choices, and decidedly, in the face of her father's and Vesta's doing everything in their power to prevent her from making any decisions at all.

They had yet to contend with her determination, she thought grimly, as the mystery pair came closer and closer. She never wanted to hurt her father, in spite of what he felt about her, but she knew she had the courage to do even that if the choice were necessary.

But Jeralee would have it all handed to her. Jeralee palpitated behind her like a native drum. "What does he really look like?" she whispered.

"Dark—and rough," Sarianna said loudly, her resentment oversetting her common sense. It happened so rarely; she had schooled herself against letting it happen because it was not the way to get things done. She barely noticed the men as they passed by the balcony, except—"And his shoulders are broad. Maybe he'll carry you off into the night, Jeralee. I'd be eternally grateful to him for that favor."

"*Hush you!*" Jeralee hissed. "Don't you ruin this for me!"

"Me? *Me?*" Sarianna whirled to face her, just catching the sharp

11

ferrety little look that turned Jeralee's expression predatory. An instant later it was gone, and Jeralee was beautiful again, her full lips smiling and coaxing, her chocolate brown eyes warm and melting. She thrust a handful of her chestnut brown hair away from her shoulder and turned away from the balcony.

"No, you couldn't ruin it for me no matter what you did," Jeralee said slyly. "I think it's time for me to get dressed. Would you like to help?"

But what she was asking, Sarianna knew as she followed Jeralee down the hall, was, would you like to see how much more beautiful *my* gown is than yours? Look at how much money your father lavishes on me.

And indeed he did. A second daughter—even a stepdaughter—was a daughter. A first daughter was a disappointment. She was everything that Sarianna wasn't, spritely, gay, full of odd little graces and flirtatious looks. She had the beauty, which privately Sarianna thought had always been spoiled by her nose, which, while it was proportionate to her face, was faintly curved and pointed. At a certain angle, that nose gave Jeralee's face a wolfish look, and if she had known it, Jeralee would have practiced before a mirror so she would never tilt her head to quite the same degree again.

Alzine was waiting. "Company's come," she announced primly.

"We know," Jeralee said brusquely, pushing her way into her bedroom, which was a huge corner room overlooking the side and back of the house, and which had a dressing room fixed up in an ell off of the bedroom solely for Jeralee's multitudinous dresses. "Where is my gown?"

"Yas'm, I done ironed out de wrinkles and hanged it back in de little room."

"Good. Go get it then, and Miss Sarianna will help me dress."

Sarianna frowned, catching Alzine's speaking look as she passed her to get to the dressing room.

Jeralee picked up on the frown. "Oh, are you busy? Was Merleen going to fix your hair or something? I thought you were already dressed."

"I'm at your disposal," Sarianna said with a trace of irony in her voice. She turned away from the hurt and the malice in Jeralee's voice, and caught sight of herself in the dressing table mirror. Oh, yes, she was already dressed, and she was well aware that her watered-blue silk was just that little bit unfashionable, with its bell-shaped skirt and fitted bodice that might have been popular ten years before. Nonetheless, the style suited her, and she hated the corsets and whaleboned crinoline cage that women like Jeralee wore gracefully as a matter of course.

"Oh, why don't you just take the netting off if it won't stay put?" Jeralee demanded behind her as Alzine assisted her into the crinoline support.

Sarianna gazed at her machinations in the mirror, fascinated by the awkward elbows and wriggling and adjustments. Jeralee was not shy about parading around in her undergarments when Sarianna was around, but Sarianna supposed that Jeralee felt by comparison she had nothing to fear from *her*. Even beside such natural abundance, Sarianna did not disappear into the wall, and Sarianna supposed that Jeralee had to try, in her mean way, to make the distinction anyway. *But I won't go away,* Sarianna thought angrily as she watched Jeralee, *and nothing she can do will make me think more of her and less of myself. Nothing.*

Impatiently she pulled at the net, tore it, and tossed it onto the dressing table while she scavenged in her unruly curls for the pins. So she was thin, she thought, assessing her reflection. And her chin was a mite too squared, and her lips a touch too thin. Still, there was a dimple that caressed the side of her mouth when she smiled, and her eyes were that brilliant blue that everyone said was the exact shade of her mother's. Her complexion was excellent, she knew, and owed its faintly gilded glow to the hours she spent outdoors without a hat, against all rules. Her hair was impossible, the same tousled golden mane as her mother's, though she seemed to remember that her mother had somehow tamed it. Nonetheless, she couldn't or perhaps, she thought ruefully as she screwed her face up at her reflection, she did not want to take the time.

"May I borrow your brush?" she asked Jeralee, who was now holding on to one of the posts of her four-poster bed while Alzine pulled at the fastening tapes of the cage.

"Don't you go mucking up my brushes with your hair," Jeralee said petulantly as Alzine pulled one last time and then quickly bowed over the loose ends. "Come help with the dress now, Sarianna. You can do your hair later."

Sarianna stood up, afraid to trust her expression, but Jeralee was

13

gazing at the dress as Alzine brought it into the room, and not even thinking about her.

The dress was dazzling. Alzine held it up against the light of the window, and through the mirror it seemed as if she held gossamer and silver in her hands, woven in pure ivory and fragile as gauze.

Sarianna turned. "It *is* beautiful," she said generously, "and you will be beautiful in it."

A mistake to say that; Jeralee thought so, too. Sarianna and Alzine lifted the creation over Jeralee's glossy brown head and slid it downward gently until Jeralee could insert her arms into each of the delicately draped sleeves, and Alzine began fastening the hooks at the back.

Sarianna brushed down the flowing skirt, tucking it here, puffing it out there, noticing without rancor how the ivory color enhanced Jeralee's skin, aware, with just the faintest feeling of resentment, how well such a dress would have become her, too.

But Jeralee's dark coloring set off the ivory drifts of material, and there was to be a pearl-encrusted length of satin wound around her waist, tied and left trailing down the train of the dress. Around her throat, Alzine fastened a satin ribbon set off by a shimmery satin flower, and in her glossy dark hair, Alzine wound threaded pearls as a headdress.

Finally, Jeralee moved to look at herself in the mirror. Her dark ferret eyes met Sarianna's in the reflection. Her expression did not change. "My gloves," she said imperiously, and Alzine rushed to hand them to her. "I wish," she said, turning away from the ivory glow in the mirror, "I had someone to carry my train." She looked hopefully at Sarianna, who shook her head.

"No, no, no, you have it all wrong," Sarianna said, modulating her voice to sound as if she were speaking to an idiot child, "someone bears your train when you get married."

"Oh."

Sarianna could have sworn Jeralee's disappointment was real. "Cheer up," she said encouragingly. "Perhaps your rough suitor will be so moved by your beauty tonight, he will propose. Or, failing that, Samuel Summers may absolutely fall into transports when he sees you, and decide he cannot live without you."

"I *am* beautiful tonight," Jeralee agreed with obvious satisfaction. "It *is* a night for fairy tales and magical wishes." She slanted a look at

Sarianna, who stood unmoving beside her. Sarianna would do well enough; she tended to remain behind the scenes anyway. She needed no further primping; all her duties required was that she greet everyone and then make sure the food was properly served. Her chocolate eyes sharpened as they swept over Sarianna's tall slender body. Sarianna couldn't hold a candle to *her*. Sarianna was too tall, too thin, too blond, and too awkward. To this day, Jeralee did not understand how Rex had borne his disappointments.

Even so, tonight was to be *her* night, and Sarianna would be relegated to the background . . . as usual. Jeralee did not consciously add that, but the thought pushed its way to the foreground of her ruminations anyway. Rex wanted her in the background, and she understood fully what her position was to be; she had never challenged her father at all in that respect that Jeralee knew.

The thought made her happy. They would enter the ballroom together, as sisters, though the one would surely outshine the other, and the rest of the night would belong to Jeralee. She would be surrounded by her loving neighbors, her would-be suitors, and her mysterious rough man who made her skin prickle every time she thought about him. She couldn't wait; even now he could be yearning for a glimpse of her.

"Come *on*, Sarianna," she cried gaily as she lifted her skirts, "let's go to my party."

From the landing overlooking the huge ballroom which occupied one whole wing of Bredwood, they could see bright pastel swirls of color moving across the room in a stately social quadrille, accompanied by black moths of men who never strayed far. At the far end of the room, on a dais, a small orchestra played bright spritely music to accompany the conversation. The great French doors on either side of the room were open to bring in light and air and to provide a place for a respite in the gardens that surrounded the ballroom wing.

Jeralee leaned over the balustrade, her face a blaze of excitement. "Just *look* at everyone, Sarianna! Oh, don't they look fine!" She turned to Sarianna abruptly. "Don't I look fine? Sarianna! You must tell me if you can see him!"

Sarianna stared at her for a long hard moment until Jeralee started to become uncomfortable, and turned her attention back to the spectacle, angry that Sarianna would spoil her pleasure with such a grim look. Sarianna said nothing, and that made it worse. It was one of those moments that Jeralee hated, when Sarianna made her feel trivial, and on a night like this, she wanted to feel special; she wanted no one to spoil the perfection of the event.

She lifted her head to look at Sarianna, but she couldn't quite meet those all-knowing sapphire eyes. "I want—" she started and stopped, thinking how it would sound to Sarianna. And then she shook herself mentally. Why should *she* care how it sounded to Sarianna? *Who* was Sarianna?

"I want to be sure he sees me—us," she amended, "when we come downstairs." Now she truly could not look at Sarianna. Her slip was not unintentional, and Sarianna knew it.

Sarianna was not looking at her however; she was looking at the throng below which had increased in size even since they had been in Jeralee's bedroom. No one could know, she thought with a little pang of expectation, what or who awaited either of them down there. It was Jeralee's party—to celebrate her sixteenth birthday—and that was all it was. It was not a slap at her, even though she had not had her sixteenth birthday celebrated nearly as lavishly. It was merely that *she* had not had a mother to intercede for her and beg for these little extravagances.

What did it matter if the overly romantic Jeralee was assuming the man she could love would be waiting for her at the bottom of the long winding staircase. There wasn't a woman alive who didn't believe that, Sarianna thought, even herself.

Jeralee pinched her arm. "Do you see him?" She knew Sarianna was scanning the crowd for her. Sarianna always did what she wanted her to; it was just she made her pay a price by her unflinching vision of Jeralee's real motives. It didn't matter. The moment was over; Sarianna's cynicism could not touch her now. She felt beautiful and confident once again, ready to float down the sinuous stairway into a lover's arms.

"I don't see him," Sarianna said flatly, but she would not have known him, she thought, if she had seen him. She hardly had any description to go by, and all she had seen was long, straight dark hair, broad shoulders and an unbending seat on horseback; in truth, that had impressed her more than anything Jeralee had said.

16

"You're lying," Jeralee accused her, leaning over the railing again. "Damn, you can hardly see a thing from up here."

"It's twenty feet ceiling to floor," Sarianna said, still in that hateful flat voice. She wasn't doing it deliberately; she hated Jeralee at this moment.

"You go down first then," Jeralee proposed. "See if you can find him."

"If I go down first, the only one I want to find is Eon to make sure he's been serving the champagne."

"You're impossible!"

"I tend to think you are," Sarianna said. "Excuse me." She marched away from Jeralee, her back stiff, her emotions ready to break wide apart. It always came to that; whatever she did for Jeralee, Jeralee wanted more, and more again. *Expected* it, as if Sarianna were a servant.

But then, wasn't that what she was in her father's house—someone who could only work off her grievous and innocent sins by servitude? She couldn't help how she had been born, but always his rank bitterness placed the blame on her. And for which transgressions? She had not been the long-coveted son and heir; she was the image of her coquette of a mother, and she had had the further misfortune to be born wrong-handed.

Even as she walked down the stairs slowly, she held on to the wall rather than the bannister, and she knew everyone watched and everyone wondered what was wrong with her. It was always the same with even the most commonplace of things: So many things she couldn't learn—embroidery, knitting, a stringed instrument—because her teachers did not know how to approach tutoring her. For a brief time they had tried securing the wrong hand behind her, to force her to use her right hand. She never could quite grasp it, not even for her father, who treated her mastering that facility as though it were the only thing that would remove the mystical black marks on her soul.

She reached the floor of the ballroom finally and took her place among the guests, turning just in time to see Jeralee come floating down the stairs like an extravagant ivory flower, her petal face smiling, her hands outstretched to her guests in feigned surprise, and great pleasure, before she even reached the lower step—and her greedy eyes searching the crowd for her rough man, and lancing through

17

Sarianna as though she weren't there.

Sarianna knew who he was the moment he walked through the colonnaded arch into the ballroom. All conversation stopped as he paused at the steps that led down to the parquet floor and stood for a long moment surveying the glittering gathering of Folquet County aristocracy of which he, too, had once been a part.

She felt a kinetic moment of danger: Here was a man who had lived in other worlds and among people unconceived of by this gaily dressed throng, and it was as if everyone were struck dumb by his gall. A sardonic line of disdain etched itself down one lean cheek as he handed his cape to the majordomo and took one more dark assessing look around the room before his inscrutable gaze settled unerringly on *her.*

She held his gaze with a calm she was far from feeling; her heart hammered so hard she thought it would explode. By odds she would have thought she would be the least noticeable person in the room. She wore no fancy clothes; her hair was not dressed. She had effaced herself into a corner where she could oversee the servants unobtrusively, where she could see and not be seen.

And yet he saw her.

And he stood insolently in the entry, commanding attention blatantly. Did they all remember him, she wondered. And what must they be thinking? How could this boy have come back to the house of the man whose wife he had been with just before she died? How did he dare show his face in the home of the man who had saved his discredited father from ruin, a father who had promptly shown his gratitude by drinking himself to death?

How *could* he?

Even she wondered as her heart thrummed under the intensity of his dark scrutiny and her body turned to stone; she could not have moved to save her life.

He knew who she was. She had been all of seven years old when her mother died, and he knew who she was.

And she would have known him anywhere, twelve years later: He was so much the same, and so very different. It was like seeing two people, concurrently, in the same body.

And then he moved. He came down the steps and strode easily through the crowd, and conversation began again, engulfing him; and Sarianna wondered then if *anyone* remembered except her.

He headed purposefully toward her stepmother, Vesta, who was deep in conversation with a neighbor. No—she amended that—Vesta *seemed* to be in deep conversation; depth of any kind was antithetical to her nature. Everything was on the surface with Vesta. At best, one always knew where one stood with her—she never minced words—at least she never minced words with Sarianna, who was very well aware of Vesta's tingling interest in the man approaching her, and the obvious way she was pretending not to notice him.

And then she looked up, in a gesture so reminiscent of her sister that Sarianna for a moment felt the old overwhelming sense of loss. And then Vesta's expression changed altogether as she sighted Jeralee bearing down on them, her face vivid with anticipation, her wide hooped skirt parting the milling guests like a biblical command.

Vesta took her silk shrouded arm proudly and pulled her forward into the little group. Sarianna watched dispassionately as Jeralee was presented to the stranger.

She was having a hard time containing herself, Sarianna thought, as expression after expression chased over Jeralee's face, ranging from pure delight to positively vulturous. She looked ready to eat the man, Sarianna thought viciously, shifting her attention for a fraction of a second to the tall elegant form of her father, who stood motionless twenty feet away, watching the scene with an expressionless face. His pale blue eyes glittered, following every nuance of the conversation he could not hear and the eager wolfish look on Jeralee's face.

Her father remembered good and well, Sarianna thought, but just what was going through his mind as Jeralee poured the viscous honey of her personality all over the man, she couldn't guess. She had thought his being forced to welcome Cade Rensell to his home would be a punishment; instead he looked as if he considered the situation scandalous and one to be gotten under control as soon as possible.

She swung abruptly on her heel and stalked to the entrance to the servants' hall. "Eon!" she called urgently through the door, and the tall butler appeared immediately. "Another round of drinks, please. Another guest has arrived."

"Certainly," he said with his stately grace, and several moments later, she saw his formally garbed figure moving through the crowd with a silver salver of champagne glasses.

"Yes," she said out loud. It was some satisfaction to her that she managed her father's home so well, and that everyone respected her and did her bidding just as she wished, and just as her mother would have wished had she still been alive.

Had she not fallen in love with another man.

Or so her father had said.

And the man was here tonight, his dark head attentively bent not to miss a single golden word issued from the mouth of Miss Jeralee Wayte.

She didn't know what she felt. She didn't even have to meet the man if she did not want to. "Alzine!" she called frantically, feeling as if she must do something. *Must.*

"Yas'm?"

Sarianna caught her breath. Alzine was like a little rabbit, popping up where you least expected her. "In five minutes, Alzine, begin serving the hot tidbits, and make sure once again that Sylvia is prepared to serve at nine o'clock, after the dancing."

"Yas'm." Alzine bobbed her head, and her bland dark face, shining already with perspiration, revealed nothing of her thoughts. But it was at least the fifth time Miss Sarianna had issued that order. She scurried away.

That's settled, Sarianna thought, wiping her damp hands on her skirt. She ought to have an apron. She edged toward the door unwillingly. She didn't want to care what Jeralee was doing, how she was captivating her "rough" man. But she had to know—she had to—because he was the man who professed undying love for her own mother moments before she died. And—damn it . . .

Once again a preemptive voice summoned her forward. But this time, this time it was Vesta. *Why?* Damn her!

Sarianna walked out of the service hall door. "Vesta? Is something wrong?" It was all she could do to keep from running. More than that, she was drowning in a feeling that Vesta had orchestrated this deliberately. *Why?*

"My dear, are you hiding?" Vesta asked, her eyes glimmering with an odd dark light. "We have another guest. Come."

"But you've played hostess for me already," Sarianna protested.

She didn't want to meet him. Vesta had brought him here for Jeralee, and only because he was rich and eligible. Not to make trouble. Not to spite her father. Jeralee had said he was rich—it was the only thing that would count with Vesta. Sarianna didn't want to see him face to face. Not ever. But he had seen her. *He knew her*. She couldn't hide, and Vesta, by the look of her, would not let her.

"I could never replace you," Vesta said with venomous kindness. "Come along. Perhaps you remember the Rensells."

"I remember," Sarianna said; how could she deny it when Cade Rensell had seen it in her eyes? She looked at Vesta accusingly, and Vesta turned away.

Sarianna pushed back her damp strands of hair and followed Vesta into the ballroom. She was not unconscious of the admiring looks bestowed on them as they made their way toward Jeralee, who was still talking animatedly to Cade Rensell. She and Vesta could have been mother and daughter as well but for their coloring: Vesta's hair was darker, verging on brown, and her eyes were that same melted chocolate color as Jeralee's. But something in Vesta's stance or the way she walked was reminiscent of her sister and, by association, Sarianna, who would have given anything to negate the relationship. Her aunt was now her mother and it made no sense to her. Vesta had never been in any way motherly; Sarianna could see right through her and she knew it.

It seemed to Sarianna that she often tried to wield parental power over her, and each time Sarianna frustrated her, she became more determined. The little cruelties got more intense, more subtle. Perhaps this was one of them, for her to see Jeralee's excessive success with Sawny Island's famous pariah, who now had something to offer that only Vesta knew.

Her foot faltered for a moment as she caught her father, Jeralee and Cade Rensell all standing together in a little tableau out of context: her father cool and removed and pulsating with anger; Jeralee frantic and vivacious all at once; and Cade Rensell, seemingly attentive, but with his dark eyes fixed unwaveringly on *her*. She knew instantly he had not come to Bredwood for a party, and he had no interest at all in the ivory spectacle of Jeralee's beauty, or the rapacious hands that kept plucking at his sleeve as if she knew he had gone far away from her in his thoughts.

And her father, with no choice at all about whether to welcome him to Bredwood—if he could have thrown Cade out of the house right then, he would have done it with great pleasure. He was furious beneath that cold façade—and furious, she couldn't credit it, with *her*, and not Vesta.

His hard blue eyes fixed on her as Vesta led her to the group. "Dear Cade," Vesta said sweetly, "here is little Sarianna, all grown up."

2

"*Mr.* Rensell," Sarianna said formally, and held out her hand which she hoped was not trembling. "I'm so pleased to welcome you to Bredwood."

Ah—a reaction, displeasure that she would not acknowledge the mutual past at all. For the best, she thought, and he must know it. How many of the almost hundred of their guests were murmuring about how familiar he looked, or wondering where they had seen him before? Formality would carry her through the meeting, and then she could escape from the haunting vision of this man whom she herself had seen with her mother five minutes before the shot that had killed her had been fired.

She would hear his voice forever, pleading with her mother to make a decision about leaving Rex if she were so unhappy. She would have forever etched in her memory the agony on his face when her mother laughed off his concern and brushed him away. He hadn't been that young then: They said that he and her mother had grown up together on neighboring plantations and that they had loved each other with a storm of fury of young love.

At the age Cade had been when she died, he would have been a good match for her. But when she married Rex, she had been eighteen and he three years younger, and she could not wait for his prospects to catch up to his innate maturity. Even if she had wanted to, her parents would never have allowed it.

He had waited seven years, biblical, faithful, unyielding. He had completed his education and taken his grand tour, and he had come back to Dona still full of hope and an abundance of love and support.

23

Which was not enough to keep her alive. Then he had disappeared, and everyone said it was a tacit admission of guilt. Someone had shot her, but the authorities could not prove who. Dona was laid to rest in a shroud of mystery, and Sarianna, who had watched her reject her beloved childhood lover, never forgot a moment of it, never forgot *him*.

And then he took her hand, and she was overwhelmed by the flashing image of the younger man's face imposed on the older, harder face before her; and she could not reconcile the two because she was responding to both of them on entirely different levels.

"Sarianna." His rough drawling voice caressed her name.

How old was he now? Early thirties? Where had he been; what had he done? What did he remember in his dreams? she wondered as she pulled her hand from his, still feeling the callused clasp to the depths of her soul.

Had he done it? Had he killed her mother in some kind of jealous rage, walking away with a show of acceptance, but with vengeance cupped in his hand, at the ready with a final rejection? How much had he loved her mother? How much had her father known?

"Something to quench your thirst, Mr. Rensell?" she asked politely, her voice even, flat; nothing could have betrayed her agitation more. She saw it in his eyes; the lively hazel color darkened ominously. But how could she not feel a certain fear, a certain disgust even. She knew what he was seeing: He was seeing her mother, not her. The look in his eyes was for Dona.

And Vesta. Vesta was watching them as if they were specimens. There was something in her expression—a war of some sort going on. She didn't like the way Cade was ignoring Jeralee.

In fact, Jeralee hadn't liked it either; she had removed herself without saying a word, and she was circling the room, speaking to each guest with a bright gaiety that she had to be hoping that Cade would notice. She could not help but see Cade's whole attention was focused on Sarianna, and Sarianna could feel her jealous heat steaming across the room.

"What did you say, Mr. Rensell?" she asked, her voice still frosty, knowing full well he had said nothing at all.

"I said yes, thank you," Cade responded, his tone as icy as hers.

Her shimmering blue eyes shot to his, and her mobile mouth made the gesture of "nicely done," as she nodded her golden head and signaled to Eon, who was circling the room once again. He came to her side at the instant and offered his tray of chilled champagne.

"Join me, Sarianna," he dared her as he took one of the long stemmed glasses.

She gave him her considering sapphire look once again; she felt calmer now that she had faced him, and she understood the curious look in his eyes. She was an adult after all; he wasn't the black nemesis of her nightmares. He was a man, tall and hard, with a raw, flat-planed face with high cheekbones that were etched with lines, finely arched eyebrows, a long straight nose that quivered slightly with impatience and a rather sweet mouth which seemed to belie that capacity for violence she had witnessed so long ago. He wore his straight black hair way too long, and it gave him an untamed aspect, like a lion who couldn't be caged. And it was coupled with a sensibility that did not suffer fools gladly.

She pulled her gaze away from him as she became aware of Vesta beside her, whispering under her breath, "Sarianna . . ." a warning, and her father's cold flat eyes pinioning her from still another corner of the room.

She took a glass from Eon's tray. "Mr. Rensell."

"Miss Broydon," he said in kind, lifting his glass to her.

"Let's *all* have a toast," Jeralee burst out gaily, suddenly appearing beside them and taking a glass from the tray with a shaky hand. "Come—to the return of Mr. Rensell to his rightful home." She sent him a bright hard look that glittered with implications. "Isn't it true, Mr. Rensell? You *have* come back to stay?"

He looked at her coldly and then turned to Sarianna. Her sapphire eyes told him nothing. "Yes, it's true," he said, mindful of his manners. "I *have* come home."

Damned gossips, he thought moodily as he watched Jeralee's antics the rest of the evening. The dancing had begun, and he had already sloughed off Vesta, who was demanding that he take one or another of the simpering belles in attendance out on the dance floor. Or Jeralee.

"But Jeralee has all the partners she could want," he pointed out promptly as she waltzed past them in the arms of Samuel Summers.

Vesta followed Jeralee and Samuel with her deep brown eyes. Interesting ramifications there, she had thought; she saw them all instantly in her mind's eyes, not the least of which was Samuel's dying within the first year of marriage and leaving his estates to his vigorous young wife who, if she had been smart, would have by then given birth to at least one son. Yes, there *was* something to be said for *that* . . . but then there was also something to be said for the latent magnetic danger exuded by the man beside her—a delicious danger, virile and blatantly sexual.

"Jeralee wants *you,*" Vesta had said boldly.

"Maybe *you* do," he had tossed back rudely, and was gratified to see her shock followed by a speculative look as she flounced away from him. He wondered how close to the truth he had come.

But after all, his motives were not of the purest either, and his fortuitous meeting with her in Savannah had eased his way back to Sawny Island. He had hardly expected to come roaring down the driveway, demanding to know how Rex Broydon had gotten hold of Rensell land and Rensell cotton. By the time he had heard that his father had lost everything in the depression of '57, it was too late. He had sent money, and it had been poured down a bottomless well. His father had never been able to recoup, his lawyer, Pierce Darden, had written. In the end, Rex Broydon had bought him out, and his father couldn't live with the knowledge that Rex had destroyed his son and taken advantage of his adversity. He drank himself to death as quickly and deliberately as possible, in exactly one week, a suicide as surely as if he had taken a gun to his own head.

Cade heard months later, months too late to save him, and the news sent him on a wild tear that lasted three more months before he regained his senses enough to assess what was left. It amounted to a moldering, unprofitable cotton plantation up on the Ogeechee River just beyond Savannah that had been run for years by an overseer who had been accountable to no one. And even then the property came down to him through his mother, and by all accounts his father had let it go to ruin.

He knew then it was time to return to Georgia, to Sawny Island, and in the ensuing months it had become a ravening need. He knew what he wanted to do, what he had to do.

He was coming home to bury the past and find a wife, no—take a wife from one of the Greek-columned plantations of Sawny Island aristocracy. Nothing less.

He didn't expect to be stopped dead on a Savannah street by the movement of a woman's body as she glided into a shop. The first conscious thought that occurred to him was Dona. And then—Dona is dead.

Not Dona. Vesta, in town to shop for the upcoming birthday party of her daughter, Jeralee. Vesta, with the astonishing news that *she* was now married to Rex Broydon. Vesta, who asked the astute questions that determined whether he was prosperous enough to be asked to join that exclusive party.

He could see her mind working—click, click, click. His lineage was impeccable, but not if he had no money to back it up. The taint of his father's death and Dona's murder could be overcome by the smell of money and his settler antecedents, as easy as that; it was so far back in the past. This was the opportune present, and Vesta had a most eligible daughter.

When she pointed Jeralee out to him, he decided instantly she would do as well as anyone else—better, in fact, because she was Rex Broydon's stepdaughter. And he had forgotten all about Sarianna. Sarianna, the golden surprise, the shocking past.

Sarianna had been the shimmery, golden-haired figure on the balcony that caught his eye as he trotted up the drive—the ghost of Dona, whom he instinctively sought out the moment he entered the ballroom.

Sarianna. He hadn't remembered the child until his eyes settled on her; and then he had known her forever, and he didn't want that. She was everything Dona should have been and more. She had a core of integrity that shone out of her brilliant dark blue eyes, and she didn't flaunt her startling beauty, and that perversely pleased him.

She was hiding and he could not figure out why. She knew him and he could not understand how.

The minute he set eyes on her, she became imprinted on his consciousness, and he was always aware of her: where she was, where she was not, and what she was saying and not saying with those speaking sparkling eyes.

Sarianna. How incredible he might be able to relive his past as well.

But where was she? His eyes instinctively shot to the door of the service hall where he had first seen her, and there he saw her again, beyond the portal, directing two burly field hands who were carrying a long spindly-legged table between them.

The trappings of wealth, Cade thought disgustedly, built partially on his father's imprudence. If he wanted vengeance, he surely had the means at hand. Had it been his intention when he conceived of the idea of coming back? Perhaps it had; there were enough young ladies to choose from. Even now Victoria Gray's eyes admired him as she danced by with an elderly neighbor; he must have thought of revenge. And here he had it all on a silver salver.

And Sarianna. How fortuitous there was also Sarianna.

Sarianna, in the dining room, silently suppressed her anger at the inconvenience of her having to rearrange the tables to accommodate her stepmother's extra guests.

Nonetheless, it was part and parcel of what she had come to expect from Vesta: little aggravations, little slights, no appreciation, no thought given to her feelings or even her desires. Vesta had moved in and taken over almost as if her sister had never existed, and Sarianna became someone to be used to gratify Vesta's every wish and whim.

At first Sarianna remembered herself as having been desperate to please Vesta, who, Rex made it clear, was to be treated with every courtesy. She did not resent Vesta; she saw her as an extension of her beloved, frivolous mother, someone she could love as well as she had loved Dona, someone who might even love her.

But no; Vesta had leapt instantly upon her wrong-handedness and the uncanny resemblance to Dona, and there was nothing a ten-year-old girl could do to palliate those faults. Vesta smiled at her a lot, and Vesta patted her head and shoulder a lot just as if she were some small animal; and Vesta never let her get one step closer than she had to, to perform some small service for her.

And now: "But my dear—there will be thirty-five to dinner; I thought you were aware of that and had made arrangements for them."

Vesta surely was not going to. She had given Sarianna that expectant look, as if to say, "Well, what are *you* going to do about it?" The fascination of the party could not be allowed to be interrupted by *arrangements*.

Sarianna stood back for a moment, trying to decide which configuration of the tables was best suited to conversation. The easiest thing to do was line them up: The dining room was large enough for that; but the rectangularity of it made the whole thing look like some state dinner, and Sarianna was not sure she wanted to attach that kind of importance to Jeralee's birthday celebration.

In the end, she aligned the two tables side by side, thinking a little maliciously that Vesta could have the task of choosing who would sit where.

She was just directing Alzine and the kitchen girls to lay the silver once again when Vesta burst into the room.

"Oh!" Vesta said, with her peculiar knack of infusing that one small word with a wealth of negativity.

"I beg your pardon?" Sarianna said politely.

"I didn't expect—*two* tables, Sarianna? Isn't that a little exclusive?"

"Perhaps you'll give me the benefit of *your* wisdom," Sarianna said, as she steadily folded napery and set the silver. Alzine followed with a tray of utensils and linen poised in her boneless hands, her fear of Vesta reflected by the way she refused to look at her and how she kept as close to Sarianna as possible.

Vesta shrugged. "It's too late to do anything about it now. I bow to *your* superior wisdom, Sarianna. Just mind how you place the forks and spoons, please."

Sarianna's head shot up, and her knowing sapphire gaze lanced like a physical blow. Vesta recoiled at the shock of its enmity, aware, suddenly, that this was one of the few times Sarianna had allowed it to show.

"Perhaps Jeralee would be more adept at a chore that requires she know the social graces, but doesn't make more demands on her intelligence," Sarianna said, bending her head once more to the task at hand. She felt Vesta's fury coming at her in waves now. Vesta had never expected this kind of retaliation from her; Vesta didn't know she had it in her.

Vesta was going to know, Sarianna reflected as she continued laying the table in a rhythmic soothing motion that calmed her temper. It was time. Her resentment festered over her father's open-handedness with Jeralee, as though Jeralee were the treasured daughter of the house and not she. But that always had been the case, ever since Jeralee had arrived at Bredwood. And Jeralee knew it.

Vesta had coerced her father into it somehow; Sarianna had always felt that. There just was no logical reason for her father to treat Jeralee any better than he treated *her*.

She laid the last gleaming knife down on the table and stared at it. She hated them. She had always hated them, ever since Vesta's express rejection of her. Nonetheless, dutiful as she was, Sarianna had never consciously allowed herself to actually think the words. But she stared at the knife, she touched it, she even lifted it to feel the heft of it and the good, thick, cool silvery sense of it, and she thought the words. And if she were that much more aggressive, she thought, she might lift that knife and throw it at Vesta, who stood watching her with a supercilious look on her face.

"Jeralee," she said suddenly, "knows everything that she needs to know to attract a wealthy husband, Sarianna. I trust you'll agree the same cannot be said of you. It's very useful that you can do other things."

Sarianna felt herself flushing, and lifted the knife tentatively. So cool in her hand, so tempting to wipe that smirk off of Vesta's face—her mother's face . . . thickened, coarsened, darker . . . not her mother, rather the hurtfulness she inflicted—but how could she be allowed to get away with it.

She put down the knife and looked up at Vesta and smiled. "Some gentlemen may not be particular," she said gently. "Anybody with some kind of dowry will do, wouldn't you say?"

She saw Vesta assessing her with new eyes. She had never been quite this openly vindictive before either; it was time, damn it. How much more should she take from them—especially after Jeralee had been handed everything at her whim—and she, nothing.

"If it were so," Vesta retorted, "you would be mistress of your own home by now, wouldn't you, Sarianna?" She smiled benignly as Sarianna flinched, and then her expression turned malignant. "Don't ever try to take anything away from my Jeralee, Sarianna; you'll never succeed."

Sarianna recoiled. What was it—a threat? A challenge? Lucky Jeralee to have this mother bear of a protectress. Her fingers itched to slap Vesta's confident, menacing face. She felt slightly unbalanced by the ferocity of Vesta's attack, as if the only way to fend it off were to tear into Vesta. Yes, it was the very thing she felt; she wanted to bite, scratch, kick—anything to wipe the growing look of insolence from Vesta's face.

Her fingers reached, of their own volition, for the cold sanctity of the silver knife on the table. Was Vesta scared? The idle thought came at her from nowhere as she stroked the knife and envisioned revenge. What an idea! That Vesta should be afraid of anything that she, Sarianna, could do . . . or could she? Could she somehow ruin Jeralee's chances—at what? What was Vesta planning that she could possibly subvert?

She lifted her golden head to meet Vesta's patronizing expression. "So you see, my dear," Vesta murmured.

Sarianna decided to be obtuse. "Well, I really don't," she said musingly, lifting the knife again, calling Vesta's attention to it, and then laying it back down gently, lovingly.

"What difference does it make, after all," Vesta said smoothly, her own hands reaching for a folded napkin to move it from its precise positioning to an even more precise alignment with the silver.

"Exactly," Sarianna agreed softly, her heart breaking just a little that her irony was totally lost on Vesta. "What difference could *I* possibly make, especially when you compare my attributes with those of Jeralee? It's impossible for me to understand what you're trying to warn me against."

Vesta eyed her uncertainly as she bent her head and her concentration on setting the next napkin beside the next plate in the exact placement as the ones before it. There was something wrong with what she had said, but Vesta could not quite pinpoint what it was; Sarianna had agreed with her, as she should have. On the surface, she understood exactly what her position was in relation to Jeralee. And yet . . . she longed to say something to refute Sarianna's words, but what could she say that would not disagree with her own express point of view?

She lifted a hand as if she could negate the words with a motion, and started as she heard Rex's voice:

"So there you are, Vesta."

She whirled to find him in the entryway to the dining room. "Rex, my dear . . ."

He stalked in, all gray and elegant in his summer frock coat that was just three shades darker than his receding silver hair. "Tell me what you mean by inviting *that man* here?" His hands reached for Vesta's bare shoulders, pulling her to him, crushing the drape of her hoop skirt against his thighs—totally unmindful that Sarianna overheard every word. "You didn't tell me it was Rensell, damn you! Why did it have to be Rensell? And that fool lawyer of his, for God's sake, Vesta! Just why do you suppose that bastard leapt on an invitation to come here?"

"It doesn't matter," Vesta said shakily as she struggled against his tight grip. "How can it matter after all this time, Rex? He's got money and prospects, and he wants a wife, and why not my Jeralee? Why not? Who but you still cares what happened to Dona twelve stupid years ago? *Who?*"

He thrust her away from him impatiently. "Damn you, Vesta, you never have learned that people on Sawny Island have damned long memories. I promise you, I'm not the only one who remembers, and that man will not be welcome no matter how much gold lines his pockets."

Vesta lifted her head stubbornly. "I can think of a few people who might relent about *that* if *they* could get their hands on that gold, Mr. Broydon. I assure you, the Grays are looking at this man mighty hard, or don't you see what's before your eyes? You can carry all the old grudges you want, but I'd do anything to be sure that Jeralee married well and married a man she could love who would care for her. And the fact it's Rensell lineage does not hurt the matter at all. And that's *my* say about it. No one is going to challenge him to a duel because of some nebulous charge of his being the last person to see Dona alive twelve years ago. *No one,* Rex. He's a Rensell, and everyone knows what happened to his daddy and how you stepped in; and there's folks here that think you didn't act quite as honorably about the whole thing as you might have. He's my guest, and Jeralee's, and she will have her chance with him, Rex—won't she?"

Rex turned away from her, his smooth face stony, his pale eyes mere icy blue chips that saw nothing in the room. He looked at Sarianna, who stood frozen in place, and for all he saw her, he could have been seeing her mother in her place, Sarianna thought frantically. He was hearing Vesta's words, but he was locked somewhere in the past; and because of it, Vesta would get her way as usual.

"You may be right," he said stiffly after a long silence. "What *does* it matter after all?"

"And all that money, Rex," Vesta said coaxingly, gliding over to where he stood and plucking gently at his sleeve. "There's a lot of money. He told me."

"And you believed?" Rex said mockingly, removing her hand.

"He was in the goldfields," Vesta said, still in that cajoling voice. "In California. That's why he did not get back here in time to save his father. Think back, Rex, Parker got hold of a lot of money suddenly, and we all thought he would pull himself out of debt, remember . . . ? Cade sent it, a lot of it, and it just got washed away, remember? But everyone wondered who was fool enough to try to bail him out when he tried to buy back the stock he sold; that was Cade, Rex."

He nodded slowly, assimilating it, making it mesh in his mind in a way that thrust out the memories and left in their place a pure golden greed to possess; and he could, through Jeralee, and he could find vengeance, too, if he tried hard enough, he thought fleetingly. The idea was there. If he offered hospitality, he could mitigate what little ill feeling remained, if what Vesta said were true. He could have Cade Rensell in his home and under his thumb and perhaps, when all was said and done, at his mercy.

It was an interesting idea, especially when he had never thought to see Cade Rensell again. He had assumed Cade had no intention of returning to Sawny Island when it became obvious he had washed his hands of his father's follies. Useful news to find out that it had not been so.

He tempered his expression as he turned to face Vesta. "Well, my dear, perhaps you did show some good sense in this matter; after all, as you say, the man saw you on the street and accosted you while you were preparing for this event. Of course you could have done nothing else but invite him down. I fully see that now, Vesta, and I do beg your forgiveness for expressing my anger before I understood the situation."

Vesta smiled.

They looked like two snakes, sinuously twining around each other with words and looks, and things that Sarianna silently looking on did not understand. They were hateful, she thought. The two of them belonged together; they were perfect together. They never acknowledged her, so wrapped up were they in their own little plans and plots, and in that same vein, they left the room together arm in arm never looking back at Sarianna, who stood with her weight leaning hard against the edge of the table, her knuckles white as she grasped the edge with the effort of restraining herself.

She had been invisible to them, a nonentity. Never had it been brought home more fully to her, her status in her father's house. He had looked through her just as he always seemed to have done. But never so pointedly. It had never been quite so real how he felt about her.

She couldn't quite believe it. He had treated her the way he would have treated Alzine, she thought in despair. She slanted a look at Alzine, who was still standing quietly by, tray in hands, waiting for her mistress to resume.

Alzine did not avoid her eyes, and Sarianna could not evade the sympathy in Alzine's, slave to mistress. Slave to slave.

3

It took Sarianna a long time to regain enough composure to return to the ballroom. She had spent it arranging and rearranging the tables to her complete satisfaction, changing the centerpieces, moving the seating—busy work for a sensibility that could not comprehend the nature of a father's callous disregard. She loved him. She thought she loved him. But when it came down to it, she realized what she felt was the duty of a daughter to a parent, nothing more, nothing less. There was no affection, and she could not feel loyalty to him. She repaid him amply by her astute management of Bredwood, her supervision of the household staff, her bookkeeping, and her being his hostess, ever efficient and out of the way like a smooth running machine.

And why? Because of Dona, because of her sex, because of her awkwardness. She had never understood his attitude, and she could never justify it, especially in the face of the moderate affection he showered on Jeralee. And it had never been anything as conspicuously overt as this party; this party made a statement. This party told the world that he considered Jeralee his daughter, more than Sarianna. Vesta should have been well pleased with such an event.

But now Vesta, the dark pale version of her beautiful mother, was threatening her; and she stood in the middle of the airy, two-story, company dining room that adjoined the ballroom, and she wondered how she could combat such enmity. More than that, why should she? If Vesta thought she were some kind of menace to Jeralee's happiness, why should she not grab for the thing that Vesta most feared?

Why not indeed? she thought later as she entered the ballroom and

35

stood in the service hall doorway, watching the glittering company moving up and down the dance floor in a spritely reel. Eon followed her, pushing a tea cart full of platters of hot tidbits and a generous service of oyster forks with which to eat them. Sarianna nodded at him, and he began wheeling the cart around the circumference of the room where friends sat and gossiped, couples whispered secrets to each other, and several of the men portentously discussed business.

She pinpointed Jeralee instantly sitting on one of the poufs of chairs in the center of the ballroom, surrounded as always by a retinue of young men, one of whom she recognized as the dark man who had arrived with Cade Rensell. The lawyer.

She studied him curiously. He had a nice face; it was open, bluff, with a ready smile and expressive eyebrows. His hair was short, shorter than his friend's; everything about him seemed neatly trimmed and nicely turned out, right down to his well-cut suit and snowy white shirt.

She liked watching him. He spoke to everyone in turn, and he made Jeralee laugh with a quip as he in his turn took a helping from Eon's cart as it stopped before them. The music ceased, and the dancing couples proceeded to crowd around the wagon, demanding a drink or some food; and it became a lighthearted scene of good-natured shoving and joking as the sounds of merriment carried across the room to where Sarianna watched.

Her father and Vesta had gone onto the dais in preparation for the birthday tribute, and they stood overlooking this lively crowd with a smug enjoyment of the fact that it had been Rex Broydon's money and Jeralee's beauty and popularity that had created this enviable moment. And none of it had anything to do with Sarianna as far as they were concerned.

And she knew it. She had only planned the party, executed it, devised the menu, arranged the seating, chosen the decorations, delegated the household tasks, and appropriated the household monies to accomplish it, as well as providing the ferry service for their Savannah guests, and opening up the guest wing of the Bredwood so that their travelers might have overnight accommodations. But she saw clearly that Vesta and her father thought that the whole thing had come about solely because of their desire to do it.

So be it, she thought; she did not have to be among the guests as Jeralee was feted by the company that *she* had invited. She moved unobtrusively out of her corner and edged around the left side of the ballroom where the French windows opened out onto the garden, and the daylight and welcome fragrant air filtered in to the cloying atmosphere of wellwishers whose attention now focused on Jeralee's gracious figure curtseying to applause in the center of the ballroom floor.

The ballroom had seemed empty without her, and when she finally returned to her station by the service hall doorway, Cade noted her face was drawn and pale, and she ran a shaky hand through her unruly curls more times than was necessary to correct her tousled appearance. She was visibly upset, and she kept clenching her jaw to suppress some deeper emotion which she could not vent in this crowded company.

So perfect, he thought. Beautiful, spirited, intelligent. Rex Broydon's daughter—he could not have planned better if he had ordained it from heaven.

And she looked as if she devoutly wished she could be elsewhere. Even as he thought it, she began to move quietly through the guests who were crowding around the center of the room as the orchestra struck up an introductory note and Jeralee stood up, her chocolate eyes glowing, acknowledging her friends and well-wishers even as she sought in the crowd for the one face she most wanted to see.

Her expression tightened just the faintest bit as she caught sight of him striding toward the garden door, but there wasn't a thing she could do about it. She was the center of attention as she always liked to be at the one moment she wished she weren't. She knew, with her radiant intuition that had scanned the room a moment before, that Sarianna had left the room as well, and she wondered, as she bowed to the applause, whether Sarianna had arranged some kind of assignation just to spite her.

But Cade wasn't even thinking of Jeralee; Sarianna was his prey, and he blessed fortune that he had these few moments alone with her on the stone terrance as she pensively gazed out at the gardens.

In the lowering light, she seemed ethereal, her golden curls like a halo around her head, her slenderness, emphasized against the mellow red brick of the ballroom wing, seemed to him throat-catching and seductive at the same time. Her arms were crossed around her waist as if she were hugging something precious against herself, and her expression was ineffably sad. She wanted to be left alone, and her tense, closed-in stance isolated her as surely as if she had fenced herself in physically.

He wanted to touch her, awaken her; she had to be aware he was watching her, but she gave no sign she knew he was there. Indomitable, he thought. She could dispense with the conventions when it suited her. Dona's child. Dona—who couldn't renege on vows, promises, on what was expected of her.

He was so conscious of the similarities—but even more so of the differences; they struck him all over again just as they had when he first laid eyes on her. That steely spine that held her so erect, the firm chin so clearly outlined in the pearly evening light, the quirky lips. Sarianna's lips, Sarianna's determination limned in the silhouette of her ramrod posture.

He wanted to kiss her. The thought didn't even shock him. He wanted to taste that tenacity, Sarianna's tenacity. *Her,* not Dona. Not the past or memories; he could hardly conjure up what that had felt like anymore. There was no confusion in his mind. He wanted that woman in that instant as she stood there so magnificently alone. He wanted her for all the right reasons, and he wanted her for all the wrong reasons; and he felt the least little pang because he knew that the wrong reasons motivated his actions *now.*

"Sarianna!"

She whirled. "Mr. Rensell." Her voice was calm, her expression changing before his eyes into one of careful civility which was not in the least what he wanted from her.

He moved toward her and she edged away subtly.

"Sarianna . . ."

"But the food and celebration are inside, Mr. Rensell. What possible interest could you have out here?" she asked warily, all her senses alert, aware. He had stepped twice toward her, and already she felt as if she was being stalked. A man like Cade Rensell didn't pursue disenfranchised daughters of women they had purportedly once loved. Men like him wanted dowries, wealth, dutiful wives to provide them with sons on whom they could bestow their dynastic ambitions. Men like him wanted a woman like Jeralee. Vesta could never have made a mistake about that; Vesta was too finely tuned into those kinds of niceties. She could figure a man's net worth to the dollar with just a minimum of information. Even her father had been impressed.

But as he came closer, she felt as if she were seven years old again, and he became the ever-present dark invader of her old nightmares.

"I merely came to ask you to dance," he said conventionally, holding out his hand to her, watching her with a piercing attentiveness that was unnerving.

"I don't dance," she said tightly, avoidng his eyes and turning to look out over the garden once again.

"I don't believe you."

"But you don't need to, Mr. Rensell. Do go back inside and enjoy the entertainments there."

"There is nothing more entertaining than talking to you, Sarianna."

"I'm delighted you feel that way, Mr. Rensell, but I truly have nothing more to say to you." She didn't dare look at him; she felt a conflict within her at his persistence. She didn't want the trouble it would inevitably bring, and she loved it. She loved it with the perversity of someone who has a supreme sense of humor, and she loved being pursued with every ounce of her femininity, and having the power to say no. Especially did she like saying no to Cade Rensell, who really was only being courteous, because he was so desired by Jeralee. The feeling was heady, powerful, challenging.

But then, she thought, it had nothing at all to do with good manners. Something else was operating, and as he came closer to her, she felt a thrill of pure animal excitement.

"I believe you have a lot more to say to me," Cade contradicted softly, ignoring her pointed rebuff. He held out his hand once again. "Dance with me, Sarianna—here, if you won't go inside."

She turned her golden head to look at the shadows of couples waltzing within, and then she slanted a look at Cade Rensell. "I don't understand, Mr. Rensell."

"Why must you?" he countered with a self-deprecating smile that softened his face with deep-etched lines. "Come, Sarianna."

"Must I?" she retorted in kind, holding herself removed from him, refusing to take his hand. Out of the corner of her eye, she could see the dancers and—wait—wasn't that Vesta circling the dance floor like a bird of prey? Was it self-centered of her to surmise Vesta might be looking for her? And what if Vesta found her in Cade Rensell's arms? she wondered, half giving in to the impulse without further thought.

She wanted to be held in *someone's* arms, she thought longingly; perhaps today the reasons why did not have to matter either.

Her vivid expression changed once again; Cade could almost—*almost*—follow her thoughts, but not quite. Her quirky smile appeared, along with a very thoughtful gleam in her sapphire eyes as she awaited his inevitable answer that would give her leave to take his hand.

And he gave it to her. "You must, Sarianna." He extended his hand once again; and this time her cool firm fingers grasped it, and she allowed him to pull her into the circle of his arm. Inside, she could hear the tempo of the music changing as the orchestra shifted into another lilting waltz for those who could not get enough dancing, and simultaneously she felt herself inexorably bound in Cade Rensell's hard embrace.

She looked up at him quizzically. "I can barely breathe, Mr. Rensell."

"Perfectly understandable, Sarianna," he said implacably, not loosening his grip one bit. He took a step and she followed, her body pliant and almost boneless against him; and then another, and another, and then slowly he swung into the rhythmic timing of the music.

"Sarianna . . ."

And why, she wondered despairingly, did he have to say her name in that beguilingly drawn out way that made it sound faintly sensual. He did it every time, as though he were savoring the sound of it, and almost as if he were reassuring himself she would not suddenly disappear because she had to answer him. But she felt real enough in his arms, close to his long lean body with the broad shoulders that Jeralee had so admired. Sarianna's hand rested lightly on the broadcloth breadth of them, and she felt the hard muscle beneath the material, and heat of his body as he expertly guided her around the parameters of the terrace in time to the muffled strains of music. She looked up into his unreadable hazel eyes, and *she* was the one he smiled at with a kind of rueful grin that she did not want to like.

She almost answered it and stopped herself just in time, catching her lower lip in her teeth and chewing on it, hard. He followed the movement with a great deal of interest, and his eyes darkened just that little bit more at her attempt to deny this little flare between them.

It was impossible that he was interested in her, she told herself sternly. He had a history with her family, and he could not possibly want anything to do with *her*. She was too much like her mother for one thing, and she was too graceless and awkward to be the kind of woman who would attract someone worldly like him. He was toying with her for some reason of his own: to annoy her father perhaps, or to make a subtle statement to Vesta that she should not be so sure of his interest in Jeralee. Whatever it was, it made her nervous; his arm around her waist was firm and inescapable, and his lion-face was inches from hers and full of some kind of portent she could not read.

"Don't be afraid of me, Sarianna."

The timbre of his voice melted her bones; no one had ever spoken to her like that.

"Should I not?" she said lightly to cover the fine tremor his words had sent shooting through her body. He could feel it; how could he not? She could be clay in his hands if he said one word more. And yet underneath all the words and awareness was still the reality of his youth with her mother. She couldn't banish it. It was there every time she looked into his face superimposed over the hard man-features that had evolved from the rawness of the boy's.

"I won't hurt you," he said roughly.

"But you have—you can—" she protested with a knowledge in her older than time, of him, of herself. It would take a touch, and she knew it. He had already stormed her defenses by merely holding her in this possessively firm way, and his touch—the touch of the mythical someone who would want her—was just as she had always imagined it.

She had only brief moments to store up the extravagant sensations she felt as he whirled her around the terrace, close and closer still, and then slower and slower until they were standing stock still and on the edge of the precipice.

They were alone there, his head tilted at just the right angle, and his mouth descended toward hers just as she desired. She watched it, fascinated by the shape of it and imagining just how it would feel when it finally settled on hers.

Then the demon within her spoke, and she was horrified. "I'm not Dona, you know."

He wasn't in the least disconcerted. "I know," he murmured with a hoarse break in his voice that convinced her, as his lips tested hers, that he really did know.

41

But then even he wasn't sure. The texture of her skin, how she felt in his arms, the lean of her long body against his, threw him so far back into the past that he felt as if he were drowning in a sea of bittersweet sensation as he taught her willing lips how to play and part for him.

And then there was the sumptuous feeling of entering her, tasting her, seeking her response from her eager untutored tongue, and he was kissing Sarianna because it could only be the honey of *her* sweet mouth that aroused him so intensely.

And she—what did she know of kisses and men, and the feel of a man's body next to hers—this was what she did not know: the heat, and the overriding voluptuousness of a man's mouth moving over hers and into hers in such a shockingly delicious way to explore her with such possessive thoroughness. She could never have imagined the billowy feelings that enveloped her, or the keen knifing of desire that took her totally by surprise—a corkscrew of sensation that spiraled tellingly between her legs and made her yearn to feel it again.

She reached for him eagerly; she felt no shame, no compunction. She did not even care at that moment that it might have been her resemblance to her mother that had provoked his kiss.

Then Vesta said behind them: "Oh, *there* you are, Sarianna! You *do* know it's nine o'clock?" And the fairy tale ended.

Sarianna moved away from him, her face averted, her body trembling with a kind of triumph that something about her had moved him to such extremes. Vesta had seen, she was sure of that; she had fully incited Vesta's fury which she knew would escalate out of all proportion if Vesta knew that she herself had wantonly desired that kiss.

She looked up then to see Jeralee standing just behind her mother, and Rex came up behind them, the apex of a triangle that boxed them in, and shut her out.

The lush pressure of his lips on hers stayed with her as Sarianna preceded Vesta into the ballroom and signaled Eon to sound the dinner gong.

The music stopped, and Sarianna disappeared into the service hall doorway, not even turning to satisfy her curiosity about whether Jeralee had taken Cade's arm, which she must have done, if only to show everyone that Cade Rensell was hers, at least for this evening.

It was small consolation that Cade had not sought out Jeralee. All right, he had come after Sarianna Broydon, and given the result, she didn't give one whole damn even what his reasons were. But that did not change the order of seating at dinner, and Sarianna could not bear to watch the stately march of guests into the dining room, and the spectacle of Jeralee hanging on to Cade Rensell's muscular arm.

Besides, she thought, if she did not appear, Vesta would be forced to seat everyone, and Vesta, who was always aware of nuances, would know exactly whom to seat where so as not to give offense.

But she wouldn't like it. Vesta never liked to be seen doing anything that remotely resembled work. They had servants for that. And they had Sarianna. Somehow they had trapped her because no one wanted her, and they made very sure she knew it, and that in her surbservient position, she could demand nothing more.

But she had always viscerally known it. There was just no escape. It wasn't likely she could become a governess, given her wrong-handedness; Rex had even said so. The only other recourse was marriage, but no one had ever asked for her hand—or so Rex had said.

I'd even walk out the door with Samuel Summers if he asked me, Sarianna thought viciously, as she made her way back to the kitchen where a stream of servants were lining up the various trays and the dishes upon them that Sylvia had already put the finishing touches to, beginning with a fragrant cold soup dusted with mint, and a fresh fruit compote to accompany it.

Would I? she wondered, testing the steaming loaves of bread cooling on racks by the window. *Am I that desperate?*

Sometimes she thought she was.

She bent over the nearby table where another servant was setting out prints of butter on individual serving plates with intense precision.

And sometimes she just didn't care.

She inspected each work table as she walked around the kitchen and forced herself not to think about herself in Cade Rensell's arms. She finally wound up at the stove where Sylvia was basting the haunch of meat to be served as entree.

"This looks lovely," Sarianna told Sylvia appreciatively, and gestured for the serving girls to begin taking the first course in to the guests. It gave her a brief respite before she knew she had to go in and attend to the service. It was her job, she thought resentfully, her responsibility. Everything had to go well for Jeralee, even the annexation of Cade Rensell.

No—there was nothing to say anything would come of that. He didn't look like a man to be forced into anything he didn't want to do, nor could she see Vesta pushing him into some compromising situation with Jeralee in order to force the issue. There *was* no issue, except that Jeralee had fallen hard for a man's broad shoulders.

But that man had pursued *her*, Sarianna, and kissed *her* in the heat of the moment, and what Jeralee wanted hadn't mattered one bit.

She touched her lips with questing fingers as if she could remove the kiss and examine the sensation in front of her eyes. But nothing came off on her fingers, and the sense of his delving, questing tongue remained sharp and true in her consciousness. And with it came the nagging feeling that she had done exactly what her giddy flirtatious mother would have done.

Resignedly, she followed the servant with the last tray of the first course out into the dining room. It was like walking onto a stage with every activity ceasing at her appearance and thirty-five and more expectant faces looking up at her, waiting for her opening lines.

But she saw no one except Vesta and her smug satisfied smile as she bent her head over her soup bowl to hide it; her father with his quizzical eyebrow as if he were saying, *What are you doing here*; and Jeralee, in all her bright gaiety pointedly seated next to Cade, holding her soup spoon in mid-air, whatever she had been about to say poised on the tip of her tongue as she waited for Sarianna to go away.

It took a stranger to pinpoint what was wrong. Pierce Darden, ever the Georgia gentleman, stood up in the ensuing silence. "Why, Miss Sarianna—let me help you; where is your seat?"

His voice trailed off at Sarianna's stricken eyes, and he looked around at both tables. There were no empty seats, and he belatedly realized his error. There was no place laid at the table for Sarianna, and nowhere for her to sit.

4

No one, *no one,* had ever mentioned the blatant omission in company. No one had ever questioned it. No one had ever cared. And Sarianna did not want to explain. Only she was not embarrassed by his question. Only she was curious to see how her father would explain away the peculiar exclusion of his daughter from the table.

But Vesta spoke first. "Sarianna is needed to direct the servants."

Pierce turned to her, plainly disbelieving her words. "But surely . . ."

"Sarianna!" Her father's whipcrack voice carried across the room, telling her as plain as words to leave.

She looked at Vesta and saw her eyes turn muddy with hate at her contrariness. Vesta had given her an out; she should have gracefully taken it, and no one would have questioned it further. She hated Vesta, and she hated Pierce Darden for perceiving that which everyone else took for granted. She couldn't move. Movement meant a defeat; it would mean she was what they were intent on making her, that the awkwardness of seating her was such a burden they could do nothing else with her. *How* had she ever given them such power?

"We would have to rearrange the seating," Jeralee said suddenly, brightly. "Sarianna eats with her opposite hand, you see, so it's best that she sits at either of those two ends." She waved her hand gracefully at Pierce himself at the second table, who stared at her, his mouth faintly agape, and at Victoria Gray at her table, who was hardly paying any attention for the slavering looks she was sending in Cade Rensell's direction. "It's sometimes such a bother trying to accommodate it."

45

"Well, let's try," Sarianna heard herself say, her voice every bit as gay as Jeralee's, her sapphire eyes hard with purpose now—oh, and it was a good one. She was going to defeat that gloating triumvirate and make a statement tonight. She turned and called behind her, "*Alzine!*"

Alzine came running, and Sarianna could only surmise she had been listening by the door. "Find another chair please."

"Take mine, Miss Sarianna."

She whirled at Pierce's kind voice. "Thank you, I will." She quickly scanned both tables. "Alzine!"

Alzine stopped dead in her tracks. "Yas'm?"

"I believe Mr. Darden will be very comfortable if you place him beside Miss Victoria. Another setting, too, please, for the second course, for *both* of us."

"Yas'm." Alzine fluttered a moment, waiting for a countermand from Vesta; but no negating words followed Miss Sarianna's orders, and she scurried out of the dining room, her mind agog at Miss Sarianna's uncharacteristic refusal to give in to Miss Vesta's demand.

In short order, one upholstered balloon-back chair appeared in the hands of Eon, who placed it painstakingly next to that of Miss Victoria Gray while Miss Gray stood, choking back her indignation that she should be made a cynosure so that Sarianna could have a place that everyone knew she did not want to begin with.

Nonetheless, Sarianna took her seat at the end of the second table where her movements would not interfere with those of the guest sitting next to her, knowing full well what the end result of this little skirmish would be: No one would by tacit consent talk about it, everyone would ignore it, and Vesta and Jeralee would punish her somehow for her insubordination.

So be it. She nodded at Eon, who stood poised by the door awaiting her silent instructions, and he disappeared to summon forth his retinue to begin serving the second course.

So Rex hated her *that* much, Cade mused broodingly as he held his wineglass to the light so he could covertly watch Sarianna, who had not looked at him once during the confrontation. He wondered if she knew. He wondered if Rex himself even knew the difference between them. How well that played into his own plans. What retaliation if he could take Sarianna from Rex as well!

Could he? He hadn't quite expected the depth of Rex's feelings about Sarianna. He had not at all expected the kind of petty despotism that Vesta and Jeralee practiced on her. And yet she was here, and she bore the brunt of their mean-spirited intentions.

Why would she? She was so beautiful, and too intelligent; it could not escape her what they were doing. Why was she letting it happen? Why had tonight happened? He wondered if it were common that Sarianna stayed behind the scenes when her father entertained. He wondered if she could not have simply walked away from it all by saying yes to any of the suitors he was sure she must have.

But if that were so, she would not be here tonight; she would not have taken what had to be an unusual stand for her.

It meant perhaps that she never intended to marry, or perhaps that Rex never intended her to marry. But that was insane; every woman's destiny was home and family. And if Sarianna had been convinced otherwise, *he* could meet that challenge.

He studied her a moment longer. It was a strange situation, and Sarianna's reactions were even stranger. He understood nothing about her or her relationship with the woman who was her aunt and the self-centered child who was her cousin. Vesta was scared of her for some reason, and so was Jeralee. They both worked hard at convincing her that her position in the house was inferior, when actually her rights superseded theirs. And Rex allowed it.

Indeed, Rex must have sanctioned it. Rex wanted it. Vesta had to be a much inferior version of Dona. And Sarianna the next best thing. Rex must hate her and love her—all at the same time. He wouldn't want to lose her; he would lose Dona altogether. So if there ever had been suitors, Rex must have discouraged them. *Really* discouraged them. Or Sarianna had not wanted any of them—but that didn't seem likely either. Why hadn't she fled from all the disdain they heaped on her?

It had to be Rex's doing. And Vesta's, for different reasons. But try as he might he couldn't picture Vesta at all in those long ago days when he had loved Dona with such an overpowering intensity. She had been a shadow in the background, that much younger, and—as was the custom—very much out of sight.

And now Vesta had everything that had been Dona's—including the fearsome reminder of what Dona had been.

Vesta hated. He caught it in her eyes just as he turned his gaze away from Sarianna's bright beauty. Vesta could kill for that seemingly effortless dexterity that Sarianna displayed among guests at the table. If she could destroy and wring from Sarianna whatever it was immutable about her that made her Sarianna, she would, and she would infuse it somehow into Jeralee so that *she* could become everything Sarianna was and she was not.

He saw it all in Vesta's eyes and in a brief spasmic anger that crossed her face as Sarianna's silvery voice flowed through pauses in conversation, sounding so much like a confident woman supremely enjoying herself.

If it were an act, it was a good one. Even Rex was looking at her through hooded eyes, almost as though he, too, were seeing the past merged with the present in a way he could not possibly like.

It was even possible, Cade thought, that Rex had kept her immured just so that the eligible men would not ever see her in just this way: as Dona's equal certainly, and still better—everything come perfectly together in one womanly being who could not ever escape the demons of her father's past.

And he would be the worst of all the ghosts that haunted Rex Broydon, he swore as he felt a hard dark anger envelop him for the way they had been treating Sarianna.

What better repayment for the way Rex had treated both Dona and his own father. The symmetry of it was perfect. He would take what Rex could not have: the reincarnation of Dona through her daughter whom only *he* was free to love.

She did not like the sense she had of Cade's watching her. There was an empathy there of something even she did not understand herself. Or maybe she did not want to understand it. No explanations were needed. Anytime she looked in the mirror, everything became clear. Yet as she sat at the table and directed the service and the conversation with equal ease, she felt the approval all around her, as if the men of her father's acquaintance had heretofore regarded her as some kind of freak and were caught off guard that she was a perfectly acceptable young woman who spoke intelligible words, had a passing amount of wit and pretty table manners.

She had to stamp down hard on her growing anger that her father had removed her so thoroughly from society that she was enjoying even this small forced taste of it. She felt no awkwardness at her table placement; rather it enhanced her ability to take pleasure in the meal because she knew she would not discommode anyone on either side of her.

But her father's active disapproval balanced her joy. She could not avoid it, nor did she have to look at him to feel it and sense it. He would have made her disappear if he could, and he had no recourse but to remain in his seat with his guests until such time as he would lead the men into the library for their hour of brandy.

She watched with dispassionate eyes when that moment finally came. He gave the signal this time, and the men rose in one body—even the unwilling Cade Rensell—threw down their napkins, and followed her father's elegant form through the door at the far end of the dining room, the one that was built so narrow that a hoop skirt could not get through it, which was no small discouragement to fashion-conscious women like Vesta and Jeralee.

She waited for Vesta to rise as well to conduct the ladies into the ballroom parlor for conversation and lemonade and wafers to cleanse their palates before dessert.

Vesta sent her a haughty look across the expanse of two tables in the long unwieldy pause that followed.

Vesta's eyes said without reservation that she, Sarianna, must carry on as the hostess now because she had had the nerve to take over, and now Vesta was willing to let her. And Vesta nudged Jeralee quite publicly when she opened her mouth to protest.

Sarianna looked beyond Vesta at the expectant faces around her, and she rose to her feet abruptly, put down her linen napkin and pushed out her chair. "Ladies." Her compelling voice commanded them to follow her to the opposite end of the dining room to still another door, wider this time, closed to the public eye, and she automatically reached out her left hand to grasp the doorknob, turn it, and push through the entrance to the parlor.

She found herself, as always, following the door and unable to turn gracefully unless she made a full circle to face her guests. She had no other choice; it looked impossibly ornate, but it was the only way to do it. Her body pivoted into the follow-through and she felt resentfully out of place in a world where objects like doorknobs and doors were made specifically for people who were born to be comfortable

49

using them.

Vesta noticed. Sarianna saw the smug look on her face as she motioned the women into the parlor and to the overloaded table set by the marble fireplace. Vesta was very happy to have witnessed that one moment of ineptitude. Vesta would celebrate it, toast her, never let her forget that grace was something she would never achieve because she was born that way.

Very well, Sarianna thought, reaching her benighted wrong hand out for a tall cold glass of lemonade. That was Vesta, and now she and Vesta were at war; and perhaps it was just as well the hostility was very much out in the open.

Sarianna stood in the grand entrance hall a little apart from her father, Vesta and Jeralee, who were bidding good-night to their Sawny Island neighbors heading home that night.

The Rudleys and the Grays were leaving as well as Samuel Summers, who made a pretty show over Jeralee before he descended the broad entrance steps to mount his fashionable carriage with three boys—two on the driver's perch and one behind—to carry the lantern light to see him home.

Sarianna could almost see Vesta counting the dollar cost of such extravagance and liking the sum she came up with very well. Behind her she could hear Victoria Gray's fluty voice, the words unintelligible, but the tone unmistakably flirtatious.

Sarianna folded her arms loosely around her waist. She knew nothing about coquetry; she thought Victoria sounded vain and foolish. No doubt the man on whom she unleashed these womanly wiles thought she was charming. The fool. She wondered who it was. And then a telling prickle down her spine and the change in Jeralee's courteous expression gave her the answer.

But the voice that spoke in her ear was not Cade Rensell's: "Sarianna." Was she disappointed? She looked up into the warm brown eyes of Pierce Darden, who seemed nicely amused by Victoria's antics.

"I trust Victoria was a stimulating dinner companion," Sarianna said, her voice just touched with the faintest irony.

"It was a lovely dinner," he agreed, looking deeply into her sparkling sapphire eyes, his mouth curved into a faint understanding

50

smile. "Victoria can be an entertaining conversationalist."

Sarianna smiled. "I'm sure you've learned more about Sawny Island and *her* family than you ever thought you wanted to know."

"It *was* very interesting," he concurred, searching her face, wondering just how much to tell her. "Especially the part about the Rensells."

Sarianna's expression froze. "Really."

He caught it. "Oh, no, Miss Sarianna—please; I meant nothing by it. I've caused you enough trouble tonight anyway. No—Cade wants to go out to Greenpoint tomorrow."

"I'll have Abel take him over," Sarianna told him, her tone dismissive. She knew little about her father's dealings with Parker Rensell, or why the fool man had drunk himself to death a week after her father had paid his debts and bought him out. She only knew that Cade was not going to like what he found at Greenpoint.

And perhaps he knew that too; or perhaps he had sensed what they were talking about, for he came up behind her, and she felt like bolting up the stairs. "I'd like *you* to take me, Sarianna," he said firmly.

She moved a pace or two away—she had to move away from him— and turned to face him. "Surely you don't need me to show and tell you what your eyes can very well see, Mr. Rensell."

"I surely need you, Sarianna."

She made a negating gesture with one hand. "My father knows your intention?"

"He knows I wish to visit *my* father's grave. As I do. Come with me, Sarianna."

Sarianna bent her head, fiercely aware of Jeralee's fulminating gaze tearing into her from across the hallway. Jeralee could not in good conscience leave her guests who were departing, but her good manners were just barely on the surface as she watched Sarianna captivating both Cade Rensell and his lawyer.

Sarianna bore the full force of the angry glances Jeralee periodically shot at the three of them. Cade could not know what he was asking. Her father would never let her alone off of Bredwood, and certainly not in the company of Cade Rensell. It was almost funny to think he thought it was possible. Just as surely, her father would probably agree to Jeralee going, she thought. Which would play right into Vesta's plans, and would satisfy Jeralee's not too subtle desire to have Cade to herself for an unspecified period of time. She would

51

even wager Jeralee would get away with going without a servant to accompany her.

She shook her head. And just why did she feel a slight longing to have the freedom to accede to his request? To spite Jeralee? Or because she wanted him to kiss her again? Because she could easily get used to the tenuous feeling of excitement and yearning she felt in his presence?

Why shouldn't she?

"I wish I could, Mr. Rensell, but you must know my father would never allow it," she said finally, meeting his eyes fully, sending a message—if she were aware of it—that she urgently wanted him to find a way that she could do it.

Cade's eyes flickered tellingly. "No, he wouldn't." He fixed his gaze on Rex as he shook hands with Victoria's father and spoke a few words with him while Vesta insincerely hugged the mother.

Jeralee's muddied gaze skewered him. He nodded at her and returned his attention to Sarianna. "We'll leave early. Very early. You ride? You must. No chaperones, Sarianna. Just the three of us. Only you."

She felt a chill of fear at the thought of defying her father—Vesta—Jeralee—and then a thrill of courting that danger and flaunting her daring after the fact. Why not? *Only you.* Whyever not?

"I'll come."

His hazel eyes flashed with approval, and he instantly perceived that Jeralee caught it. Damn. "Six o'clock tomorrow then. Here. Hell—here comes Jeralee. . . ."

Every guest had his own bedroom to which he was shown by Eon with his usual courtliness, but not even he could dissuade Miss Jeralee from her taking Mr. Cade up to his room. Her manners were disgraceful, and the worst of it was she showed no remorse, and so he said to Sarianna as he escorted her upstairs as well.

She thanked him for his concern and assured him that once Jeralee had some responsibility her manners would improve, but Eon knew better.

"She ain't never going to improve, Miss Sarianna, I don' care even if she catches dat Mr. Rensell in her net."

"Then it will become Mr. Rensell's problem," Sarianna murmured as she closed her door, but she didn't like the thoughts conjured up by the notion of the two of them together. Jeralee could be very beguiling as even she well knew, and Cade Rensell could be playing some kind of game that none of them could fathom by his actions. She wasn't sure, on reflection, that she altogether trusted him, but the thought of sneaking out in the morning with him was not without a peculiar kind of excitement.

Alzine came very soon after to help her with her dress and pull down the bedcovers, but even as she climbed into her venerable four-poster, she felt too keyed up to sleep. She listened idly to Alzine's low voice as she folded clothes and hung her dress carefully in the chifferobe. "All am quiet, Miss Sarianna. Dey all is gone to sleep; dey is tired from all de dancing after. I believe dey didn't stop till past midnight, and dat be a good party, folks is gonna say. Miss Jeralee be mighty pleased no one done wanted to go. Ain't that so, Miss Sarianna?"

Sarianna's lips curved into her quirky smile. "I hope and pray Miss Jeralee was pleased." But she would be the last to admit it anyway, unless her solitary moments with Cade Rensell tonight were the stuff of her romantic dreams. And if they weren't, Sarianna concluded with a heavy heart, Jeralee would claim they were anyway. No matter what the truth, Jeralee would have it all her own way.

But then again, Jeralee wasn't going with him to Greenpoint tomorrow. Mutiny upon mutiny, she thought wryly. Vesta might well put her into some kind of solitary confinement after the coming escapade. She supposed she had been lucky even to still occupy the room she had slept in as a child. She had wanted it, even though it was smaller than some of the upstairs rooms, and for the reason that it overlooked the flower garden and the long vista of the fields beyond. Far and away was the distant sparkle of water from the boat landing on the intervening river between the island and the mainland, and it was the only place in the house that gave even a glimpse of it.

She loved her room, it was so manageable and contained. No one had tried to change it, or convince her to move—yet they thought they were putting something over on her by letting her stay in it.

Vesta was a fool, Sarianna thought suddenly, stupid and petty, and nothing like her sister, and perhaps her vindictiveness stemmed from the fact that she herself knew it and she thought Sarianna didn't.

I know it, Sarianna thought, and she knew that and more

instinctively about Vesta. Something had changed tonight, and she wasn't sure it didn't have something to do with Cade Rensell's arrival. Even if he were the catalyst, she was absolutely sure she had been very ready to break free of the constraints that Vesta and her father imposed on her. She had thought about it so much, and she could not stop thinking about the events of the evening for almost the rest of the night.

The wonder was, she was able to awaken early, even though she knew she had fallen asleep barely past two o'clock. Some internal excitement jolted her upright in the depths of the dark as a far-off clock chimed a half hour.

Instantly she jumped out of bed and began pulling underclothes and her riding habit from the chifferobe, brushing aside the morning gown that Alzine had laid out for her. And damn the hooks and tapes she had to fuss with before she could don the wide-skirted dress, which, without the minimum whalebone support, hung limply around her legs.

But there was no time to tend to anything but convenience. She performed the quickest toilette, secured her hair with yet another net snood pinned tightly, pulled up the skirt and fastened it with a belt, and dashed into the bedroom hallway and then down the wide curving stairs.

The grandfather clock in the family parlor read a quarter of the hour as she sped past and toward the front hallway adjacent to the ballroom. No one was up, save perhaps Sylvia in the kitchen preparing the morning's gargantuan company breakfast. But in the sleeping silence of the house, not a soul was about except Sarianna, who pulled open the connecting door to the hallway and crept carefully out from behind it.

"Shhh . . ."

A hand reached out for hers, and for one hysterical moment she believed it was her father in the shadowed curve of the front staircase, looming so tall and dark.

She grasped Cade's hand without a word, and they cautiously opened the front door and let themselves out.

"Pierce is getting the horses," Cade whispered as they made their way down the broad steps and cut across the wide lawn toward the stable. When they were clear of the house, they broke into a run and arrived breathlessly as Pierce brought their mounts out from the stalls.

They mounted and walked the horses, with Sarianna in the lead, to the outlying road by a shortcut she knew; from there, it was about a half hour ride around to the opposite side of the island.

As they came closer and closer to Greenpoint, Cade's nerves began to tingle, and it was impossible not to relive old memories. Everything seemed familiar and nothing. He couldn't even tell which direction the old Wayte plantation lay, but that could hardly any longer exist: Hadn't Wilmot Wayte sold up after Dona married Rex, and gone off to Charleston to live with his sister Sallie? He couldn't remember anymore. All those details. All those frenetic yearning nights. All the anguish.

Hadn't there been two stone columns marking the entrance to Greenpoint? But for miles now there was nothing, just fenced fields, planted and picked. And the sun rose over a different kind of desolation as Cade finally was able to pick out what remained of the stone pillars that his father had so lovingly built at the entrance to the drive to Greenpoint.

The trees remained. The long gravel drive still wound gracefully under a double row of tall leaf dripping oak trees that looked hardy and welcoming. He cantered up the drive expectantly, followed closely by Pierce and reluctantly by Sarianna. She knew what he thought he was going to see: the homey two-story house where he had been born, with its long comfortable porch, and sweeping green lawns. And she knew what he would find.

Nothing.

"Sarianna!"

She couldn't mistake the rage in his voice. As she cantered into view, she saw he had dismounted and was pacing around the field that once had contained a house. A field that grew wheat now—and memories that lived only in Cade Rensell's mind. And that had been accomplished in only two years—by her father. So what did he think she could tell him that he couldn't see for himself?

She unhooked her leg from the pommel of her saddle and slid to the ground. Cade was standing directly ahead of her, and it was as if he heard the thud of her feet as she hit dirt; he wheeled on her angrily. *"Why?"*

She didn't answer; she made a show of tethering her horse to a nearby bush to gain a moment's respite.

"Look at it."

"I see," she said quietly, finally approaching him. She had not seen it before; her father had discussed it with Vesta, and she had overheard. He had put every last board and brick of the house to use somehow on Bredwood, but she couldn't tell Cade that—not with that look on his face that said he was almost ready to tear apart anyone named Broydon who had had a hand in this betrayal.

But after all, Cade Rensell had not been around to stop it. Rex had done what he thought best—for himself first, surely, and then for Parker Rensell, who had been drowning in debt and whose property would have been foreclosed anyway. Parker had sold off his stock of slaves first before he had considered that he would have to sell Greenpoint as well. He had found he couldn't afford day labor and couldn't get the crop in by himself with one or two loyal field hands who had stayed. Parker had been a drunkard then, or so Rex had said, so it really had been a matter of time before things came to a head with him. And not nearly enough time for Cade to come to the rescue personally.

Or maybe her father had been just a little too self-serving, and after just a little too much in the way of vengeance. Sarianna would never know, but the look on Cade's bitter face told her plainly that *he* was going to find out.

"Tell me what you know," he said harshly.

"I know very few facts, only what I've heard and what I've conjectured," she temporized, hoping he would not settle for gossip and overheard conversations she might or might not have comprehended accurately.

He motioned for her to continue, and she sighed. She could not play the simpering lady with him; he knew already she was far too intelligent, and reliable for that matter.

"All right. Your father ran several years of bad crops; he expanded too fast and apparently drank too much—everyone said he did. He borrowed against future income, and he finally got caught. At that point, there *were* rumors that someone was trying to bail him out, but he apparently did not have the acumen to know the best way to make use of the windfall. So the slaves went first," she added hesitantly as his expression darkened. "You don't want to hear the rest."

"But I do," he said stonily, tracing a long line with his boot that might have been the wall to his boyhood home around a foot of the perimeter of the wheat field.

"He sold off the slaves, he had to, even though he knew he couldn't afford day labor. He thought he and two of the older hands who had stayed could manage enough to get by that year. But he was never around to work it, and he lost it, and the land had to go."

"And Rex seized the opportunity, he was such a good friend," Cade put in rambunctiously.

"Did he?" Sarianna said coolly. "Mr. Darden?" She turned to Pierce.

"You know," Pierce said firmly, "your father came to me, Cade. We drew up the condition of sale, which included house, land, implements and restitution of debts."

"And any number of Sawnians were after that land, Mr. Rensell; you should be aware of that. Father outbid them. He was determined, especially after Samuel Summer got the Wayte place ten years ago when Wilmot sold up and went to Charleston. Father bought out Greenpoint by bidding just a little higher, and your father took the money—I don't know how much it came to—and went over into Savannah, rented a room, bought himself a case of bourbon and drank till he dropped." She found the nerve after telling him that to look into his burning eyes. "That's what everyone said, Mr. Rensell. He drank himself to death in that room, and everyone knows it."

He didn't like hearing it either; a muscle jumped in his jaw as if he were keeping back an explosive anger with great effort. His hands clenched and unclenched in futility, but there was nothing he could do now, nothing. Sarianna had not been the cause of the tragedy, but his own precipitate removal from Sawny hadn't helped matters either. And nothing, if he were honest with himself, could have helped his father once he took to drinking; he had known that himself, and still *he* had allowed himself to be persuaded to go. If anything, he bore more blame than anyone else. He had been glad to be free of Sawny and Dona's spell. Maybe he had even looked for a way out, and his father had handed it to him, knowing what he was sacrificing.

Damn and damn. "What about the house," he asked after a while, leveling his voice to temper his growing frustration.

And how did she tell him about that? Sarianna wondered, collecting her wits. His contained fury over the truth of his father's demise was enough to cope with for one morning. She wondered that she had thought she would be participating in some kind of romantic adventure. There was a wall between them now: She was Rex's daughter and he was the victim.

"Father did not want or need another house on the island," she said finally, plainly. "He decided not to make the mistake your father made, and one of the reasons he wanted the property was the proximity to the water on two sides. He diversified into rice. He kept the workers' accommodations and the overseer's house, and since he is only a short ride away . . ."

"Yes, of course," he said, as her voice trailed away. His tone was flat, opaque. He understood fully the why of it; he just could not forgive it. "Pierce!"

"Cade?" Pierce's voice was reassuring, calm. Sarianna marveled at his even-handedness; it wasn't as if he had not known most of what she had told Cade. Perhaps he had even laid out the very same details to him from his own point of view and what *he* had heard. "It can't be changed," Pierce said firmly.

"Don't I know it!" Cade wheeled and started to walk away from the field that was all that was left of Greenpoint. And then he pivoted back. "Where is he buried?" he barked at Pierce.

"Up on the bluff, of course," Pierce told him, and Cade felt a buzzing in his ears: fate laughing, a darkness descending, or that fateful symmetry? He didn't know. He heard Pierce say from a distance, "You know how he loved it there."

Somehow he found the wit to reply, "I remember," but he didn't remember. He remembered only his own history there, no one else's, and all the agonizing hours he had spent there on that rise overlooking the ocean, yearning for Dona, meeting with her, loving her in secret. He looked at Sarianna, his hard eyes assessing the slender body of the woman who could have been her double. Maybe retribution and redemption did lie in her unknowing hands.

For an instant he felt time reeling backward once again, and he shook himself. He *knew* this was Sarianna, and he knew she was aware of his dark invasion of her soul. She would be the end and the beginning both—he swore it, for he knew he was about to deliberately and painstakingly create a history with Sarianna—and he reveled in his lust for the vengeance he would take.

They climbed the bluff into the wind, and the energy he expended

58

dissipated all his initial fury and left a cold little knot of determination in the pit of his stomach. He could accept what he could not change; he had mourned months before. The wonder was that as they topped the rise that faced the water, he felt no memories rushing over him to incapacitate him. He felt nothing but a sense of calm and purpose, and an inner strength to do what needed to be done.

After all, he thought, watching Sarianna's golden head as the wind tousled the loose tendrils of hair around her face, it would be very easy to love Sarianna. Very easy to make her want him. Not so easy to get her away from Rex—and to do it before his very eyes. To have him relive the past. To make him suffer.

He had absolutely no conscience about that; Sarianna would not die a spinster in her father's house, a too vivid double of the woman who had betrayed him. If he did nothing else, he was determined to get her away from that.

But he felt her wariness, almost as if she sensed he was plotting and scheming somehow. She distrusted him; she thought his fury had melted away much too fast. She saw nothing in his eyes for the loss of his father whose small, square marble tombstone he stood over that moment. Nothing of the resentment derived from what Greenpoint had come to—they could see so very clearly from the bluff the flooded fields and the workers already knee-deep in water raking the stalks.

But he felt nothing. Yes, his eyes were dry. Pierce had been the one to bury his father, and Pierce had picked up the pieces and found him an inheritance he did not want. What emotion could he show for that? Gratitude to Pierce only, but even then, his father had not trusted Pierce enough not to kill himself.

Come to that, one part of his businessman's mind could applaud Rex for taking the bold step of turning the fields to rice, for making profitable the verdant land that no Rensell would ever own again.

It had not been quite so real to him in California and Nevada. But here, on the wind-buffeted bluff, in a place that had been steeped in memories, here it became real and clear and his purpose plain.

He buried the pain as far as it would go and turned to Sarianna. "We'll leave."

She smiled uncertainly and followed him as he turned down the path from the top of the bluff.

She was totally uncertain how to proceed with him now. There was something chilling about his expression as he viewed his father's grave. She wondered how he really felt about what he saw. How could he remove himself and view it all so dispassionately after his initial bitter anger? Rensells had lived at Greenpoint for generations. But her father had had no love for Parker Rensell, who couldn't even control his own son's passion for his neighbor's wife. Oh, her father had set out to ruin Parker Rensell—she was almost sure of it—and it wouldn't take much wit for Cade to figure it out.

His calm acceptance was unnatural.

Damn, she did not understand men and their ways, she didn't. She would have expected Cade to come after Rex with a gun after all that had happened, and instead he honorably accepted hospitality from the man he must hate. She saw nothing of his lust for revenge except the cold mask he presented to her as they picked their way slowly down the path.

When they reached the horses, he turned to her. "This is what *I* know, Sarianna. My father started drinking even before he made me leave. I knew I was abandoning him to it, but he was adamant I had to go. Damn it, what did I care what everyone would think about the circumstances of Dona's death? Do you know how much I *really* lost, Sarianna? *Do you?*"

She shook her head mutely. She couldn't speak; she would scream if she opened her mouth. She didn't want to hear about her mother—and him. *Never. Ever.*

"Neither do I," he said abruptly, and she felt as though she had climbed a precipice and had been pushed off. Her heart was pounding wildly as he went on in that same flat voice: "I'll *never* know if she were what I thought she was. He would have made me leave in any event, my father. It was too much, Sarianna, and it was obvious she was not going to leave your father. I became reconciled to that. And that is what happened."

But not all, she thought, because she knew. She had seen them together once, the night he had met with her mother for the last time; she had found the note, and she had gone after them. It could not have been all just because of that, and she would never tell him that she knew.

She did not refute his story; as far as it went, it was probably true. And she would never question it. Why should she? He would be gone after a few days, with or without Jeralee in his pocket, and the dangerous attraction she felt would dissolve into the fairy tale that it was.

For now, she was at the mercy of the lion and whatever he chose to tell her or do with her. But even so, the contained power of his masculinity spoke powerfully to her in some elemental way. She could not let herself succumb to it. There was too much to him, and too much tied up in him with her family. *He* was the realist, after all. He would never let her dream, and his golden words: *come with me . . . only you,* had proved to be just a ruse to lure her to a place where he could take out his fury on the least culpable person in her family, and the one who would feel it the most.

Damn it, she did; it overwhelmed her even as she knew there was no reparation for his pain. Or perhaps he wanted to cause pain—and the thought shocked her. Her romantic image had clouded her judgment altogether; he *had* known—she was sure he had known—exactly what he was doing.

5

They had been gone about two hours, Sarianna estimated when they pulled up at the stables. In the distance, beyond the trees that separated the house and lawn and gardens from the working area of Bredwood, she could see movement, and she knew the servants were setting up the long tables on the lawn for Sylvia's massive breakfast *al fresco*.

And she knew that Vesta would have come to wake her so she could supervise. She didn't know quite what to expect as she took the servants' staircase up to the second floor, but she certainly didn't reckon on finding Vesta waiting for her in her room.

Vesta was livid. "Why, Sarianna, you sly puss, sneaking out after Mr. Rensell this morning. How we all have misjudged you."

Sarianna moved past her briskly. There was no way to talk with Vesta now, nothing to say to excuse her inexcusable behavior; but why should she be accountable to Vesta, after all, who was only protecting Jeralee's rights. "Perhaps you all have," she agreed noncommittally, seating herself at her dressing table. God, she did not like what she saw in the mirror; her own cheeks were flushed as if she were admitting some kind of culpability, and Vesta stood three feet behind her, consumed with an ill-concealed rage that was about to go out of control.

"Of course," Vesta went on, "I only came to see you to remind you to . . . but that's irrelevant now since I took care of it myself. Imagine my surprise when I found the room empty."

"Imagine," Sarianna murmured, forcing herself to put her hands to her head to pull the pins from her snood—anything to occupy herself so she did not have to face the full brunt of Vesta's oncoming explosion.

"Two *hours*, Sarianna."

"Yes, it takes that long to get to Greenpoint and bury a man's childhood," Sarianna said—futilely, because she knew Vesta didn't really hear a word of it.

"And it takes five minutes for—certain other events to be consummated," Vesta retorted, her muddied eyes boring into Sarianna's reflection.

"I have no idea what you are talking about."

"The hell you haven't," Vesta spat. "So obvious you are, just like your mother, Sarianna; no wonder Rex has had to take precautions all these years. And still—! A ravishing man comes into view, and his little nun goes tearing off in the small hours of the morning when she thinks no one will see, and has her way. My dear—a nunnery is surely where you belong."

"Do suggest it to father since *his* old-fashioned methods seem not to have worked," Sarianna retorted out of shock. She was utterly stunned by Vesta's attack. It went beyond anything Vesta had ever said before in public or private about her limitations. Like her mother? *So* like her mother? Maybe she was; maybe it was that part of her that felt the enormous pull toward Cade Rensell. Maybe that kind of thing was passed down through birth and she had no control whatsoever.

Maybe she was getting hysterical.

"He asked me to go," she said suddenly, even though she knew Vesta would never believe it.

And plainly she didn't. "He asked *you*? *You*? Not your father? Not me, to arrange a carriage and Abel to drive him? *You*? So early in the morning? Please, Sarianna, your lies are going beyond belief. *You*, to take *him* to Greenpoint at six in the morning? It's laughable. My dear, it's pathetic; I think you are becoming unbalanced."

Was she? Or was Vesta, contemplating what might have happened after she witnessed the delicious prelude the evening before? Sarianna clenched the brush which she had picked up and had not yet used. She watched her knuckles turn white, and felt her face drain of its color. Her head whirled at the bald directness of the attack; and she knew she had to retaliate or Vesta would go on and on with her poisonous vituperation, and there would never be an end to it, not even after Cade Rensell walked out of their lives—laughing.

She put down the brush because otherwise she would have thrown it at Vesta's preternaturally calm mask that belied the viciousness that issued from her mouth—Dona's mouth—and one of the few real similarities of feature between them.

"I see," Sarianna said slowly, turning her body so she could look Vesta full in the eye. "You mean to tell me that if Mr. Rensell had approached you about going to Greenpoint, you would have been perfectly satisfied to arrange transportation for him there, and would not have been averse to providing him with some *other* feminine company—*even* so early in the morning—and you would have considered it proper and right that Jeralee accompany him instead of me?"

Vesta's eyes glittered, and she took a step forward. "You *are* a little bitch," she hissed, and her arm snaked out and whacked Sarianna across the side of the head. "You're absolutely right; that is exactly what I would have done," she added for good measure. "I told you not to get in her way." And she whirled and stalked out of the room.

Sarianna did not move. Her head was ringing with the force of the blow, and her mind refused to function. And she had thought the thing was out in the open finally. She had had no conception of the virulence against her that festered in Vesta's soul.

My God, my God, my . . . Lord—she shook her head. It hurt. That horrible woman had really hurt her and had meant to hurt her like that. She pushed aside her hair, and there was the evidence of it—her ear and part of her cheek were blood red, and the mark of Vesta's fingers stood out like the mark of Cain.

She just sat looking at herself. Vesta might kill her if she could find a good enough reason to exonerate her. But why? Why why why? The loathing and the malice . . . and her father allowed it, participated in it, and Vesta could even get away with physically assaulting her because of it.

God.

She sat; she could not move. It all overwhelmed her, and she knew without even analyzing it, that it all had to do with Cade Rensell and the past and her mother.

She *had* to get away from them. She had never felt so frantic or

64

hopeless before. Helpless. Either she had to get away, or Cade Rensell had to leave, and quickly. If he were gone, her life would become outwardly more peaceful. Yes. She would go, or he would go.

Maybe she could ask him. Maybe he would do it. Maybe she was becoming crazed with stupid ideas because the blow to her head had already deranged her.

She could not arrange Cade Rensell's life. The only thing she could do was save herself. She could run away.

She laughed out loud at the absurdity of that—with no money, alone, and from an island. How? How? How, without her father coming after her instantly or her secreting herself under one of the long, landing docks.

God, she was getting crazy. . . .

Her father hadn't even known she was gone this morning. Two hours—what could she accomplish in two hours if she were running away? She could get to the Sawny mercantile at the dock, wait for them to open and somehow convince Arvill Summer—Samuel's indigent nephew who ran the store with his uncle's money and lived at Summerton on the other side of the island with the family—that she really needed to book passage to the mainland and she really was going alone—unthinkable—and her father approved.

The perfect plan—doomed to failure. . . .

She felt her head nodding, and somehow she roused herself to just enough energy to stumble to the bed. Perhaps, she thought woozily the instant before she dozed off, she could convince Cade Rensell to take her with him when he left.

Alzine woke her an hour later. "What happen to yo' head, Miss Sarianna?"

Sarianna shook her head fuzzily and collected herself enough to say, "I expect I slept on that side and the cover wrinkled up under me."

"Don' look like dat to me," Alzine muttered as she began removing fresh underclothing from the walnut bureau. "I done ironed dat purty white dress fo' you. Lookit." She motioned behind her to the chifferobe door where she had hung the dress on the hook over the mirror.

"That looks fine," Sarianna murmured, not in the least willing to try to stand upright at the moment.

"You don' look fine, Miss Sarianna. You sick?"

"I'm fine."

"All dem fine folk is readyin' deyselves fo' one huge breakfast, ma'am, an' you got to be readyin' yo'self now, too."

"I will, Alzine."

"Now, Miss Sarianna. You know Miss Vesta expects you down dere fo' direction."

"She expects too damn much," Sarianna muttered, easing her body upright. Duty pushed her; until their guests had gone, she must present an amicable if not enthusiastic face to them. No one must get even a whiff of the discord between her and Vesta, and she knew Vesta was counting on her feeling that way.

Why should she? she wondered as she swung her legs over the bed. Vesta probably would treat her in that same sanctimoniously condescending way; why should she bear the burden of smoothing over Vesta's bad manners?

She could hardly answer that question when she could not even decide what pair of shoes to wear with the dress. A pretty dress it was, if a trifle girlish. Vesta had commissioned it, adding the ruffly touches and the high neck and the virginal, blue satin ribbon, while Alzine when she "done ironed" the dress, reshaped the sleeves and neck and removed the telling blue sash, substituting a narrow white belt that she had garnered from somewhere—from Jeralee's discards, Sarianna thought to herself. But she could not even find amusement in that today.

Curious, she stood up and made her way to her dressing table. She looked a total shambles: Her hair was a nest of unmanageable curls flying in all directions, her riding habit was a mass of wrinkles, and her face was puffy.

She pulled back the telling hank of hair, and there, visible under it, was still the remnant of Vesta's fury: the fading blotch with the fingerprint.

"I help you," Alzine said behind her. "I see what we got to do, Miss Sarianna. You let me do de work, and you is gonna be just fine."

Sarianna stared at Alzine's reflection. That look was there again, that sympathy and kindness. Empathy of the oppressed.

She closed her eyes so she wouldn't see it and signaled for Alzine to begin.

* * *

66

In the bold morning light, it was easier to take count of those who had chosen to remain. Sarianna paused as she came out onto the long, side porch, caught by the gracious spectacle of Bredwood's guests crowding around the bountiful buffet tables, helping themselves to gravy sauced meats, corn bread, muffins, fruit, platters of ham, potatoes, eggs, hominy, coffee, tea, and lemonade, something for every taste, to be heaped on fine china already laid on individual trays to be taken to smaller, congenial tables set up under the trees, to be eaten in the convivial company of each guest's choice.

The sun beat down, an all enveloping blanket beneath a brilliant blue sky, and in the leaves, the wind whispered ancient secrets in a soughing underscore to the lively conversation.

It was a moment out of time, a picture framed by the soaring tree trunks and grounded by the emerald green lawn, reassuring, elegant, ongoing and unchanging.

Sarianna stepped off of the porch and onto the lawn, feeling just a little burdened by the weight of her long-unused hoop, and choked by the feel of the erstwhile blue satin sash that was now wound around her neck and tied around her bosom in a way that called attention to the newly lowered neckline, as well as heightening the color of her eyes.

She felt conspicuous and overdressed, and she knew Vesta would not miss the sophisticated changes and would mark these, too, against her in her ledger of hate.

At a far table, under the sighing trees, she could see Jeralee surrounded by their childhood friends, Eula and Peter and William Rudley who, along with their parents, Victoria Gray and her parents, and Samuel Summers, had returned for the morning repast. Gaff Gilmartin's long gangly figure hovered above them, comically seeking a place, and Jeralee's head turned covertly this way and that, seeking first view of Cade Rensell when he finally would join them for breakfast.

Sarianna paused. No one yet had taken notice of her. Her father's back was to her, and Vesta pretended not to see her, or else Samuel Summers' repartee had become vastly more amusing than it had been in the past. Whatever it was, she felt isolated from them all, and physically unable to take one step forward to join in their gaiety.

And then: "Sarianna?" His rough caressing voice at her elbow startled her.

"Mr. Rensell?" she said coolly, just glancing over her shoulder where he hovered like some dark bird of prey, congratulating herself she had enough presence of mind to answer him civilly.

"Can't it be Cade?" he asked gently.

"I hardly think so," she said, frantically searching for a place to escape to that he could not follow.

"Sarianna . . ."

Oh, his voice! Did he *like* saying her name so much? It was so tempting to encourage him to take his obvious momentary admiration and store it against the future cold winter. She saw herself, a mangy hungry squirrel with a golden bushy tail, ferreting in a dead tree for the remnants of that moment of warmth.

How sad.

"Yes, Mr. Rensell?" Thank goodness her brain was still operating on some social plane that knew exactly when to answer properly and what to say. She felt giddy. Only the wired cage of her hoop supported her, she thought or she might have toppled flat over.

She felt his firm fingers grasp her bare elbow. The contact, to her, was electric. She didn't want him touching her. She didn't want him anywhere near her this morning. She wrenched her arm away, but he only took it again, this time in a tight grip that brooked no resistance.

"Pierce has saved us space at that table," he said firmly, the tone of his voice now edging on harshness. He felt as though he had captured a leery butterfly whose wings would tear with a single tug of his hand.

"I don't particularly want to sit with you or Mr. Darden," Sarianna said carefully, slanting a sharp look at his set face.

"Pretty manners, Sarianna, for a hostess. Of course you do. And you don't want to make a scene about it."

Sleeping beauty, he thought, pushing her deliberately forward and finally into the corner chair that Pierce held out for her. Time to awaken her.

"Good morning, Miss Sarianna," Pierce said pleasantly as if nothing were amiss.

"Good morning," she replied civilly, fully aware that everyone had watched their progress through the maze of tables to the one Pierce had deliberately chosen that was set farther away and just a little apart from the others. Of course everyone noticed. She felt skewered by their knowing looks.

"What will you eat?" Cade asked her, bending over her shoulder once again to hear her response, but he knew it was fruitless to ask. Nonetheless, he appeared solicitous and caring to those watching, and

Sarianna seemed stonily rude as she stared past Pierce's head at a vista of perfectly trimmed bushes and precisely aligned trees that edged the lawn and separated it from the stables.

Her hands, clenched in her lap, felt like iced stone. She had the feeling at any moment her father, Jeralee and Vesta would converge on their table and yank her up and bear her away. She wasn't even aware that Cade left, or even when he returned, until a tray was set down in front of her containing a steaming cup of coffee, eggs, a slice of ham, two fragrant beaten biscuits dripping with butter and a dish of fresh peaches steeped in brandy.

Her hands reached automatically for the coffee to cup it in her palms, and with its heat, a welcome warmth flooded her veins and galvanized her to life. She looked across the table at Pierce's kind face and concerned gaze, and everything returned to normal.

She was overreacting; she had let Vesta scare her, threaten her, frighten her beyond measure. And over what? The fact that Cade Rensell was momentarily intrigued with her. How could he not be? And what could Vesta or Jeralee do about it anyway, here? Now?

She smiled reassuringly at Pierce and sipped from her coffee cup, keenly aware of Cade's heated gaze following every movement. She had not said a word to him, but she knew she didn't need to; the thing between them even she in her innocence recognized, and she knew there was nothing she could do to prevent it. It was almost as though it were foreordained that he should return and she should be the object of his interest because of her very history, because of her face, because she was after all her mother's daughter.

How could she stop it? She didn't want to stop it, the more so because Vesta and Jeralee so desperately wanted her to.

Oh, no. She touched her face tenderly at the very place where Vesta had struck her. Oh, no. It was her turn now; she would take the moment while she could—and damn the future.

"Walk with me, Sarianna." His first words to her, through a long hour of desultory conversation between her and Pierce and the two others who shared their table; she had not spoken to him at all, but the awareness simmered between them. And something else. Some resolution on her part, something that had aroused her from that earlier torpor and made the erstwhile china doll set of her face come alive again with her speaking blue gaze and quirky little smile.

"I would like that," Sarianna said conventionally, but her heart was pounding already from the sheer force of imagining Jeralee's steaming rage. She knew Jeralee was watching her; she knew Vesta had not missed a single movement she had made and counted every one of them on the slate of slights against Jeralee's interests.

No matter. Cade held her chair as she slid upright, and he took her arm, just as other couples were doing, and guided her past the buffet and dining tables toward the rear of the house.

She shook off the vague feeling of discomfort. It wasn't as if there were no tacit chaperones; servants flitted everywhere, attending to their clean-up tasks, keeping a covert eye on everyone. She could almost feel Alzine's eyes following her, ever vigilant; and beyond her, Jeralee's fiery gaze scorched her back with every step she took.

But her malaise had nothing to do with Jeralee either. If anything, she felt a flaring excitement at challenging her. No, it was something else, ingrown and internal and not, it turned out, very well concealed from Cade Rensell's perceptive eye.

"Sarianna?"

Again that bending caressing note in his voice.

"Mr. Rensell?" The polite tone of her words belied just how deeply she felt the distinctive way he pronounced her name. She needed a shield from him, and what better deflector than sheer good manners?

But he did not like it, and she knew it. She was bothered in some strange indefinable way, and he could not have that, especially with Jeralee and Vesta looking on and marking every nuance of their conversation—such as it was so far. "Are you uncomfortable with me, Sarianna?"

"Not in the least," she said smoothly.

"Nervous?"

"I should think not."

"Scared of me, Sarianna?"

"Should I be?" she countered.

He grinned at her, that unrepentant smile that creased the deep-etched lines on either side of his face. "Probably."

"Your honesty is refreshing, Mr. Rensell."

"So would yours be," he returned in kind. "What's wrong, Sarianna?"

She knew, and it was at once both silly and very real, and the wonder was she felt it when she wasn't even used to walking about with a man, whereas Alzine was very used to her eccentricities, and Jeralee ignored them altogether.

"I would feel a whole lot better if you were walking to my left," she said frankly, wondering what he thought of this odd request. He didn't discount it; he promptly changed sides, and she felt a deep sense of relief and more, gratitude for his sensitivity.

"Better?"

"More than I can tell you."

They walked on in silence a moment or two more, rounding the far end of the house which led to the broad sweep of the rear lawn, the fragrant groves of fruit trees, the arbors and the kitchen gardens. Everywhere, despite the presence of guests, there was a buzz of activity.

Cade watched her expressive face as she watched the bustle of the workers. So easy to love Sarianna, he thought, and he knew he did not have the time to pursue her the way she deserved. He didn't have the time for anything but insulting directness, and he felt compelled to say, "And will you want to be on the left side of the bed when we sleep together, Sarianna?"

Her sapphire eyes shot to his in shock. "I beg your pardon, Mr. Rensell? Did I hear you correctly?"

"Cade, Sarianna."

"Mr. Rensell," she said severely, "you are either mocking me or this is some kind of new form of flirting; either way, I can't possibly handle it. I don't know anything about flirting, and I most assuredly will never sleep with you; and the question, furthermore, is positively insulting." Perfect indignation, she thought with rising excitement, while her heart hammered wildly at just the suggestion he might *want* to. But why? she asked herself realistically as she assessed his reaction to her prim little speech. To compare her with Dona? To gossip still more about her deficiencies?

Why?

"My dear Sarianna, of course you will sleep with me." He grasped her shoulders suddenly and turned her against the nearest tree so that she was backed against its trunk and could not move past his muscular length.

"I see," she said coolly. "And you mean to tie me to the tree until I submit, is that it, Mr. Rensell?"

71

He had to admire her poise, he really did, especially in the face of the gamble he was taking; but she couldn't know that. Her curiosity and playfulness stunned him; but under it was a tense quivery wariness, as if she were telling herself it wasn't real, and she mustn't let herself believe it was real. "Oh, no," he murmured, "I mean to capture your lips and prove you are capable of the kind of feeling that will lead you to my bed," and he lowered his head meaningfully, slanting his mouth across hers, feeling the softness of her lips with quick tentative little kisses, waiting for her to deny him and sure that she wouldn't.

She felt a simultaneous reaction with each pleasurable foray of his lips: *Oh no, oh yes,* and somewhere between those brief awakening pressures, she sighed. "Mr. Rensell . . ."

"Cade."

"I couldn't," she murmured against the next light coercive caress.

"So proper, Sarianna. Of course you must. Try."

God, *was* she really standing in the middle of the gardens at Bredwood kissing this *man,* this stranger, this person who had known this place before?

She had to be dreaming; she hadn't yet awakened from that dizzying blow Vesta had dealt her. She felt his teeth firmly tug at her lower lip and his long fingers slide sensitively from her shoulder to her neck to her mouth to feel the texture of her lips, to compel her by his touch.

"This is hardly proper," she managed to say with some asperity.

"We don't have time to be proper, Sarianna," he said roughly. "We have time . . . we only have time to know each other's names." His mouth hovered over hers for a long breathtaking moment before he crushed her lips beneath his, seeking to imprint her with his urgency and his ever growing desire. How delicate she really was, and how slender and long against him, made—he thought then—to fit in perfect apposition to his angularity. He would be her seducer and her lover both, at the same time; there was no other course, and there was no other end to the burning sense of recognition he felt within him—and her.

She could not refuse him; she did not know how, and she did not want to know now. Her quiescent passion was like a long-burning fuse, to be lit with great care and caretaking for just how and where the explosion would finally come.

She had an innocence, an eagerness, a purity and a radiant

womanly instinct for the right movement, the right expressive little sound that conquered every inhibition he felt about his chosen course. Possession was everything, and he possessed her now as he delved deeply into her mouth and made her come to him willingly, made her seek his tongue with a hunger that was growing greater than his own, made her yearn for the very thing she thought she never would have—someone who could love and desire her as she was for all she was.

Each time he relinquished her ardent lips, he felt their swollen texture with sensitized fingers that waited to catch their movement as she breathed a response, a sigh, an encouragement, his name.

He captured her mouth again, and this time his kisses were not respectful; they were voluptuous, hard-driving male declarations of overpowering need and overriding intention. They left her breathless and begging to taste of more of him, and still more, deeper and more heated, more demanding than anything she had experienced in her life. She gave him everything and it was not enough, and she had the dawning awareness there would be more—not here, not now—and that the surging hunger she felt was a prelude to it. She adored his lusty kisses and the way he teased her with his tongue and lips and fingers, thrusting one or the other of them between her parted lips almost mindlessly, in concert with the hoarse echo of her name: Sarianna, Sarianna—like a litany of desire so tangible she could take it into her mouth and savor it as well.

She was totally his now, and his damp fingers and urgent mouth explored every inch of her that he could reach. He held her golden head quiescent with both hands, and then one hand at just the angle that he could delve deeply into her sweet wetness, and taste and feel the contour of her mouth, so insensate with the erotic feel of her response that in those fevered hot moments he could conceive of nothing else he wanted more.

He held her provoking intoxicating mouth away from his, inches away, for a long moment to contemplate her swelling lips. "Sarianna?"

She opened her eyes slightly, and he watched, fascinated, as her lips formed the words, "Yes, Cade?"

"Say again, Sarianna?"

Her quirky little smile appeared, and he touched it wonderingly as she murmured again, "Yes, Cade?"

He smiled, and she was utterly captivated by that smile and the softness of his eyes as he gazed down on her and brushed back the hair over her left ear.

She felt him stiffen, and she knew why.

"Who *did* that?" His voice, steely soft, demanded an answer.

She shook her head. "It doesn't matter."

He released her and tilted her head sideways to take a better look. "Oh, hell, it matters, Sarianna; there's a nice raised welt there." He touched it and she winced. "Who, Sarianna?"

She jerked away from his gentle fingers. "I won't continue this conversation, Mr. Rensell."

"Oh, mister now, is it? I won't forget, Sarianna. There are only three possibilities, and only two of them are really so desperate that they would lash out at you."

"I won't deny it," she said finally, "but that is as much as I will talk about it."

"Loyal little thing, aren't you?" he jibed. "And to whom, and for what, Sarianna? How can you let them treat you like that, damn it—"

"And how *do* they treat me so badly?" she asked icily, her chest heaving. She didn't know where her fury came from, when a moment ago she had melted, hot as butter, into his arms. What right did he have to question *her*, and damn him, why had he spoiled the voluptuous communion between them?

But his body still held hers confined against the tree, and his expression turned stony hard as he considered an answer to her question. "You're right," he said finally, "it's amazing how they do it. They depend on you for everything, and they treat you like a servant. They give you cast-offs, feed you put-downs, and make your life miserable by aggrandizing differences that make no difference whatsoever; and on top of that, they pretend you're not Rex's firstborn daughter. Otherwise, you have it perfectly delightful here, Sarianna. A true belle, and the most eligible catch in the whole of Folquet County."

A neat encapsulation, she thought, terrorized; he caught it exactly, and she could find no other outlet for her frustration at his perception than to kick him.

"Hell, Sarianna!"

"Go to hell," she hissed, stalking away. "Who are you to say what's what about *my* life? Where is the honor in yours, Mr. Rensell?"

"Why don't you leave?" he called out from behind her, nursing his shin and ignoring her barb altogether.

She whirled to face him. "What an eloquent suggestion, Mr. Rensell. To do what, and go where?"

"Governess? Relatives?" he shot back, glowering, stepping toward her with each word to emphasize it.

"My dear Mr. Rensell—how illogically you think. I hardly can teach Spencerian script now, can I? My embroidery stitches go left to right, and Father never allowed me to learn the piano because SHE played it; of course any stringed instrument would have to be restrung and the fingering charts rewritten before *I* could learn it, and since I'm mostly self-taught to begin with since Father thought I was too awkward, and possibly too backward to be schooled, I expect, Mr. Rensell, no one would hire me. I suppose, too, you don't imagine that I even thought about that myself because I'm too slow, or wrong-brained or something? Well, I'll tell you, Mr. Rensell, I have thought of it, and much much more, but I'd have to corrupt myself to live as mean a life as I have here, and possibly worse. As for relatives, Mr. Rensell, I have two. All of father's family is gone, and there is only an elderly great-aunt in Texas, and a cousin in Charleston, who, by the sound of her letters to Vesta, is busy raising her own brood of children and couldn't possibly take on the nebulous problems of a distantly related member of the Wayte family. I hope that satisfies your curiosity, and you won't pry any further into the details of my situation, Mr. Rensell. I expect it would be much more profitable to inquire into the why of your inexplicable return to a place no one expected you would ever want to see again." Her fury totally and suddenly dissipated, and she looked at him helplessly, as close to tears as she had ever come in her life. He had no right to force her to bare her soul like that, he had absolutely no right. No one knew those things nor the hidden rage in her heart that she camouflaged so carefully with her dutiful obeisance to her family's wishes.

And now he knew; he had made her vulnerable, and that was all it took. How lowering. How humiliating. She had to cover her mortification with aggression and divert him completely. "Well, Mr. Rensell? What *is* the why of it?"

He smiled at her again, and this time, in the bold late morning light, it was not at all a pleasant smile; it was the lion on the trail of his prey.

"The reasons are simple and straightforward, Sarianna, even

though I can see by that militant light in your eye you'd like them to be a lot more complicated. I came to visit my father's grave, and to take a wife from among the sanctimonious Sawnians who rejected him."

She fell back a step at this bald declaration, her shock plain in her eyes. But she didn't expect what came next.

"So, Sarianna . . . will you marry me?"

6

"You're crazy!" Sarianna exploded. "Utterly deranged. Out of your mind—" She stopped her castigation abruptly and stared at him consideringly. "Just anyone would have done, wouldn't she, if she had been from Sawny?"

"I expect that's true," he agreed. "Just my luck to happen on Vesta in the middle of Savannah the very day I was taking the ferry over."

"Just your luck Jeralee wasn't the only daughter of the house, or you'd be asking *her* to marry you at this very instant," Sarianna said tartly, crushing down the numbing feeling of let-down she was beginning to feel. But why should she have been first choice next to Jeralee? And why even should she be second if he had, as she could infer, fully intended to ask for Jeralee during his stay on Sawny?

"I doubt it," he snapped. "I want you, Sarianna; you can't tell me that with this morning's events you don't feel something for me, too."

"I won't tell you anything. I don't know anything. I'm ripe for use by someone as unscrupulous as you, Mr. Rensell."

"You put yourself in the position, Miss Broydon. Keep drowning yourself in pity, and I won't be the only one who will take advantage of that provoking tongue of yours—but I *may* be the only one who offers marriage."

"Maybe you're the one who is desperate," she countered angrily. "Maybe you're the one who needs saving, Mr. Rensell. You must be unhinged if you can mistake *my* physical attributes for Jeralee's in broad daylight." And then she regretted her brash words. His hard eyes traveled an insultingly bold path over her slender body, resting finally on the thin adamant line of her mouth.

"I could hardly make that kind of mistake, Sarianna. There's a lot more of Jeralee to get in my way." His gaze rested on the perfect line and swell of her breasts. "And I don't doubt she makes you very well aware of it either."

Sarianna pivoted away from him abruptly. Damn the man, damn him. "Nonetheless," she said over her shoulder, "Jeralee has been led to believe you have come because of her attraction. I really feel you had best not disappoint her—or Vesta." And that was the end of it, she thought—what Jeralee and Vesta expected. She was tired of the conversation. She began to walk away.

"Nonetheless," Cade called after her, "I'm only leaving here with you."

She ignored him; his words and his kisses were so glib. Wishes didn't make them real, or passion or despair. If he could render her so helpless now, she could become utterly worthless when he left. With Jeralee.

She turned to look at him; he stood a hundred feet away where she had left him.

"With *you*," he called out with supreme male arrogance. "Count on it."

"So—Miss Bold as Brass, now you hide in the arbor to practice your little seductions," Vesta sneered from the doorway of Sarianna's room.

"Oh? Were you watching?" Sarianna retorted, watching her carefully through the chifferobe mirror as Alzine carefully unhooked the dress.

She felt a little frisson of doubt in the next moment that she should push Vesta quite so far; but how could she help it? And Vesta needed it.

"My dear, we *all* were watching that distasteful display in the garden. Really, all that disgusting carnality—"

"Which wouldn't have been *quite* so disgusting had it been Jeralee in his arms, do I read that correctly?" Sarianna interrupted, her voice dripping with false sweetness. *Don't goad her*, a part of her mind kept begging. *Don't push*. And yet she had to; she felt reckless, intense, keyed up to a fever pitch by both her response to that disgusting carnality and her exacting awareness that nothing would come of it.

"Jeralee is a lady," Vesta said sharply. "She knows when to keep private moments private."

Jeralee was a barn cat, Sarianna almost retorted, and she would have done far more with Cade Rensell in the arbor than had happened there this morning. Jeralee didn't care one whit *where*, and Sarianna had good cause to know it while Vesta probably had good cause to ignore it. Maybe, Sarianna thought viciously, she should prod Gaff Gilmartin into some bold reminiscences this evening before dinner.

"Perhaps Jeralee can give me lessons in how to discourage Mr. Rensell's attentions," Sarianna suggested.

"A sound 'no' might do it," Vesta said nastily, "but then, you're just like your mother; she never could say no either, and of course it *is* perfectly obvious why he is pursuing you."

"Perfectly obvious," Sarianna quoted, her hackles up.

"My dear, he was obsessed with your mother, and you are the spit of her, more's the pity."

"But if he were still after someone as like Mother as possible, wouldn't he come after *you*?" Sarianna asked reasonably—unreasonably, she thought as she watched Vesta's face drain of color and then wash over with a delicate pink. "You're more like Dona than *I* could ever be, since you're so much nearer her in age and mannerisms—"

"Bitch, oh, you are a little sneaking bitch," Vesta growled. "Don't turn it around, Sarianna. He's going to work out his obsession for Dona on you, mark my words; he's going to finish what he started with her all those years ago, and it will take him just one day and night to find out what a bitch and a tease she was, and you can be, and that will be the end of it. He wants a Sawny-bred woman for his wife, and he will have one; and her name will be Jeralee Wayte, and nothing you can do will stop it, my girl. *Nothing.*"

"Such a challenge," Sarianna murmured, stepping out of her dress now. "It really *is* a challenge, Vesta, since it is me he has been kissing and enjoying it most thoroughly."

"Men don't care what they kiss or who they bed, Sarianna; don't bless the man with finer instincts than he has. He is not going to fall in love with you of all people in the space of one day unless he has some other motive on his mind. And do remember, dear, men can be awfully convincing when a body is the means to get something they really want."

"Of coures this sage advice does not apply to Jeralee who is above the baser needs of most men? They look at her and fall over themselves to win her for love of her alone?" Sarianna retaliated. She lifted her arms as Alzine lifted the steel cage of her hoop over her golden head, and her fury mounted. "I expect Jeralee would be more prudent," she added in a pointed aside to Alzine, whose face was beginning to reflect a subtle terror at the undertone of violence in the room, "if she could see that weasel face of hers. I guess when she is practicing her sweet smiles in the mirror, she doesn't quite turn her head in the right direction to catch it."

There was a hard moment of killing silence as Vesta swallowed rage, pride, and hate, all those things so that she would not reach out and choke the life from Sarianna. She smiled then, she really managed a smile, and afterward, she never knew how she did it, but it was that condescending smile that patronized Sarianna, belittled her, as she so desired to do, and didn't soften her cutting words.

"So you say, Sarianna. Oh, my dear, you are so transparent. My Jeralee has what every man wants: a lush body to bear him sons, a dark sensual beauty to entice him, the knowledge to manage his household and servants, and the breeding of the Waytes and the wealth of the Broydons behind her. Dona would have better served *you* if she had been a little less flamboyant and flirtatious."

"So she would," Sarianna agreed, "because you would not now be married to my father." She bit her lip as the words came out; she could not have kept them back. Vesta could talk all she wanted of breeding and dowry, but had things gone one iota differently twelve or fifteen years ago, Rex would never have been in a position to marry her. God—and think of the ramifications of that!

Even Vesta had: Sarianna could see it all in her face, flashing by with each twitch of a muscle and finally coming under Herculean control by sheer mother wit and strength. Vesta couldn't afford to strike her again, and she knew it.

"You have got a mouth, Sarianna. Who would have suspected?" She paced backward to the door, feeling with her right hand for the molding. "I'm a formidable enemy, Sarianna; you had best take my warnings seriously. Don't get in my way."

Sarianna shrugged. "We do what we must," she said airily, knowing her laissez-faire answer would infuriate Vesta all over again.

"Some of us have to get our fingers burned," Vesta said philosophically. "Forewarned is forearmed, my dear; don't forget." She smiled at Sarianna's slender, chemise-clad figure standing in the center of the room, and turned quietly out, closing the door gently behind her.

Sarianna stared after her suspiciously. She had won that round much too easily. She caught sight of herself in the mirror. And what did she see now? A childlike figure in white lawn undergarments who hardly looked strong enough to combat an opponent like Vesta.

And to be so foolish as to goad a woman like that, when she was obviously as obsessed about Jeralee and Cade Rensell as she claimed Cade was about Dona! It was crazy. The whole merry-go-round of the past and present was crazy. And obscene.

"Alzine!"

She had to move, to do something.

"Yas'm?"

"My dress."

"Yas'm. Merleen done washed it; I'm gonna get it." Alzine opened the door and then turned back to her. "Dat Miss Vesta be one witchy lady, Miss Sarianna. She don't know nothin' 'bout Miss Jeralee, or she wouldn't be sellin' Miss Jeralee fo' lady to no man."

"No gossip," Sarianna protested half-heartedly, but it was a token objection at best; even she could see after Cade's neat little seduction this morning how easy it was to succumb to a man's mouth and hands.

"Mind you change dem white stockin's, Miss Sarianna," Alzine reminded her, ignoring the remonstration as she closed the door behind her.

Sarianna climbed up onto her bed. How convenient to have a servant perform each inconsequential little task and fulfill each trifling wish.

And how nice to be alone for a moment, and to feel safe and somewhat sane now that she was back in her own room again. Here, none of it seemed real. None of it. When Alzine returned with her serviceable calico dress, she would put it on and she would go downstairs, and everything would be precisely as it had been before Cade Rensell arrived.

But how *had* it been? she wondered, as she gazed out the window adjacent to the headboard.

Bearable.

Monotonous.

And not fraught with that terrible excitement and the tenuous thread of danger and the forbidden.

A person's heart could fail from all that agitation, she thought acerbically. Her days were much better spent tending to Jeralee's needs and her father's wants. There really was no other way.

She bent her knee up to her chest and began unfastening the garters that secured her stockings.

He heard no voices emanating from behind the closed door of Sarianna's room now. In truth, he had heard too much already, eavesdropping on Vesta's attack. What a feisty cat Sarianna was! But he knew now she had that passion in her. He was hovering at her door because he wanted still more of it, because he could not get enough of her.

He tried the doorknob, and it turned with greased ease in his hand. He pushed the door open a crack. His furtive reflection looked back at him, and it startled him. He pushed the door still farther. A mirror. A dressing table. He was hard put to picture Sarianna there, gazing at her own image in vanity.

An inch more and he could see her seated at the head of her plump bed, virginal white against the deep blue of the candlewick bedspread, one leg pressed against her breasts, the other angled out and braced against the side rail.

She wore only her chemise and pantalette, and as she bent forward to roll down her stocking, her body shifted, and one perfect rose-tipped breast, taut with unconscious desire, slipped from the loosely tied neckline of her camisole.

She was supremely unaware of her subtle erotic pose. Her hands briskly worked the one stocking down her curvaceous long leg and tossed it aside, before she lifted her leg and extended it fully outward and then up as if she were stretching each muscle to its fullest extension. A moment later, she braced that naked foot against the side rail and lifted her right leg to her breasts and began the same sensual motion of removing her other stocking.

He watched every movement; he could see everything from where he stood, motionless, just behind the door. Nothing was hidden from him, not even the lush triangle of darker hair that shielded her femininity and showed plainly through the opening between her pantalette legs which pulled tightly against the stretch of her thighs as she lifted each leg.

She raised and lowered this leg in the same way, and then hooked this bare foot into the side rail as well, so that she was sitting with her legs spread out to brace her body and her breasts thrust out in subtle invitation to some imaginary lover.

Even he, from his covert position, could see her taut, lush nipples pushing against the tissue-thin material of her camisole. She stared down at them and, in a kind of innocent curiosity, lifted her hands to touch them.

Then she looked up, stunned, as she heard him step into the room and close the door behind him. And lock it.

Her hands fell, and she grabbed for the bedspread. "How come I am not surprised, Mr. Rensell?" she hissed, pulling the cover up and around her.

"Sarianna—"

"Get out!" Her voice trembled. Already she was feeling the radiant raw male power of him, and all he was doing was leaning against the doorjamb, waiting for her to speak, the lion—patient—stalking his prey, dressed for pouncing.

"Get out!" How *puny* words were against the lion; even with his arms crossed over his chest, he looked dangerous and sensual to her. He wore no frock coat, or tie, to impede him, and his shirt was unbuttoned just enough that she could see crisp hair curling out from beneath it. The sleek line of his lion body was more apparent now, from the broad shoulders Jeralee so admired to his narrow waist. And he had her cornered.

She licked her lips nervously. She hadn't forgotten a moment of the morning and her utter surrender to his mouth. She had only to look at him and her body tensed with memory and, more than that, yearned for a repetition of it—demanded more, craving the thing that came next, a completion, an absolution.

And all because she sat there so defiantly looking at him; no, abandoning herself to imagining the "more" she would never know because her cooler head would prevail and she would make him leave her room, with both of them unsatiated.

"Don't be absurd, Sarianna." His voice was so gentle, and so tellingly firm, as if she were some scared animal that had to be cajoled to bring about a capitulation.

"Just get out," she said with as much dignity as she could muster from within the depths of her frail cover. And what did she suppose she could hide from *him*, the man she had characterized as worldly the moment she laid eyes on him. He surely had known other women, women bolder and more well-endowed than she, women less modest and more brazen. Women who would have gladly invited him to their rooms and undressed *for* him, rather than conceal their wretched nakedness from him.

She found she didn't like those thoughts at all, and that the thought of him kissing another woman altogether could almost destroy her. She could not let things go another step further.

"Don't you dare tell me this isn't proper." His voice cut through her chaotic fantasies, and she came back to reality.

"You're right—I wouldn't dare. I don't dare speak to you at all."

"Yes," he agreed with that peculiar bend in his voice, "we do have other ways to communicate." He began walking toward her, and she scrambled to the other side of the bed, pulling the bedcover with her, tangling herself in it and finally yanking it totally off of the bed.

"Don't come near me."

"Sarianna—"

"I don't want any more of that. I *don't*."

"You want it."

"*You* want it."

"I do." He lunged across the bed and swiped at her cover; it came away in his hands as she darted across the room and grasped a chair.

She looked entrancingly medieval as she lifted it threateningly. She had no dearth of nerve, he thought admiringly; damn, he wanted that mouth again.

"Come, Sarianna—throw it at me," he taunted her, his voice edged with amusement. He extended his hand, and she didn't doubt that he could catch the damned thing. She must look a ridiculous sight brandishing an upholstered chair at him. Would any other of his women have done that to him?

She lowered the chair to the floor and draped herself over it, folding her arms over the finger molded back. "This chair's too good to waste on you," she told him roundly. "Why don't you just leave before Alzine returns?"

He flashed a wry smile at her. "Alzine will return when Alzine will return," he said obliquely. "Now, why don't you sit down on the bed,

84

and we'll talk?"

"*That's* what you call it these days?" Sarianna said helplessly, unable to stop her mouth from saying idiotic things. Her chest felt tight and her whole body prickled. Where could she hide? There wasn't even a door on her dressing room. If he caught her there, he could spill her to the floor among the cottons and serviceable summer silks, and tumble her there.

And why was that notion so exciting? Forbidden. A heightening of the feelings his shattering kisses aroused. Things she should not know nor ever want to know if she were truly a lady.

She did not know what she was; standing across the room from him, clad in the thinnest of undergarments through which she was sure he could see quite clearly, she was aware only of her clamoring body and his dark invasive eyes. His hands. The morning. Everything, beyond his discovery of the discolored skin of Vesta's assault, was subordinated to the shaking excitement that possessed her as she gazed into his eyes.

Eyes and memory, and his driving male desire—he was here with her now, she thought triumphantly. There was no thought of Jeralee in his mind here. Whatever his reasons, he wanted her, and she wanted to provoke him again. Fine. With a gleam in his eye, he began pacing deliberately to her side of the room, and she edged away from him slowly, suggestively, toward the bed as if it drew her hypnotically; but she climbed onto it like a child, even to the point of centering herself in it and folding her legs under her, looking up at him with sparkling, expectant sapphire eyes.

"Well?"

The question was older than time, with a wealth of feminine and womanly vanity contained in it. She knew the picture she presented now; she wriggled slightly to get the shoulders of her camisole set just right, then she played with the ribbons of the neckline, subtly loosening them still further, laying the ends with sensual precison over the swell of her breasts and then between their twin perfect, rose-tipped curves.

Oh, Sarianna, with her golden halo of hair and the elusive whimsical smile. He held himself back a moment more to watch her, restraining his own rising desire to further incite hers by making her wait, and she looked at him questioningly, with an incomprehensible longing in the deep blue depths of her eyes.

85

Every pore in her body wanted his presence on the bed beside her, but she felt a curious inexplicable understanding that he wanted to watch her, too, and that all her movements, deliberate and innocent, were as provocative to him as kissing her, and that her barely clothed body was as enticing to his eye as if she were naked, more so because he was required to imagine the exact shape of her quivering breasts, the slant of her belly, and the satin slide of flesh of her thighs. Yes, she knew that instinctively, and that if she touched herself here and there with just the right air of knowledgeable innocence, she would arouse him past all endurance.

And she wanted to. Somewhere inside her, she wanted to because that would make her unforgettable to him, and she wanted him to remember her long after he had gone.

He didn't move. His eyes moved, devouring her with a gigantic hunger to possess; he ached to taste her and touch her, to strip away the barrier to her nakedness so he could see and feel very inch of her. But slowly, and softly, and very . . . very . . . soon, as he watched her fingers flirt with her neck, touching her mouth, brushing her hair back from her ears, sliding down the long column of her throat to the flat of her chest just above the tempting swell of her breasts; and then pulling the taut fabric of her pantalette away from her trim little bottom. . . . Oh, she knew exactly what she was doing now, he thought; here was Eve—and voluptuous temptation—and what would she do next? How would she compel him to her side if nothing else so far had done so?

He waited. The sensual tension between them thickened unbearably. She lifted her left leg upright so she could wind her arms around her knee. The fingers of her left hand settled lightly around her naked ankle, and she twisted forward slightly to get a firmer grip, and then sent him a provocative look.

His eyes flared as her fingers gently slid down her bare foot to her toes and back again to her ankle, and she saw it. Catcing her lower lip between her teeth, she slanted another heated glance at him and repeated the movement again, slower this time, sliding her hand slowly up past her ankle to her leg, up and up to her knee, and then down the naked flesh of her calf to her foot again, returning to her toes where it rested provokingly.

He would never forget the picture of her sensual goading eyes, her taut body inviting him and inviting him, and her enticing posture that revealed everything, and nothing. It took just one more movement—the faint, knowing, elusive smile, and her slender fingers, sliding down between her naked toes—and he was on the bed, his hard hot hand grasping the alluring ankle, and his other hand grasping her hair to position her mouth for his erotic invasion. She felt as if her body would explode as his tongue slicked wetly all over her willing lips and slid heatedly into her mouth, seeking the wanton response of hers.

He pulled her up to him as he knelt over her on his knees, molding her slender body against him so she could feel his huge pulsating length, and she wound her arms around his powerful neck and reveled in the hot hard maleness of him. His hand had moved as he lifted her to the firm fleshy line of her buttocks, and he held her there, his fingers digging into the lush flesh, thrusting her tighter against his erection, harder against his granite strength.

He murmured love words into her mouth and onto her lips, refusing to break the kiss, to leave her voluptuous mouth. She heard his hazy words and felt his rock-hard manhood and his hands caressing her writhing body everywhere he could reach, and he felt her everywhere, everywhere; between her legs, the soft alluring roundness of her thighs, the enticing firmness of her buttocks, and the taut nippled perfection of her breasts.

He held her head firmly, angled to him because he wanted—he needed—her hot wanton kisses above all.

"Sarianna," he breathed against her lips.

"Don't stop . . ." Her pouty little plea enticed him back to her mouth, and he delved luxuriously within to her avid response. He kissed her tongue, her lips, he nipped her lower lip all the way across, and then gently laved each bite with his tongue; he played with her and dueled with her, and he could not get enough of her honeyed sweetness. He parted her lips more fully; he teased them with his fingers and his tongue, exploring her with his lips and fingers deep within the sensitive recesses. It was the taste of her, the luscious Sarianna taste he couldn't define and would never stop wanting. It was the quirky smile that turned wanton temptress under his lips and tongue so he could possess it and learn it.

It was all of that and the insatiable craving to know her nakedness so well. He felt for it with his free hand as his tongue tasted the nectar of hers over and over again, and she twisted her body around him and with him to ease his way.

"Sarianna . . ." he moaned with his tongue just resting between her lips.

She licked it. "What . . ."

"Let me undress you."

She groaned and he kissed her lips. "You'll have to stop kissing me."

"I can kiss something else."

She made a little sound in the back of her throat, a sound of excitement, invitation, or denial. He didn't know.

"Sarianna . . ." he murmured against her mouth. Her lips parted and he slipped his tongue between them. "Tell me."

"What will you kiss that will feel so wonderful as this?" she whispered. "Or taste so good?" She reached for him again, boldly inciting him with her sensual movements against him and her wanton demanding tongue.

"All of you," he murmured into her searing kisses. He could have kissed her all day and exploded with pleasure at the end of it. He wanted her body now—*now*—elementally, man to woman. The lush mound of her femininity thrust against him, unconsciously demanding the satiation only he could give.

He needed her there, to know her there—to touch her everywhere.

"Sari-anna—"

His hoarse voice reached her in the throes of her pleasure. She opened her sapphire glazed eyes and smiled at him. "Undress me," she whispered, "now."

But the loss of his mouth was shocking and in concert with a new kind of rapturous feeling of his hands sliding all over her, skimming over her tight taut nipples that were still shrouded in the mystery of their cloth covering; over her hips and legs and up again finally to take hold of the sleeves of her camisole with such intense deliberation that she thought he was going to rip the whole away in one mighty sensual motion.

He saw it in her eyes, and that erotic light flared in his in response. He moved his fingers to her neckline and inserted them between her breasts, and with a short, sharp jerk, he tore the thin material away from her body and threw it on the floor. Only her pantalettes remained, draped over her hips like the dress of a houri, seductive and revealing. Another sharp tug, and they too were lying on the floor, leaving Sarianna naked in his arms, her golden head on his chest.

"You're beautiful," he whispered, sliding his hands over the perfection of her body.

"Kiss me," she murmured, loving him for saying that; maybe he meant it—but she couldn't stop to think about that.

"I will," he whispered, touching her lips first and then tilting her head and holding her so he could explore the hollow between her shoulder and neck, and down farther to her chest and the mounds of her breasts, his fingers touching the sensitized nipples, almost sending her into a spasm of pure ecstasy.

Nothing else could feel like that—nothing. And then—something, as his mouth closed around the taut tipped peak and he began gently sucking it.

She arched her back and leaned into him, silently groaning with delight, and then she felt his hand sliding downward toward her most secret place, inching along, so gentle and so arousing. He knew just how firmly to enter her silken promise; what did he know—how did he know—she was going to dissolve from the pure rapture of it. He knew everything. Her hips moved, enticing his hand deeper still, and his mouth moved from one breast to the succulent delights of the other hard peaked nipple.

She moved with him, his hand and his mouth. Pleasure suffused her body, building in some indefinable way that she understood even without having ever experienced it. His touch was perfect, perfect; the suckling of her nipple, perfect; everything he did, holding her, kissing her, perfect . . . how perfect, and mounding, the feeling heightening unbearably. She moved with it, totally unconscious of the urgency of her body as the explosiveness in her escalated.

His expert hands, his incredible mouth at her breast—if he had never come, she could not bear to think of it in the height of this sensual storm—she would never have known it. Never. And that mouth—that ravenous mouth pulled and tugged on her nipple almost in rhythm with his hand and her movement. Any moment now. Any moment . . .

She had never felt anything fine and loving about her femininity, but she felt it now; there could be nothing else she was born for but to feel this, naked in his hands, *just*—she felt a glittering culmination—*like*—it exploded with the last hard pull of his lips and tongue on her satiated nipple—*this*—and cascaded all over her body, sparkling pinpoints of pleasure showering all over her. She hung on to him, unaware she was pulling his hair, pushing his mouth away from her, pushing his hand away—just totally enthralled, and finished at once. Then she finally sank into the bed, and he gathered her into his arms and covered her face with gentle kisses.

Suddenly reality took hold: She had enticed this man, flaunted her body and found forbidden enchantment. *What had she done?* What was that stunning upheaval that stormed her body? "What," she demanded into his chest, "was *that?*"

His arms tightened around her. "*That* is a taste of what you will experience when you agree to marry me, Sarianna."

She felt cold suddenly. Marry him. She had not known him a day, and he had done this to her. And to ask her to marry him, shockingly, out of the blue in the morning, and now, unrepentent in the afternoon.

Vesta was right. He wanted something.

She felt cold suddenly, and she reached out a hand blindly to pull the sheet up to her to conceal her nakedness. How fruitless to cover herself now—he knew every inch of her, and the sheet would hide nothing from his burning gaze. Not even her intentions.

"Sarianna—"

"I think you should propose to Jeralee as soon as possible and then remove yourself forever from Bredwood."

"There isn't a chance in hell I will propose to Jeralee. I want *you.*"

She slanted a skeptical look at him. "You want *something,*" she said coldly.

He pushed her backward, away from him, and she fell on her elbow and lay there looking up at him, wrapped in her sheet and looking impossibly exotic. "I want a wife and a lover, a partner, children— yes, I want *something,* Sarianna." He felt a rising fury as he looked at her and knew he could not have her again, not like this first time, and never again with that pure aching innocence. Damn her. And damn it all. "You can give all that to me, Sarianna, or you can stay here the rest of your life and be a wife to your father in every sense but one. Or haven't you understood what you've been doing?"

She wriggled into an upright position. "Oh, you are deranged. A wife? You must be overwrought by the heat, Mr. Rensell. My father has a wife, thank you. Nothing could be more senseless. I really think it is time you leave—with or without a wife, Mr. Rensell."

"A *wife,* Sarianna," Cade repeated firmly. He wouldn't let her deny it; he couldn't, if he hoped to convince her to marry him and win her away from Rex Broydon. He had riled her terribly by his accusation. He could see her turning it over in her mind, hating him for bringing up the implausibe proposal and ending the magic of her capitulation, and he could see her rejecting it, too. But the notion was planted, and he knew it was rooting itself in her mind.

"Oh, you are impossible, Mr. Rensell. You should have heard every word Vesta said to me, because you persist in doing the very thing she warned me about—and you seduced me into the bargain. You aren't very clever if you think you are now going to scare me into accepting the first proposal—any proposal—that accompanies such tactics."

"I want you to see the truth," he said.

"As I said," Sarianna concluded triumphantly, "you *do* want something." She slid her sheet-wrapped body back against the headboard and favored him with a sultry blue look. "Please leave."

"We are not finished, Sarianna."

"Oh, but we are finished, Mr. Rensell."

"Just as long as you don't forget what just happened, Sarianna," he reminded her, as his warm gaze slid over her bare shoulders and the alluring drape of the sheet over the curves of her body. Her arms crossed defensively over her breasts, and he smiled crookedly. "I see you don't, Sarianna. And I will remember you pleaded for my kisses; so we'll see who comes begging first. I intend to stay until one of us does," he added for good measure, and she visibly bridled at the assumption it would be her. He left her to her indignation and her growing humiliation at her shamelessness.

She would never capitulate to such high-handedness, *never*. She lay in the bed in a tumble of sheets, seething at his insinuations, his disgusting inferences. Really, there was nothing to remember; he had stormed her senses, that was all. He had caught her at a vulnerable moment and had taken advantage of the situation, just as he had before.

She would not let it happen again. It was out of her mind already. When Alzine returned with her dress . . . when Alzine returned—! She would find Miss Sarianna naked in an unmade bed, and how would that look? Or had he planned that as well. What had he said? Alzine would return *when*—had he bribed her *not* to? Did *she* look so desperate she would submit to any man who walked into her room—

or even *let* any man walk into her room?

God! She leapt out of the bed and swept up her torn undergarments. She couldn't even look at them. It was the damned charm of the man: He made her forget everything and regret it afterward. Drat the man! She thrust the offending underwear into her dressing room, behind a pile of mending that neither she nor Alzine intended to get to any time soon.

She needed new undergarments; she dragged the first thing that came to hand out of her dresser and slipped on the drawers and tied them swiftly behind her back, making sure the ends of the split material between her legs overlapped properly, before she donned the lace-trimmed camisole with the blue ribbon. Yes, that would do. And a pair of flesh-colored lisle stockings—where were the white ones? She scrambled around the bed frantically looking for them, found them under the heap of the candlewick bedspread, and picked the whole up and piled it on the bed.

Alzine would have questions about *that*. She picked up one lisle stocking and rolled it onto her foot quickly. He had seen all that, her thoughts narrated. God, she could not let herself think about *what* he had seen or not seen. What he had *done* was dismaying enough; her unbridled reaction to it was positively wanton.

She rolled up the other stocking briskly and secured it under the finely tucked knee of her drawers. There. The bed. She threw her white stockings aside, making a mental note to burn them, tossed the bedspread over the blanket railing at the foot of the bed, and began a hasty reassembling of sheets and pillows.

It didn't look quite as neat as Alzine did it when she had done, and she wondered how much Alzine would notice when she came into the room.

She positioned herself against the headboard to present a picture of—what? Someone who might have unwittingly messed up the cover while in the course of wrestling with her stockings? Someone who had taken a brief little nap and perhaps tossed and turned enough to wrinkle the coverlet—just slightly? Someone who was trying desperately not to remember what had happened in her bed, and her own stupidity in coping with a man's perfidy?

Ah, yes. But then the soft material of her camisole would shift with her body movements and softly rub against her protruding nipples, and how could she forget? Her lips still felt swollen from his unconscionable kisses—how could she forget?

But *beg* him? *Never.* Succumb again? *Never.* Besides, he looked like a man who did not like to be crossed, and she fully intended *not* to live up to his expectations for the brief time he would remain at Bredwood.

"Thirteen to dinner, Sarianna," Vesta said gaily as Sarianna came downstairs an hour later into the bustle of more guests departing from Bredwood, and with Alzine's scolding ringing in her ears. She had not fooled Alzine one bit. And Cade had indeed made sure they were to be alone for a short period of time. She didn't like learning that, and she could barely concentrate on Vesta's neat accounting of the remaining guest list because she was still fuming. But Vesta's words finally penetrated.

". . . Mr. Darden, Mr. Rensell, Jeralee, the Gilmartins, your father and myself. Just an informal, neighborly dinner to show Mr. Rensell how we do things nowadays on Sawny. Sylvia believes there are some fresh chickens for a fricassee, so—if you would check the henhouse and tell Abel. And then the cellar for a bottle of my father's port. I think there are a couple of bottles still of the vintage he gave Rex twenty years ago. And, let's see . . ."

Sarianna stared at her. Vesta was acting as if nothing had happened, as if she had never issued threats in her room. As if she never claimed that Sarianna might be trying to seduce Cade away from Jeralee.

Why?

What if she knew that Cade had only left her room moments ago and had seduced her—under Vesta's very nose—and brought her to the peak of that mysterious shattering pleasure?

Would she be pretending that everything was back to normal and as it should be, with Sarianna in her proper place?

And what was her proper place?

Vesta issued the orders and *she* carried them out? But *she* carried the keys and doled out the supplies, took care of the servants and field hands, kept the key to the medicine cabinet, and sat with the sick and the lamed; she laid in the stores and ordered what was to be brought from Savannah on their twice yearly trips. She dictated the clothing allowance and supervised the cutting of the patterns and sewing and knitting, and she listened to complaints and gave succor or advice where needed.

She kept up her father's correspondence and tended to his accounts. When he was away, she even went out in the fields with McInerney, their overseer, who had a healthy respect for her intelligence.

The kitchen garden was hers—and Sylvia's—and when she had free time, she tended the flower garden as well, which was her special delight. But there was always mending to do, which Alzine helped with, and which she also did in order to participate as fully as possible in caring for her extended family; they did respect her, and they did not like Vesta and Jeralee at all. She knew it.

They loved Miss Sarianna, and they tolerated Mr. Rex and that was the end of it. Mr. Rex was a god who could drastically change their lives on a mere whim. And he had.

And so, Sarianna thought, as she counted out the keys to find the one to the cellar, she did many of the tasks that Vesta should be doing. Why couldn't Vesta have asked for the key and checked the wine cellar herself after all?

She had no answer for it, and Cade's firm voice echoed in her ear, *Wife*, as she picked her way down the cellar steps into the cold underground vault. No—she could never go that far in defining her duties. But Vesta was relying on her to make up the menu and choose the wine, and once again she was to be excluded from company.

Wife?

Or wife to the sumptuous pleasure that Cade Rensell could conjure up with a mere touch?

She lit the lantern that was kept hanging by the stairs and held it high as she perused the rows of bottles. Why wasn't Vesta doing this?

She plucked out one without even seeing it, and then went in search of the revered port which was at the far end of the cellar. She took one bottle, picked up the other and grasped the lantern to light her way to the steps, and then blew out the wick and felt her way up to the door.

It swung open unexpectedly.

"Oh, there you are, Sarianna." Vesta's voice, menacingly near.

"Yes, Vesta? Do you want something?"

"Oh, I think you could say that."

Vesta stood at the top of the steps, the light behind her, looking like a terrifying asexual hulk. Sarianna felt a moment of pure blinding fear.

"You could just give me those bottles, Sarianna."

"And next time you could just get them yourself."

"No, no, Sarianna. I want you to understand something. Right now, I could take those wine bottles from you, and I could push you down the stairs, and you could break your sweet little neck. I want you to—understand that I have that power . . . if you get in my way."

Was Vesta going mad? "I don't understand it," Sarianna said boldly.

"Mr. Rensell was seen emerging from your room this afternoon, Sarianna. You are hardly being discreet, and I beg you to consider Jeralee's feelings in the matter."

"But *not* Mr. Rensell's?" Sarianna hazarded, aghast at the thought someone had *seen* Cade.

"Most assuredly not, Sarianna. I'm sure you're a tasty little morsel, the more so because of your resemblance to Dona. Don't forget whom he is thinking of when he is making love to you, Sarianna. Don't forget, my dear. He waited seven years for her. And he can have my beautiful Jeralee now."

"And she can have all his lovely money," Sarianna added tartly, easing herself up the next several steps. She could not back down from Vesta. The only plan with her was attack. "Get out of my way, Vesta," she commanded.

Vesta didn't move. "Just understand, Sarianna," she said as Sarianna came level with her, "you interfere, and I will be waiting in one dark stairwell somewhere in this house."

Sarianna thrust the bottles at her. "Beware I don't arm myself in defense," she retorted, pushing by the older woman. Vesta was going crazy; what *was* it about Cade Rensell that was making everyone crazy?

She raced into the kitchen, one place she was sure Vesta would not follow her, and sagged her body against the nearest table. Damn her mother. Curse Vesta, and damn the man with the bewitching hands and beguiling mouth. She had never expected this, *never*. Of course he said he wanted her. If she just stood still and never opened her mouth, she was Dona to the life. He wanted a replica doll to put on a pedestal, and a substitute in bed, and that was *all*. Anything else was the heat of the moment; even *she* had lost her mind in the heat of the moment.

Who had seen him—or was that a Vesta-lie? Someone was spying on her: *Would* Alzine, whom she thought to be wholly loyal to her. . . .

And if not Alzine—who? Jeralee, spying on her?

Jeralee seemed more likely than Alzine. And Vesta herself seemed like a more likely candidate for skulking than all of them. Cade Rensell seemed to have suddenly become some kind of prize, and Vesta was determined to win him—annex him—for Jeralee.

But she knew Jeralee wanted him, too, and the reason was obvious: He was a damned attractive man, and the fact he had money—or so Vesta kept saying—didn't hurt matters either. Jeralee would have caught a paragon, if Vesta could engineer it, and of course that would raise her standing in the eyes of their Sawny neighbors.

Could it be as simple as that?

The man was too magnetic, too rich, and sweet little Jeralee Wayte was going to tame him?

She almost felt like laughing. Jeralee in the hands of the lion. In his jaws most likely. Oh, God, she couldn't bear the thought . . . not after today.

What had he done to her?

And what would Vesta do to her if he left Sawny without Jeralee?

Wife.

She sent Abel to the hen house, and then went to the family dining room to choose the linen and the china and arrange a centerpiece.

Wife. Where was Vesta? Resting? she wondered acidly, as she brought an armful of flowers in from the garden and began slicing down the stems to fit into the flow blue bowls and china export vases she had chosen to match the blue, transferware dinner set that Rex himself had imported from England for Dona. Why not? Everything else had the taint of Dona, she thought venomously. *Wife.* She set out the cobalt blue saltcellars to match.

Wife.

She took a selection of pressed glass goblets from the shelf in the hunt board where they were kept. The cane pattern was intricate and interwoven—like their lives, she thought, setting them carefully out above each nest of plates and silver. But she had to rummage in the pantry for the slightly smaller port glasses which had not been used in a while, and prepare a silver tray with the beautifully faceted brandy decanter and matching miniature snifter. How many men? She counted on her fingers and added the correct number to the tray.

She placed these on the hunt board in readiness and stood back to admire her handiwork. She knew how to set a lovely table—just like a wife.

Oh, damn him!

She would never look at *anything* routinely again. *Damn him.*

Sylvia bustled in. "We can select de vegetables now, ma'am. Abel have de chickens by den."

"All right," Sarianna agreed, and followed her down the long enclosed hallway and through the kitchen, out to the gardens. She wandered up and down the long rows of staked and mounded plants, thinking. Sylvia hung behind, at the edge of the plot, a huge basket in her hand.

Sarianna turned to her. "Biscuits, I think, Sylvia, don't you— instead of the long loaf of bread." She didn't wait for an answer. "Greens with it—the haricots dresesd in vinegar with tomatoes, stewed okra and carrots with cheese, and the onions in cream sauce. That sounds lovely."

Sylvia followed her into the planting beds and began picking the necessary ingredients, and Sarianna knelt beside her and proceeded to do the unthinkable—pull carrots from the ground, brushing aside Sylvia's protest: "Oh, ma'am—I can do dat—" with a firm hand.

Wife didn't do *that*, she thought with satisfaction when she had finished and was wiping her hands on the hem of her skirt.

Servant did, said Sylvia's reproachful gaze as she picked up the overloaded basket and picked her way carefully through the planting beds. She turned to Sarianna at the kitchen door. "Fo' dessert, ma'am?"

"Fresh fruit with fresh whipped cream," Sarianna snapped. "Coffee and lemonade. No pies or cakes or anything like that, Sylvia. This is a plain company dinner."

"Yas'm," Sylvia said. She walked slowly back to the house, debating whether to tell Sarianna that Miss Vesta had already ordered one of her famous lemon pies for the dessert tray. She decided not to the minute before she reached the kitchen door. It was much easier to push it in and disappear altogether from the arguments between Miss Vesta and her ma'am.

Sarianna stared after her. So now she had chosen the menu, selected the dinnerware, created the centerpiece, pulled the damn vegetables. . . . Damn it, what *was* she—daughter—no, factotum with all the responsibilities Vesta should be shouldering, and the status of a servant—*and* in her father's house.

She clenched her hands in frustration and felt the garden grime that was still smudged on them. A mistake to do that; one had servants to do that. That was what Vesta understood, and she had not. There were servants and spinster daughters whose fathers had all but disowned them, but were relied on nonetheless by tacit consent to do the things the *real* wife had been allowed to relinquish as her obligations.

And all because Cade Rensell had unexpectedly walked in the door, she reluctantly acknowledged the deficiency in her father's system that had allowed her the only kind of independence she believed she ever had a right to expect.

She rubbed her hands abrasively against her calico skirt but to no avail. She wished she could smear the dirt right in Cade Rensell's face.

She turned toward the front of the house as the noisy leave-takings became more noticeable. No, she could not go out there, dressed as she was, with her hands in the state they were in. She rushed back into the house, through the kitchen, and ran straight into Pierce Darden.

"Whoa, Miss Sarianna. Where you off to? Miss Vesta sent me to find you. I believe the Wendells wanted to say a few words to you before they left."

"Did they?" Sarianna murmured abstractedly, folding her hands under her arms. "I wonder why?"

"Beg pardon?"

Vesta must have seen her in the garden, Sarianna theorized as she followed Pierce through the long center hallways of the house. Vesta was looking to embarrass her, nothing more.

She stepped into the entrance hallway behind Pierce, and there stood Vesta with Elmore Wendell. "There's the little lady," Wendell boomed, and Sarianna thought she would sink through the floor. And he came toward her, too, his hands outstretched, and she had no choice—none—but to take his hands in her own with as much warmth as she could muster.

He never noticed her hands; his engulfed them, and whatever Vesta might have thought about them was lost in the effusiveness of his farewell. The words he used were incomprehensible to her—words like "charming," "beautiful," "knowledgeable little lady"—words not normally applied to her in the course of company visits—and by

98

the company. She murmured self-deprecating little sounds, aware that behind her, Pierce Darden was enjoying her discomfiture more than just a little bit, and that Vesta hated it.

Finally, she was released from the bear-grip of the well-meaning Mr. Wendell, and she stepped back to stand beside Pierce. "You enjoyed that?" she demanded.

"*You* enjoyed that," he assured her.

"Never. I was totally embarrassed," she contradicted, thrusting her hands into the folds of her skirts, which looked decidedly more graceful than her holding them under her arms.

"You shouldn't be, Miss Sarianna." Pierce turned to her seriously, and she was warmed by the concern in his eyes. "Everything he said was true: You *are* beautiful and charming, and very knowledgeable, and I don't underst—" he broke off, and lifted a negating hand. "It's not my place to question anything, Miss Sarianna. I beg your pardon."

She smiled at him. "I understand we are to have the pleasure of your company for at least another evening, Mr. Darden."

"Yes, I'm afraid so," he answered, his eyes on the departing Wendell carriage which they could just see through the open door.

"*Afraid?* Afraid, Mr. Darden?" she teased gently. "Shall it be said that we kept you, and Mr. Rensell, here against your will?"

"Oh, no, Miss Sarianna. Forgive me. Bredwood's hospitality surpasses anything I've yet experienced. No, I'm not a farming man, and while your own lovely company is most invigorating, and your table is the most tempting I have sat at, I do have business in Savannah; and I find the vagaries of growing cotton and rice don't interest me in the least."

Sarianna smiled. "Perfectly understandable, Mr. Darden." She slanted a cool blue look at him. She was going to ask the question she swore she was not going to ask. "And where is Mr. Rensell this morning?"

"Can't you guess? He's in the fields, of course."

"Of course." She felt a tremor of foreboding. So he had gone into the fields. She knew what he would find there: more that would not be to his liking. She felt a hellion urge to grab Pierce's hand and pull him to the stables where they could hop in a carriage and drive out in the fields—where she could, if she were lucky, forestall any explosion on Cade Rensell's part when he saw what it was likely he would see.

"Mr. Darden," she said carefully, keeping her voice neutral and her eyes focused on him so that they would not reveal her fear, "have you seen our fields yet?"

"Why no, Miss Sarianna," he said in kind, smiling at her.

"Perhaps if you were given a tour," she suggested, "you might find the growing of cotton a little more fascinating topic . . . ?"

"I believe I might," he agreed. "Would you be so kind, Miss Sarianna?"

"I would. Come." Really, she *was* being kind—to Pierce, and to herself. It had nothing to do with wanting to see Cade again, nothing. She only wanted to diffuse the anger he would surely feel when he discovered the presence of his father's best field hands laboring on Sawny for his father's enemy.

Pierce listened to every word she said and did not understand a blessed thing except that *she* knew an incredible amount of information about raising and selling cotton. He was much more interested in her grace and her beauty, the pure profile she turned to him as she expertly guided their gig through the ripening fields that were lush and green, bursting with bounty through excellent management and labor. That was the core of it, he thought; the labor.

Neither Rex Broydon nor Sarianna had seeded the fields of Bredwood, nor pulled and pulleyed the water to irrigate it; nor would they labor the required many hours and days under the sun to reap the harvest. Sarianna's pride was understandable, but he wondered why she should care about anything other than what the sale of that harvest could buy for her.

But then, she was an unusual young woman. And she held an unusual position in her father's house. He wasn't quite sure he understood that either, or just why she was taking him out into the fields when he had only acquiesced to her veiled suggestion when he realized *she* wanted to go. She had said nothing about her reasons. He wondered if it would be judicious to ask.

He decided it was enough for him to bask in her pleasure in the productivity of the estate, and to listen to her soft voice explaining details he would never remember.

And then she said, "You knew, of course, that father bought many of the Rensell hands at the auction?"

He came to attention at once, casting his memory backward to think whether he had or hadn't. "I believe so, Miss Sarianna. And I do think I sent Cade an accounting of who went where as well."

"Oh?" She kept her eyes straight ahead, amazed at the feeling of relief that washed over her. He expected it, then, she thought; he wouldn't be angry. There was no need for her to save his feelings. She could just turn right around and go back to the house.

Except, of course, Mr. Darden was still consumed with interest about Bredwood, and it would be bad manners to abruptly terminate his little tour. In fact, she insisted on expanding it, and she subtly directed the gig toward the outer rim of the fields to show him the field hands' housing, which were trim but small wooden cabins, placed far enough apart that each one had some room for gardening. The overseer's house stood slightly apart from these, larger and more commodious, with a front porch and a little fence surrounding it.

"Nicer than most," Pierce commented, as she guided the gig in a wide circle around this far grove and back toward the main house.

"Yes, they are," Sarianna agreed, forebearing to say that she had fought for the houses to be kept in good repair since there were men among their field hands who had shown some talent for carpentry. She had also discovered a shoemaker and a dairyman, and a blacksmith who now oversaw the stables. "Our woodworkers see to them and make the furniture for the interiors as well as repairs to the house when required. If anyone shows promise at any of these mechanical skills, father takes him from the fields for training. Ah— you see ahead of us now the dairy and the smokehouse, the summer kitchen, which father moved from the basement, the storehouse— everything convenient, wouldn't you say?"

She was prattling, she knew she was; but she did not want to go back to the house yet, and she must if Pierce showed just the slightest hint of boredom. There was no sign of Cade Rensell in the east field, and she hurriedly cut across the road past the outbuildings and took the track out to the west field.

She saw him first, and just where she feared he would be: with Big Henry and Joshua and Darby—slaves he had grown up with at Greenpoint—and now was surrounded by, in the company of the overseer McInerney.

She knew him by his elegant posture before she even saw his face. "Why, there's Mr. Rensell," she said lightly, reining in and slowing down. "I expect he has found some old friends."

Pierce shot her an odd glance. So here was her prey—but why? Cade had shown no interest in her whatsoever apart from the random comment about how like Dona she was, and the brief walk in the garden that morning.

Was that enough?

He watched McInerney indicate their presence, and Cade wheeled his mount around, and then slowly picked his way up the track to meet them. He was hatless, and he wore a leather vest over his shirt.

He wasn't smiling either, Pierce noted, and so he could see did Sarianna.

"Sarianna, Pierce." His voice was still, dry.

Sarianna quivered under his dark inscrutable gaze. He didn't even look at Pierce, and she could not tell if he were angry or not. "I see you've seen Big Henry," she said, lifting her sapphire eyes to meet his just a trifle defiantly.

"Yes, I have," he said noncommittally, and looked at Pierce. "You could have warned me."

"I'm sure I sent you an accounting of the auction," Pierce said stiffly.

"Then of course you did," Cade conceded instantly, but he didn't sound convinced. He turned to Sarianna again. "So, Sarianna?"

She decided not to answer him. He saw too much, he really did. And he wasn't a gentleman either. Maybe they were too much alike, she thought, as his eyes rested thoughtfully on her prim mouth.

"Did you come to try to spare my feelings?" he asked suddenly and none too gently. "Or, my Sarianna, did you come to beg?"

7

She was totally nonplussed, and then she gathered her wits together. "*Beg?* Beg for *what*, Mr. Rensell?" she demanded haughtily. "Perhaps you meant the reverse—that *you* might beg for my father to sell these men back to you?"

She cracked her whip to punctuate the question, and the gig moved forward, forcing Cade to back away and to the side of the field to let her pass. "The nerve," she breathed furiously. "Never mind," she interrupted, as Pierce started to comment. "Don't say a thing. My intentions were misread, as I should have expected they would be, Mr. Darden."

She hoped her words carried; she doubted they did. Pierce looked bewildered, as he had every right to, and she felt a familiar sense of humiliation wash over her again.

She drove the mare that pulled the gig in her growing anger. How *could* he! And in front of Pierce Darden, too! Let him suffer then, knowing the complete extent of Rex's perfidy. Let him sit at her father's table then, smiling at his hospitality, admiring the little empire her father was building on *his* father's demise.

She wouldn't be there, and wasn't that a pity. She would have liked to have seen him squirm. Beg him, indeed! Beg him to leave more like.

She reined in the mare suddenly as the gig pulled into the stable yard. "Here we are, Mr. Darden. I hope our little jaunt was enlightening."

"Uh, indeed," Pierce said as Earl the blacksmith came forward to take the reins from Sarianna's hand and unhitch the mare. "Shall I see you at dinner then, Miss Sarianna?"

"I think not," she said just a trifle wistfully, as he helped her down from the driver's seat.

"Really? But I had hoped . . ." His voice trailed off. There was no use talking to *her* about it. Her face had set in a peculiar expression that said to him more clearly than words: Don't press the issue.

"Thank you for your excellent company," she said, holding out her hand, and then almost snatched it back again. Damn, she had forgotten it was still dirty. But no matter, he took it anyway, and she appreciated the gesture.

She waved to him as she left him standing in the stable yard and went in through the kitchen to ascertain how far along in the preparation of dinner Sylvia was.

She found the chickens roasting in preparation for deboning, and a soup simmering. She found the sauces mixed and stored in crocks at the ready for final presentation. She found Oresta, one of the kitchen helpers, vigorously churning butter, and Merleen, whose duties were varied, punching down a rising loaf of bread and then picking up the biscuit batter and beating it yet another go-round before setting it into baking tins.

She found all was as it should be, and that she was not needed here as well. The only place left for her to go was her bedroom.

She found Jeralee pacing on the bedroom landing, her nose quivering with anger, her handkerchief a damp knot in her hands. If the square of cotton had been her neck, Sarianna thought in dismay, her father would be holding funeral services for her at that very moment.

"So," Jeralee said, her voice tremulous with suppressed fury, "so—you usurp Mr. Darden as well now. And did you chase out into the fields for Mr. Rensell? Did they entertain you well, the two of them? And don't we know *where* this wanton streak of yours comes from? Don't we? You cannot have Mr. Rensell, Sarianna. I forbid it!"

"You credit me with more allure than I could possibly have," Sarianna said temperately, holding her own anger in.

"No, I credit you with being your mother's daughter."

"As you are yours!" Sarianna snapped. "There is no point to this, Jeralee. I am not pursuing Mr. Rensell or Mr. Darden. *You* may have either or both with my blessings and if you are capable of it—which I think you are." But she didn't think that, she thought in amazement as she tried to brush past Jeralee and was caught in Jeralee's talonlike grip. Jeralee wasn't capable; *she* was. *She,* the one for whom they professed an unaverred kind of shame. She was the one.

She stared into Jeralee's chocolate-mud eyes, unfathomably deep with hate, and she heard Jeralee's words and couldn't believe she was hearing them. "You are *just* like Dona. I know all about what Dona was like. All her men. All her lies. Mother told me, Sarianna. She told me I had to beware of you; you have Dona's taint. You want everyone, no matter who it is, as long as someone else wants him, too—don't you, Sarianna? Isn't that what you're like? But you'll have to fight me, Sarianna. Father was forced to bring you into company to fend off questions about why he doesn't allow you to come in company, but you know now, don't you? He won't relive that pain again, Sarianna. And I swore I would protect him, too. So you leave off running after Cade Rensell, you hear? You leave him to me. Stay in your room, Sarianna, until they leave. *Stay away.*"

She dropped Sarianna's arm abruptly and pushed her away. Sarianna stared after her as she flew down the stairs.

Jeralee was insane. She had to be insane to say all those things. None of it made sense. Her father had limited her social life because he was afraid she was like Dona? Dona chased other men? Everyone?

Jeralee was mad. Sarianna inched her way down the hall until she came to her room. She was almost afraid to open the door lest she find Vesta there, waiting to attack. Her room was empty, a haven for the moment. She collapsed wearily onto her bed, which had been remade, she noted with the functioning side of her brain, the one that wasn't horrified by Jeralee's desperate innuendos.

Thank God she did not have to appear for dinner, she thought, burying her golden head in her arms. Imagine—all of this had happened because Cade Rensell had been precipitately invited to Bredwood. And what had Vesta hoped to have happen—that he would fall crazily in love with Jeralee in the space of two days? *Vesta* had to be mad.

Or had she been pinning her hopes on something else?

What?

That Cade was so thirsty for vengeance that marrying into the Broydons would be revenge enough? Never. He wasn't that kind of man. He would never have allowed himself to be railroaded into marrying Jeralee. Anyway, Jeralee would not suit the purpose if his goal were revenge. There wasn't anything he could do to Rex *now,* and

Jeralee's urgency seemed even more misplaced when she considered it in that light.

She was tired of thinking of it in any light. They were all crazy, Cade Rensell most of all for walking into a hornet's nest and hoping to come out alive—even after he had seduced her and perhaps led on Jeralee.

How far? her unruly thoughts wondered. No!

Had he kissed her, too? Like *that?*

Given *her* that same exquisite mindless pleasure . . . was that why Jeralee was insensate with rage . . . ?

And wouldn't Sarianna be, if she had even the slightest suspicion that any of that were true?

Oh, God, would Sarianna be, she thought, her body beginning to tremble at the merest glimmer of the picture of Jeralee in his arms, naked, straining for his caress. No! Not like that. *Not like that!*

Innocent! she castigated herself. Anything was possible. Anything. She knew nothing of men or sensuality except this brief awakening hour in Cade Rensell's arms. He was just as capable of duplicity as any man—or any woman. He was just as capable of lies and deceit.

He—

"And what you doin' layin' abed, Miss Sarianna, when you got to be gettin' ready fo' dinner with yo' guests?"

Sarianna turned on her elbows. "I'm not going to dinner, Alzine. Vesta made it very clear."

"Den she done made it unclear. You is expected to dinner, Miss Sarianna, and she done tole me to tell you. Mr. Cade and Mr. Pierce be wantin' to know if you was gonna join dem fo' dinner, and she had no choice unless she want to be rude. And since she want Mr. Cade, she sent fo' you. Now, what you gonna wear, Miss Sarianna?"

Even with Vesta's express invitation, Sarianna did not want to join the others for dinner, but she allowed herself to be fussed over by Alzine. She *needed* to be fussed over; her nerves felt jangly, and her stomach knotted. Vesta was planning something. Vesta would never let her off that easy, nor would she accede to pressure unless she were up to something.

Vesta was planning to humiliate her somehow.

Her tension suddenly lessened, as if defining the thing hovering on the edge of her anxiety made it easier to deal with.

She watched with calmer eyes as Alzine prepared an abbreviated bath for her, and stepped into its cool lemon-scented depth gratefully. She allowed Alzine to wash her heated body and pour the even cooler rinse water over her to surround her with the tart refreshing scent. She stepped out and into a towel that Alzine held for her, and she wondered why Alzine had all this time to tend to her needs when it was usually Jeralee whom she dressed.

Alzine's face was impassive as she withdrew yet another camisole and set of drawers from the scented dresser drawer and laid them on the bed. She said not a word as she retreated into the dressing room wardrobe to hunt out a suitable dress which both of them knew would be slightly out of date or somewhat the worse for wear—or even a made-over cast-off of Jeralee's.

Well, she wasn't concerned with how she looked tonight anyway, Sarianna thought, regarding herself in the chifferobe mirror. She was not trying to impress anyone. She was merely being polite.

Oh, yes, but what would Cade Rensell think when he looked at her across the table tonight, her niggling little inner voice demanded. There wasn't much he hadn't seen this afternoon, she reminded herself tartly. What had he thought? she wondered, staring at her towel-wrapped figure. What *had* he seen?

She could tell right then; she let the towel drop to her feet and boldly looked at her reflection.

And she saw clearly what he had seen: the tall reedy slenderness of her body, the long legs and narrow hips, the perfect conical shape of her breasts with their thrusting nipples that seemed to have a life of their own. Her slender arms and huge, darkening blue eyes. Her ever-unruly hair. Why did he want her when Jeralee's lushness was available for the asking?

She turned sideways, to examine the pert curve of her buttocks and the flat swoop of her stomach to the inviting vee of her thighs with its dark golden concealment. Her body was so lean, so taut, every inch of flesh finely defined and not an inch of excess anywhere.

And all of that Cade Rensell had seen and desired at the moment. He would come to his senses, she thought humorlessly, but she would never forget what it felt like to be in his arms—how her body had hungered for what he gave her to the point of ignoring all propriety and demanding it. God, what she had missed! It was almost as if the afternoon with *him* atoned for some of the neglect and lack of affection from her father. Even as she thought about it, she felt the aching demand of her very skin to be touched again and caressed, by some hand—by his hand. The sensation was so intense she could have screamed in frustration.

What did it mean if she yearned for it now after one hour of pure temptation? Did it mean she would begin to seek it out anywhere, anyhow from anyone? Was every man susceptible to the wanton display she had put on for Cade Rensell? Would every man affect her like that?

Would she want just anyone to touch her that way as long as she felt the things she had experienced with Cade?

Oh, God, what a question! Where had that come from? From the mother part of her, the secret self that screamed to be held and fondled, that wanted to be loved, that pleaded to be desired?

But she knew now what it meant, no—something of what it meant. It meant losing all sense of self. It meant tempting and revealing, giving up the decorous side of herself, the civilized side; it meant floating on a molten cloud above propriety and not giving one good damn about it. It meant feeling and touching and holding and that spiraling sensual foray by a stranger's hands which now knew her body more intimately than she did.

And he wanted it; even if it had been the lustful desire of the moment, he had wanted her and the imperfect body she saw in the mirror.

She folded her arms around her naked waist, her arms pressing against her breasts, pushing them farther outward and making them look larger. She wished suddenly that they were larger, lush and full and billowy like Jeralee's and that her hips had more of the coveted curve that betokened successful childbearing.

Yes—Vesta had said it. Jeralee had everything, including the cherished symbol that men revered: the wide hipbones that would nurture and bring forth the much coveted male heir.

But it wasn't a contest, after all. Cade Rensell had tendered a proposal which she had refused. It was now up to Vesta to bring him to the point for Jeralee. How amusing that would be.

How heartsick she would be if it came to pass. She was almost tempted to try to thwart it. Almost. The dictates of her hungry body almost superseded the overt threats Vesta had made.

She considered it for a moment. Sheer folly. She was outnumbered for one thing, and they hated her wildly on top of that, a hate that would imbue them with an uncanny ability to defeat her.

She shivered at the notion. If there were a way out, she thought, she would grab it and damn the consequences.

Even accepting that proposal? her niggling little voice asked snidely.

Even that, she allowed reluctantly, truthfully and only to her innermost thoughts. Even that, if it meant lying naked in his arms again and—

"Miss Sarianna! What you doin' like dat in de mirror?"

She whirled. "Damn, you scared me!"

"It ain't right fo' you to be standin' and lookin' at yo' self like some painted woman flauntin' herself. You go sit yo' self on dat bed, and we gonna get you ready fo' de dinner."

"I don't want to get ready for the dinner," Sarianna said, moving reluctantly to the bed.

"I done found you a pretty dress, Miss Sarianna, and everything is gonna be just fine, you gonna see." Alzine disappeared for a moment and came back bearing a flowered muslin gown and its several petticoats.

"Oh, that one," Sarianna said, fingering the material with a show of interest. It was a remodeled dress, one she had not worn in several years, and it was supported by layers of petticoats that did not require a hoop. Moreover, the material was lightweight and the neckline was cut low, with the bodice fashioned in the princess style which, while it was slightly out of mode, was nonetheless flattering to her.

Alzine, she reflected, was a wonder, as she began slipping in to her undergarments. "Why," she inquired over the rustle of petticoats slipping over her head, "aren't you dressing Jeralee tonight?"

Alzine pulled down the layers one by one before she answered. "Why, dis be de most imp'tant night fo' Miss Jeralee. Ain't nobody gonna dress her baby but Miss Vesta."

Sarianna descended the stairs to the anteroom, fully aware of the waterfall murmur of voices below. Thirteen to dinner, and her. She felt as if she had fallen into a flowerbed, and that the soft riotous print made her conspicuous, a target. She felt wary of her reception by her father and Vesta, and knew she had to be on her guard with

Cade Rensell.

And yet, from the eleven waiting guests, he was the one she picked out instantly, and she hated herself for settling her sapphire gaze on him like some kind of lifeline.

Whether he felt her grazing look or he was watching for her anyway, she did not know, but when she appeared, he immediately raised his eyes and watched her slowly waft down the stairs, his hazel eyes curiously soft and his expression—dared she think it?— appreciative. And he, of all the men, instantly moved forward, even in advance of Pierce Darden, to offer his arm.

"Sarianna?"

"Mr. Rensell, I *beg* that you don't trouble yourself," she said deliberately.

"It would be beggarly of you to refuse," he answered in kind, holding his arm out once again.

She looked up at him, and he was keenly aware of her discomfiture. There was tension in her slender body and a faint wrinkle across her smooth forehead. Her gaze focused beyond his tall black-garbed figure and noted frantically that neither Vesta nor Jeralee was there. It was impossible as well to miss her father's icy blue disdain.

"Sarianna!"

"Mr. Rensell?" Her response was cool, distant, and he felt like throttling her.

"You *will* beg, Sarianna," he said suddenly to force her attention back to him.

She heard the words; they sounded ferocious in her ears over the thin thread of a threat she felt emanating from her father. She did not know how to play word games, but she did know that she must keep him as far away as possible from her this night; she wondered why she had the impression he was bent on staying close.

"I am not a beggar," she said tartly, her body tightening as they all awaited Jeralee's entrance. Why would he court disaster by hanging all over her, she wondered fretfully. It was enough he had wanted her at the table. It was too much. Vesta meant to show her something tonight, and she was taut as a bowstring as her mind ran riot over all the possibilities.

"But I am the chooser," Cade reminded her softly in her ear, leaning so close she could feel the barest whisper of his breath against her skin. The ethereal contact made her tingle. The truth made

110

her shiver.

He was the one who would make a choice, and he had already said it would not be Jeralee. She looked up into his lion-face and his inflexibly set mouth. He had a raw look about him tonight, reckless, just daring a challenge. He was different from all these Sawny men in all ways, and they all knew it. They were tolerating him for her father's sake, and they all remembered the story of his father very well. She could almost read their eyes: Rensell was the son of his papa and just as stubborn; he wasn't wanted there, and they were too polite to condemn his unorthodox manners and ill-conceived dress.

He dominated the room, so full of energy was he against all these soft planters who had others to toil for them. He reeked of a sweaty muscularity that was anathema to them. He had worked, he wore plain clothes, and his hair was unkempt and his skin tanned; and they all felt he might be more at ease in the overseer's house than at their host's table. They couldn't cope with the notion of his callused hands using the same utensils in concert with them. He was a man of crude cabins and thick ironstone plates, not elegant Greek-columned mansions, silver and fine china.

Nonetheless, he was among them as Rex Broydon's guest, and they honored that; but nobody spoke with him, and he liked that just as well.

It was curious to Cade that Pierce was the one they conversed with; they had no problem with Pierce. He was learned, in a way Cade himself was not; he had something to offer them that they could trade in fair coin, and they could respect that. Cade thought them all hypocrites and didn't give a damn about a single one of them but Sarianna, and she was making her scorn obvious as well.

But he had shocked her just then, saying he was the one who would make the choice, and she had never considered that, only the consequences should he persist in the fool notion that he wanted *her*.

Oh, but he wanted her, and no more so than this afternoon, when she had wantonly let herself surrender in his arms. And how he had had to tamp down tightly on his bursting desire as he left her in her room to contemplate the folly of her life at Bredwood. He could have taken her the moment before his rash words, but to what effect? Nonetheless, her mask of civility was back in place, and no one would have guessed that Sarianna had been in his arms, consumed by lust, just a few hours before.

No one would have guessed the pain that fed her brief, wafting little smile. Only he, and he meant to have her one way or another.

He meant to get both of them out of Vesta's clutches.

"Gentlemen and ladies!" The voice came from behind them, and the great double door from the anteroom to the parlor slid open to reveal Vesta within, and Jeralee standing near the fireplace, behind her.

What a picture she made, Sarianna thought venomously, poised as though one of those head clamps held her head for a picture-taking, with Vesta sweeping backward in five quick steps so that for one brief moment, Jeralee was framed by the ornate door frame, an elegant marble fireplace as a backdrop for her dark beauty and her obviously new golden gown that dripped tiers of ivory lace all over her lush body.

But if it were a setting for a jewel that was meant to impress Cade Rensell, it had missed its mark. Cade still stood by the baluster with Sarianna as the guests moved into the parlor, and he and she were the last to come in, Jeralee's expression by then turning faintly petulant.

"Oh, Cade." She pouted, catching sight of him with Sarianna, and her mood turned inexpressibly darker. She appropriated his black broadclothed arm immediately and left Sarianna adrift in a sea of formless faces.

So much for the chooser, she thought viciously; and what did *his* fine words come to? He was nothing but a choice bull himself, and Jeralee was making every effort to make sure he knew it.

"So, my dear," Vesta said beside her. "A lovely dress. Alzine remade it, I collect? It's perfect for you."

"Sarianna," another voice chimed in behind her—Pierce, a welcome respite from Vesta's snideness, which she had been about to unleash.

"Mr. Darden," Vesta acknowledged. "I was just about to tell Sarianna that she will be seated tonight between you and Mr. Rensell, such a fortuitous arrangement, don't you think, to find oneself between two such handsome gentlemen?"

"*We* are fortunate certainly that we shall have Miss Sarianna's company at the table tonight," Pierce said gallantly, as his appreciative eyes swept over her flowery gown. "You look mighty

112

fine, Miss Sarianna—and you, too, Miss Vesta," he added punctiliously to Vesta's curt little nod. She moved away before he could say more, and Sarianna looked at him with a dawning respect.

He shrugged. "Well, I'm not . . . quite . . . acceptable, Miss Sarianna. She could explain it better, I expect, but it does come in useful when she's badgering you."

"Thank you, Mr. Darden. It must be your lawyer's skills honed to a fine point that can deal so successfully with Vesta."

He bowed. "May I have the honor of escorting you to dinner as your thanks?"

"I would like that."

"I beg to differ with you." Cade's voice broke into their mutual accord. "You wouldn't like it half so much with him as with me."

"But then Jeralee's favors would go begging," Sarianna countered before she could stop herself, "and Vesta would never permit that. No, it's better this way, Mr. Rensell."

"Cade," he corrected gently.

"That wouldn't be proper under the circumstances, Mr. Rensell. I don't—" Sarianna paused, thinking how her next words would strike him—"know you well enough."

His mouth quirked humorlessly. "Perhaps I should beg for an introduction, Sarianna?"

"I beg your pardon?" she shot back, helpless to combat her unruly mouth. She wanted to goad him, and she wanted him to just go away. Such contrariness within her boded deep trouble and warred with her deep feeling of enjoying her elegant sparring with him. She was holding her own well enough, she thought, as Cade looked at Pierce expectantly, and Pierce, with his ever present good manners, took up the gauntlet.

"Miss Sarianna Broydon, may I present Mr. Cade Rensell, late of Sawny Island, and parts west? And Mr. Rensell, Miss Sarianna Broydon," he intoned with a humorous inflection in his voice, and Sarianna felt a moment of exasperation.

Cade bowed formally, and she snapped, "*Really*, Mr. Rensell . . ."

"Cade, please, Miss Sarianna," he said gently, "and I would be honored to escort you in to dinner." His hazel eyes were soft now as he took in her stormy expression. Oh, she was damned right, she did not know how to play, not to any great extent. She was out of patience with him already, and her heady enjoyment of their conversation had toppled into something more deadly serious. She looked uneasy now as Vesta's and Rex's guests milled around, sipping a glass of champagne before the dinner gong sounded. Vesta was nowhere around, and Jeralee was occupied with the Gilmartins.

"I should think Vesta will designate those arrangements," Sarianna said, keeping her eyes fixed on Cade's face. She saw his expression change, almost as if he had divined what she was not saying—that she was afraid of what Vesta might do if Cade were to continually pay such marked attention to her.

He shrugged. "So what, Sarianna?"

"You've caused enough trouble by merely requesting my presence at the table tonight," she told him—or maybe he had guessed anyway; maybe he had thought Vesta would be goaded into some other little vindictive act, and he had demanded her presence because he knew it would annoy her. Was that possible? Oh, with a man like this, anything was possible; hadn't he admitted he had come to find a wife? He had told her just that, and that Jeralee was to have been the candidate. Vesta inferred it, Vesta expected it, and Vesta would not like anyone tampering with *her* plans.

"My dear Sarianna, I merely wanted you to benefit from the result of your efforts; surely the wife in spirit deserves to be seated at her own table."

She froze. How did he have the insolence to bring up that which she considered a closed issue. He had made his point; he *knew* he had made his point, and he must have been aware how deeply his words had cut. She hated him at that moment. "I should slap your face for that," she said tightly, her sapphire eyes blazing—but with what? The admission she *had* thought about it? Loathing for his perception?

"And I could kiss you for *that*," he retorted impudently, "right here and now, and let everyone know just where I stand."

Her knees buckled. "Oh, my God, don't do that. You're impossible, Mr. Rensell." She felt Pierce's hand at her arm and caught a fleeting glimpse of his disturbed expression. Worse and worse; Pierce knew nothing of the flaring attraction between them. He mustn't know.

He raised his hand warningly. "Cade . . ."

Cade stared at him, the lion-look that said, *Don't say a word, don't interfere.* "I'm very possible, Sarianna," he said, turning his

114

ferocious gaze on her just as the dinner gong sounded. "I suggest you get used to the idea."

Pierce escorted her to the table after all, and here, she thought, was part of her punishment for having commanded this consideration from them. She was seated between Pierce and Cade, on the long side of the table, with Cade to her left in a position where she was sure to bump elbows with him throughout the meal.

And didn't the settings look lovely—but she had chosen them, she remembered, and there would be the chicken fricassee and all those fresh vegetables. *Had* that been today? Time had stopped in her bedroom, with her wanton invitation to the man beside her; nothing existed before that, and nothing, she thought, would exist after—no matter what he said.

Pierce seated her with the greatest of care, and she was amused to see Jeralee seated to Cade's left, and Samuel Summers beyond her. Perhaps Vesta was intent on playing all the angles. She wondered that Vesta didn't feel she was a threat to a possible liaison between Jeralee and Samuel.

They were all crazy, even Cade, who watched with a mocking smile as Samuel Summers guided Jeralee into her chair. Jeralee flashed him a speaking, chocolatey look as she settled her golden skirts around her with too much attention to just how smooth they lay around her legs. When that was finally done to her satisfaction, she nodded at both Cade and Samuel Summers, and they simultaneously seated themselves.

Sarianna unclenched her hands, which she had held tightly in her lap during this maidenly display. Jeralee was a one, damn her; no doubt she intended for them all to try to imagine what lay beneath that silky gold material that draped so tantalizingly around her. She had seen Sarianna watching, and she meant to make the most of her moment as the center of attention. Too bad she couldn't have seen that wolfish little look appear on her face when she looked at Cade; it had spoiled the effect, Sarianna thought in great satisfaction. There was no mistaking its meaning, and its intent was not lost on Cade. He said something to her, and Sarianna itched to know what.

How was she going to contain herself during this meal? It was

115

perfectly obvious Cade would have conversation with Jeralee and could ignore *her* with impunity. That was what she wanted, wasn't it? she demanded of herself as Eon and Merleen wheeled in the mahogany serving cart and began ladling out the cold consommé.

And now the first test, she thought. Vesta's eyes were on her, and Jeralee's, obliquely, from around Cade's shoulders.

Sarianna looked up at Cade as Rex lifted his spoon and signaled his guests to begin the meal.

Cade nodded, and she took up her own spoon, dipped it in the fragrant liquid, and lifted it to her trembling lips.

The soup was followed by a course of fish and egg in aspic, which was removed by the chicken fricassee, served in vol-au-vent pastry and accompanied by the haricots, tomatoes in vinegar and the creamed onions, as well as a wild rice casserole and corn bread stuffing, biscuits with butter or honey, cold sweet potato puffs, and the stewed okra and carrots with cheese. There was an uncooked cranberry sauce made with sugar and oranges, spiced grapes, pepper relish, pickled watermelon and Sylvia's chutney. Accompanying these successive courses were sherry, white wine; and with the fruits, lemon pie and whipped cream, champagne once again.

Sarianna ate sparingly and covertly watched her father enjoying his guests taking pleasure in his bountiful table. He was known for it, and it was a point of honor with him that each subsequent contingent of guests should experience even more lavish hospitality than the last.

And what did Cade Rensell think of all this, she wondered, pushing her fruit and pie around on her plate. Her father's Sawnian friends expected nothing less and returned her father's open-handedness in kind.

But Cade had been away from this unstinting munificence for a long tme. Did he condemn it as too prodigal a display when it had been presented to *her* as a simple family dinner—and for what? To impress him with its abundance and simplicity both? *Was* he impressed?

She felt his eyes on her and turned her head. And why did she care when it was Pierce who was making light inconsequential dinner conversation with her to divert her mind from her father's critical eye which fixed on her every time she lifted her fork. Cade, in fact, was

116

unusually silent, neither responding to Jeralee on his one side, nor speaking at all to *her* on the other. And Vesta watched them all like a hawk eyeing a chicken.

Cade was aware of it. The currents swirling around the table could pull him into an undertow, he thought wryly, and he half expected to see Vesta leap over the neatly appointed table if he so much as turned his head in Sarianna's direction.

She was deadly serious about snaring him for Jeralee, and he was just waiting to spike her intentions. Jeralee was a piece of fluff, a decoration, good for no more than minimal table conversation and only if that were concentrated solely on *her*.

And yet, he thought disgustedly, he would have taken her, and gladly, if he had thought it would punish Rex for his treachery and avenge his father's death. But he saw clearly now that that never would have done; Rex had almost as little feeling for Jeralee as he had for Sarianna. Vesta made the difference in the way he treated Jeralee, and Vesta hated Sarianna.

And they were all watching her, waiting for one misstep on her part, as if she were some incompetent relative they had hidden away and were now allowing out to test her adroitness in a social situation.

He felt a flaming anger spewing inside him at the way they treated her and the way they were praying for her to commit a solecism.

They hated her grace and her beauty, and the elegance of her movements beside him, and the way his right arm shifted in concert with her motions almost as if they had orchestrated it.

They despised her, every damn one of them, from Rex down to the Gilmartins; they couldn't stand seeing her shine, and that the thing they considered such an aberration was no more than a minor inconvenience to anyone else.

Damn them all, damn them.

He had so little time, so little. He had to reject Jeralee and win Sarianna all in one night, and somehow convince Rex to give her up. And he had to take a stand soon, he thought, which was no mean feat given Jeralee's inane repartee. Nonetheless, he unbent enough with her to say a few words to her in answer to some comment or the other, and he was bemused by the pleasure that flooded her expression. Oh, she wanted him, all right. How good that would look to her Sawnian neighbors—all that Sawny heritage of his, and all that money he had

117

made in the West. And best of all, he knew, was that he was the sole surviving child of his parents' union. Jeralee liked what she saw, the full package, and Vesta liked it even more.

Finally Rex stood up and stood gazing benignly at his company. "Gentlemen?" he said, and once again the men rose, Cade reluctantly, as if one body, and Rex nodded at each of the women in turn. "My dear Jeralee, Vesta. Olivia, Dorothy. Josephine." He moved out from behind his chair. "Oh—Sarianna . . ." he added from the door as he opened it and motioned his guests into the hallway.

Cade's jaw tightened at this blatant discourtesy even as he followed Rex across the hall into his narrow portaled library where Eon was already dispensing brandy.

None of the men, except perhaps Pierce, had even noticed the slip. Only Pierce sent him a meaningful look over his cut crystal snifter as he cupped it in his hands to warm the liquid within.

Only Pierce understood because of his gaffe at the birthday dinner the magnitude of the shameful way they treated Sarianna.

The rest were fat, overindulged Sawnian planters, even Rex in his elegant slenderness was fat with their misplaced regard and the triumph of his success. And who were they after all? Samuel Summers, who had buried two wives already and fed his conscience by supporting indigent relatives; Dr. Hammond, who had risen from nothing and married into a Sawny planter family; the Gilmartins and the Grays, who had inherited their acreage and probably sat back on their fat rumps letting their slaves work the land for them while they did nothing but spend the profits.

And of course there was always the question of whether there were profits, if his own father's experience was anything to go by. Maybe they were all living on credit and borrowed time, and the future didn't matter to them—only the lavish exhibition of the day to throw a smokescreen up for their neighbors whose good opinion counted more than their own integrity and worth.

He hated them, and he hated that Sarianna was being sacrificed to this lust for appearances, and her father's perhaps unwitting (he granted) desire to keep the essence of Dona with him always.

He could destroy Rex if he took Sarianna, he thought, as he sipped his own snifter of superlative brandy. And he wanted to. He wanted to desperately. Sarianna was his, and if his reasons for wanting her were entwined with the past and his thirst for vengeance, he must nonetheless have her. He couldn't leave her, not after these two days and nights.

She was in his blood, in his heart. He saw her as all that she was, and he saw her as Dona's child, forever to be offered up on the altar of her mother's follies. And—God—his own. Yes, his own, and his downright insanity for his ever thinking he could have the likes of Dona, and wanting it all those years, when the perfect symmetry of fate had created Sarianna for him and him alone.

Would he have found her? It was unthinkable that he would not have known about her. He would have come straight to Bredwood in any event to demand answers from Rex Broydon; he would have discovered her. It was ordained he would find her; why else had he been so obdurate in his desire to return to Sawny?

And what was she doing now, he wondered apprehensively. They had left her in the den of the she-dogs who were ready to tear her from limb to limb because of their envy and hate.

She wouldn't let herself in for that, he thought; she would escape it as reasonably soon as she possibly could. She wasn't a martyr; she was downright scared of Vesta for some reason. And while her room was no refuge from Vesta, she could surely count on not being disturbed while Vesta was entertaining.

He envisioned her there, her flowery dress heaped on the side chair, looking like a brilliant bush of roses growing from the floor. He saw her there on the bed, as he had seen her this afternoon, scantily dressed, wondering about her body, wondering now, he hoped, about *him* and what he had said and all the voluptuous feelings he had aroused in her.

He closed his eyes, visualizing her innocently erotic pose and her sensual flaunting as those feelings made her yearn for his touch. He wanted to go to her, instantly; his body reacted, remembering the feel of her in his hands, the taste of her lush nipples in his mouth, and suddenly nothing seemed more important than Sarianna.

But nothing was, he thought, setting down his snifter. All the pompous man-talk swirling in the air around him had nothing to do with Sarianna.

He waved Eon aside as the stately butler approached him. "I think I'll forego a second round," he said, motioning him away.

"But Mr. Rensell . . ." Rex came instantly to his side, protesting as a good host must. "We can't possibly let you abstain from having another drink with us. I propose a toast, gentlemen, to my daughter, on her birthday." He sent Cade a goading look as Eon began passing around a tray full of fresh drinks.

Cade was obligated to take one. The men surrounded him and Rex, and Rex lifted his own snifter and stared straight at Cade. "To Jeralee, gentlemen, to Jeralee."

8

The ladies had removed to the parlor once again, and Merleen served sherry, lemonade and plain little coconut cakes. Vesta blossomed under her neighbors' approbation. "Lovely, Vesta, so refreshing these little sweets. Not filling though. Perfect after such a lovely dinner. . . . How does Sylvia do it every time, Dorothy? Perhaps she can give her secrets to our cooks? Vesta?"

And Vesta laughed them off, nibbled at her cake, sipped lemonade and watched Sarianna, who sat slightly apart from them, her sapphire gaze fixed unrelentingly on her hands.

But the coup de grâce was yet to come, Vesta reflected. Soon Merleen would wheel in the cart with coffee and tea, and she would ask Sarianna to pour. That would do it, she thought with satisfaction; that would diminish her in the way that Vesta had hoped dining with company might do.

Sarianna nursed a tall glass of lemonade, which she had taken to ward off the stifling, hot atmosphere in the room. Vesta's active dislike was like a fog hovering over them, waiting to devour her, Sarianna, into oblivion. She had only to wait, and Vesta would present her on a platter for her guests' delectation, to scorn and to gossip about.

She didn't intend to wait, but there seemed in the initial fifteen or so minutes of the gathering of this feline conclave no opportunity for her to gracefully excuse herself.

She had a grim feeling that Vesta would not let her go.

And it would always be like this if Cade Rensell walked out of Bredwood without Jeralee on his arm.

121

It didn't have to be like this, she reflected. He had offered her a way out. *She* could walk out of Bredwood on his arm and away from this repressive family forever.

What a cool breeze of hope that thought sent wafting through her! But it was just the merest possibility; she had rejected his bald proposal already, and she hated the thought he had been willing to spitefully pick whichever Sawny belle would have taken him. Not her. And with no love. Cold-bloodedly he would have wooed whomever had been offered, and fortuitously it had been the rapacious Jeralee.

There was no room for the fumbling Sarianna Broydon in that romantic story. She had been a mere sidestep, someone enchanted with his momentary desire and her own latent longings and covetousness. Oh, yes, she had liked it very well that she had kissed him before Jeralee. Yes, she liked what he did to her body, and yes, damn it, she would have given much to have him come to her in her bed again. But for what? To arouse the sleeping desire once again, so that when he left, she would live in a morass of anguish knowing she could never experience that potent culmination ever again?

How silly of her to want what was not possible. She was not someone whom men swooned over and fought duels for. They did not write poetry to her, or beg her favors, or storm her father's door for permission to address her. They never begged her kisses, or devoured her lips in broad daylight, uncaring of who was watching.

Cade had done that; *he* had awakened her to the notion that she conceivably could be desired by a man, in spite of Jeralee, in spite of her heretic wrong-handedness.

She wasn't sure she was grateful for it. She could have slumbered forever, laboring in her father's home, and known none of it and been perfectly content.

He was only answering that within her that spoke of Dona and his long lost love, she thought; he never saw *her*, despite his protestations, otherwise he never would have made love to her.

She watched with impassive eyes as Merleen wheeled in the tea cart that was loaded with delectables: a second helping of Sylvia's lemon pie, a platter of lemon cookies, a frosted cake, an almond cake slathered with a layer of rich almond paste and covered with white icing, a gingerbread and a brandied peach tart. There were fresh fruits, and containers of heavy cream, whipped cream, brandied cream and cognac for flambé. There were delicate bowls of nuts, raisins, dates, and sliced peaches and plump strawberries, while sliced plain pound cake was provided for those who wished to devise their own dessert concoction.

There was coffee, tea, more brandy, lemonade and sherry, all to be served on Dona's delicate dessert set with its fluted cups and saucers made of the finest thinnest bone china, and the matching cake plates.

And there was Vesta beside it, motioning to her, Sarianna, to come help her serve.

So here it was, Sarianna thought, and she wondered how in the world she could refuse without admitting her fear of making a gaffe. There was no way. She slowly rose from her seat and moved to Vesta's side.

Treacherous Vesta; she had arranged the cart so that it was to Sarianna's left, and her serving hand would have to stretch awkwardly across the bottles and coffee and tea service in order to pass out the drinks and cake plates.

How vicious she was, Sarianna thought, as she turned to Dorothy Gray.

Mrs. Gray fluttered and waffled back and forth between the almond cake and strawberries and whipped cream heaped on a piece of pound cake.

Sarianna turned politely to Mrs. Gilmartin. She at least was a no-nonsense woman, courteous to a fault, and plain as a pikestaff in spite of her grooming and expensive clothes. She had never been discourteous to Sarianna in all the years she had visited Bredwood, but Sarianna perceived instantly that tonight somehow was different. Tonight Josephine Gilmartin had aligned herself with Vesta and Jeralee, and tonight she hoped that Sarianna would humiliate herself completely.

"I'll have the peach tart," Mrs. Gilmartin said, and Sarianna knew she had chosen it because it was the most difficult to portion out and cut. "And some coffee—with the heavy cream and a tea-spoon of sugar." She waited.

Sarianna, aware of her rank awkwardness without room beside her to wield her knife, cut the piece of tart—a small piece of tart as it happened—placed it on the doily in the waiting plate, put the knife down in order to hand the plate comfortably to Mrs. Gilmartin, and then proceeded to pour the coffee.

Even then, she felt all eyes on her, telling eyes, angry eyes. Envious eyes, she thought; she wasn't ungainly or inept. Vesta had deliberately placed the cart to make things as unmanageable as possible for her.

She handed the coffee cup to Mrs. Gilmartin, who retired from the fray. Mrs. Gray then requested the almond cake, and Sarianna cut that from the same awkward position and served her a cup of tea, all the while aware of Vesta's devouring eyes waiting, hoping, praying for one disastrous mistake.

"Vesta?" Sarianna said politely, holding up the knife in a way that Vesta could not misunderstand that she knew what Vesta intended.

"Oh, my dear, let me see, everything looks so good," Vesta said, pretending to ignore the threat of the knife that were she pushed far enough, Sarianna might fling over the table and into her gut. "Oh, the lemon pie, Sarianna, and top it with some of the whipped cream. It does taste better that way. With tea, please."

Sarianna cut the piece of pie and Vesta watched, and Sarianna wondered why she did not just push the piece of pie in Vesta's face. The thought hovered around her mind for a moment, tantalizing, active, satisfying even in the dying moment of its conception.

"Oh, you stupid girl, you tilted the plate and the whipped cream dripped all over my dress."

She heard the words—was that Vesta? Merleen rushed forward with a napkin, her eyes wide with fear. "Here it is, Miss Vesta, no trouble, no problem. It clean clear away, look now, ma'am. De little bit of cream is gone, see?" She flashed a look at Sarianna. *You got trouble,* it said, and Sarianna knew it, because Jeralee was next to be served after she paid assiduous attention to her mother's small accident.

"Try to keep a steady hand, Sarianna," she said snidely, as she approached the cart. "Tea and the almond cake, if you please. A thick slice. No one makes almond cake like Sylvia," she added, turning to the other women, and then back again to Sarianna.

What happened next Sarianna was sure was deliberate: Jeralee's hand stretched out to take the delicate saucer of her teacup, and Jeralee's hand tilted the saucer at just the faintest angle, enough so the tea sloshed over and splashed onto her dress. "Oh! You clumsy *lump!* My dress! Stupid, stupid, why didn't you look where you were putting that saucer, Sarianna? My dress is spoiled because of you and your stupid hands."

Sarianna stood still as a statue. Everything in her was frozen into one one tight knot that shut out Jeralee's wailing, "My dress, my dress." She felt as if there was a coil inside her ready to spring up and lash out. How dared they! How *dared* they! As if she were mentally deficient somehow, as if she were nothing in this house, nothing to them, nothing to her father . . .

But she was, she thought, she *was* nothing. She could never fully credit it before. She was worse than nothing to them; she was someone to be abused or ignored, on their whim, at the instant, except when they needed something from her or wanted her to do something for them.

Oh, no, she thought, *never* again. She would *beg* Cade Rensell to take her from this house before she would buckle under to them again. She would have her own revenge, and it would be sweet. Sweeter, because she didn't care now what they thought or wanted, or how she betrayed her wrong-handedness.

She wanted to hurt Jeralee, she wanted to kill Vesta, and she almost had it in her to wield the knife that she had unseeingly, unthinkingly picked up in preparation to cutting the cake.

But if she used it, she thought, the thing would be over, and she would be liable and her life would be forfeit. No, the better way, the better idea was to humiliate Jeralee the way Jeralee had wanted to humiliate *her*.

Her hand moved, apart from her brain, apart from reason, and out of pure animal self-defense as she lifted and brought the knife down into the thick creaminess of the almond cake and, very precisely, sliced the healthy portion that Jeralee had requested.

Painstakingly, she lifted it onto the doily decorated china plate, all while Jeralee was still making a commotion and the other ladies were succoring her, and just as deliberately, she moved out from behind the torturous serving cart, and over to where Jeralee stood. "I believe you forgot the cake," she said stonily, and lifted her arm.

Jeralee didn't have a moment to foresee her brazenness. She swung the plate up and into Jeralee's face and smeared the contents downward and onto the stained silken folds of her golden dress.

And then she turned, and with the music of Jeralee's shrieks accompanying her, she walked out of the room.

* * *

It was like swallowing bile to drink the toast that celebrated Jeralee. Cade put down his glass almost instantly after his lips touched the mellow liquid. He wanted no more of Broydon hospitality, and he wanted desperately to find out how Sarianna was faring.

Pierce joined him. "Excellent brandy," he murmured, lifting his snifter to the light to admire the color of the liquid within.

"He's an excellent son of bitch," Cade growled. "We're leaving in the morning, Pierce. Or—" he amended as he perceived Pierce's unvarnished enjoyment of the brandy—"you could stay as long as you like."

"Oh, no, by no means. I'm rather sick of the way Broydon treats Sarianna myself, but do tell me, Cade, how you intend to avoid Vesta's snare?"

Cade looked at him. "Damned if I know. I wouldn't put it past Jeralee to come bouncing into my bedroom tonight—" He stopped short as an interesting idea occurred to him. No, it wasn't an idea, it was a situation that could only further humiliate Sarianna—and force the issue the same way that Vesta seemed to want to impel him into a compromising position with Jeralee.

He couldn't do it, he couldn't. But on the other hand, if Vesta and Jeralee came searching for him and found him with Sarianna . . .

Jeralee might kill him. Or Sarianna, he thought humorlessly.

He had to do it, maybe he would even tell her, *beg* her to cooperate—*beg?*

"Do me a favor," he said to Pierce in an undertone. "Go talk to Broydon so I can get out of here without his noticing."

Pierce's eyebrows rose, but he obediently turned and sought out his host and, with some maneuvering, managed to speak to him with his back facing the door so that Cade could effect his escape.

Out in the hallway, he heard chaos emanating from the parlor: Jeralee crying, and the babble of concerned voices surrounding her. Damn. The men were due to join them at any moment for dessert. He hadn't much time; he had to ascertain Sarianna's whereabouts.

No one saw him poke his head into the parlor briefly, just enough to be sure Sarianna not only was gone, but what was causing all the commotion. Jeralee was crumpled on a small couch, surrounded by her mother, Alzine, Merleen and Dorothy Gray, who fluttered uselessly around the amazing sight of Jeralee with cake and icing dripping off of her hair, face and dress, and crying copious tears.

126

Josephine Gilmartin was not in the room; presumably she was organizing a cleanup before the men finished their brandies. He had a little time. Just a little. And what the hell had happened to Jeralee?

He raced into the hallway and up the steps, hoping it had been Sarianna who had dumped the cake all over Jeralee. No, he was sure it was she, fed up, bitter, resentful, enraged by their supreme desire to belittle her still further, and showing her mettle and the fine burning spirit that he—perhaps the only one of all of them in this house—saw deep within her.

Sarianna! Her name throbbed in his pulse as he took the last steps two at a time. Sarianna. God, he wanted her, and he wanted her away from the gross cruelties inflicted on her in her father's house. And he wanted—

Hell, what right had he to want anything, he thought, as he slowed his pace midway down the upstairs hallway. Vengeance was not nearly so sweet now that he had no time at all to persuade Sarianna of his very real desire for her.

He edged down the hallway toward her room. There was a thin line of light under the door which was adamantly closed. Sarianna. He tried the knob. It wasn't locked. Sarianna. Was she expecting repercussions? Awaiting them?

He knocked softly on the door and awaited her answering call.

Josephine Gilmartin knocked hesitantly on the library door, only to have it thrust open almost before she had touched it. Rex halted on his way out, his face a hard mask of fury. "Josephine." He shook his head, trying to regain his cool civility before his old, and unexpected, friend. "We'll join you momentarily," he said, his tone patronizing and chiding both.

"No, no." Josephine held up her hand. "No, there's been a small accident. We're not ready to have—"

"What do you mean, a *small* accident?" Rex demanded, as his guests crowded around behind him. What the devil was going on in his house? That bastard Rensell had the nerve to absent himself from their company without so much as a word, and now—accidents? Yes, of course, accidents, he thought instantly, the first thought that crossed his mind: Sarianna.

"What happened?"

"She—no, don't come. Sarianna spilled tea and cake all over Jeralee, and she's just a sight. I don't think she wants anyone to see her until she's cleaned up," Josephine told him as succinctly as she could.

"Don't be stupid; of course I'll see her." He turned back to his guests. "Please—help yourself to another glass of brandy, gentlemen. This will only take a moment, unfortunate occurrence though it may be." And to Josephine: "Come."

He wasn't even aware as he took Josephine's arm and scurried across the hallway with her that Pierce was following them.

The sight that met their eyes had elements of the comic in it, but it was clear neither Jeralee, Vesta nor Rex thought there was anything funny about the smeared cake and stained dress.

"It will never come out of my hair," Jeralee wailed, as Alzine patiently worked a comb and towel through the sticky mess. "My dress is ruined. My life is ruined. Father—I can't have anyone see me this way. I want my room and a bath. I want—" Her voice took on a vicious cast—"Sarianna. I want her punished. I want her out of here. I hate her, I hate her, I *HATE HER!*" Her voice ended in a shriek, and then hysterical sobs shook her shoulders as she buried her flushed face in her hands.

"No one will see you," Rex soothed, raising his hand to comfort her and then lowering it as he realized there was nowhere to touch her that had not been smirched by the sweetly smelling sticky cake, except her back. Awkwardly he patted her at the nape of her neck.

"I want to see Cade tonight," Jeralee cried, instantly lifting her head. "Everyone is supposed to come back, and Sarianna was to have been gone by then, and I would have had Cade to myself tonight. I want that, Father, I *want* it; I don't want him to see me like this, what that little bitch did to me. I swear I will get even with her, I'll get her back, I will—I'll *KILL HER* . . . I'll—"

Vesta clamped her hand down over Jeralee's mouth. "You're getting hysterical, my dear, do you hear me? You must calm down. You *must*. Mr. Rensell will still be here in the morning, and we'll find a way to punish Sarianna for this treachery. I promise you, Sarianna will not go unpunished because her jealousy drove her to such violent lengths." She looked up at Rex. "Really, Rex, you would think you could have exercised some control over Sarianna in all these years. Such envy to incite such a reaction. Look at poor Jeralee. How desperate Sarianna must be, how pitiful that she could imagine that Mr. Rensell would even look at her, let alone evince some interest in her. What about *her* could possibly arouse *him*, I ask you? No, no, Jeralee. We will deal with this in the morning, when you are calmer and Sarianna has answered for her perfidy."

"Where *is* Sarianna?" Rex demanded, as Vesta continued wiping the remnants of the cake from Jeralee's shuddering body.

"She went away, the only decent thing she could have done; I suppose she's in her room. Where else could she have gone?"

"She could have gone after Cade," Jeralee cried, her voice sounding on the edge of derangement next to the calm practical voice of her mother.

Vesta's eyebrows lifted questioningly. "Indeed, and where *is* Mr. Rensell, Rex?"

"He left," Rex said shortly, meeting Vesta's pointed chocolatey gaze.

"Nooooo!" Jeralee screamed, launching herself upright. "No! They're together; I know they're together—he'll . . . no, she's a witch, she's got her mother—" Her raving voice died out as Rex fixed his hot pale glance on her.

"You were saying, Jeralee?" he said coldly, noting that Vesta looked at Jeralee nervously, because she couldn't protect her, couldn't feed her the answer he wanted to hear. He wondered if Jeralee had any native wit at all.

Jeralee took a shivery breath. "I was saying—" she swallowed hard, clamping down on the rash foolhardy words that were forcing their way up her throat—"I was saying—just what Mother said: She's desperate, and she is not above throwing herself at him in the most blatant way."

"Just so," Rex said approvingly. He sighed. "What a cross to bear has been my Sarianna. I will deal with this, Vesta."

"I will as well," Vesta interrupted, and he agreed with a nod that she should indeed.

"I will send your husbands to you, ladies, and I beg that you all will continue to partake of dessert. We will join you, I promise, shortly." He turned to Jeralee. "You, of course, will go straight to your room, and Alzine will attend to you there." He raised his hand again as she took a breath to contradict his orders. "No more, Jeralee. Tomorrow you shall have your chance."

He turned, and only then did he see Pierce. "So, Mr. Darden. Would you be so kind," he said, ignoring the knowledge that Pierce had heard every word, pretending he hadn't, exorcising the scene totally with his request, "as to ask the gentlemen to join the ladies?"

"What are *you* doing here?" Sarianna demanded insolently.

"I think I would like to congratulate you for drowning Jeralee in tea and cake," Cade said. "Let me in."

"Oh, no. No. They'll be after me in another moment or two. They can't find you here. They might lynch me," Sarianna said, holding the door tightly against the pressure of his large hand.

"Really? Let them get past me, then. Open the damned door, Sarianna."

"Why?"

"Oh, God, I'm not going to beg you, Sarianna. I'll break the damned thing down if I have to. Stop wasting time, Sarianna."

"You're wasting time," she said grudgingly. "Please, Cade—you don't know—"

"I *know*," he contradicted roughly. "They fed you to the damned vultures, and you didn't let them eat you alive. You're wonderful, Sarianna, and I want you. Together we'll defeat them. Now, damn it, *let me in*."

She was so startled by his words that she fell backward as he shoved against the door once again, and the door opened. He pushed her in and shut it behind them.

"You're crazy," she breathed.

"I still want you, Sarianna."

"*Begging?*" she asked tauntingly.

"Offering an honorable proposal, *again*. Say yes, this time, Sarianna. It's the only way."

She moved backward toward the bed, her emotions in turmoil. Hadn't she promised herself she would just ask him—beg him—to take her with him when he left? "Is it the only way?" she asked, sparring for time. The back of her knees touched the bedrail, and she sank onto the mattress almost as if her legs would not hold her any more.

God, how appealing she was, he thought, and firelight only enhanced her beauty and made her seem that much more fragile. Her dress lay like a blooming garden on the side chair she had threatened to throw at him, and she was dressed in a thin, well-worn silk wrapper and nothing else. He watched her wriggle her way onto her bed, the little girl side of her that entranced him for the moment as she pulled up her bare feet and settled herself against the headboard, as though she needed it to support her very bones.

"It was insurrection, Mr. Rensell," she said, her voice cool and collected now. "I believe they shoot rebels."

"Yes, I'm sure they feel like it, too," he agreed, moving forward toward her.

"Mr. Rensell—?" Her voice stayed his progress. She didn't want him one step closer to her. His proximity was dangerous to her, even halfway across the room. She had a vision of Rex bursting in at that very moment, gun in hand, his fatherly rage as his justification. No, it was her burden to bear, whatever Rex chose to do. The only thing Cade could do was leave, and even if he departed Bredwood alone, it would be better for him than if he left with her. Now that she was calmer and saner, she knew it.

And she said it. "Your best course is to leave as soon as possible. You must know that."

Cade swore under his breath and took another step toward her. She looked like an elf with a mop of curly golden hair and her legs crossed under her in that seemingly comforting way. She looked like a woman, fully able to handle the likes of him and his warring motives. She looked as if she could even handle Rex if she had to, but why, he wondered angrily, should she have to.

He moved again, and this time she did not stop him. He was at her bed in a moment, and on it with her, frozen by her cold blue gaze. He stripped off his jacket and threw it across the room, and settled himself against the blanket rail, with one knee braced against his chest and the other foot hooked on the bedrail. It would take as long as it would take, he thought, and he waited.

She sent him a rueful look. "We have nothing to talk about, Mr. Rensell."

"I think we do," he said calmly, pulling at his tie. "I mean to take you with me, Sarianna; you can't say anything to dissuade me. And frankly, after today—everything that has happened today," he added meaningfully, "I don't think you want to."

"Your arrogance is appalling," she said, but there was no bite in her words. "I'm no damsel in distress, Mr. Rensell. I don't need you to rescue me."

"Don't you?" he asked, with the faintest hint of challenge in his tone.

"I don't believe in fairy tales, Mr. Rensell."

"Yes, you were taught early on dreams were not for you to dream, I know," he said cuttingly. "And it's sheer stubbornness for you to keep on denying what already is between us."

"And what *is* between us, Mr. Rensell?" she asked maddeningly before she thought about it. Oh, but here was the danger, she collected, now she understood; his back was to the fireplace so that she could not see his face in the shadow. There was an intimacy already between them because she had allowed him so close to her, and now he would weave it tighter with words. And she was so susceptible to him already!

"I should coerce you into telling, Sarianna; deep within you, you know, don't you?" he said, watching the firelight play over her face and resistance settle in a firm line around her mouth. "I have held you in my arms, and I have held your essence in my hands; I know every inch of your mouth and every quiver of your breasts. I know the feeling of your body when I touch you—and I know your body wants me, wants more of what I make you feel. That is what is between us, Sarianna. Deny that if you can."

She waved her hand at him. "Transitory, Mr. Rensell. It's merely an exercise in mind over body. When you go, the desire will disappear." What was she saying? *What?*

"The desire will never disappear," he said, his voice hard with frustration. Stubborn woman, intractable, wrong-headed, mulish *woman* . . . rigid . . . denying them both, damn her. Damn her. He felt the minutes ticking away, precious minutes he could be nurturing the desire she so cavalierly dismissed as unimportant to her. It *was* important to her. Her untutored body had its own urgency, its own demand. The room was heating up with it, in counterpoint to her denial.

One bold move, he thought, and her could win her—or lose her.

"Shall I go then, Sarianna?" he asked gently.

"Yes," she said instantly and then covered her mouth as if she could call back the word. "No."

He stopped in mid-motion and sank back onto the bed. "Which is it,

Sarianna?" he asked edgily, knowing that in this one moment everything was on the line. "What *do* you want?"

She looked at him with huge shimmering eyes. "I don't know," she whispered shakily, but she knew. She did not want Cade Rensell to walk out of her room.

But he got to his feet anyway, and her heart caught in her throat. He came closer to her and closer, and her heart began an erratic pounding that he must have been able to hear. It thrummed in her ears, it answered her questions, and it urged her into his arms as he reached for her and pulled her up against his hard body. "*I* know," he murmured against her mouth and touched her lips with his. The faintest touch, and that and the flagrant male angularity of him destroyed her resolve.

It was all the same, and it was totally different, the way he held her; and she didn't know, in the moment his mouth covered hers, if she could live without the opulent sensation of his body against hers for the rest of her life.

"Sarianna . . ." The rasp of his hoarse voice breathing her name in that sensual drawn-out way excited her. He kissed her again, reaching deep within her luscious mouth to taste all of her—*all*.

The touch of his tongue was new to her, staggering in its arousal. Her hands reached this time to hold him immobile, to feel the scrape of his skin against the pads of her curious fingers. Her body pressed against his in a timeless voluptuous invitation. She felt explosive, lit up, incandescent with indescribable feelings.

Her body surged against his, feeling his maleness, needing his heat. She was on her knees, on the bed, her thinly clad body seeking him with an innocent surety. She was naked under the wrapper, and he could feel every nuance of her body against him, from her taut nipples to her slender hips grinding with slow enticement against his.

His hands threaded through her hair to keep him from reaching for her body. His mouth devoured hers, her eager kisses and playful tongue enchanting him. He had time, he thought, abandoning himself to the dizzying conquest of his mouth. He wanted only to kiss her now, to taste her sweetness.

Finally his hands moved. He needed to touch her, to wrest from her body the one impediment that prevented him from holding her nakedness against him. And she moved, she helped. She wanted his hands on her bare body, arousing those glimmering sensations that culminated in that bone-melting pleasure.

She wrenched at his shirt, pulling at the buttons as his hands coursed up and down her body, feeling the long line of it, the hollows and indentations that were so beguiling to him, the texture of her skin that was so erotic to him.

His shirt fell away, and her hands swooped up his hair-darkened chest as she basked in his heat and the roughness of the wiry hair, and pressed her breasts against him, rubbing her sensitized nipples against his.

Could anything have prepared him for her perfect response to him? Or that she would be the one to unbuckle his belt and release his manhood into her inquisitive hands.

He felt her shock as her fingers encountered his hardness; her mouth pulled away from his, and she looked into his eyes, as clearly as she could see them in the flickering firelight. They told her nothing.

She reveled in the lovely sensation of feeling his nakedness against her skin. What was this? This was the huge bulge she had felt each time he held her against his hips. This was the root of the thrusting movements he made; this was the secret of his masculinity.

She saw it in his face as she overcame her reluctance and touched him there. And there. He loved it, her skimming fingers gliding all over the velvety length of him. How curious and fascinating, she thought, watching his expression. She wondered where else she could touch him to give him that pleasure, as he shucked his trousers and pulled her mouth back beneath his.

"Just hold me, Sarianna," he whispered, as he slanted his mouth across hers and took it voraciously, and her fingers wrapped around him with an innocent assurance that almost sent him spiraling out of control.

His hands began sleeking their way down her body, sliding in a roundabout way all over her buttocks and thighs, and up her arms to her breasts, then back down again. His mouth settled on hers in a most permanent disquieting way, as if he never meant to move it again, and finally his questing fingers slipped between her legs, from behind, and touched—just touched—her provocative femininity.

Instantly she reacted, thrusting her lower torso backward to invite his caresses, reveling in the incredible sensations he aroused. Her body writhed against him, wild with wanting, but wanting what she did not know. She felt as though the space within her were empty, that something must fill it, something more than his erotic touch, and suddenly it was obvious she held it in her very hands. The wonder of it, the perfection. The symmetry: her empty straining center sheathing the living heat of his towering manhood.

She caressed him lightly and felt his sensual groan down to her very core and, with it, the sense of him lifting her off of the bed, cradling her against the strength of his chest, holding her so tightly, and finally, laying her down on the bed with his long lean body beside her.

"Sarianna," he breathed once again, taking her lips, cupping her breast and exploring its exquisite contour, its taut erotic peak.

She wrapped her arms around him, and her legs around his legs, her body straining toward fulfillment. Her mouth slid all over his, tasting anew the firmness of his lips, the luscious taste of his tongue, nipping him, goading him, demanding his kisses just as he had said she would.

She didn't care. Her hands moved, feeling his heated skin, memorizing the shape of his flanks and the tempting line of his thigh that rounded into the crisp hair that shielded and framed the essence of him.

Her fingers slid downward toward it, toward the mystery of his sex.

Her hand trembled; there was more, still more. Discovering him was an unending quest. Lord, his body was amazing, as tactile as her own, fabulous in its response to her exploration. But still that was not enough; it only excited her more in preparation for what was to come. And she knew it was to come; she could feel it in the tensile movements of his body against hers, the brisk little thrusts of his lips and surging manhood, in the frenzy of fevered exploration by his hands.

Finally, finally he poised himself over her. "Sarianna . . ."

"Yes. *Yes*," she whispered, pulling at his naked hips, forcing them downward. This . . . this . . . how did she know what to do, where to guide, how to brace herself for the initial entry. She didn't know; something primal within her knew, but nothing prepared her for the thrust, the overwhelming sense of invasion, the stabbing pain, brief as it was, and the utter fullness of his manhood possessing the waiting space within her.

How strange it felt, she thought, as the pain subsided and he waited with all the patience in the world for her sign that she was ready for the rest. Strange and full. Strange and exciting.

His lips touched hers questioningly, and she answered him eagerly.

She wanted his kisses, and she wanted what came next. And she thought that if he only remained nestled within her in just this way, it would be enough and she would be connected to him for all time.

But there *was* more. As he possessed her ardent mouth once again, he began his carnal possession of her body. The briefest movement excited her, and then there was another, and another, short thrusts, letting her feel his power and his fullness within her. But then a long, slow slide, and another, and her hips moved, lifting against him, thrusting with him, beguiled by the shimmering sensations, answering the smoldering love words he whispered against her lips.

"Sarianna," he groaned. "Sarianna . . ."

"Yes," she murmured, affirming with the one word the answer to the question he did not ask. He did not need to. She wanted him as elementally as he wanted her, and it was enough. Everything else went out of his mind. She was his, in the most carnal primitive way possible, and he would never let her go, never.

She rocked against him, loving the voluptuous stroking of his torrid maleness; it filled her, possessed her, sent extravagant sensations spangling through her, feelings that were just starting to build into something else, something different—the thing she strived for.

He felt the critical change in her. She shifted, almost as if she were positioning herself perfectly for the final cataclysmic climax, and he poised himself for the first potent lunge—and the door burst open.

Somewhere, behind the roaring in his ears, he heard Vesta shrieking, "Oh, my God, oh, my God, oh, my God . . ." and he felt Rex's iron hands pulling at him, forcing him off of Sarianna, his voice beating a counterpoint to Vesta's frenzy: "You bastard, you bastard, get off of my daughter, you son of a bitch bastard . . ."

He heaved himself upward and onto his feet as Sarianna grabbed for the bedspread and pulled it around her. He stood at the edge of the bed, his hands on his hips, his blatant maleness protesting its abrupt removal from its nesting place, and he felt a twinge of guilt and a wash of satisfaction.

Rex was in a fine rage, sputtering imprecations, pretending, Cade thought, a concern he could hardly have felt. All the hell they cared about was that Jeralee would not, for once, have her way.

But whether they would consent to his marrying Sarianna was something else altogether. He did want to marry her; he distinctly remembered he had asked her before they tumbled headlong into that erotic carnality. It didn't matter; she was his now as fully as if a service had already been performed.

He had planned it just so; it had worked, and he was gambling that Rex could not refuse his offer to redeem the Broydon honor.

And she—? She looked horrified and stunned, and bereft. Her eyes were resentful as they moved from Vesta to Rex to him. He knew what she was thinking; he understood her feeling of deprivation, her utter frustration.

"Get dressed," Rex said shortly, avoiding Sarianna's eyes. It wasn't possible she wanted this animal who would take advantage of her under her family's own roof. He would never forget the sight of her writhing, ravenous body under the taut straining maleness of Cade Rensell, oh no. Everything, he thought dazedly, was all and one the same. It could have been Dona. Once, it had been Dona. He could kill Cade Rensell, and he might still do it.

Vesta stood looking glazed and tormented as Sarianna's cold gaze knifed through her. All she could think was, he had had Sarianna, Sarianna had won, Sarianna got him first, and for the first time, she felt defeated and as murderous as she had ever felt in her life. Sarianna had gotten in the way, and she had to be punished.

Cade waited, not moving until they finally understood in their mutual rage that he wanted them to leave, and all motivations would be called to account only when Cade was ready to do so.

9

He waited until the door closed firmly behind Vesta and Rex before he turned his attention to Sarianna. She had moved to an upright position once again, with her back against the headboard and her body huddled in the comforting, woven cotton bedspread. She looked lost and sad, and utterly desirable, even perhaps a shade skeptical, now that the enchantment had been effectively wiped away and her common sense had asserted itself.

It was astonishing to her that she had surrendered so much of herself to him, inconceivable how sense and morality bowed to a loving caress and the feel of a man's naked body desiring hers. And it was utterly devastating that her willing capitulation had not led to the complete culmination she had desired—no, still wanted desperately —even in the chilling wake of Vesta and her father's finding them together.

But it was also obvious that he was not going to be able to continue. His face was set, his body had reacted, as it must, to the nocturnal visit, and he was girding himself for a confrontation.

Sarianna knew what that would be about. Her father had to demand he do the honorable thing. Or—she might demand he do the honorable thing and leave her to her father's wrath and save himself.

He didn't need to marry her, she thought. He had not seduced some unwilling virgin; she had wanted his caresses, demanded his kisses, made it very clear she wanted the full experience of his lovemaking. She might not have consciously decided it and gone after it; but she surely wanted to thwart Jeralee and Vesta, and she definitely wanted the volcanic pleasure of his hands feeling her body. All that had led to this, and she would have the memory of their incomplete union and the possibilities of it forever.

Maybe it was enough; she hadn't, in her life, expected even that much. But how could she have survived without it? she wondered. And what would she do afterward, when the yearning overtook her and she *needed* it? Who would be the next Cade Rensell? Or the next man she might seduce away from Jeralee?

What a thought! But she knew how to do it now, with disconcerting directness. She had savored the excitement of a man's response to *her* sensual exploration, and it was heady and positively erotic, and arousing beyond imagination. She wondered about other men, all men, even as she knew if she had a choice, she wanted only him in this intoxicating carnal way. It had nothing to do with love, not yet, but she could live on it and with it, she could.

What if she asked him? She opened her mouth, but the words stuck in her throat. He had been watching her so closely, he fully expected to hear her say something, but she couldn't find the words.

He sat down next to her on the bed and took her hand, wondering himself what he ought to say. He felt little triumph that his hastily conceived plan had worked, and elated at her surrender to him. And he felt no little trepidation about the tactics he planned to use on Rex Broydon. Would the revenge be as sweet if he hurt Sarianna in the process? He had said enough to her already on the subject of her cloistered life at Bredwood. She did not need to know the rest. The rest was for Rex Broydon's ears alone, to bury the past and cement a future—with Sarianna.

He looked at her for a long time, wondering what she would say now that he was forcing her to make a decision. For a brief instant he hated himself; but he thought he wanted her more, and now was not the time to tell her.

"Will you marry me, Sarianna?"

"You don't—" she started to say helplessly, and he interrupted her.

"I *want* to."

"How *can* you?" she burst out, negating his words with a hard movement of her hand.

"I want to," he said again. "How can I give up your mouth and your kisses, your incredibly responsive body? Tell me how, and I won't walk out of this room."

She couldn't answer him, not for a few moments, and even then she thought that it didn't matter what he wanted. "They'll never let you," she said finally, and he shook his head.

"They'll let me," he said with assurance. "You're mine, Sarianna, and even Rex, in his heart of hearts, knows it. *He* is the one who has to relinquish the past."

You're mine . . . you're mine . . . the words reverberated through her body as she painstakingly watched him dress, a pure pleasure that could not be undercut by her fear of his sincerity and Rex and Vesta's tenacity at not disturbing their most comfortable circumstances.

When he kissed her again, her doubts flew out the window, and when he left her, she scrambled to find some underclothes and an old pinafore so that she could follow him down the stairs and hear every syllable of his conversation with Rex.

The guests had been sped on their way; only two long tapers at each end of the hallway lighted Sarianna's way as she crept downstairs, berating herself for her suspicions. She wanted to leave them, she had deliberately created a scene over the way they treated her this very evening, and now she was pulling back from that decision when an honorable alternative—of sorts—would deliver her from Vesta's subtle little retribution. She was crazy, but *she had to know.* There had to be a reason that Cade Rensell was so willing to marry her out of hand after two days' stormy acquaintance.

Whatever it was, she would marry him—just to get out of the house, just to get away, to be on her own. Marriages were consummated every day for less particular reasons, she thought. Had her father not married Vesta because it was a point of honor for him to do so, and take care of his deceased wife's sister?

She edged down the hallway toward the library where she knew Rex would be waiting and where Cade would accost him. Nothing needed to be said: Gentlemen somehow knew these things, and she never could figure out how. It was some kind of code that women were never given the key to, even down to the express exclusion of them by the architectural detail of the narrowed doorway.

But she wore no hoops tonight; she could squeeze herself into the door frame and listen with impunity. And she had come just in time to hear Cade express his intentions, clearly, decisively and in no uncertain terms.

"I will marry Sarianna," Cade declared.

Rex poured himself a brandy and settled back in his leather armchair. "That's not a choice." He sounded so cold and sure, but even he had to admit to himself he did not know whether Rensell had culminated the act with Sarianna; he was banking on the fact he might not have, that there might not be a threat of an illegitimate child.

"Excuse me, it isn't?" Cade said easily, helping himself to the brandy without Rex's invitation. "Why not?"

"It's for her own protection," Rex said sanctimoniously, hiding his truth by sipping from his snifter. "A wrong-handed wife is no asset, Rensell."

"Truly?" Cade murmured, much taken by the speciousness of Rex's statement.

"It's possible she might produce a child of the same bent. You see how awkward it is, how ill-mannered she has become because of it. How hopeless she is, how desperate to taste of some normalcy in a life that couldn't possibly be normal." Rex paused, thinking about that tack, liking what he was saying—he almost believed it, and Cade was listening, listening hard. "When Vesta and Jeralee came to live with us, I think Sarianna became resentful. Here was a normal, beautiful child, beloved of her mother, like a daughter to me. I don't think she knew what she was doing, but there were always little incidents, things that were blamed on Jeralee that Sarianna had instigated. Such a jealousy could only ripen into something destructive, anyone would concede that, but she *is* my firstborn daughter; I could not send her away."

"Oh, hardly," Cade conceded in a hard voice. God, he thought, the gall of the man, the absolute puling nerve of him to do this to Sarianna.

"Well, Rensell, you yourself know how man-mad the Wayte sisters have always been. Even Vesta—saddled with a child whose father she barely knew who died precipitately. I have always believed she rushed into marriage because I proposed to Dona. But that's neither here nor there. I suppose it would be easy to believe that Sarianna inherited some of her mother's traits—certainly her looks, although I have always felt she is much too thin—however, this kind of headlong confrontation has never happened before. She has never challenged

141

any of Jeralee's beaux, and in any event, I can assure you that none of them would have thought twice about her anyway. So I suppose, too, it's possible to surmise that it was this party, your appearance, for whatever reason you chose to return, Sarianna's perception that Jeralee was old enough to accept a proposal of marriage, something Sarianna might—in fact I can say assuredly she would *never*—have; all of this I believe, came to a head in her disordered mind, and she began a studied pursuit of *you* in order to hurt Jeralee as much as possible." He smiled faintly, sliding his fingers over the crystalline cut decoration of his snifter, enjoying the feel of it and the knowledge of its cost, and the exquisite color of the expensive liquor within—a brandy, he thought belatedly, that Sarianna had chosen and stocked in his wine cellar. Superlative, he thought; but then she did everything superlatively, and that was something Cade Rensell would never know.

"And she has. Look at the end result tonight," he continued, still in that creamy, faintly righteous tone. "I suppose I must consider an asylum for her, but I really hate . . . I think, Rensell, if you left, and Vesta took Jeralee to Savannah, things might be better. I definitely think things would return to some kind of order, and I can consider what is the best course to take with Sarianna. She might, for example, stay here, and I would arrange suitable help to keep an eye on her, and turn the running of the estate over to my overseer. Yes, that might work. Or perhaps—" he frowned into his glass, still not having looked once at Cade, or perceived his growing rage which he was about to ignite with his inflammatory words—"I might build a new home— over at Greenpoint—and sequester her there. . . ."

Cade's fist came down on the library table.

"Oh, I'm sorry, Rensell; I tend to forget that Greenpoint hasn't always been mine," Rex apologized, enjoying the anger and the power he now held over a Rensell, *the* Rensell.

"I bet you conveniently forget a lot of things," Cade said unpleasantly, restraining himself, clamping down on his fury because he could see there was more to go, more to be said, and that there was a palpitating evil in the room, the consequences of which he could just envision, and he swore he would kill Rex Broydon before he would let it happen.

"Now, now, Rensell. You have nothing more to do than to leave Bredwood, and perhaps, if you feel like it, pay your respects to Vesta and Jeralee when they arrive in Savannah. No obligation, you needn't saddle yourself with an imperfect wife, nor think any more about Sawny Island. I understand you have independent wealth, and you have a home and land to work—from your mother, Vesta said?—yes, I thought so. We could arrange to move your father's remains as well, if that would satisfy you. . . ." he let his voice trail off as he finally looked at Cade and perceived that his carefully worded speech had made no dent in his determination, and in fact the mention of his father had only exacerbated his temper.

"I'll tell you what will satisfy me," Cade said tightly. "Sarianna will satisfy me, nothing more, Broydon, and nothing less."

"Well, I can't give my consent," Rex said with great finality.

"But do you need to? Sarianna is of age, Broydon; I could take her away from here easier than you can prevent me. But I don't want to spirit her away in the night. For one thing, she deserves better than that. And for another, I want you to know the full force of her choice and decision to marry me. I want you to see me taking her from you, the way I took Dona from you years ago. I want you to face that fact, Broydon. *I* am free to love and to make love to Sarianna, and *you are not.*"

He watched his words sink in, and he had the momentary satisfaction of seeing Broydon pale and his glass almost slip from his hand. He could almost see him assessing how much he could deny and how much Cade had conjectured. It couldn't be much; he had been away too long.

"You'll never have her," Cade cut into his thoughts, thrusting the knife in still further, "not now that she has had *me.*"

"Go to hell," Rex muttered, and drank deeply from his snifter, seeking to collect his scattered wits and shattered excuses.

"I mean to make you live in hell," Cade hammered on. "Sarianna is your wife—she does everything for you, you depend on her, in your cold hard way you adore her—she's Dona to the life and better. *Better,* Broydon, and didn't it scare the life out of you when you realized *I* could see it? You've spent years trying to destroy her sense of self so that she would have no course but to turn to you. And you could wait—you could have a dependent, broken Dona in your life eventually—maybe even in your bed, you bastard, after Jeralee was successfully married off and Vesta went with her because Jeralee could never manage anything on her own. You son of a bitch, it *was* your damned bad luck Vesta chose the wrong man, a man who had loved Dona and could plainly perceive what you were about—your huge hidden-secret that you belied by every lie you told about Sarianna. Oh, damn you, you should live in hell for what you planned to do to her, what you've done already. I could kill you for almost destroying her."

"Fairy tales," Rex spat, slamming his snifter down on the table. It broke, and the amber liquid within dribbled onto his hand and soaked into the wood grain of the table, and he didn't even notice. "You're such a choirboy, Rensell. You ruined my marriage, you ran away when things got hot, and you never came back to do a good goddamned thing for your daddy. If you mean to punish me for taking advantage of that miscreant's adversity, you'll never do it. It's a closed issue. Sarianna marries *no one*—" he swept the dripping shards of glass from the table to emphasize his words—"*EVER*."

He got to his feet and looked into Cade's hard-set face. "And no one will question my reasons, either. I've made damned sure of it, Rensell, damned sure," he added with more bravado than he felt. He didn't like the expression on Rensell's face; it was savage, primitive, not the face of a gentleman raised on Sawny. It was the face of a man who would fight to win at any cost, and not even his confident words could wipe away the surety he read in Cade's glittering eyes.

"Sit down, Broydon," Cade commanded harshly. "You don't think you're finished with me, now do you? No, you don't know about fighting, Broydon; you know about undermining with snide words and critical looks. You think no one else can play your stupid cruel games. And you think I won't fight for Sarianna. Oh, yes, I want the pleasure of taking her from you all right, I don't deny it. But I want *her*, Broydon, and that's what you'll have to live with for as long as I let you live. So—" He pushed a finger into Broydon's chest, and he edged backward into his chair again.

Rensell didn't scare him, he thought. He had no proof, nothing he could use to convince anyone of his own intentions toward Sarianna.

"I won't let you punish her for Dona's sins, you know," Cade continued, but his voice sounded far away to Rex in his shock that Cade understood fully, with those words, what the underlying motivating force of his treatment of Sarianna was. "I won't let her become your Dona, chained to you forever by virtue of your perception of her desirability. You arrange the wedding, Broydon, and let her go. Vesta's a decent enough substitute, not as lighthearted or pretty, I grant you, but the voice, certain movements, the way she holds herself, things she says sometimes, and the way she says them—don't you agree, Broydon, that if you closed your eyes, it could be—"

Rex leapt at him, his clawed fingers aiming for Cade's throat. Cade hadn't expected that; he hadn't thought he could goad Rex quite enough to get some kind of reaction. Rex was hardly proficient in any manner of self-defense. Rex had sat on his damned rump and let others fight for him and make his money for him. Rex could only victimize someone like Sarianna, and that thought made Cade see red.

It took him five minutes to pin Rex, and he was a little awed by the animal intensity with which he fought. He rolled Rex briskly onto his stomach and pulled his flailing arms behind him, wrenching his wrists together.

He liked the idea of having this power over Broydon, and he was about to exert still more.

"Let me create a story for you, Mr. son of a bitch bastard Broydon," he grated, yanking his arms as Rex began to struggle again. "Let me make up a fairy tale, a real possible it-could-happen-to-you story, you monster. You just think of the ramifications of a story like this, Broydon. The story goes like this: The king refuses to give the hand of his daughter to the knight who wants her. There is no apparent reason: he has a handsome heritage, he is wealthy, he can provide a good home; he has bedded her, and she might even be with child—" He broke off as he felt Rex stiffen, as if he had not considered that their union had been consummated before his precipitate entry. *All to the good then,* Cade thought humorlessly, *let me tantalize him with the thought of Sarianna's child—and mine.*

"Oh, yes," he went on, "in a monumental breech of good manners, the king had thrust himself into his daughter's room at a most critical time. Of course, it was incumbent upon him to feel rage that the knight had taken his daughter without the legal binding of their marriage, but then to deny her suitor her hand after the fact was, in the knight's mind, a gross injustice. It seemed obvious that the king would rather imprison his daughter in some ivory tower than let her give in to the more earthly pleasures of marriage and motherhood.

"Nothing would sway the king; but it so happened that in his royal domain there were many who had met the knight, many with daughters who were casting unconscious lures to a most desirable suitor, and many mothers who were not averse to entertaining the lovelorn knight in order to show their daughter as a prospective bride in a favorable light. After all, love had nothing to do with alliances.

"The thought gave the knight an interesting idea. He accepted the invitations willingly, and he sat at the table of the peers of the king's realm and wondered why the king was so reluctant to give over his daughter to someone as eligible as he. He pointed out that they had all seen for themselves how beautiful and gracious the king's daughter was and how elegantly she comported herself. Why in the name of all that was holy did the king not wish to contract an alliance with the knight.

"Of course, none of this stopped him from outrightly pursuing—oh, Miss Victoria Gray for example, and accepting her parents' hospitality while he spread the gossip, the intimation that the king perhaps had something in mind for his daughter that was faintly incestuous. Even Miss Eula Rudley—her parents were eager to welcome him and hear of the goings on at Bredwood castle while the knight paid tender compliments to their daughter and whispered of dark secrets from the past coming back to haunt Bredwood's ruler. . . .

"Need I say more, Broydon? You perceive you are not the only one who can be destructive with words, you bastard. I'll kill you with words if you prevent this marriage. I'll make you into the monster you are. Everyone will know what you have done and why. They'll talk about you for years, Broydon; they'll drive you from Sawny and force you to sell Bredwood and Greenpoint, and by God, Broydon, I'll be there to buy them out from under your very nose. I promise you it will happen, Broydon; I'll make sure it happens just that way if you lift one finger to prevent Sarianna's marriage to me. You hear, Broydon?" He reached forward to pull Rex's head up and around.

Rex choked.

"You hear?" Cade hissed, pulling his head back still farther. "I'll ruin you, Broydon, with the same kind of innuendo you would have used to ruin Sarianna. And I invite you to test whether I'm capable of it, you bastard." He shoved Rex's head down onto the floor and got off of him in total disgust.

He was so tempted, as Rex dazedly climbed to his feet, to shove his boot right into Rex's nether region. His fury was explosive. If Rex said just one wrong word, he would commit mayhem.

He stood in the center of the room, his arms akimbo, his expression stony. Only his eyes were alive, watching every move that Rex made, waiting for his challenge, his hostility just a scratch below the surface.

Rex eyed him warily when he was finally upright. The man was a maniac, totally deranged if he thought he could ruin a Broydon's reputation on Sawny by implying . . . nonsense, utter nonsense.

He staggered back into his chair and sank into it. How far could he push this Rensell, he wondered. What if he denied that anything he said could harm him? What if he denied him Sarianna anyway? How far would he go?

He stared at Cade, trying to gauge the depth of his determination. He saw nothing but rock-hard resolution, and he saw the man who had conquered a western dream and made a fortune. A physical man, he thought disdainfully, but capable of paying him back in his own coin?

But he *was* educated; Parker Rensell, damn him, had seen to that. He had the words, but what—really—could he say to destroy Rex's reputation? His eyes narrowed as he contemplated a scene very close to the one that Rensell had envisioned, and he didn't like the words that he could hear issuing from Rensell's mouth.

He could just see him at Graydon Hall, instantly beside Miss Victoria Gray, whose flirtatious glances had not been lost on him at Jeralee's birthday dinner, whispering in Victoria's ear about the strangeness in Bredwood, insinuating that he had gotten away from the Broydons as soon as he could because he wanted no part of the odd relationship between Rex Broydon and his eldest daughter. God, he groaned inwardly, wouldn't the Grays love to hear that! *Had* there been questions about his relationship with Sarianna all these years? Had they gossiped about them, and Dona after her death, and his return to Bredwood ultimately with Dona's sister? No, Vesta's status in his house was the expected thing. There was no one else he wished to marry; he had even said that to his neighbors just before he went to Savannah so many years ago.

No, it was the question of Sarianna and how he had maligned her all these years, and how they had all accepted his assessment of her and treated her accordingly. What a treat, then, if Cade Rensell came into their midst and gave them something new and juicy to chew on.

Goddamn him. Cade knew—just the faintest hint of something unsavory in a closed island society like Sawny could ruin him. And just as surely Rensell knew that what his neighbors thought was important to him. The son of a bitch had been born and raised here, goddamn him. He knew, he knew, just as he was very well aware of the ostracism of the Rensells when his father was found dead and reeking of bourbon.

Damn him to hell—*why* had he even taken it into his head to return to Sawny? It was as if Dona were destined to haunt him every which way, from her daughter inheriting her body and perhaps her soul, to her erstwhile lover wresting from him the last of Dona that he had within his power.

It was totally untenable; he thought in that moment he might collapse under the burden of it. He had never questioned why he had immured Sarianna; he had only felt the desperation to closet her away, for whatever reason, to give her responsibility and then deny her the things she had a right to expect, and then salve his conscience by showering it all on Jeralee.

He looked up at Cade, who had been waiting him out with a grim murderous patience that followed his thoughts intuitively. And he knew in that moment that Cade had won. He couldn't risk what Cade might unleash with a few carefully chosen, carelessly revealed words. He couldn't risk that Sarianna might have conceived during this ill-timed night of seduction and betrayal. He couldn't risk anything, especially his reputation after all these years on Sawny.

Cade felt the tension coiling within him as he waited for the one moment when he knew instinctively Rex had caved in.

Rex fixed his contemptuous pale blue eyes on the austere face of his enemy. What was Sarianna to him, after all, he thought, and he said, "You can have Sarianna."

10

You can have Sarianna . . . you can have Sarianna . . .

The words beat in her brain like mallets as she raced down the hall,
suppressing the primitive scream of negation that gorged in her
throat. The parlor was closest at hand, and she ran into its darkened
recess and slammed the rear service door behind her and sagged
against it. Then, then the bitterness poured out of her, the tears and
the long held-in hysteria at the nature of the truth of her status in her
father's house.

The darkness was a balm as she slid bonelessly to the floor and
released the pain with one keening grieving cry.

All that vengeance, all the hidden reasons and meanings of
everything; all the years she had labored under the burden of being
not quite good enough. All the years of swallowing the pain over her
father's lack of affection, his intolerance, his . . . the list was endless,
endless, and now the man who had loved her mother and broken her
father had given her even more pain and heartache.

And all to pay Rex back for what he had done to Parker Rensell. She
had known it, hadn't she, when she had accompanied him to
Greenpoint. She had sensed his perception of her father's hand in
Parker's downfall. How stupid of her not to look beyond that. How
stupid to think that Cade's delicate seduction of her was any more
than part of some plan to avenge his father.

It was too much; it really was too much for one person to bear.

And then Rex had given her—*given* her? *Bartered* her in exchange
for his reputation! Oh, God, was there ever a father like this? She
hated him. She *hated* him.

She felt a cold knot of pure loathing settle in her gut, in her brain. He could never reach her again, her miserable excuse for a father. She would never be vulnerable to the mitigating thought that she had come from his seed, and of his love for her mother, a love that had turned into roaring obsession which had been misplaced on her. Oh, God, she couldn't *think* about it. Her tears would never stop: She would die crying and perhaps they both might be at peace.

Her torrent of sobbing abated suddenly. She did not want to die—not for his mistake, his delusion. She would not let him make her into the final sacrifice.

What did she want, then?

So many choices, she thought bitterly, and every choice led to her being bound in chains once again. Which of those choices was the lesser of all the evils that vibrated within the walls of Bredwood?

She wiped her eyes, and it was not a comforting gesture; she had no more tears for the likes of those in her home. She hardly had tears for herself at this point, only an instinct to save herself.

And what was the means at hand? The vengeful son of the man her father had ruined. Why not? Why *not?* He would take her away from Bredwood, take her to Savannah, and she could somehow convince him to leave her there. She could enlist Pierce Darden's help; she was sure Pierce admired her, even beyond the sympathy he felt for her situation. After that—what did it matter? She would be far away from Bredwood and Vesta, Jeralee and retribution.

He didn't need to marry her either; she would go with him just as she was, with the very clothes on her back. She wanted nothing from Bredwood except the freedom to leave it.

Her anguish caught in her throat, and her tears poured down her cheeks, her silent sobs shaking her body, her only witness the cool and unyielding dark.

He heard her tormented cry the moment he closed the door of the library behind him.

Sarianna! Oh, God, where? Here, close. Too close. On this floor? Damn the lights. Why here? He felt panicked. Sarianna here? She had followed him? Could she have? And heard everything, he concluded frantically, a hollow place within him filling with anguish at the thought of what she was feeling. *Where* could she have hidden?

150

No, she would have run—instantly—when? When Rex gave in, he wagered. What agony to hear her father so cavalierly give her away, to have revealed to her as well *his* non-too-altruistic motive for wanting to marry her. Oh, God, Sarianna.

He paced slowly down the hall, clamping down on his first urge to run, to find her. He would find her—and make it right.

And then he heard her quiet sobbing behind the service door at the rear of the parlor, alone in the dark, he thought, pausing with his hand grasping the doorknob, terribly alone, abandoned by everyone—even him.

He waited, aching to soothe away her pain, and not wanting to make the wrong move, the wrong gesture.

He pushed against the door and felt her weight against it, as if she were barring his entrance—but how could she know it was him—or just blocking everyone out altogether.

He made his way resolutely down to the anteroom and paused before the great sliding doors that led into the parlor. He hesitated only a moment before making the decision to intrude on her pain. The connecting sliding doors were closed, and only the lonely darkness filtered through their etched glass panels.

He moved one sliding door soundlessly on its track and entered. There wasn't a speck of light to guide him, but he knew by his fine sense of her where she was. He groped his way across the room, feeling like the blind man he was, cursing his insensitivity and the fate that had led her down the stairs to find the unpalatable truth.

He heard her very quiet sobs, and he felt a stabbing in his heart. She was like a wounded animal, licking away the hurt; she was on the floor, huddled away against the inhumanity of the ones she thought she could trust the most.

"Sarianna," he called out to her, his voice low, getting down on his knees and inching his way toward her.

She didn't answer; why should she? He had betrayed her worst of all, and his voice grew urgent with the thought she would reject him, too.

"Sarianna!"

"I'm here."

He felt a wash of relief and trepidation at the calm note in her voice beneath the reedy remnants of her tears. He found her leg, and then her arm, and he reached out in the darkness and crushed her against him.

Her resistance was unnerving. "You don't need to pretend with me any more," she said unsteadily.

"Oh, God, Sarianna . . ."

"It's all right. It's all right, I tell you. Let me up, Cade, please."

"No," he countered forcefully. "I know you heard everything. Listen to me—"

"No, you listen to me. I'll make a bargain with you."

"No bargains," he said roughly, pulling her against him. "Listen—"

"You don't have to marry me," she interrupted. "Just take me away from here." She pulled at his shirtsleeve. "Please—that's all I could ask of you; all I want."

"You don't know what you want, Sarianna, damn it . . ."

"I do, I do; don't touch me—just—take me with you tomorrow."

"I will *not*," he growled, fighting her resistance. "I will marry you, Sarianna, nothing less, just as I told your father. Hear me—you're mine, do you understand, you're mine, and Rex will never come near you again—ever—I promise, Sarianna. I promise."

She sagged against him. She didn't know what she felt except that his body was comforting and warm and she needed that contact. She felt his lips brush her tangled curls. "I'm not Dona," she cried suddenly. "I'm *not* Dona. . . ."

"You're not Dona," he said soothingly. "I promise, Sarianna, you're nothing like her. Your light never shone out of her eyes, your strength, your passion. We, Sarianna, your father and I, made her into something that maybe she wasn't. And look at what she did to us. All of us. She wasn't you, Sarianna, she wasn't. Trust me."

"No," she moaned, pulling away again.

"Yes."

"I don't believe anything anyone says any more. Nothing. Everything is blank inside me, and I want to build something new in there, without my family—without you, without anyone—just me, just me, me . . . me . . ." She started crying again. "I'm me, and he never ever gave me the chance to exist as myself. Oh, God . . ." her brokenhearted voice tailed off into uncontrollable sobs.

He held her; he held her so tightly he thought they would fuse together just by his will, and he waited—he would always wait, he thought—until she was able to talk, even though the tears coursed down her face and onto his hands.

"It was always—Dona's child; here comes Dona's daughter; oh, here's that awkward child again. And don't touch this, and don't do that, and watch your feet, Sarianna, and don't set the table wrong, and no, we won't accommodate your wrong side, you stupid—" She swallowed convulsively. "Always stupid, always . . . always—" she choked. "Just an excuse . . . because I was just like her . . . he didn't want me *just* like her. He took away temptation, but what he said was, h-he was protecting me from other people's misunderstanding and talking about me—and . . . it was all one damn, gigantic, horrible stupid—lie. . . ."

Cade couldn't speak; he held her, he rubbed her arms, her back, her hair, he touched her soft vulnerable mouth that revealed her father's unspeakable deceit, and his whole body shook as he comprehended that there might still be one thing that Sarianna did not know.

"It was a lie," he murmured, "it was a lie. You're beautiful and desirable, and loving and perfect, Sarianna. I swear to you; it doesn't matter, it never mattered."

"It mattered to *him*," she cried fiercely.

"Yes, it did," he agreed hoarsely, "because *he* is a cruel stupid man. And—" he added tensely, because he didn't know if she knew; he didn't know, and he was taking a chance telling her.

"And?" Her voice was as taut as his as she sensed the hesitation.

"You have to know . . . or did you know, Sarianna?" He waited a moment because he honestly didn't have any idea whether she knew. "Dona was left-handed, too."

It was so simple after all, Sarianna thought as she approached Rex the next morning. He was a futile old man who had caused her a great deal of suffering, and now she was going to pay him back. She understood now Cade's thirst for vengeance. And she understood unyielding unforgiveness; it was cemented in her soul.

"I have agreed to marry Mr. Rensell," she began summarily, her voice devoid of expression.

"Sarianna . . ." Rex made a small fruitless motion with his hand.

She ignored him. "I wish to be married from Bredwood as soon as possible. I want all of our old friends to be invited, Father: the Grays and Rudleys, the Gilmartins, all those fine friends who celebrated

Jeralee's birthday so enthusiastically. I mean to fill up the ballroom, Father, for my wedding, and I beg you to arrange things as expediently as you can. And I wish to have Jeralee to attend me."

Rex's eyes suddenly came to life. "No!"

"It would be a mistake to leave her out," Sarianna said calmly. "Everyone would wonder where Jeralee was. I'm sure it would look very strange if she did not attend my nuptials, Father, even you can see that. Your friends would talk. They would wonder about what happened in our home, or why Mr. Rensell did not choose Jeralee. They would wonder a lot of things, Father. They would talk about us."

She broke off as Rex sagged back in his chair. "Very well, Sarianna. What else?"

"I would like Sylvia to prepare the wedding dinner, and it would please me very much if Vesta would choose the menu."

"Would it," Rex murmured, with about as much energy as he could get up at the moment.

"And I would very much like it if Alzine could be spared to make a dress for me."

"Very well," Rex agreed, wondering where he could draw the line, and how he could break through the emotionless shell she presented to him. He didn't know what that scoundrel Rensell had said to her about their confrontation. All he knew was this cold husk of Sarianna who was making demands in a way and in a tone of voice she had never used before, and he could only conclude that Rensell had briefed her well. The threat was now on her lips, issued with impunity and with no thought for the family whatsoever.

He didn't hear Cade and Pierce Darden enter the library, and he only looked up when Sarianna greeted them.

"Father, Mr. Darden is about to leave for Savannah to make arrangements. Is there anything you can think of that he might attend to for us?"

"I think not," Rex said coldly. "Our minister will be called upon to perform the ceremony, and everything else can be done from Bredwood, I believe."

Sarianna turned to Pierce. "I thank you then, for your efforts in our behalf."

"No trouble, Miss Sarianna," Pierce told her with his customary kindness. He didn't understand it either; but Sarianna herself had assured him that she wanted to marry Cade, and he knew Cade wished to wed Sarianna. Who was to say what feelings had developed in the short space of two or three days? He had never been in love, but he believed at that moment as he gazed into her sad eyes that he was half in love with Sarianna himself. He shook his head slightly to clear away the vision of his touching her in a loverlike way and her responding to his plea.

He reached out and took her hand. "May I play for your wedding, Miss Sarianna?"

"Play?" she inquired, her voice coloring slightly with curiosity, her lifeless eyes staring right past Cade.

"I—um—have some small talent with a guitar, Miss Sarianna. I thought—"

She smiled then, and his heart turned over. "I like that thought, Mr. Darden; I hadn't thought about music. Music would be delightful, wouldn't it, Father?" She turned to Rex. "*Wouldn't* it?"

Rex looked at Cade, and Cade's grim expression prompted his answer. "Whatever you want, Sarianna."

"Good. Then we'll see you back here by the weekend, Mr. Darden. I would like the ceremony to take place on Sunday." She turned to her father. "That gives us enough time to prepare, doesn't it, Father?"

"Whatever you wish, Sarianna," Rex agreed, with a tinge of resentment in his voice. But then, he would not be handling the details. He had only to hand over all of Sarianna's wants and wishes to Vesta and let her cope with them. He didn't know why Sarianna seemed even more remote than usual; he would have thought she would be dancing all over the house because she was the one Rensell was determined to marry. Not even Vesta knew about that yet. Good God, Vesta . . . she would have apoplexy. She would have to break the news to Jeralee . . . he hadn't thought of all the ramifications, only of Rensell's sensational threat.

He watched Sarianna bid good-bye to Pierce Darden. She didn't *look* loverlike, he thought; she looked—determined—and pale as if she had not slept. Damn, what had Rensell told her? What did she know? Was it what she wanted, this marriage?

He knew she would never give him a straight answer. She had made up her mind, and he knew her well enough to know she would not change her course once it was set. The loyalty she had given him, despite its constrictions, had been fierce, forgiving even. But now he did not sense that in her. The coldness of her manner flayed him. It

155

was as if she had repudiated him altogether and was only looking forward to the next moment and the next. He felt no happiness emanating from her, only unswerving resolution. She was living moment to moment, he thought. But then, with this announcement, so were they all.

It was so easy, Sarianna thought as she left her father and walked back to the hallway with Cade, to pretend. All she had to do was pretend that everything was normal, sanctioned, happy, and everyone would take their lead from her.

On the surface, she thought, everything would look the way it was supposed to look. No one would dare gossip within the confines of Bredwood—that was for later. If they wondered why Cade had proposed to *her* instead of Jeralee, they would not speak of it until weeks later, and it would be Vesta who would have to answer the questions and defend Cade's choice.

The notion gave her pleasure. She was in control for the first time in her life, to some extent at least. She could not refuse, after the ceremony, to accompany Cade to Savannah, but after that—oh, after that loomed blessed freedom. He knew nothing about it either. He was looking as grim and unrelenting as she.

"I still do not understand your decision to have as big a ceremony as possible," Cade said after a little while, when they had traversed the hallway and gone out the front door onto the white-columned verandah.

"There's nothing to understand," Sarianna said. "I merely thought it would be nice for everyone to celebrate this happy occasion."

Cade's lips twisted. He caught her arm and pulled her back to him. She did not resist, and he tilted her face up to the bright morning light. "Yes," he murmured, "your happiness positively radiates out of your eyes, Sarianna. I wonder how you plan to convince Vesta when you tell her your news."

She pulled away from him. "Perhaps I'll find I'm able to pretend convincingly. What do you think, Mr. Rensell?"

"I think I don't like your still addressing me so formally, first of all, and secondly, I don't like—oh, hell what I don't like. Sarianna, you've turned into a block of ice overnight."

"What did you expect?" She shrugged. "It was rather an emotional night, after all. It isn't often one learns one has been betrayed by both one's father and the man to whom she has given her virtue. It's rather stunning, in fact. It makes you wonder." She flashed a hard look at him. "As I said, you don't need to marry me now."

"You're right. I don't need to. And I am going to," Cade said definitely.

"And for the purest of motives," Sarianna added before she could stop herself, and she wondered if she would ever forget his words. They overrode everything, even the comfort she had found in his arms, even his express determination to marry her. The reason for everything, she thought, was Dona. And that was fine; she would live with that, as long as she could get away.

She saw him flinch at her words. "And your pure motives?" he shot back. "A marriage for love, Sarianna? Or a marriage to escape?"

"A marriage for the respectability that everyone thought I would *never* have," she retorted, her sapphire gaze darkening in anger, the first emotion he had seen from her the entire morning after a broken night of endless crying. But no one could have discerned that: Sarianna's eyes did not puff up or turn red. There were smudges beneath them, and her face was pale, the lines etched deeper around her mouth and her forehead. She looked faintly unkempt, as though she had slept in her clothes; and the actuality was, she had slept in his arms, finally, and he had slept not at all.

"Truly, marriage to me will give you all the respectability you could ever want," he said, a touch of irony in his voice.

"But there is all that money . . . ," she murmured, and then felt appalled. She hadn't meant to say that, but he was pushing her; she really felt he was pushing her. He seemed to want something from her, and she did not know what she had to give him. She wasn't even sure she could give him her body now, either. The memory of the rapture had diminished into a tight little coil inside her, still there but compressed to a point where no feelings could take hold that would spring it to life.

"I see," he said expressionlessly. She didn't mean it, he thought, but still—it was a fierce little gouging point against his gut. The money. Amazing no one had mentioned the money. The money could soothe an ocean of tears, even Sarianna's. The money bought the normalcy she had craved. The money was as good a reason as any for her to consent to marry him.

And he didn't believe her. Sarianna didn't care one whit about money. But everyone else would say she had, and wonder why *he* had wanted to marry *her*.

There was an awfulness about her composure. Her face had schooled itself back into that blank emotionless expression. Her quirky little smile had settled into a bitter line. She could not be talked to, he thought; she would never in this mood hear a word he was saying.

Sarianna could not even look at him; she sensed his retreat at her callous words, and she did not feel like trying to make amends. She had Vesta to contend with, and Jeralee, and she was steeling herself for that confrontation. She didn't need one with Cade.

"It's your wedding, after all," Cade said finally, wondering if it would be kind or cruel to tell her that her Sawny neighbors would not be any too happy to celebrate it with her. But she wanted it, and whether her desire was sincere or it was meant to show up Jeralee, it didn't matter. It was time someone made reparations to Sarianna. "Sarianna!"

She stopped short at the command in his voice and turned to look at him. "I don't care," he said forcefully. "I just don't care why you think you want to marry me, Sarianna. *I* want to marry *you*, and it's not important that it wasn't what I was after when I came here."

Sarianna checked a reaction, and he noted it with a brief humorless smile.

"Be aware, Sarianna—I'm after *you*." His words were both shocking and warming. She didn't know quite what he meant, or even how to respond. "But you've got me," she pointed out with a false sweetness.

"Oh, no, Sarianna; I've got the circumstances, but I promise you— I'll have you, too, not here perhaps, not now, not tomorrow—"

"Maybe not ever," she threw in, bridling, and whirled as she heard still another voice behind them.

"Dear, dear, Sarianna—what a way to talk to the man you're going to marry."

"Vesta." How did she remain so calm, when Cade's words had rocketed through her with the force of a tornado. He wasn't going to let her go, she thought frantically. She didn't know what he intended, what he felt. But it made sense. Why *would* he allow his Dona-doll to walk away from him? She felt a fulminating panic overwhelm her, both at the thought of being trapped by him for the rest of her life, and being surrounded by Vesta's evil aura.

And Vesta was smiling, a thin pasted-on smile that made her face look like a mask. Rex had made the announcment. Rex had told her everything. Why had he saved her that? she wondered. Why would he be so kind?

"My dear," Vesta went on, holding out her two hands and grasping Sarianna's in a cold hard grip. "I'm just delighted." Her words sounded hollow, and whatever life she tried to infuse into them fell into a dead space from which she couldn't reclaim them. Nonetheless, she was an adamant proponent of doing the right thing, and doing the right thing meant tendering her congratulations to Rex's deficient upstart daughter. She was doing her duty, nothing more, and she was aware that both Cade and Sarianna were watching her with wary eyes.

"Thank you," Sarianna said, trying very hard to pull her hands away, but Vesta's hands held her like eagle claws.

"So clever of you to appropriate Mr. Rensell right from under our *very* eyes. And you, Mr. Rensell—I wish you well with . . . your choice." She smiled up at Cade as if she hadn't said something insulting about Sarianna, and about him. "Jeralee, though . . . well, she's packing for an unexpected trip to Savannah."

"Is she?" Cade said smoothly. "She will miss our wedding, then."

"I'm afraid so. The Grays invited her—"

"No, no," Cade said, as Sarianna stood there helplessly, unable to combat Vesta's opening foray, "the Grays cannot be leaving until Monday. Sarianna specifically requested they be invited to the wedding. Surely you misunderstood, Vesta?"

"Oh—" Vesta looked uncertain. "Perhaps I—"

"And then of course," Cade interrupted her, "it would certainly look odd if Jeralee missed the ceremony. Everyone would say she couldn't face Sarianna. I can't believe she would open herself to that kind of gossip."

"No," Vesta said, her mind working furiously. "Indeed not."

"Some might say she was sulking," Cade went on, his burning hazel eyes on Sarianna, who was looking very discomfitted. He himself wondered why Rex had broken the news. Rex wasn't kind; he would not have wanted to save her from Vesta's wrath. "Some might say," he added, "that she couldn't stand to watch Sarianna get something she had coveted."

Vesta's head snapped up. "What nonsense! Jeralee hardly knows you—neither does Sarianna, but I won't dispute that. Some people do believe in love on first sight. Perhaps that is your story, or is it something else? It doesn't matter. Jeralee privately told me she thought you were a little uncouth—my apologies, Mr. Rensell, but we are plain talking here—and she was rather overwhelmed by you. You two would never have suited. I think Jeralee's delighted Sarianna will have a chance to experience the normal married state, something we never expected to happen."

Sarianna reacted as if she had been slapped, and Cade grasped her hand before she could retaliate. Her impassive face became militant, and her fist balled up in his hand.

"Indeed, Rex was so afraid to lose her, he kept her from meeting the full complement of young men who might have taken her from him," Cade interpolated smoothly. "So tragic that he was so misguided on that point, don't you agree, Vesta? Sarianna might have married a long time ago but for that. But that is *my* gain. I've got her now"—he sent Vesta a meaningful look—"and no one will ever hurt her, misuse her or demean her again. I trust I make myself clear?"

He smiled at Vesta, not a pleasant smile, but one that held her motionless for a long moment. It held a threat, implicit in its meanness. His eyes were hard, and she didn't care at that moment to challenge him at all.

"Of course," she said, "of course, certainly you feel that way. Don't we all?" She leaned toward Sarianna. "I am so happy for you, my dear, and I will be so happy to choose the menu and direct its preparation. I'm sure Jeralee did mistake the day she was leaving, and we will have Alzine immediately begin working on her dress."

"Alzine will be working on *my* dress," Sarianna said in a frozen voice.

"But—" Vesta held up her hand. "Alzine is—"

"Going to be busy making up Sarianna's dress," Cade said, and Vesta bowed her head.

"As you say, Mr. Rensell. I'm sure Merleen will be happy to assist Jeralee." She threw a haughty look at Sarianna as if to say she would not get away with usurping Alzine's services no matter what Cade Rensell said. Nonetheless, she was burning inside at how much Sarianna was getting. By rights Sarianna ought to have gone off to the minister's house at the far end of the island to get married. She ought

160

not to have been planning such a lavish little wedding, complete with reception and all of her—and Jeralee's—friends. She should never have been able to attract a man with the power and money of a Cade Rensell. Damn her, she fumed, aware of the same fierce resentment she had felt before: Sarianna had gotten in the way, and she was going to pay.

11

Sarianna had a throbbing headache after their encounter with Vesta, and she hardly had the energy to climb the stairs to her room and lie down. Where *was* Alzine, she wondered fretfully as she rinsed out a handkerchief and pressed its cold comfort to her head as she sank onto her bed. She felt **wrung** out; it was too much emotion for her to cope with after years of no emotion whatsoever from her father or Vesta. She hated it; she felt out of control again. Thank God Cade had been with her; she might have swung a fist right at Vesta's condescending lips.

And wasn't it nice, she mused, to have someone to defend her? Just for that small space of time, she had savored Cade's parrying all of Vesta's supercilious thrusts; even in her anger and distress, she appreciated having someone so fully on her side that nothing anyone said could make a dent in his support. It was lovely, lovely— something was lovely—thank God, something was lovely; she was beginning to think everything was black, cold and ugly.

It might not be so bad, she thought. Whether Cade really wanted her as he said, or a second chance with a Dona look-alike—how hard would it be to live with that? She might even find it pleasant, particularly since he had demonstrated very amply today that he cared about her and that no one should denigrate her any more. Ever.

Oh, yes—ever. She could sit wherever she wanted at her own table, or do whatever she wanted without anyone suggesting she was reaching for the moon. It was such a burden relieved to find that Dona had had to cope with her wrong hand—such a huge burden to bear with no one ever having told her.

162

Her thoughts whirled around in her head, disjointed, frenetic. She felt such gratitude to Cade, and such ambivalence, and even that was overlaid by a fine sense of fear. But why? She had spent the whole night in Cade's arms, going over and over this, devastated, inundated by tears that wouldn't stop, and she had trusted him enough to reveal the depths of her sorrow and grief.

It was too much to think about. Too much. But inside her she felt a galvanizing frenzy to get it done, to run from Bredwood, to leave everything behind her as if it had never existed.

"Miss Sarianna?" Alzine's soft voice intruded. "Mr. Cade said you want to see me."

"Yes." Sarianna summoned and found some stamina to raise herself to a sitting position. "I'm getting married, Alzine," she said baldly. "I need a dress, and I want you to make it."

Alzine stopped in her tracks. "You is *what?*"

"Getting married, Alzine. Mr. Rensell has asked me to marry him, and I agreed. I want a special dress."

"Oh, yas'm, I be mighty glad to make a special dress fo' you. But—"

"Alzine?" Sarianna prompted as she hesitated and a look of uncertainty flitted across her face.

"Miss Jeralee ain't gonna—"

"Miss Jeralee will be fine," Sarianna said briskly. "Miss Vesta agrees that my dress takes precedence. The wedding is Sunday."

"Oh, lawd—but *dis* Sunday weekend? Oh, Miss Sarianna—we got work to do."

And she supposed, Sarianna thought later, as they went through the material in the storehouse and chose something appropriate, that was the saving grace: Work to do meant she did not have to speak with Vesta, or direct the servants. Work to do meant concentration on an all-consuming task so she did not have to think or surmise, or even wonder whether Vesta were going to go to any lengths to ruin what should be a happy day for her. Work to do meant she didn't have time to speculate where Cade was or what he was doing. Work to do meant silence and busy hands, the snip of the scissors, the soft huff of the material as Alzine draped it around her to determine weight and color against her skin.

They settled finally on a length of pure white, swiss muslin and they spent the rest of the morning making a pattern which Alzine would cut out after lunch.

Alzine, Sarianna noticed suddenly in the midst of this work that meant she did not have to think, was unusually quiet.

They were in the upstairs sewing room which was at the same end of the house as Sarianna's bedroom, and the windows were open, with a soft breeze and liquid sun warming the room. There was a large worktable, well scrubbed, in the middle of it, and on this lay the paper on which she was transcribing Alzine's measurements of her, which Alzine would then translate into a pattern.

She could only watch as Alzine drew lines and connections on the paper in ways that seemed illogical but for which Alzine seemed to know exactly the configuration.

And Alzine never said a word.

Sarianna forced herself to go downstairs and push food around on a plate under Vesta's scornful gaze. Cade was nowhere about, and her father sat morosely at one end of the table just as uninterested in eating as she.

"Well," Vesta said, "Mr. Rensell is nowhere about this afternoon." She turned to Sarianna. "I have been busy writing invitations, Sarianna. But please don't expect that the same large number of people will want to attend your nuptials as came to Jeralee's party."

"Perhaps they will," Sarianna said blandly, "out of curiosity."

Vesta shuddered. When had Sarianna acquired such cattiness that she delivered in the most expressionless of voices? Oh, yes, they would come, she thought venomously, and for exactly that reason. So smart of Sarianna to see that. So aggravatingly perceptive of her. "In any event," Vesta went on, "Sylvia and I have conferred on the menu, and of course we'll find the appropriate decorations. We'll use the company china; we have a selection of wine, champagne, whiskey . . . well, you know, Sarianna—this is more your sphere than mine, but I hope my choices will please you."

"How could they help but please me," Sarianna said. "Look at Mr. Rensell."

She had the great satisfaction of having finally discomfitted Vesta to the point where she flushed, threw her napkin down on the table with a resounding thump and in a choked voice excused herself.

Rex looked at Sarianna. She sat erect, impassive, her fork digging into the ham on her plate, her eyes not meeting his. Such strength, he thought, in the face of Vesta's insults; had she always had such fortitude? But he didn't care to dwell on that thought; he would have to admit some culpability, and he had admitted as much as he wanted to when he had consented to Sarianna's marrying Cade Rensell.

Sarianna waited until he was no longer in view. With his exit, the air seemed to freshen, the atmosphere to lighten. Her decision was not a mistake, she thought, cutting herself a piece of the lukewarm ham and eating it with relish. Her decision was a lifeline with which she would save herself.

She heard the snip of the scissors as she paused at the door. She could just see the length of material pinned to the pattern pieces. A second later, Alzine's small figure appeared, looking curiously lumpish and defeated. She pushed open the door and Alzine looked up.

"Miss Sarianna," she acknowledged her presence.

"Alzine?" She put the question in her voice. Something was wrong if Alzine was not chattering away as she usually did when she was in the midst of cutting out a dress. Alzine distinctly did not look happy. "You know," she said, moving into the room, "I could swear you are not happy about my coming marriage."

"No," Alzine said staunchly, lowering her eyes. "I be happy fo' you, Miss Sarianna. You rightfully got to leave here; you got de freedom to leave here . . ." she broke off as if she had said too much.

Sarianna watched her as she picked up the various pattern pieces with their shaped material pinned to them and fit them together almost like a puzzle on the table. "Dis is good," she breathed, making an adjustment here and another there. "Now we take away de pattern, we pin dis together, and you gonna try it on, Miss Sarianna, and den de sewing work starts."

Still she did not look at Sarianna. Sarianna helped her unpin the muslin pieces from the patterns and then helped her assemble it once again on the table.

With Alzine's help, she shucked her pinafore and let Alzine lift the pinned dress over her head and felt it drift down over her head and shoulders.

"Now," Alzine said, directing her arm into a sleeve, "you don' like dem hoops and all, but we got to get some span fo' dis here skirt, Miss Sarianna. You could do fo' one day havin' dat old hoop 'round you, just fo' de weddin', sure you can do dat." She delicately pushed and pulled at the plain bodice, and held out the skirt so that Sarianna could see the difference in the mirror.

"I suppose you're right," Sarianna said obligingly.

"And den when you finish, you can take it off, put it away," Alzine said with satisfaction. She was proud of how Sarianna looked, even in the pinned-up dress. The wide skirt made her torso seem even more slender, fragile, and the low neckline gave her bosom a hint of promise to tempt Mr. Cade. Yes, he would like that, Alzine thought, and she would drape two swaths of contrasting satin over the bodice, and trim the elbow-length sleeves with lace which she would also use to trim the hem of the overskirt. Somewhere, she thought, there had to be some veiling, or netting might do for the makeshift veil. She could frame it with lace, attach it to a crown of Miss Sarianna's flowers, and trim it with more lace; then Miss Sarianna would look like an angel.

Miss Sarianna was an angel, she thought, as she began helping Sarianna remove the delicately pinned dress. And Miss Sarianna would leave and never come back to Bredwood again—ever. She knew it.

She laid the dress on the table to hide her emotions, and Sarianna slipped back into the pinafore, not insensible to Alzine's distress.

"Alzine . . ."

"Now, Miss Sarianna," Alzine said brightly, "I got to tell you, you is gonna have to wear one of dem corset things you don' like so much with dis here dress. You got to have dat shape fo' how I'm gonna make it. You got to promise you do dat fo' me, and I'm gonna dress you dat day, too."

"Of course you are," Sarianna agreed, touching Alzine's shoulder. "Now tell me what's really the matter, Alzine."

Alzine turned to her, gauging her expression, her sympathy, how much or little she could say. Perhaps, she thought, she shouldn't say anything, and then the words rushed out. "Take me with you, Miss Sarianna. Please take me with you."

Men. Damn them! Damn them, damn them, *damn them!* Sarianna stormed out of the sewing room in a fury, leaving Alzine quaking in her wake.

Unspeakable, she thought, running down the stairs, the kind of thing that everyone accepted and no one protested. Why? *Why?* And was this what she could count on expecting from Cade after their marriage? Sneaking, lying, abusing, stinking men! Her hands were trembling. Nothing was ever enough, nothing. Here was an example; here was a lesson. A woman had to be wary. A woman had to protect herself from caring too much lest her life come to a welter of lies over something like this.

She wouldn't forget; never would she forget. It was the only safeguard, her only shield from a man's duplicity. It didn't matter which man—Cade, her father—it was all the same; they were all the same. The temptation of the moment was to be assuaged at the moment and damn the consequences. Wife or slave, it made no difference. Wife was slave, come to that, but that they never acknowledged; they did something worse. They pretended no one knew.

Well now she knew, and she was forewarned. She charged through the formal downstairs room and raced like a whirlwind into Rex's sanctum, the library.

"Sarianna?" He might have been sleeping; even he didn't know. Luncheon had not been that filling, but he remembered he had felt lethargic.

He struggled upright in his chair, the chair, he thought belatedly, where Rensell had cornered him, and now Sarianna, looking as if she had been shot out of hell. "Now what?" His old dislike asserted itself as she paced furiously around the room until he woke up enough to face the confrontation. "Something else, Sarianna? Another demand? I have given you everything I intend to give you as of now."

"I'm taking Alzine with me," Sarianna said, wheeling on him, clenching her fists at her sides lest she strike him. She felt like striking him. He was so righteous. His will directed everything. He was lord and master, and no one dared stand up to him. Except, Cade had stood up to him. Cade had told the truth and freed her, and now she must tell the truth and save Alzine; and she wondered if she were strong enough to fight him.

No, she was, she would.

"I'm afraid not," Rex said regretfully. "Alzine stays here."

He looked so smug she had to contradict him. "I wish Alzine to come with me to Savannah. I will need her there."

"But Vesta needs her here," Rex pointed out reasonably.

"Vesta has a whole corps of servants to do her bidding," Sarianna snapped. "She won't miss two."

Rex overlooked that sniping remark. "Alzine cannot go with you. I'd rather you take Merleen or Minda. Or Lucy," he offered in a tone of an adult trying to be reasonable with a child.

"Neither of them are carrying a child," Sarianna countered, her own voice rough with the frustration she felt.

"Well then, you see my point."

"No, I don't."

"Don't be obtuse, Sarianna."

"Surely I'm missing something; it *is* your child?"

"It's my property," Rex contradicted callously. "There is no question that Alzine must remain here."

"So you'd rather have a child in your home by your servant than your own granson from me," Sarianna said quietly, knowing Rex would miss the thread of anger under her words in his haste to justify his behavior with Alzine.

"This is not uncommon, Sarianna. You're not naive enough to think things like this never happen."

"Oh, no, I believe they happen, and all the time, Father. I believe that Vesta will be furious if Alzine remains here and the baby is born with any identifiable Broydon characteristic. More than that, I believe I could do much damage if I openly state the case at my wedding and demand that the minister do something to legalize Alzine's status."

Rex snorted. "What could *he* do?"

"Probably nothing, but I think the wives of all your Sawny neighbors could do something very drastic," Sarianna said. "I hate to keep threatening you with spreading innuendo, my dear father, but I do believe in an eye for an eye. It's a new philosophy that Mr. Rensell introduced me to. I find it very satisfying to think there is some power in my hands, that I'm not entirely as helpless as Alzine, that I'm not your slave as well as she."

"I will not let you have Alzine."

"Call it a wedding gift, Father, some property in my own name."

"It's *my* property," Rex shouted, enraged by Sarianna's boldness; her shocking disregard for the proprieties and her express blackmail drove everything else from his mind.

"Oh, it is," Sarianna agreed quickly. "It's for you to decide."

"You may have Alzine *after* the baby is born," Rex countered.

"No, no. You can't have her baby when you were within a stone's throw of preventing your own daughter from ever having her own. No, Alzine and the baby come with me."

"You are demented," Rex said. "Rensell doesn't know the half of what he is getting into. I do believe I'm glad he is taking you off my hands."

"And if there *is* a baby?" Sarianna queried with a false sweetness.

"I'll send you a congratulatory telegram, my dear. What more can you expect?"

"As much as Alzine's child will get," she threw out bitterly, as she turned her head and left the room.

She held it all in, all the rage and hostility, all the resentment. There would be a time to cut her father's legs out from under him. She wasn't afraid of seeking retribution any more. She felt strong and very able to overpower his puny excuses and excesses.

The chance came that evening. She could not believe that luck was playing her way. She had changed into a slightly more formal dress that was some years old and usable still, and she had spent some meditative time in her flower garden, which relaxed her and dissipated some of the murderous anger she felt.

She saw Cade return, and she was surprised that she was not even curious about where he had gone or why. She felt blank once again, as if the effort of confronting her father had drained away all her blood and left a shell that might crack in a thousand pieces if someone so much as touched her.

It was too much, the idea of her father sneaking into Alzine's room, giving her no choice, no chance, and merely taking whatever he wanted, with the end result that Alzine had now become to him a thing to be bartered and her baby something to add to his list of possessions at Bredwood. Item, she thought rigidly, one Broydon baby boy, born—when? Within six months' time, send her father a bill of lading for labor, and put poor Alzine back to work before she had finished nursing it. His *son*, if it would be a son, with bloodlines inconsequential if he chose it to be so and with Alzine having no claim to her own flesh and blood. It was monstrous, and even more so because Rex would have denied her that fulfillment, and accepted Alzine's son in place of her own.

He *was* a monster; she kept coming face to face with the fact and kept denying it over and over, as if her refusal to recognize it would turn it into some kind of truth. The only truth was her father was selfish and Cade Rensell had been the only one who could sway him from his course.

But the cost to her was catastrophic. She had as little choice as Alzine in point of fact. She didn't love Cade; she didn't even think she could summon up any kind of response to him after all that had happened, all that she heard.

She would don her white gown and promise to love and obey him, and her vows, like everything else at Bredwood, would be part and parcel of still another lie.

She felt as if she was being pulled into a self-perpetuating vortex of deceit, and she could do nothing to stop it.

She didn't at that point even want to join them all at the dinner table, but for some reason Vesta had made it mandatory, no doubt because Cade was still at Bredwood and didn't look as if he were going to spend more than an afternoon away at any one time before the wedding. It almost looked as if he were guarding her, she thought abstractedly as she finally dressed for dinner with Alzine's dispirited help.

"He ain't gonna let me go," Alzine said mournfully, after she had briefly detailed her conversation with her father.

"Nonsense," Sarianna said with more surety than she felt. "I haven't left yet, nor have I told Mr. Rensell about this development. It may be that he can persuade my father when I can't."

"It may be yo' daddy is gonna take a switch to Alzine fo' talkin' too much," Alzine said, as she pulled the dress down over Sarianna's head. "Dat is one tired old dress, Miss Sarianna. Ain't nothin' we can do to make it lay better—and you is too thin by half now, not like me," she added dolefully, pushing Sarianna toward her dressing table so she could attend to her hair.

"I'll think of something," Sarianna promised, her eyes huge and dark as she watched Alzine's ministrations, but she wondered what more she could do to pry her father's grasping hands from one more helpless servant.

She had to try. It wouldn't be easy, but it would be harder for Alzine to stay and watch her firstborn son become one of the cadre of field hands, a cipher in Rex's account book. She had nothing better to offer herself, but at least Alzine's body would be safe in her house, and

Alzine's child would have no obvious identity to set him apart from everyone else.

When she entered the dining room, everyone was seated, including Cade, whose lightning hazel gaze swept over her like a thunderbolt.

What did he see, she wondered as he held out her chair. He saw her drawn face, she supposed, and her ill-fitting dress, a brown silk, high-collared affair with very little in the way of decoration or contrast in collar and cuffs; he saw her tense mouth and bloodless cheeks, and her unruly hair which curled wildly in the sultry air. He saw the woman he supposedly really desired to marry in stark contrast to the elegant room and the fresh ivory appearance of the woman he had rejected.

Jeralee didn't for a moment look as if she had been second choice; somehow she had come out of the debacle of Cade's choosing Sarianna with some rationalization that comforted her enough to put in a smugly righteous appearance at the dinner table.

Her chocolatey eyes glowed and landed on Sarianna like a physical blow. She wouldn't forget either, Sarianna thought, as she picked up her spoon to taste the evening's cold soup.

In the end, after an hour of very tepid conversation during which no one said anything and everyone looked from one to the other as though they were thinking things they would never say aloud, it was Vesta who finally looked at Alzine, after spending the evening looking *through* her, and said, "Surely Alzine is wearing the same dress she wore last night to serve?"

Rex's pale blue gaze shot to Vesta and then to Sarianna. Sarianna held his gaze, goading him, making him wonder whether she might answer what obviously was a rhetorical comment.

No one spoke, and Vesta went on, "Well, I suppose I must talk to her about it. We can't have our servants looking slovenly, especially with the big—event—only days away." Having settled that to her satisfaction, she helped herself to a piece of peach tart, and looked up at Sarianna, and smiled. It was an unpleasant smile, Sarianna thought, but no one noticed it. Rex was struck dumb by the thought that Vesta might hear what Sarianna already knew and Jeralee was devouring Cade with her eyes.

"I hope," Vesta said suddenly as a thought seemed to occur to her, "that all of our staff will be properly outfitted for the occasion?" Her question, as always with things relevant to the house and servants,

171

was directed at Sarianna, who hadn't given the question of what their household servants would wear a single thought.

Sarianna swung her heated gaze back to her father. "It seems to me that if Alzine has to resort to wearing her dresses more than once when she usually is so neat and clean, she must have a reason."

"She's being fractious," Vesta said, dismissing the subject entirely.

"Or she has a reason," Sarianna insisted, as she saw relief flood over Rex's face.

"Don't be ridiculous," Vesta snapped. "What possible reason?"

Rex sat bolt upright waiting for her answer. Sarianna smiled, aware that not only was Rex's attention fixed on her, but also Cade's. "I expect she would tell you if you asked her," she said softly. "I think you should just—ask her."

12

Pierce returned on Friday, his guitar in hand, and all the necessary papers in hand. Sarianna was glad to see him, too glad, Cade felt, but he himself was not impervious to the hostility in the air. As the day approached, Sarianna became more and more edgy, and Rex more reclusive. Only Vesta fluttered about, Alzine trailing her, with yards of netting and satin in her hands, draping everything in sight in white, or tying satiny bows around anything that wasn't festooned in satin.

Two more days, Cade thought, as he prowled the house following Vesta to make sure she did not foul up anything relevant to the wedding. He watched her sort the responses to the invitations which collected into quite a pile on her desk in the morning room. He watched her supervising the mixing of the cake and eavesdropped on the discussion of its decoration.

He conferred with Pierce over the marriage agreement, which was merely a matter of form and only gave him something to do to pass the time, besides watching Sarianna enraptured by Pierce's delicate playing of the light, lilting baroque piece with which he planned to escort her down the steps to Cade's side. And he hated the fact that all her attention was centered admiringly on Pierce and that she had barely spoken to him at all.

At one point, her delighted appreciation of Pierce's skill brought him up short as he traversed the hallway toward the front door.

"I love that," he heard her say with as much warmth as he had heard in her voice in days. "I wish I could do that."

"It's not difficult." Pierce's voice and a strumming sound, simple chords, and then his voice hummed a simple air.

"But for me," Sarianna said, and Cade could imagine her indicating to him that the instrument would have to be turned upside down for her to play it.

"It could be restrung," Pierce said consideringly. "The chords are easy. If you could master three or four of them, you could play a lot of songs. Perhaps when you come to Savannah, I could teach you."

Really, Cade thought, immediately discarding his plan to ride, and pushing into the parlor.

There, Sarianna and Pierce sat across from each other in the sun-bathed bay window at the far end of the room, and on his lap, Pierce balanced his mellow dark-wood guitar.

Sarianna's face immediately schooled itself into a mask of polite interest, and she stood up to greet him. "Mr. Rensell." Her two cool hands grasped his. "Mr. Darden plays beautifully, did you hear him?"

"I heard," he said shortly. "Come for a walk, Sarianna." God, he hated her remoteness; sometimes he thought the only thing that kept him going until the wedding was his memory of her surrendering to him, a child and a woman all at once, destined for him and no one else.

"I can't," she started to protest, but he took her hand and pulled her from the room. The lion, she thought resentfully, feeling his power and her yielding to it. There was always that . . . as he marched her past her father's library and out the front door and down the flagstone path, away from the encroaching walls of the house.

Finally, as they neared the stables, he slowed down. "You look ready to run at the first instant you can escape me," he commented harshly, pushing her ahead of him.

"I won't run," she said. "We made a bargain, Mr. Rensell; I intend to keep it."

"Only a bargain?" he questioned. "There's nothing more?"

"How can there be?" she answered bitterly. "I'm the most convenient one, didn't you say so? The one whose defection will hurt my father the most? The one that *you* have the freedom to marry?"

"Hell," Cade swore.

"Yes, it is a match made in hell. Nevertheless, I will be leaving my father's home in a most seemly manner, Mr. Rensell—as someone's wife—and that has become the thing of major importance to me." She sent him a considering blue look. "Are you sure that is enough for you?"

She quailed under his long searching look. Here was the part of him she did not trust, did not know. He was the lion, the hunter, and he might, she thought, lie with a lamb if he couldn't lie with her. His violent response confirmed it. "It is *not* enough, Sarianna. It is hell. And you stupidly risk everything by encouraging Pierce Darden."

She drew back farther from him. "I see. That's what this is about. I'm not to have any friends either. I can't extend a moment's friendship to anyone, even the man who supposedly is *your* confidant and presumably your friend."

"Exactly right," he said tightly.

"I won't be dictated to," Sarianna said angrily, totally put out with him. What, was she exchanging one tyrant for another? Why not, she thought humorlessly; wasn't it true—men were all the same, *all* the same. Her father secretly wanted to be her lover, and her lover actively desired to be her father.

"You don't scare me," Cade said warningly.

"Nor do *you* scare me," Sarianna retorted, and stalked away.

She was so tense she had no time to wonder what Jeralee or Vesta were doing, and she did not know if Vesta had spoken to Alzine, who was now busy putting the finishing touches on her dress.

She was upset, too, that she did not feel the triumph she had expected to feel once all the responses had been returned to Vesta and she could point to all the guests who were planning to come to her wedding. It didn't matter suddenly, and she was at a loss to know what did.

Since Vesta had relieved her of the household duties for these remaining days, she was at loose ends to know what to do with herself, and it seemed safer to remain in her room than to look for trouble. She might find it, too, if her encounter with Cade were anything to go by.

It was true she had to pack her meager possessions for the forthcoming trip to Savannah, but the whole of that chore barely took one morning. There were pitifully few dresses and trinkets to be taken with her, and the sense of that reflection of the barrenness of her life made her feel an alien violence, and a vital pulse to get away.

One more day. One more half day, and then the evening meal which she had to suffer through, enduring her father's tight pale looks, Cade's stony expression and Jeralee's smirks.

One more night, she thought wearily, her nerves strung to the breaking point. It was easy to perceive over dinner her father's wary glances at Vesta, and the particular way she avoided meeting his eyes. Alzine's absence was not even remarked upon, and Merleen took her place serving the table. No one cared.

She cared. But she had no power; her threats had not intimidated Rex, her innuendo had rolled over Vesta's head, and her determination could not even sway Cade.

Only Pierce's presence saved the dinner from being an unmitigated disaster. He had such pretty manners, she thought; he knew how to fill a hole in the conversation, and relieve the thick atmosphere with a kind word. He was both observant and complimentary without being overly ingratiating, and it was very clear that Jeralee was enjoying his attention.

One more night.

Cade looked utterly forbidding, his lion-gaze fixed steadily upon her, daring her to back down, to say something, to renege.

She felt an overwhelming moment of terror, and he saw it.

One more night.

She would never be able to sleep. She could stay up all night and ruminate on her future that was now as fixed as the stars. She felt like crying.

One more night.

Alzine woke her. "Yo' daddy need to see you, Miss Sarianna."

She shook her head groggily and slipped her weary body upright. How strange. "He can come in, Alzine."

Alzine scurried out the door as Rex entered, and he closed the door behind her meaningfully.

"Father?"

"Sarianna." His expression was cold; he wasn't there to make some fatherly prenuptial speech to her. He reached into the pocket of his morning coat and removed a folded paper. "You win, Sarianna. You and Cade both; you've beaten me down, my dear. Alzine goes with you. Vesta took your enlightening suggestion, and now she will not have her in the house." He tossed the paper negligently onto the bed. "That should make your day complete, Sarianna. You and Rensell both have blackmailed me into submission—but I warn you—it's the last time, my dear. The very last time."

176

Sarianna picked up the paper and scanned it quickly. It was a simple document, a transfer of property in its simplest form, drawn up by Pierce that very morning, and an eloquent statement that her father was not invincible. "This is a generous wedding present," she said finally, willing to pretend if it made the appearance of it easier for him. She knew her statement was generous as well, and she waited to see how he would receive it.

He chose not to be gracious. "Be kind enough, if you will, *not* to inform me if Alzine should give birth to a boy," he said stiffly, and ignoring the look of utter shock on her face, he turned and stalked out of the room.

Pain. There was pain; she felt it in her head, in her heart. She saw it on her father's face, and the yearning for the son he would never have. She couldn't move, couldn't feel. She managed to put down the paper, and she swallowed the gall that rose in her throat over her father's last defection.

She had to get married; she had to leave this house. She had to be ready, her emotions under control when Alzine returned with the copper tub and bath water, and Alzine must never know more than what she had told her father: It was a generous wedding present.

Five minutes later, Alzine charged back into the room, dragging the tub behind her and balancing an ironstone pitcher full of lukewarm water on her hip. "It be time, Miss Sarianna. You got to take yo' bath and be gettin' ready. De minister be comin' fo' eleven o'clock, and it nine now."

Sarianna shuddered and slowly got up and went to the edge of the tub. She shucked her nightgown, feeling as though she were removing all vestiges of her childhood and her feeling for her father, and she stepped into the tub and sat. Alzine poured the water over her head and began soaping up her hair just as Merleen entered, followed by Lucy and Minda, in a round robbin of toting heated water from the stove top in the kitchen.

Each long pour of water warmed her and took some of the disbelieving stiffness out of her bones. The lapping water against her skin soothed her.

She would get married. She would leave. At that very moment, the words did not strike her with reality. She felt as if she were watching herself go through the motions, and she wondered when—or if—it would ever seem real to her.

177

Alzine tenderly washed her hair and scrubbed her body and rinsed her off with a warm pitcher of lemon-scented water. Sarianna stood and was wrapped in a huge enfolding towel and guided to the dressing table chair where Alzine brushed her wet hair into some semblance of the order she wanted it in when it finally dried.

Sarianna watched her reflection in the mirror, savoring the one moment when she would tell Alzine the only good news today, listening to Alzine's soothing murmur and the care and love her hands expressed in the handling of her hair. "You is gonna be one beautiful bride, Miss Sarianna. I done made de mos' beautiful dress fo' you, and dat Mr. Cade gonna take one look and love you fo' sure; and it don't matter what done gone befo'. You hear, Miss Sarianna? You be kind to dat man, and you gonna be just fine, just fine. I know. I be thinkin' of you. I be prayin' fo' you, Miss Sarianna—"

"You'll be coming with me," Sarianna interposed gently, and it took Alzine still another moment to assimilate what she had said. The brush fell out of her hands, and she stared at Sarianna.

"Truly," Sarianna confirmed.

"Praise God," Alzine murmured fervently. "Oh, now fo' sure, Miss Sarianna. We goin' to get married, you—and me!"

She allowed herself to be tied into her underclothing, the chemise, drawers and the bothersome corset, and finally the crinoline cage she so loathed. Over this went a petticoat—an underskirt—and then she waited breathlessly for Alzine to bring out the gown.

Oh, the gown, the beautiful, never envisioned gown, with its tight low-cut bodice that was swathed in draped satin over her shoulders and arms; with its long, tiered drift of a skirt being patiently straightened out over the cage, and arranged just so around the petticoat, which peeked through the ruched-up hem—held up by satin bows—at intervals. Satin ribbons streamed from her waist down her back, and the slightly puffed tiers were hemmed in lace and ribbon to match, and dotted with twinkling glass teardrops.

Her satin kid slippers had a lacy decoration across the vamp which was fastened with a miniature satin bow that matched the dress. As she stared in the mirror at her elegant figure, Sarianna could not count the hours Alzine must have spent sewing and decorating her gown and shoes. She looked like a bride, and for one magical moment, as Alzine brought in her headdress, she felt like one.

The veil, a lightweight length of woven net, had been appended to a stiffened circlet of satin that was made with pasteboard and material and sized to fit snugly across her forehead. It too was decorated in lace and glass drops, and the veil hung straight down behind her back so that she looked like some medieval demoiselle; and she liked the way she looked very much.

"You is beautiful, Miss Sarianna," Alzine said reverently.

"Thank you, Alzine," Sarianna said, but her gaze was fixed on her reflection in awe. Color washed her face and heightened her fragile beauty. Her eyes glowed, almost as though she could pretend she were meeting her lover down those stairs to take the last step to consummation. Her mouth smiled, and it felt a little strange to be according this ceremony the joy it should engender in spite of the circumstances.

Alzine talked and she barely heard the words. "De guests is comin' once mo', Miss Sarianna; it be just like de day of Miss Jeralee's party. Dey is swarmin' in de house, dey be so curious. Dey want to see yo' beautiful self, Miss Sarianna, and you gonna show dem what dey never done see befo'. You is like a queen today, Miss Sarianna, and you don't let nobody make you be less den dat, you hear?"

"I hear," Sarianna said, her eyes never moving from the Sarianna in the dress who was a creature she did not know and might never know. She felt as though her mirror image were going to be summoned from the room any moment, and it would take her place on the stair landing and ultimately walk down the stairs to mate with Cade Rensell.

"Yo' daddy gonna come fo' you," Alzine went on. "He all decked out fo' dis occasion like he never did befo', and I don' understand why. He never done nothin' fo' you befo'."

"Alzine . . ." Sarianna cautioned.

"You know dat be true, Miss Sarianna. You is doin' de right thing, and Mr. Cade done chose de right woman fo' him, and dat is all I is gonna say."

Sarianna drew in a deep breath. Maybe the waiting was the worst, knowing people were arriving, but not being able to see them; or maybe the worst thing was knowing her family didn't care one bit about this wedding, and that Jeralee might be spiteful enough to try to ruin it. Or maybe the worst thing was her desperation, both to get it over with, and to escape the prison of her childhood home.

But the woman in the mirror felt none of that desperation. She looked calm, cool even, her eyes bright and steady, her hands—trembled just the faintest bit, she perceived as she held them up to the mirror to brush back one of the golden curls that lay in artistic disarray over her shoulders. Her hands betrayed her as the time dragged slowly on and she waited for the knock on the door that would summon her to her future.

And then, the summons came sooner than she expected. Alzine flung open the door to admit Jeralee, dressed in a gown the duplicate of her own.

Sarianna screamed and she leapt at Jeralee, and she didn't remember doing either, only her hands thrusting out, grabbing, pulling. She heard a tear, material giving—oh, God, not *her* gown—and then she looked at her hand where a long piece of muslin had materialized in her palm. Jeralee was sobbing in Alzine's reluctant arms.

Sarianna reached out again and pulled the satin from around Jeralee's shoulders, pulled the skirt, the bows, the lace. Pulled Jeralee's hair, without ever knowing quite what she was doing.

Why was Jeralee crying? she wondered. Why was she shrieking and running from the room?

"She has another dress," she heard herself say to Alzine. "She has that birthday dress, that beautiful birthday dress. She can wear that; make her put that on, Alzine." She didn't recognize her voice.

Alzine looked wildly from her to the door, trying to decide whom to succor first. "You stay right dere, Miss Sarianna, don' move now; what she done was bad, and you is right to be angry, but . . . don' move, hear? I be right back. . . ." She edged uncertainly out of the room.

Sarianna didn't move. The Sarianna in the mirror, she moved. She went back where she belonged, beyond the mirror, into that other life that she had been preparing for these last several days.

It seemed to her that she couldn't move. She was the statue, and the mirror image was real.

It was a mistake, she thought, all a mistake. Maybe she had dreamt everything; Jeralee was really the bride, and it was she who had dressed herself in the disastrous duplicate gown. Very likely she had imagined the whole thing.

Or else she was going mad.

Alzine came running back into the room. "I found Miss Vesta; she gonna take care of dat viper of a daughter, de she-devil. How you be, Miss Sarianna?"

"I'm all right," Sarianna said, and now she recognized her voice. It seemed normal, lodged in her throat and not coming from somewhere outside of herself.

"Any minute dey is gonna call fo' you—you sure you all right?" Alzine's warm brown eyes were misty with concern. Miss Sarianna didn't look right, didn't sound right. That cursed Miss Jeralee, trying to spoil things. Like they hadn't been spoiling things for years for Miss Sarianna. But never no more, she vowed. Now she knew; she would take care of Miss Sarianna right and tight. Miss Jeralee and Miss Vesta would nevr hurt her again.

"I'm ready," Sarianna said just at the very moment her father rapped on the door. Alzine admitted him, and he stood in the door frame and waited for her to move.

"What in hell did you do to Jeralee?" he hissed as she came into the hallway. There was no admiration in his eyes, no pride in his heart for her. *She* had done something to Jeralee; she had not been the victim.

It was as if she were in a place where everything was backward and upside down. Maybe, she thought whimsically, it was a last-ditch effort to drive her crazy. Maybe they were desperate to keep her exactly where she had been her whole life and were willing to use any means to accomplish that end.

Her father didn't touch her as they walked together down the hall and through the connecting doors that led to the ballroom wing.

"We are so well rid of you," Rex went on roughly. "God, I can't wait, I cannot wait until Rensell takes you away from here. I can't live with this chaos, Sarianna, with your impotent jealousy and destructive ways. Don't ever try to come back, my dear. There will never be another place for you here once you give up the one you have now."

"It's my dearest wish," Sarianna said stonily, her glazed eyes on her shoes as she paced down the hallway with her father, her eyes seeing only the movement of her skirt as her legs propelled her toward the ballroom staircase.

"At that," Rex continued, "you've created quite a sensation;

everyone has come to witness the spectacle of *you* marrying the man who should have been Jeralee's. It's rather amusing as long as you don't think of the repercussions, and how much of a story they are going to make out of it for God knows how long. Well, that's as may be. I suppose they may conclude that Rensell is deficient, too, if he wants you for a wife."

She felt his knife-edged words prickling all over her skin, unforgivable words, never to be recanted, always to be between them. "Or they may conclude that Mr. Rensell made the right choice," she said stiffly. "I suppose you think that no one has ever noticed Jeralee's drawbacks, that everyone sees her as perfect, especially next to me? I'd wonder about that, dear Father. You might do well to watch her sometime with your neighbors' eyes. You might see something that will remove the blindfolds."

The door was just ahead of them, and she sensed an anger in him that only wished to push her through it and, if he could, down the stairs to her demise so that she would haunt him no longer.

He held the door for her, and she swept through onto the balcony. Below her, two dozen guests and more waited, their avid eyes scanning the balcony every now and again to try to catch a glimpse of her.

"Well, Sarianna," Rex said, his expression unyielding.

"Father. Don't exert yourself trying to find something pleasant to say. I think we understand each other. I will join you downstairs in a moment." She watched, her eyes glimmering with tears, as he turned away from her and made his way down the steep curved staircase without another word and was welcomed into the congenial fold of his neighbors as he stepped down into the room.

Her tears fell. They understood each other. She understood nothing. She never had, and she had never felt as isolated from everyone in her life.

No one saw Sarianna. She waited in the shadows and she did not know for what. Suddenly, behind her, Jeralee whispered, "Aren't you the little bitch? A regular she-wolf, Sarianna."

She turned her head slightly, and she could just see Jeralee in the door frame and the skirt of the warm ivory dress that she had so coveted not one week ago.

"Father thinks it's your fault," Jeralee said mockingly. "I believe you requested I attend you."

"Had I?" Sarianna countered coolly, gathering her scattered wits and blinking away her tears. "What a mistake; I thought you would mind your manners enough not to try to trip me. But that's open for debate now. Perhaps you could precede me and signal to your father that I am ready to begin?"

"*My* father will be happy to know about your feelings in the matter," Jeralee retorted. "Don't think I won't try to get to you anyway, Sarianna. You've taken what was to have been mine."

"You're right, the key word is *was*, Jeralee. Remember, all of Sawny is watching. You wouldn't want to do anything to disgrace the Broydon name."

"Nothing overt," Jeralee concurred nastily and pushed her way out from behind Sarianna so that she stood poised on the topmost step of the staircase. There, everyone saw *her*, and the conversation languished as a thrum of guitar strings began.

Jeralee began her slow descent, milking every moment of being the momentary center of attention, regretting that she could not have gotten away with wearing the duplicate gown, and relishing what might have happened had she resisted goading Sarianna with it. Her restless eyes searched the guests who had now lined up on the left side of the staircase as she walked down. Right below, Rex waited. Beyond him, near the makeshift altar, Pierce sat playing the bittersweet music of some bygone era.

Between Pierce and her father, Cade waited, tall, dark and forbidding in severe black broadcloth that was relieved only by his stark white shirt. His eyes were raised, and Jeralee knew he was not looking for her. And she sensed exactly when Sarianna moved to the topmost step. There was even a sigh of admiration as she stepped down once, twice, and then began her own descent in time to the music.

Suddenly Jeralee's part was over. She hated it. She hated them all looking at Sarianna as if she were perfect and totally unexpected. *She* had looked a damn lot better in that gown; that gown had been *made* for her. Sarianna was a stick, a pale, mop-topped stick, and nothing could save her, nothing. Resentfully, she walked to the opposite side of the room to wait now with Vesta, who had slipped in through the service door entrance.

Sarianna watched her carefully to make sure Jeralee was well out of her way before she continued downward. She saw white faces, none of whom she could identify. She saw Alzine by the service door, her face transported. She saw Rex awaiting her at the bottom step.

And finally she saw Cade, or maybe she had been loath to meet his eyes first, she didn't know. But in that instant contact, she found all her answers in a way she hadn't thought possible. In his eyes was all the caring and appreciation she had ever wanted, and the total, complete concentration on *her,* and in his expression, she read his determination to make it all that it seemed at that very moment.

She didn't know when she reached the bottom step; she only saw that suddenly Cade was there, pushing Rex aside, shaking off his hand and protestation: "I'm supposed to escort her, Rensell."

"No," he said, looking deep into Sarianna's huge sad eyes, "no, you don't give a damn about Sarianna, Broydon. I'm the one who wants her. I'll take Sarianna to the threshold of her new life." He held out his arm, and she took it with a feather-light touch. The guests fell back as they began walking down the aisle toward the dais and the minister, and then they crowded around to hear every word.

She supposed she was aware of it, but the only things she noticed were disjointed, odd: Jeralee right in the front line of spectators to their vows; her father nowhere around; the glow of the candles the minister handed them as he met them. The light music behind them. Cade's heat, his warmth, his raging anger. His voice was so calm as he recited the vows in such a way that no one could mistake his desire for this union—not even she. Her own voice tremulous with tears, sounded childish in her ears, not nearly as strong as his, not as sure. Not nearly. The minister's voice, intoning prayers, came from far away.

She rather thought she was more aware of Jeralee than anything else, wary that Jeralee might shove her into the minister or grab a candle and do something disastrous with it.

And finally she heard the binding words, "I now pronounce you husband and wife," and she knew nothing Jeralee could do would hurt her any more.

Cade turned her toward him and just drank in her ethereal beauty as the minister introduced them as Mr. and Mrs. Cade Rensell. Her knees gave slightly, but to the crowd it looked as if she were leaning into him, filled with the ultimate joy of becoming his wife.

Cade slipped his arms around her. "Kiss me, Sarianna. Show them we were lovers, Sarianna, and that we will be lovers when we leave here, so that they can spend their nights imagining how it is for us. Sarianna!''

She heard him. She lifted her face to his, close to tears once again, inviting his lips, in spite of all her feelings, inviting the lie that all of Sawny would remember for as long as they talked about her.

His lips touched hers tentatively at first, and then with masterful assurance as he delved into her open mouth and took her with his tongue, showing them, all the gaping Sawnians, what a sensual creature Sarianna was.

She didn't expect it; she heard voices behind them—dismay, shock at how thoroughly he was possessing her mouth—and she didn't care. She was drowning, pulled by an irresistible force that gave her no quarter. He wanted them to see, to talk, to feel the kiss, the emotion, and finally the guilt.

She wrapped her arms around him fiercely and gave herself to him, mouth to mouth, body to body, deliberately and because she couldn't help it, and she reveled in their consternation at this overt display.

She heard Jeralee somewhere behind her screaming, "I can't take this!" and felt the gentle touch of the minister's hand as he reminded her—and Cade—where they were and what they were supposed to be doing.

She heard the murmured disapprovals as Cade thoughtfully maneuvered himself to her left side and tucked her arm in the crook of his. "Brazen," someone whispered. "Arrogant." "Indecent." "Shameless," a feminine voice hissed, perhaps, Sarianna thought, in envy.

Cade drew her with him, and the crowd around them separated to let them pass. Vesta threw open the formal dining room doors and beckoned them in.

The room behind her looked so festive, with satin bows and flowers everywhere, and a bower built over and around a towering bride's cake in the center of the room. The food was arranged on tables to be chosen, once again, and taken at a guest's leisure and whim to the linen-covered table of his choice. It felt almost real, Sarianna thought, as she inspected the beautifully decorated tables with their piles of snowy linen, white flowers and satin bows whose lavish ties floated to the floor.

Vesta's choice of menu was to serve everything: platters of ham, turkey and venison vied with baskets of biscuits, breads, corn cakes, and platters of thin pancakes over which a guest could pour a variety of dressings, fruits and syrups; there were steamed vegetables, fried vegetables, cold vegetables. There were oysters and shrimp, crabcakes and soups. Bowls were heaped with fruit—a table piled high with Sylvia's pies and tarts and cakes. There was a table laden with potables: wine, whiskey, jugs of coffee, tea, lemonade, champagne. It was a display of Jeralee's birthday party on a more lavish, almost tasteless, scale. It was too much, as if everything had been thrown on the tables with no forethought as to complementary food and wine.

It could only be interpreted as "here it is, this is the best I could do for *her*," and Sarianna felt it to the marrow of her bones. It wasn't even the final insult; she truly believed her father had earned the right to that. But it was a devastating slap in her face in front of her father's Sawnian friends, people she had known all her life who had lived by her father's perception of her. The triumph of her being chosen by an eligible man had been turned into a vulgar joke.

She touched her ring; it was beautiful, thick, with a delicate chased design all over it, and it was *real*, the only thing about this celebration that was, she thought, fingering the incised decoration. She had been stupid to think anything concerning *her* would be treated with legitimacy in her father's house.

Their Sawny neighbors had followed them slowly into the dining room, and she could hear the little squeals of disparagement as the matrons inspected the tables; the husbands went right for the liquor, and their offspring crowded around either Jeralee or Cade.

She felt outside it all again, invisible to everyone but Cade, whose restless eyes constantly searched for her, and she just as consistently ignored him. It was almost too much to expect that his feeling for her wouldn't change under the pressure of such negativism surrounding her. What if finally, ultimately, he came to pity her?

She moved among her guests, accepting the cool and measured congratulations as they were offered, and tried valiantly to make her way to Cade's side. But Vesta intercepted her. "What do you think, Sarianna?"

She looked at Vesta's smug expression and muddied eyes, and she said, "You set a bountiful table, Vesta." It was all she could say to preserve appearances and not reveal her utter humiliation which she knew Vesta was aching to see.

"Thank you," Vesta said, her gaze swinging to Jeralee, surrounded by her grown childhood friends. "I knew I could depend on your appreciating it." She moved away, and again Sarianna was left alone—the unwanted guest at her wedding.

But not for long. As she reached for a glass of champagne from the tray that Eon was circulating, Jeralee approached her, took her own glass and lifted it to her. "He really married you," she said in awed tones. "I'm really amazed, Sarianna. In fact, I'm dissolving with curiosity. Everyone's talking, you know—they really expected it to be me."

"I rather think *you* thought it would be you," Sarianna said dryly, putting down her glass.

"Or you decided the minute I pointed him out to you that you *were* going to ruin things for me," Jeralee accused her.

"Really? As if Cade were some mewling idiot that couldn't make up his own mind about things, Jeralee? Or was that what you wanted— broad shoulders with no brains? Someone, in other words, with attributes to match your own?" Sarianna turned away, and Jeralee stamped after her.

"Don't you turn your back to me after such an insult!" she screamed.

Sarianna kept walking and felt her veil catch, pull and finally tear away from the circlet around her hair.

She whirled on Jeralee, whose foot was caught in the hem of the netting. "I'm so sorry"—Jeralee pouted—"really I am. I stepped just a little too fast to try to catch up with you."

"Please—I'll pick it up." The voice was Cade's, and he knelt down next to Jeralee and picked up the fragile net which, as he held it up, they could all see now had a big hole in it.

He smiled at Jeralee, that unpleasant smile. "It was obviously an accident," he said, as he rolled the net up hand over hand and compressed it so he could put it in his pocket.

"Yes," Jeralee said, "it *was* an accident." She sent a meaningful look at Sarianna, and Sarianna looked at Cade, reading instantly the imperceptible shake of his head.

"Of course it was an accident," she concurred, taking her cue from Cade. "Jeralee wouldn't consciously do anything to spoil my reception, I know that."

Cade looked disgusted at her dissembling; Jeralee looked smug. "Truly, I am very happy for you," she said, putting her hand with

187

seeming impulsiveness on Cade's arm.

He gave her that quick unpleasant smile and patted her hand. Jeralee turned away, and there was the most horrendous tearing sound that stopped her dead. She reached down, jerked a handful of her skirt away and turned at the same time, her eyes flaring with anger, to pinpoint Cade's foot placed heavily on the hem of her dress and a huge triangle of the ivory material hanging down over his leg.

"Oh!" she shrieked, and pulled backward, only to hear the dreaded ripping sound as the skirt detached from the bodice of the dress and fell to the floor. "You bastard!" she raged, "you did that deliberately, you . . . you—"

Cade shrugged. "A man's foot can get caught awfully easy in a lady's long dress, Miss Jeralee," he said in his flattest drawl, making no attempt to mollify her as she gathered an armful of the skirt in an attempt to cover her visible petticoat.

"Oh! Really! You stupid man. A gentleman wouldn't stand near enough to a lady to get his foot entangled in *anything*," she shouted. "But everyone knows what *you* are, Mr. Rensell."

Cade smiled that same flashing unpleasant smile again. "I'd surely like to hear exactly what I am, Miss Jeralee," he drawled with a thin thread of impatience underlying his words.

But they only fanned her fury, and she didn't hear the threat. "I'll tell you, Mr. Rensell; I'm the only one who will tell you. You're the man who walked out on his father and came back to show off, and everyone here knows you've married a pale imitation of my mother's sister becaues you couldn't win her for yourself. That's what you *are*, Mr. Rensell, a pale imitation—of a Sawny Islander, and a man. And you can do no better than Sarianna. No better."

He felt the shock of her words hit behind him, and a murmuring swept through the guests—approval? Denial? He couldn't tell, but again as always, the insult, the belittling was directed solely at Sarianna; and he thought that Jeralee didn't know what a real opponent was, but she was about to find out.

"Seems to me, Miss Jeralee, the only pale imitation in this house is your mother, coming into Sarianna's mother's house and trying to take her place and warm her side of the bed. But she can't do it, Miss Jeralee; she doesn't have the beauty and the kindness—and above all, Jeralee—she doesn't have Sarianna for her daughter."

Jeralee heard that and her jaw dropped as if he had dealt her a staggering blow: to compare Sarianna to her! To choose the impaired when he could have had the perfect—it was too much for her to comprehend. And he defended her—he *defended* the fact that he had made that choice. Her impotent rage left her no outlet.

"Oh!" she shrieked again; she couldn't win with him. He was impervious to her insults, and she couldn't claw his face as she so dearly wanted to do. She knew what she could do—she could punish Sarianna, who was the cause of it all. If it weren't for Sarianna, she would be the one Cade was defending. If it weren't for Sarianna, this would be the most glorious day of her life. Everything came down to Sarianna and what she had done to her, Jeralee.

She reached behind her and grasped the first thing at hand—a platter of fish aspic that she hurled right at Sarianna. The platter fell to the floor, the aspic landed with a satisfying little whoosh on the front of Sarianna's gown, and Jeralee thought that only half paid Sarianna back for destroying her own duplicate dress. The cold potato soup was for Cade ruining her gown, and she grabbed for it with relish and poured it all over Sarianna.

Sarianna just stood there as if she were part of some mad nightmare. Cade couldn't even defend her without disastrous repercussions, she thought, her sense of unreality heightening. The fight wasn't between her and Jeralee; it was between Jeralee and Cade. Cade stepped up behind Jeralee and obligingly poured an entire pitcher of lemonade all over her.

She lost all power of speech as the sticky sugar liquid dripped into her eyes and soaked into her dress, and everyone crowded around to watch every moment of her distress and disgrace. She wiped the residue out of her eyes with the sleeve of her dress, and when she finally looked up, she saw that both Sarianna and Cade were gone.

13

Savannah!

She had never seen so much activity, so much vibrancy; she had never been away from Sawny in her life, and the accelerated pace of Savannah entranced her. Her oncoming future there dismayed her.

They traveled by hired hack from the ferry landing, with minimal possessions—only that which Alzine had been able to fit in one trunk in the half hour it took to clean up Sarianna and find Ben to order the carriage. Pierce remained behind, and Sarianna could still see his whimsical expression as he came out of the dining room to bid them good-bye. "I believe they are celebrating the fact that Sarianna is gone," he said plainly, and Cade shook his hand and clapped him on the shoulder. No other comment was necessary. "I'll see you in Savannah," he promised, and kissed Sarianna on the cheek before he returned to the party.

It was all one in that house; whoever was a guest was infected, Sarianna thought later, her great liking for Pierce diminishing somewhat in the face of that flat farewell.

Nonetheless, not even Cade could have adequately described the delight of the city as they bowled down the long tree-shaded streets that were crowded with *close,* iron-ornamented houses surrounded by verdant gardens that beckoned to even a passing stranger. And there were streets full of side-by-side row houses, with beautifully detailed pedimented doors and windows that were shaded by thick ancient trees planted right into the walkway, and there were larger, clapboard houses sitting high on stone basements, crammed together one to one down still another street. People strolled beside carriages with a purposeful destination. There were shops along the way, and churches, the custom house, and the Savannah Theatre, an array of possibilities that Sarianna had never known existed.

She was rather discomfitted by Cade's indulgent expression as he watched her assimilating her new and temporary home.

She licked her lips and tried to avoid his eyes.

"I promise you'll get used to it," he said lazily, "and very soon."

She made a nervous movement with her hand; she did not know what to do. Now that the marriage was a fact and she really was as far from Sawny as she could reasonably travel in one day, she did not know how to say to Cade that she was sorry and she had really intended to walk away from him all along. In fact, Savannah exhilarated and frightened her both so much she was afraid to take one step toward independence. Her emotions felt so fragile, she thought she might dribble away into a useless little puddle altogether, and she thought that Cade knew it.

She looked down at her limp hands which rested in the lap of the blue, watered-silk dress in which Cade had first seen her. Her hands were fine—no nerves there. Alzine was beside her, as she should have been, her brown eyes liquid with concern for her, while Cade sat opposite, with what there was of their luggage piled beside him, and she couldn't for the life of her fix on his feelings or what he was thinking.

It was easier to watch the scenery. She had determined that, even as they boarded the ferry that would take them across to the mainland, and she had kept her eyes averted almost the whole trip. But this Savannah! It seemed magical to her; she could make some kind of new life here, and maybe she could even do it with Cade. She could forget Jeralee and Vesta and cut away that piece of her heart that still wanted to love her father. Maybe here, she thought, she could finally become whole. Maybe here she could forget the insults and knife-edged words. Maybe here the distressing resemblance to her mother would blur to a shadowy similarity, and Cade would never mistake one for the other.

The hack drew up before a block of row houses that were each confusingly similar but for the shutters on one, an ornate door on the other, or some delicate ironwork on the balusters of the third. Each had a high stoop with the steps turning to the right so that the entrance of the houses faced a little balcony, and they each had two windows on the entry floor and three on the succeeding two floors. There were no side gardens, or front gardens. There were only the everlasting thick-trunked, ancient trees guarding the houses, shielding them, providing shade and frontal greenery.

One of those houses belonged to Cade. "This is Malverne Row, Sarianna, and the third house from the corner there is ours."

She turned her head to stare at it, but there was nothing to differentiate it from the others except that it was white and had the dark shutters on the windows of the parlor and upper floors.

Cade climbed out, paid the driver, and ran up the steps to summon his household help. The first to the door was the elderly housekeeper, Amanda, who unabashedly held out her arms and hugged Cade, and behind her came the butler, Herod, who bore himself with the same stately grace as Eon. Almost instantly there was a flurry of figures emerging from a door underneath the stoop, swarming around the carriage, pulling out the luggage, and assisting Alzine.

Cade came back for her, holding out his hand to ease her way out of the carriage. "Ours," he had said. It didn't feel like hers; it felt like nobody's.

She followed him up the stairs and into the entrance hall. Her eyes widened with admiration of the high-ceilinged hall with its thick moldings that were painted white and looked like vanilla cake. The floors were dark and covered with rich oriental carpets, and two stately columns divided the hall from the stairway anteroom to the second floor. To her right was the front parlor, access to which was through a sliding door, also painted white.

Amanda took her hands as she came in the door, and bent forward to kiss her. She was a little old lady, dry and wrinkled and the color of a raisin, with knowing dark eyes and a prim mouth. She stood a foot shorter than Sarianna, and two feet taller in dignity. She felt Sarianna's distress, and her strong dry hands tightened around Sarianna's. She led her into the formal parlor where a huge Turkish carpet covered most of the floor and a gilded mirror hung between the two front windows. An opulent glass chandelier was suspended from a rosette in the ceiling, and small sofas and wing chairs were placed before a thickly carved marble fireplace to insure comfort and conversation.

Sarianna sat on a gold-covered couch with undulating arms and back, and Amanda clapped her hands.

Instantly a maid appeared with a tray which she set on a tripod table that she brought forward from beside a wing chair.

Where was Cade? Sarianna looked around her anxiously while Amanda poured tea and noticed her frenzied movements, her agitation. And where was Alzine, and what was this place—and *what had she done?*

She took the cup that Amanda offered her and took a reassuring sip. Tea was normal, a ritual that calmed the nerves and settled the stomach. Tea was warm and helped her trembling hand. Where *was* Cade? Amanda said nothing, sensing her distress and fear.

Sarianna drank her tea and surreptitiously looked around the room. It was a lovely room, well proportioned and not quite square. There was a bookcase and desk at the far end, and still another of those curve-backed sofas nearby, and a chair beside the desk itself to be pulled forward as needed.

It was a comforting room, not awesomely elaborate, but still formal enough for entertaining. But it wasn't nearly as spacious as Bredwood. She wondered how Savannah women managed in their hoopskirts in rooms of this size. She wondered a lot of things to keep herself from thinking of the enormity of the day and what she had done and what had been said to her that could never be redeemed.

Then Alzine appeared, and some semblance of her rational world reasserted itself. Alzine looked at Amanda questioningly and Amanda nodded. Alzine held out her hand to Sarianna. "You come with me now, Miss Sarianna. We going to get you to bed and you rest fo' dis afternoon. You done had a day to wear yo' brains away, and you got to give yo'self some rest. Come, Miss Sarianna. Dis be one beautiful old house, so different from what you been used to. Maybe," she added, as she led Sarianna into the stairwell hallway, where the stairway curved gracefully upward to the second floor, "dis change be fo' de good. You didn't need no Miss Jeralee tellin' you what's what fo' de rest of yo' life. You didn't need Miss Vesta actin' like she never heard of yo' mama, and you didn't need dat Mr. Rex makin' out like dey was always somethin' wrong with you. You hear, Miss Sarianna? We done finished with dat now. Fix dat in yo' mind, child. We finished with dat business now."

Alzine's words rolled over her. She heard the sense of them, she knew they were true, but her ineffable sense of loss totally disarmed her. She felt adrift, alone. Cade was nowhere around, and she couldn't understand why he had abandoned her already.

Alzine led her to the front room on the second floor and threw open the door. "Dis Mr. Cade's room, and now you, Miss Sarianna. Ain't it somethin'?"

Sarianna peeked in. The marble fireplace in this room, which was directly opposite the door, was fronted by two balloon-backed chairs face to face with a small tea table in front of them. On the floor, as below, was a large Brussels carpet, and on the far wall beside the fireplace, she saw as she pushed the door open a bit more, was a highboy with beautifully polished handles. She ventured still farther into the room, and the door bumped against what she saw was a bureau washstand with a marble top and teardrop pulls.

In the ell of this room, which was the size of the parlor and hallway together, stood a burnished walnut bedstead, with an elaborate carved and molded headboard that stood, she reckoned, almost as tall as the ceiling. Against the wall that backed the hallway was a matching wardrobe with the same height and molded decorations, and beside the bed, by the window, was a small matching lift top commode. A small tufted medallion-backed sofa sat in front of the two windows that were not in the ell, and there were pots of greenery in these windows which seemed to get a lot of sun.

There were interior shutters as well as the casement of the windows, and Alzine began pulling these out and fastening the hooks. "You is gonna rest, Miss Sarianna, and I don' care how het up you is."

Sarianna sighed. "I won't argue."

"You wouldn't win," Alzine said, pushing her onto the soft bed. "Close yo' eyes; you don' even have to undress yo' self."

Sarianna stared at the ceiling, her eyes following the line of the thick corner moldings all around the room. Hypnotic, doing that. Restful. It filled her thoughts. "I don't think I even have the stamina," she said.

The room darkened; her eyes closed.

Alzine settled herself in one of the chairs by the fireplace to await Cade's arrival.

She surfaced from an ocean of despair that threatened to drown her, and sat bolt upright in a strange bed in the middle of the day.

Dona—Dona had been in her dreams. Dona, she thought, was the beginning, the middle and the end. Her mother would haunt her forever, the crux of everything that had ever happened to her—her father's obsession, Cade's youthful indiscretion, her own repression, and finally, ultimately, the reason why Cade had been adamant about marrying her. Jeralee wasn't far wrong, she thought in her dreams; no other reason made any sense.

Her indescribable sense of loss was magnified by Jeralee's words and her father's rejection. How could she ever hope to remake her life when all that had gone before had been a denial of all that had made her what she was?

Or maybe she was, in reality, Dona. Maybe if she were like Dona, Cade could come to love her, too.

And she didn't know later when she woke whether that thought was the nightmare or the reality.

Cade sat watching her at the far end of the bed, his arms propped up against the footboard, his jacket hanging on the opposite end, and his face expressionless.

She was so very beautiful, even in sleep, he thought, and she had automatically positioned herself on the side of the bed toward the window, which would put him at her left. The notion made him smile, though he had found little to smile at in this day full of disaster. The only saving grace was that Sarianna was his, her slender body slept in his bed in his house, and her father would never touch her again.

And how, he wondered, did he salve the wounds she had been dealt this day? How did he take her to his bed and arouse the only part of her he could reach and show her the foundation they could build a life upon? How did he do that when her own kin had shattered her soul and he was the stranger whose motives were suspect?

Well, he thought, he had surely destroyed Rex Broydon's little world, but that little triumph might cost him Sarianna, a thought he had never considered when he had confronted Rex with his emotional blackmail. Damn. But then, there might never have been Sarianna had he not gone back to Sawny. How goddamned circular, how frustratingly just: He might lose her because he married her. Goddamned fate. If he had just left her alone, even, if he had risked nothing and taken Jeralee as his bride, if he had said no to everything and just walked away from Sawny alone, Sarianna would not be left picking up the shattered pieces of her insular life on Sawny.

Oh, she was so much better off now, he castigated himself. She had no family at all now and the satisfaction of knowing her father hated her because she knew how deep his obsession cut into his soul. She was in a strange place in a strange city surrounded by nothing familiar, not even him—thank God for Alzine. Alzine understood the truth of it. Sarianna might have died from neglect in that charnel house, she might have died young, unloved and disparaged, and she would not have been any better off than she was now had he picked up and left her there.

He believed it. She was born to be loved, and he was born to be her lover. There was no doubt in his mind. When he thought what he might have left her to, he knew there could have been no other choice. Sarianna was his; he had known it the moment he laid eyes on her, and if she had stayed in Bredwood, there would have been exactly the same backlash against her over some other man, or some other imagined usurpation, and the end result would have been the same: None of them would have been happy until she finally died.

In his mind he saw that as the end result of the ravening envy they felt against her. They never would admit it either, and Rex had encouraged it to keep Sarianna by his side forever. It was altogether gothic, what had gone on at Bredwood, and the wonder was, he thought, that Sarianna had had the courage to even accept him and leave.

And now there were the ramifications to be dealt with: her broken heart, the fact she had used him every bit as much as he had used her, and finally the fact that he wanted her beside him—forever.

"Hello," she said, as her eyes focused and she saw him, and it seemed for one moment out of time natural to see him there, watching her. It was much darker in the room than could be accounted for by the closed shutters, and her heart accelerated as she thought she might have slept away the day into the next night.

She had been weary, right down to her bones, and unable to cope with the whole of what had happened. And it didn't go away, not even in her deepest sleep. She wondered if she had the strength to just push it aside and go on.

"Sarianna." His voice was grave, and it scared her a little. She had the stunning thought that maybe her part was over now—that it had been enough for him to take her away from Rex, and that was all he wanted. It was a heady thought that played into her idea that she would want to leave him once they had reached Savannah, and it scared her to death that it might be true. "Can we talk?"

She started to shake, and she nodded her head rather than speaking, lest he hear the desperate uncertainty in her voice.

"It was a damn hard day for you," he said. "Are you all right?"

"I don't know." She bit her lip. He sounded so concerned, so *there.* "I don't believe I told you how much I appreciated your defending me."

"Who wouldn't defend you against those vultures?" he demanded violently. "Damn it, Sarianna—"

"I can't—" she whispered. "I just can't go over it any more than I've done already in my mind, in my heart. I don't understand it, and I never did; and it was worse this time . . . horrible—"

"Because of *me,*" Cade said forcefully, leaning forward now and grasping her hand hard. "Because of *me,* not because of you."

"All right. I believe that. I even thought about that. They hate you. They hated my mother. They hate me. How can anyone live with such hate?"

"I don't know. They punished *you,* but that's over now, Sarianna. You don't have to do anything you don't want to."

"I don't know what I want. I feel blank, like a torn-up piece of paper that someone pasted back together. There's nothing written on it, and whoever has the pen can't think of a word to say."

He felt jolted by the depth of her sorrow. "Maybe not today, Sarianna, but there are good words to be written on that page, about you. Maybe about this marriage, if you can find a way to give it a chance. But not today. No one could ask that of you today. What I want to ask you is, what do you want me to do for you today?"

She felt a glimmer of hope. He had been so strong for her, he had married her against violent opposition, and he had—were she to allow herself to remember it—aroused her and made her *feel* a most undeniable pleasure. He had held her in his arms, and she had felt some small, small measure of the affection long denied her. Perhaps, she thought, all she needed was the comfort and warmth he could offer tonight.

She swallowed her tears; she had cried enough with him already. Tears did not mend broken hearts; but the words she needed caught

197

in her throat, and her tears spoke for her anyway.

He moved down toward her side of the bed and took her in his arms, tasted her tears, and let her cry.

The next day it was better, and the day after that better still. There were places to go and things to do, a wardrobe to buy, streets to explore, and a whole city the like of which she could never have imagined. Cade wanted her well dressed, and she found a dressmaker and spent hours over pattern books and bolts of cloth with Alzine by her side steaming and muttering how she could have done better for no money at all.

As the days sped by, she felt less like a cipher and more like herself, a competent young married woman, and often she would rub her ring as if it were some kind of talisman. Cade had been kind, and he had been good enough to sleep in the guest bedroom; but she knew the time would come for him to assert his right to sleep in his own bed— and more.

He was waiting until she was ready, and she did not know, as she raced here and there to various appointments, throughout the city, whether she would ever be ready.

And yet she had been ready to assume the duties of a young matron. Amanda immediately deferred to her the moment she showed she was ready to take over the household duties, and she learned very quickly how easy it was to run this minimal upkeep town house, and how convenient it was to live in the midst of the city.

But a part of her still yearned for the country life she had known. Even though there was a rear garden and a carriage house beyond, there was barely room for a vegetable garden, let alone a flower garden. There was no room to roam, or to ride, no gracious verandah to shield her from the midday sun; and there were hardly any major decisions to make about the ongoing simple menu that was catered in the city. Cade had one set of china and very little in the way of table decoration. It had been after all a bachelor establishment of a man who rarely entertained.

There wasn't that much to do. Alzine took care of her, and Amanda directed the several young servants who comprised the housekeeping staff: one cook and one helper, Herod the butler, and Owen in the stable who cared for the horses and drove the carriage whenever Mr.

Cade required it.

It was a meager staff compared to that at Bredwood, but it was a pleasure to be in a position to direct them, to use her skills. No one commented on her wrong hand, and she learned very fast that when she was the mistress, she could do whatever she wanted without creating the kind of sensation she had caused at Bredwood. She found it curious at first, and then later it made her furious that she had suffered so much from their viperish need to tear her down.

A week later, Pierce came to dinner, having only just returned from Bredwood.

"Well, it was some party," he told them over a glass of wine in the second parlor. "By the end of it, that Gilmartin son and the two Rudleys were on the verge of making the whole thing into a food fight. I don't believe Miss Jeralee ever recovered for the whole of the time I stayed there. You destroyed her, Cade, saying she had Miss Sarianna to live up to when everyone knows she hated Miss Sarianna. A wonderful stroke. She didn't stop talking about it for days."

He sipped his wine, forbearing to tell them that he had been her active listener and only because he himself had been searching for some sign of the inherited magic that made Sarianna so desirable in Jeralee. He didn't know yet whether he had found it.

"And that Rex. Oh, he is one; he is gracious as he can be, but with just that little bit of him removed from company. You don't ever get to know that man, and I tell you, that is dangerous when you accept hospitality from a man. He was devastated by the whole scene. He wasn't unkind enough to take Vesta to task for it, but he was broken up, he surely was." More than that, Pierce thought. Sarianna's defection had destroyed him. After the reception, he had taken to his study, and he had had a bottle to keep him company the entire week. He wondered if Sarianna were to know this whether she would want to return to Bredwood, and for a moment he wavered about playing God and putting the decision in her hands—in spite of what he had seen and heard.

And then he went on, "And Miss Vesta was beside herself trying to figure out what those damned guests were going to be saying about her and Jeralee. It's a shame when your neighbors come to help you celebrate an occasion and are only hoping something nasty will happen that they can gossip about. You're well rid of the lot of them, Miss Sarianna; it was not a pleasant several days following the ceremony."

"And why did you stay on?" Sarianna inquired. She didn't want to know—it was just polite conversation.

"Miss Jeralee asked me to," Pierce said, smiling at her. "How could I turn down a beautiful woman?"

He didn't know why he thought she would want him tonight. He wasn't even sure he would ever again see the impish, voluptuous Sarianna who had enticed him to her bed knowing nothing of the sensual delights that awaited her there. She had been cool and attentive as if she were standing back from herself and watching what she was doing in order not to make some misstep for which she might be called to account.

He was amused to watch her gain some degree of confidence over these two weeks. He gave her freedom, never intruding on plans, or hovering over her like some concerned parent, and at dinner she was full of fresh observations and a new excitement about things he had already come to take for granted. The talk was always topical, and he never questioned her about what had happened at Bredwood except that first night. But he was pleased that she was looking happier, less strained and more energetic, and he thought the evening of Pierce's visit and artless disclosures about the events at Bredwood that this might be the night she would need him.

But she clearly was not expecting him. She was surprised to hear the brisk knock on her door, and even more startled as he stalked in, his lion-face in place and his demeanor utterly forbidding. And she knew how she looked, too. She had become too comfortable with the routine they had established in these first weeks. She had grown used to having these hours before bedtime alone and unencumbered—by the propriety of her new clothes, or by him. She came to expect the freedom he had allowed her by day and by night. She spent those hours with her mind a blank, healing, not thinking beyond the next minutes, reflecting on the simple joys of the day she had spent, however she had spent it. She hadn't even been all that concerned to know, after the first days, what Cade was doing. She knew it had something to do with Haverhill, and those first days, she hadn't even wanted to know about that.

She had been so sure he would make no demands on her this soon.

And she knew what he saw when she opened the door. She was enfolded in a thin silk wrapper the color of her eyes, which trailed down to the floor and just covered her bare feet. And it didn't look as if she wore very much more. The silk clung to her torso, hugging her curves as she folded her arms around her waist, outlining her breasts and the long sumptuous line of her legs and thighs. When she turned to let him follow her into the room, he was entranced by the movement of her derrière beneath the thin silk that concealed virtually nothing.

He felt that immediate jolting shock of desire, and his expression turned darker.

She climbed into bed, into her favorite cross-legged position with her back up against the headboard, and regarded him with a wary curiosity.

He allowed himself to sit at the foot of the bed on her side, with his feet propped up on the side rail. He allowed himself to say, "I thought Pierce might have been a bit much for you tonight."

Sarianna shrugged to cover her ambivalent feelings about his revelations which she had still not sorted out in her own mind. Bredwood felt so distant, and her family like some characters she had read about in a book. "Pierce is a nice man," she said noncommittally. "I suppose he thought I might like to know that my going was not taken with the equanimity they wanted me to believe when they chased me away. And I am pleased to know that."

She paused, and then added, "I'm not sure I have any more feelings about it. *Do* I have any more feelings about it?" she asked, sending him an oblique look that was almost sultry.

"I expect you do," he said. "You could bury them so far inside you, it would take dynamite to blow them out. You could deny that you hate them every bit as much as they professed to hate you. Or you could be honest and try to go on from there."

"I hate them," she said promptly, "but when I think about it, I feel like it never happened to me, like it was something I read about. They've become as far away as figures in the wrong end of a telescope. It happened to someone else. It wasn't me. It *wasn't* me." She heard her voice rising, and she broke off abruptly and took a deep breath. "So it's not over, is it? I still feel pain."

"It's only been two and a half weeks," Cade pointed out. "You're getting stronger . . . you'll get better and better as time goes on. I won't let them hurt you again, I promise, Sarianna."

His words moved her; he hadn't tried to touch her. His words touched her. "I know," she said softly, and a small part of her wanted to reach out and touch *him*. It was startling to her that she felt that, when she thought she had no feeling left whatsoever. She turned the notion over in her mind as she waited for him to speak.

She wasn't sure what it was about him tonight. The harsh aspect was still there, but she sensed a kindness in him, and a leashed yearning. More than that, she felt herself responding to it, and she hadn't intended that.

He was still dressed as he had been for dinner, with the exception of his frock coat and tie, and she felt a keen awareness of him as a man even as he sat so casually at the foot of the bed. And she hadn't expected that either.

"It's time to go on," he said finally as she did not speak, and he saw just a momentary dart of fear cross her face.

"What does that mean?" she asked after a moment or two, but what she really wanted to ask was why things could not remain as they were now, with her nestling in the cocoon of the town house and the city environs, where nothing reminded her of anything and he was the perfect husband who never made any demands. But she couldn't ask for that. That was a dream that most certainly had to end, and she was scared that he was about to announce its imminent demise.

"It means that next month we will go to Haverhill." He watched her reaction, but she gave nothing away. "It's time to gauge the harvest, and I would like to be there. But apart from that, I need this month to refurbish the house as much as possible before you come. It's about a two-hour ride by horseback, and I will be going back and forth several times a week now that Pierce and I have settled the financial details and hired on a new overseer."

"That sounds fine," Sarianna said, her voice not giving away the depth of her relief. She even felt a wash of gratitude that he had thought of her comfort, and that she would be going back to the plantation life she so loved.

And soon—very soon.

"The other thing is," Cade went on and her heart dropped. She knew what was going to come next. "The other thing is, I want to move back into this bedroom."

"I see," she said after a long, long pause. "And that means with all

202

that entails?" she managed to ask, and how much those words cost her he would never know. Even she didn't know whether she wanted the answer to be yes—or no.

Neither did Cade; he hadn't expected she would welcome him into the bed with wide open arms, or with any enthusiasm, and he was feeling his way carefully through all the emotions he felt hovering in the air, first and foremost the explosiveness of the last two weeks. She couldn't be afraid of him, he thought. She just wasn't ready to take a new step forward yet—not yet, while he was aching to race ahead. That would gain him nothing, he knew, and he searched for a way to present it to her that would make it acceptable.

He said slowly, "It means I want to sleep with you, Sarianna." Her gaze flew to his, wide, startled, astonished he had phrased it so boldly. "And it may mean nothing more. I might be gambling it won't. But I want to share this bed with you."

His words held all the sensual power in the world. He didn't command her, and he didn't plead with her, and she was overwhelmed by his respect. Deep inside her a little tendril of sensual awareness uncurled and tentatively reached outward. She felt it, examined it, and felt breathless and excited by it all at once, and then scared all over again.

"It's your bed," she said finally, knowing her oblique answer gave him the permission he sought. She wasn't ready, and she didn't know if she would ever be ready for him—or she might be very ready a minute from now. She thought she hadn't wanted it, and her body denied it. Whatever she felt, her body wanted some contact.

She watched with impassive eyes as he got up and walked to the opposite side of the bed and lay down next to her.

You will sleep with me, he had said, and he slept beside her just as he had predicted; and she lay awake in a frenzy the entire night. Would she sleep on his left? she remembered him asking, and she lay to his left, frantic with feeling she had thought deeply submerged; and it drove everything else out of her mind. He slept, and she watched him and squiggled down into the cover next to him to assess the sensation of actually sharing a bed with someone—a man—*him.*

Finally she slept, and awakened with a jolt late in the morning to find Cade gone and a different atmosphere altogether in the room.

She saw immediately what it was—traces of Cade all over the place—a slightly open drawer in the highboy, the edge of a jacket peeking out of the wardrobe, beads of water on the washstand bureau. Oh, yes, Cade had been and gone, and she didn't know if she were reassured by how simply he had requested to stay and how easily he rested and then left her.

And what would tonight bring, she wondered as she dressed in a sturdy but lightweight walking gown made of crepe, with tiers of flounces on the skirt and as decoration on the sleeves; it was a practical brown with an ivory stripe running through it, and was relieved with touches of ivory lace at the undersleeve and rounded neck of the tightly fitting basque.

She did like how she looked, and how the ingrained lines in her face seemed to have smoothed out, and her lips were able to smile at the picture she presented as the well-dressed Savannah matron about to embark on a round of morning calls. She added to that a wide-brimmed straw, leghorn hat trimmed with flowers, ivory lace and ribbons, and only she knew that the balance of her morning was to be spent walking all over town, with Alzine in her wake, walking off her heartache and strengthening her for tomorrow.

She loved this freedom, she cherished it, and when Cade joined her later in the bedroom after dinner, she felt much less apprehensive. Every day would get better, he had said, and she almost believed it.

She had changed already, being careful this time to don her businesslike cotton nightgown before she put on her wrapper, and they spent a few moments talking about his day. He had gone, finally, to Haverhill to supervise the unloading of materials he had ordered for the renovation of the house—which, he said, was in terrible disrepair. She was not going to find there a house the size and elegance of Bredwood. It would be comfortable, suitable, and they would, over the course of a year, spend a great deal of time in Savannah as well. He hoped she could be content with that.

She thought she could. And was that all? She watched him disrobe, all her senses piqued, and felt a moment of exasperation when he settled himself under the cover and closed his eyes.

But that was what she wanted, she thought, as she climbed in next to him. That was precisely how he should be treating her. He should be respecting her wishes not to be touched. He was behaving like— a gentleman.

The next night was a repeat performance. And that was fine, she thought, settling down next to him, hip to hip, a breath away from a tenuous awareness of him. There was a strength lying next to her, a firm male presence that reached out to her without his even lifting a hand to touch her.

She hadn't anticipated she would have feelings about that. She felt an unexpected tension. What if she were the only one experiencing these feelings? It wasn't possible to ask either. She lay beside him in a palpitating silence.

And nothing happened.

She didn't want him, she thought the next day. She didn't quite know what she wanted, or why she felt so disappointed. He was giving her room to recover and to heal.

She *had* healed. Well, no, she couldn't call it healing; it was more like a resolve just not to think about it, and if she didn't think about it, it would recede more and more into the background until it became a pin dot of memory.

That was one resolve. What remained unresolved was the tenor of this strange marriage. As she lay beside him, she felt her vigor and her youth, she felt the faintest unfurling of that carnal part of her that remembered with awesome clarity the prowess of his living heat within her.

She had thought she had died; instead she was being reborn. She wanted to feel it again; she felt pliant, willing—if only he could see. But he slept, and she simmered in a kind of proprietal frustration that warred with all the reasons why she had married him in the first place.

She was stunned she felt this burgeoning desire.

She decided *not* to give in to it.

14

Pierce came to visit several days later, and Sarianna was especially glad to see him after three more abortive nights of lying next to Cade's inanimate body. But that was fine. That was what she wanted.

She welcomed Pierce in the parlor and sent Amanda to prepare refreshments, and she was delighted that Pierce had brought her a gift. But it was one she could not accept: a guitar.

"But you see, Miss Sarianna, it's been restrung so you can hold it comfortably, and here—I rewrote the chord chart—you can see, just three simple chords. The trick is learning to finger them and switch among them with dexterity . . . but I'm sure—"

"No," Sarianna said, vastly pleased as she ran her fingers over the strings. "I can't."

"Of course you can. Why not?"

"A gift like this, for a newly married woman like me?" Sarianna questioned just a trifle coyly. She hated herself; she was desperate to find a reason to keep the thing.

"All right," Pierce conceded. "We won't call it a gift; we'll say I lent it to you since I knew of your interest in music."

Sarianna smiled, the first genuine smile she had been able to summon up in all this time.

"You are the clever one, Mr. Darden. I would be most pleased if I could indeed borrow this wonderful instrument from you—for a short time—to see whether it would profit me to learn it."

"Sarianna . . ." Pierce shook his head, not fooled for an instant. Oh, she knew all the right words and all the little graces, and she wasn't even aware of it. There was irony under her very proper words, and he didn't think she was aware of it. "It's yours, and Cade will have no problem with that, I promise you."

"I'm sure he won't," Sarianna said with more confidence than she felt. "I thank you. I will really try to learn to play it."

"And you will," Pierce said as Alzine wheeled in the serving cart.

When Cade returned home early that evening, he found Sarianna and Pierce tête-à-tête by the parlor windows with Pierce arranging her awkward fingers on the strings of a guitar that looked appallingly familiar to him, and Sarianna laughing and grimacing with a liveliness he had not seen in her for two weeks.

"Sarianna, Pierce." He was amazed he could keep that much equanimity in his tone, and he felt a primitive urge to brand Sarianna as his own right before Pierce's eyes. The most he could do was drop a hard unexpected kiss on her lips which curved into that quirky little smile—and not for him.

Sarianna looked startled, and then the smile appeared again. Did he feel the faintest edge of envy, she wondered as she attempted to splay her fingers far enough apart to press down the horrendously thick steel strings. She hoped . . . she hoped . . . what *did* she hope? She strummed her left hand downward on the strings, and a strangled chord sounded oddly in the silence. "Not yet," she said to Pierce.

"Practice," he encouraged her. "It will work. Meantime—Cade, I should be going. I'll see you tomorrow at the factor's?"

"I believe so," Cade said coolly, but he didn't believe anything at the moment but his deep feeling of dislike that Pierce had found the thing that would give Sarianna pleasure—and he had not.

In the following days, she poured all her energy and all that sorrow into mastering the three simple chords until she could move her fingers fluidly among them and play a coherent melody. And in those days, Cade did not come near her, did not make an overture, did not even seem to notice how far she had progressed.

She felt like a doll on display, fashionably dressed, who could be wound up to say the proper words and disposed of when the words ran out.

Everything was perfect then, ordered just the way she wanted it. And she was becoming desperately unhappy again.

The guitar came up to the bedroom with her, and she wasn't sure if it were a symbol of some kind or just plain rebellion.

Cade plainly did not like it. "Would you like to put it between us in bed?" he asked acidly as she sat on the couch, strumming it in an undertone to the tension building in the room.

"I can wrest more emotion from these strings than I can from you," Sarianna retorted brazenly, a sentiment that had bubbled up from nowhere—from everywhere inside her at her increasing frustration.

A snapping silence followed her words.

"The hell," he swore at last. "You think the emotion isn't there? You think I haven't been lying beside you night after night consumed with lust—*lust*—my delicate Sarianna. Tell me what I *should* have done, damn it. Tell me now I should have just grabbed you and forced you into my bed." He stopped abruptly as a quiescent light flared in her eyes. And then, "Tell me, Sarianna . . ."

He waited, his hands on hips, and in that breathless moment when she hesitated, he exploded. The guitar went flying, and he pulled her ruthlessly into his arms and ran one hot hard hand all over her face. "Kiss me, Sarianna . . ." he whispered, as his questing hand centered her mouth beneath his, and his lips touched her, gently, delicately, demanding nothing, taking nothing.

Her body was so slender against him, so perfect, her mouth so inviting. He didn't know how he had kept away so long. He savored the touch of her lips again and again, and he knew she was not unwilling for him to take more.

Perhaps it was a punishment—for himself or her—but he wasn't willing to do more, not much more than play with her lips, nipping them, pulling them, running his tongue all over them, teasing her silky inner lip, biting them when she became too demanding on her own. Just that, that little foray, and when he could finally stand it, he pulled away and left her adrift.

And she didn't understand why. It didn't matter. He touched her. His hands wound into her hair, held her head immobile, and almost as if he couldn't help it, he began the assault on her mouth again.

"Oh, God, Cade . . ." she groaned, opening her mouth to him. But he resisted the blatant invitation.

"Enough for today," he breathed, his lips just hovering over hers. "This is all for today, Sarianna, Sarianna—" he crushed her lips again—"that mouth, Sarianna . . ." He was on the edge of seeking her tongue, he wanted it so badly, he wanted to drown in the taste of her . . . and he thrust her away abruptly before he could succumb to the ravening need to go on and on and on.

She felt shattered by the loss of contact, and he sensed it. He tilted her head up. "I want your kisses, Sarianna," he said gently.

"Then why . . . ?" she started to say.

He shook his head. "Come to bed, Sarianna. There will be no more tonight. Tomorrow we'll talk about the rest."

She was restless the entire day, her mind occupied with the voluptuous memory of his mouth on hers, and her body in a frenzy to have more of him while he was seemingly at great pains to let her have less.

The night had been impossible. To lie next to him like that, to have had his kisses and that ravenous sensual contact, and then not to have had anything further was tantamount to being imprisoned in a cell with succulent delights just beyond her reach. He was punishing her, she thought; she was sure he meant to tempt and reject her beyond anything she could stand.

However could she contain herself enough to wait for the night?

Then Pierce called in that day to see how she was coming along with her chording, and Cade walked in on that conversation. She had a terrorized moment of believing that Pierce had done it deliberately, that he had known when Cade was to return home and had timed his visit accordingly.

No, not Pierce. His soft brown eyes were so innocuous, so full of concern that he was helping her, that the simple songs that she was now able to stumble through made her feel a sense of achievement. She couldn't conceive of another reason.

Cade could, and Cade said nothing. Pierce sensed his impatience and tactfully withdrew, reneging on the invitation Sarianna had issued for dinner. He knew when to retreat: He saw the look in Cade's eyes.

The rest of the evening tumbled headlong into a sweltering contest between Sarianna and Cade to see who would give in first. She played the guitar; he read the paper. She paced the room and looked for books. He sat back in his chair and pretended to sleep. She called for some refreshments and pretended to want dessert. He stalked out of the room and into his office in the back of the house.

There was no choice after that but for her to retire. She thought for sure he was not coming to bed. He came later, much later, and she was all worn out wondering and yearning by then. She lay stretched out on the bed, wrapped in her silky kimono, feeling inordinately petulant.

He wouldn't want to kiss her tonight.

But she had left the guitar in the parlor.

When he finally came to the room, she was half asleep, curled up like a kitten, with her legs exposed under her drawn-up nightgown and kimono.

He stood by the bed, admiring the line of her body in the light of the dimmed bracket lamp by the bed. He swore not to touch her. He ached to put his hand on her satin skin. Not yet. Not yet. Anticipation shot through him, heightening his senses. Sarianna was healing. Sarianna wanted . . . Sarianna remembered.

He turned down the lamp and lay down next to her. He felt an unbearable moment of pure primitive lust that expanded luminously with every beat of his heart and the knowledge that tonight he would not take her either.

And then she turned to him, seeking his kiss, as if she had been waiting for that one attenuated moment when the waiting became too much for them both.

The darkness became a shroud and a benediction. The night was long, slow. Their lips touched, retreated; he licked her lips, enticing her back, winding his arms around her shoulders to pull her closer and to keep himself from exploring the narrow hip pressed against his own. She answered in kind, her body shuddering as her tongue lightly rimmed his lips with a teasing moistness. He caught her tongue between his lips and sucked it gently.

She felt his hands draw her closer and then the heat of his mouth move away from hers. "Cade . . ." she breathed.

"Shhh . . ." His fingers touched her lips, brushed over them as soft as a butterfly wing, and felt their texture and their movement in distress as he denied her the kisses she so desperately wanted. He felt her trembling and her growing need. Not yet, not yet. "Sarianna . . ." God, he loved saying her name—Sarianna—it was like music, a rhythm pounding in his vitals. But not yet, not yet.

She made a passionate little sound, and he stopped it with his mouth. Now, now—he caught her yearning, he sought the root of it, and he didn't know how he would stop himself when the time came. Her response was perfect, wild and wanton. She fit against him perfectly, body to body, mouth to mouth, and it felt insanely exciting, unendurably tense.

"Open your mouth to me, Sarianna," he whispered against her lips, and they parted sweetly to admit him. "Sarianna . . ." he groaned as her tongue brazenly sought his. He gave in to its lush promise. He gave in to Sarianna just this way, just this dark night. He loved kissing Sarianna. He didn't want to move, to do another thing but taste the sweet honey warmth of her willing mouth.

"Sarianna . . ." A long time later he called her name in the depths of the molten excitement that had possessed her. "Sarianna . . ."

"No . . ." she cried; she knew what he was going to do—he was going to abandon her again—and she couldn't bear the thought. Everything within her cried for continuation, for release.

She felt him ease away from her, and she couldn't believe it. "Cade . . ."

He touched her cheek. "No more tonight, Sarianna."

And she asked the same question again, the agonizing, "Why?"

And he said again, "We'll talk tomorrow about the rest."

His own body was screaming for relief when Cade left her in the morning. The heat between them the whole night was nothing short of sensational. He could have taken her at any moment; he knew she suffered, he could hear it in her fretful movements as she lay awake beside him all night. And he was sure she knew that he had not slept either. Tonight, he thought. Perhaps—tonight.

But while he had an invigorating horseback ride and hours of hard work ahead of him, Sarianna had a whole day stretching before her to be gotten through before there was a possibility of recreating the shimmering sensuality of the night.

It was a most amazing day for her. Her whole focus was a fantasy of what might happen at night, and how she could make it happen. That vixenish side of her that had seduced Cade that one morning in her

211

bedroom totally possessed her. She remembered the feeling, the mindless sense of directing every thought, every movement, every twitch of her body toward enticing him beyond his endurance. She remembered how instinctively she had perceived what would please him and what would arouse him. And she remembered most of all that he had broken and that his initial possession of her was as pleasurable as the actual fact.

She wanted to tease him and deny him all at once, and a furious excitement took hold of her at the thought. She remembered the way he looked at her when he had first come to her room three days before. She didn't know how she would get through the day.

Nor did she know as the day progressed just how she planned to seduce Cade that night. She only knew that her lips were swollen from his kisses and that her body demanded the culmination that only he could give her. The rest, she thought, she would leave to her imagination.

She retired to their room even before he returned home. The waiting was intolerable; possibly it was worse upstairs not knowing when he might come back. Nonetheless, it gave her time to prepare, to remove cumbersome wire hoops, and have Alzine unfasten buttons that she could never have reached herself. She removed the constricting corset she was required to wear with the tight-fitting basques of the newer fashions, and she found her hands were shaking as she slid her arms back into the sleeves of the dress.

The waiting drained her excitement and magnified it. Her desire turned feverish, intense. She waited.

She waited, and time turned into something tangible and fragile. She felt as if there would not be enough time in the whole night to lure him to her bed.

She sensed his presence before she heard his frantic call. She heard Alzine speaking with him, and she heard his footfall all the way up the steps. Without consciously planning exactly what she was going to do, she sat down on the bed and kicked off her elastic-sided ankle boots before he reached the door. When he opened it and thrust himself in, he found her sitting on the bed, daintily removing her arms from the sleeves of her dress.

The sight arrested him in his tracks. "What the hell are you doing, Sarianna?"

"I'm hot," she said, avoiding his blazing eyes and trying very hard to keep the faint pout out of her voice. She wondered if she didn't resent him keeping her waiting so long as she pulled the bodice downward to reveal her thin cambric chemise with its strategic lace inserts. It was a trousseau item, the dressmaker had told her; surely she wanted some enticing scraps of lingerie to tantalize her husband. Alzine, she remembered, had been very sure that she did.

Now, feeling his heated response to her simple movements, she felt grateful for Alzine's foresightedness. She never could have conceived she would want to tempt Cade Rensell to the point of breaking weeks after their wedding.

And yet—she slipped her arms behind her to unhook the waistband of the muslin dress she wore, and raising her body slightly, she shimmied out of the skirt and let it drop on the floor.

She sensed him watching every movement; did she exaggerate the sway of her hips enough as she wriggled out from under the dress? She knew the silky ties of her matching drawers fluttered lightly and settled nicely just in the opening that revealed a narrow expanse of her derrière. She hoped he was noting every detail. She sat back down and wriggled against the headboard in her favorite position.

"Isn't it hot?" she asked, making a show of pulling the fabric of her chemise away from her heated skin, her hands intentionally brushing her taut nipples pressing against the revealing lacy insert, and deliberately sliding upward to lift her hair from her neck.

He didn't move, he didn't react, and she thought she might scream. She swung off the bed and stood facing him, her hands on her hips. Nothing in his expression discouraged her. But nothing encouraged her. Her body felt explosive. She lifted one leg and propped her foot against the side rail.

The movement spread apart the edges of her underdrawers just enough so he could glimpse her nakedness. She needed to see his reaction, to feel it, to know she affected him and aroused him. She saw in his eyes and the muscle working in his jaw, in the faintly uncertain expression on his face, as if he were not sure how far to let her go.

She held his gaze as she reached behind her and pulled apart the ties that fastened her drawers. The material slid down her hips and stopped at her angled thigh. She bent over and eased the leg over the garter of her white lisle stocking, deliberately stroking her leg as she slid the thin white material of her undergarment slowly downward to her white sheathed foot. As she lifted her foot from the confining material, she felt the rest of the undergarment slide down her other leg and pool on the floor. She allowed herself a long moment to remain in that position, bent over her angled leg, adjusting her stocking, the curve of her body blatantly visible in the light of the bracket lamp.

Her hands, her body, were trembling as she slowly lifted to face him with her left hand still braced on her hip, her glowing sapphire eyes challenging him, daring him to come for her.

She felt his hot gaze sweep over her, from her eyes down to the revealing lace insets that clearly defined the thrust of her taut nipples, down to her naked hips, and along the line of her legs to the white stockings that were rolled just above her knees, and he looked like a lion waiting to devour his prey.

He didn't move. He wasn't sure he could. He had never seen such a sensual creature as Sarianna stripping for him. She wanted him to reach for her; he knew it, and the same hot caution that had provoked him into spending two nights only kissing her prevented him from throwing her on the bed and burying himself in her wanton heat.

It felt like a battle between them: He was determineed not to give in; she was determined to make him. Her scornful eyes skewered him as she started walking forward, and he watched her deliberately provocative progress across the room to the closet where she ripped out her kimono and donned it—and left it untied.

"I believe I'm ready for dinner now," she said huskily, leaning against the door, barring his way with her brazen nakedness. "I find myself in the position of hoping as well that Pierce will rethink his decision not to join us." She felt his hot anger as she opened the door. She didn't know how far down the hall she might get undressed as she was—maybe not a step, she hoped not a step.

She walked out into the hallway, and his hands wrenched her back into the room and slammed the door. She felt him wrest her around to face him, and his body crowded her against the molding of the door, his arms surrounding her, not touching her—damn it, *not* touching her—his face so close to hers she could see every line in it.

"Oh, no," she said, squirming backward and plucking at the edges of her kimono. "Oh, no. No. You can't—"

"Don't tie up that wrapper, Sarianna. I want to see everything you're offering," he growled.

"I won't let you see another inch, another—"

"No, you'll just go down to dinner like some whore and offer it to someone else . . . God, Sarianna . . ." He bent his head, and she felt his tongue graze her lips. "Tell me, Sarianna . . ."

"There's nothing to tell," she countered goadingly. "I was hot. I got undressed. You happened to walk in the room." *Why* wouldn't he touch her? *Why* were his lips so close she could touch them but he wasn't kissing her?

"Don't lie, Sarianna. Tell me . . ."

"Don't do this to me."

"I see—only you can do it to me?" he retorted.

"I don't seem to be doing anything to you," she shot back, her voice reedy with tension.

"What do you *want* to do to me?" Cade murmured, his gaze now fixed on her mouth. "And what makes you think you aren't doing it already?" He lowered his head to her still farther, still not touching her, standing so close to her fevered body that she felt covered, even though there was an inch between them.

She lifted her eyes to him and made the slightest stressed move toward him. His mouth settled on hers and she felt a long moan of completion start from deep within him. She didn't need anything more; she needed just that mouth kissing her in just this way, overpowering her, delving deep within her, feeling her, tasting her as if he had never kissed her before. He played with her lips, loving the pliant softness of them. And he loved the sense of her flaunting her nakedness a heartbeat away from him and him resisting her tantalizing flesh. He loved the firm seeking tip of her tongue begging for his. He loved the audacious way she had bared herself to him.

Somehow, he pulled away the confining silk kimono, and it pooled at her feet. Gently, as he kissed her, he slipped his arms around her and under her buttocks and lifted her up hard against his body. Her arms and legs wound around him, bringing him closer.

She was so slender, and her womanly curves nestled exactingly against him. He felt her hips writhing against him, and his hands held her buttocks and felt every movement, exploring her, pulling way the

215

impeding material of the chemise to run a long sensual line down her back.

Her mouth grew violent as the thick molten desire flooded every pore. "Cade . . ." Oh, she wanted him to keep on doing just what he was doing, feeling her, exploring her in new and different ways that intoxicated her.

He shifted her slenderness in his arms so he could carry her, and he brought her to the far chair by the fireplace and settled into it gently, positioning her on his lap. He never broke the kiss, never stopped feeling for her with his tongue and his hands, all over her now that he could hold her and reach her, could cover and excite her womanly mound, could feel the long slender line of her thighs and legs, and could slide his fingers inside the tantalizing stockings to feel the slim curve of her ankle and foot.

Her hands pulled frantically at his clothing as he explored her nakedness, and her excitement heightened at the feeling of his thrusting manhood beneath her buttocks. She squirmed sensuously as he lifted her and settled her down again, straddling his legs so that her femininity grazed the hard long length of him that was still confined beneath her. It tempted her; she found herself bearing down on him, inciting him by the movement of her hips above him.

His hands confined her hips and began directing her in her torrid seduction. Her arms pulled his mouth tighter against hers as she writhed in a primitive dance of supplication that enticed his hands away from her hips to explore the temptation of her sultry sex. She was so hot, so enfolding as his fingers began their deep erotic exploration; he couldn't get enough of her. Never enough of her.

He felt her brazen hands pulling at his trousers, pulling at his shirt; if she had the strength, she would rip it all away, but his wanton hands delayed her, enchanted and excited her.

She swallowed convulsively as his fingers sought deeper into her velvet heat. "Cade . . ." She was afraid suddenly; the feelings were building all tenuously, spiraling out from that molten heat that pulsated at some ravenous core within her, the thing that couldn't get enough of him feeling her and caressing her, the thing in her that still was not satisfied.

"Sarianna . . ." He broke the kiss, and they spoke in whispers and breaths, on a secret level of awareness punctuated by her moans as his

216

fingers explored her so deeply, and by his mouth as his tongue kept demanding hers and seeking it over and over again, as if he couldn't get enough of kissing her, tasting her, touching her. "Sarianna . . . God, you are . . . you *are* . . . don't let go. . . ."

"I won't," she breathed, but she wasn't so sure when he was sliding his hands all over her like that, avoiding the tempting quivering tips of her nipples that pushed against the fabric of her chemise as if they had a mind of their own. "I won't . . ." She surrendered to his mouth again, her hands reaching to caress him, to feel the hard, lean strength of him.

"Sarianna . . ." A whisper in the erotic haze surrounding her. "Sarianna . . . Sarianna . . ." He did love savoring her name, she thought.

He groaned as her delicate touch grasped him. "Sarianna . . . let me see you . . . all of you." His urgency excited her. She could just see in the flaring lamplight what he saw: the lush contour of her breasts against the thin lacy material, the luscious thrust of her nipples clear beneath the transparent lacy inserts, and the hunger in his eyes to have her bare herself to him.

It was a moment to incite him. Slowly she untied the neckline of her chemise and let the ribbons fall in a long stream between her legs. And slowly she pulled down the translucent material that covered her breasts until they were naked.

His eyes feasted on them, with a knowledge of their erotic nature, of *her* erotic nature, and she reveled in the hunger she saw in his eyes. She arched her back to invite his kiss in a bold demand that shocked even her. And he obliged her. The moist heat of his mouth surrounded the taut left nipple, and his tongue licked the very tip and almost caused her to go into a spasm.

He felt her reaction. One hand freed itself from its voluptuous exploration of her and lifted her up against him, bracing her buttocks, so he could taste that succulent nipple and pull it deeper into his mouth to suck it.

Simultaneously, he positioned her over his rock hard length, and as he licked and sucked her lush nipple, he eased her body downward, thrusting himself upward into her satin sheath.

Then there was a moment, a deep filling moment where he held the taut nipple bud in his mouth, and her body rested against his, filled with him, totally enfolding him so they were connected in the most elemental carnal way.

She loved the hot sense of his long hard length inside her. She loved facing him this way, offering him her body, her breasts, anything, anything he wanted as long as he kept this perfect joining with her.

His mouth moved from her breast to join with her mouth and her tongue, and they sat this way, feeling each other, for long exquisite moments. She loved this perfect fusion with him, enjoying how tightly and deeply she held all of him inside her. She loved the gentle probing of his tongue as he deepened the kiss. She loved his hands sliding all over her back and buttocks, her legs and hips, slowly upward to her breasts where as delicately as a breath, his fingers encircled her nipples and held them.

"Oh, God, Cade . . ." she moaned as every separate sensation assaulted her: her nakedness, his massive manhood inside her, his fingers barely squeezing her nipples, her legs straddling him and the feeling of him tight against her. She had to move. *She had to move.* She wanted to stay in that torrid configuration forever, and her body shifted as the intense sensation shimmered through her. "Do that," she murmured, winding her arms around him, aware of his delicate touch on her turgid nipples more than anything else as she lifted her body and thrust it downward again and the spiraling pleasure shot through her like a blinding light. "Do that," she whispered against his lips as she gyrated her hips in an elemental feminine demand. "And that," as he shifted upward and thrust into her in concert with her downstroke.

"I love your mouth," he murmured, seeking her lips with his tongue, thrusting between her lips and between her legs in an increasingly forceful rhythm, his hands on her buttocks guiding her movements, feeling the torrid twirl of her hips as she met each long thick thrust with wanton abandon.

"Oh, yes," she groaned, as each potent lunge heightened those feelings that billowed out all thick and hot inside her. He captured her tongue again as each thrust became deep and powerful, and she moved with him, bracing her hands on his shoulders and her body on her knees so she could move freely. His hands on her buttocks still guided her, slowly now, faster, faster, deeper, and she whirled around this hard center of her being, seeking the precipice, climbing toward it, hot, hot and molten, thick and heavy, an incandescence that

218

expanded and spread outward and outward until her body couldn't contain all the explosive heat and convulsed in glittering spasms of pleasure beneath his hands.

He needed nothing else, he thought, as he savored her response and her culmination. Sarianna was his. Only his. All his. With one more virile thrust, he claimed her forever as his.

15

She woke up the next morning in her bed, naked, with her long white stockinged legs entwined with Cade's, her body flushed with yesterday's memories. Such memories, such undreamed of depths of passion within her. Where had it come from? she wondered as she stretched her body luxuriously. A legacy of Dona?

The thought chilled her. Imagine thinking of Dona after such a night as she had spent with Cade. She wasn't over it yet; if she were truthful with herself she might even admit she wanted his lovemaking again. There was something so erotic and arousing about lying next to him this way, with him half-clothed and she all naked. When she moved her leg, she felt the rough texture of his trousers. Against her arm, she felt the softness of his shirt. Inside her, she felt the depth of his maleness. And her body reacted, demanding a reprise.

She wriggled her body tentatively closer to Cade's. No hope there; he was sleeping too soundly. She lay quietly next to him, enjoying his warmth and the sense of possession she felt. It was really quite extraordinary, she thought, that drive to be possessed, to give and give and ultimately find that luminous pinnacle that was only obtainable because it was Cade driving her, Cade bringing her to culmination.

She never in her life could have conceived of such a connection between two people, but it was fascinating to her that her body had known; her body knew just what to do and how to respond. All that yearning, and in the end, her body had taken over and rendered her mindless with that driving need.

Her body tingled with it again. Her mind recreated all the separate enthralling sensations, and instantly her body craved them. What was it about the thought that incited her? The pleasure, the kissing, the touching—the contact? The pure naked intimacy of being handled by someone who wanted to hold her, to caress her, who wanted her caresses in return . . . she had never known such affection before, and yet it was not affection: He didn't love her. She didn't love him. They had used each other, and yet underlying this motivation for their marriage was something else that drove them to this explosive union.

She could live a life feasting on that carnal closeness. She didn't need love. She needed what Cade had given her last night. She needed his tactile possession of her body, not her heart.

She needed him right at that very moment.

She lay next to him, naked and yearning as the early morning light slid through the louvres in the shutters. In a moment, she thought, she might nudge him slightly; she might try to wake him somehow and make her desire known to him. She might. On the other hand, he might not want to make love to her again. It was unthinkable; she needed it too much.

She raised herself on her elbows and looked at herself in the shadowy morning light: her long slender body, her flat hips and long legs encased in the rather erotic white stockings, the contrast of her golden feminine thatch against the whiteness of her skin, the lush curve of her taut tipped breasts . . . she was ready for him. She wanted him.

She eyed his recumbent body. He seemed so large next to her; if she touched him it would be like a lamb assaulting a lion. How could she dare?

She moved her leg so that it was touching his thigh. She felt her breath catch at the excitement of it: her rampaging need and his slumberous indifference.

And when he awakened?

She shifted herself slightly, so that the whole line of her body was just touching his. There was something infinitely frustrating about connecting with material, she thought, and wriggled herself a little closer.

He lay on his stomach, his face away from her and his arms surrounding the pillow, when—she thought restlessly—they should be surrounding *her*.

How? *How?* His upper torso was bare, and she could not bring

221

herself to touch him. Her body reacted feverishly at the thought of it; she could run her hand down that dark, smoothly muscled male back, feeling all the intriguing little hollows and bulges . . . the crisp hair on his chest . . . touching the fascinatingly turgid male nipples . . . Her body expanded with her lush yearnings; her ferocious imaginings excited her even more. Her hips undulated, prodding his leg. She licked her lips agitatedly as nothing happened.

She jumped as his body moved and he rolled onto his side facing her. She swallowed hard, her body quivering, and she shifted toward him still more, into the curve of his body and his sensual male scent.

Yes. His heat enfolded her, and she angled her body so she could slide backward against him, slowly, anticipating the contact of her nakedness against the roughness of his trouser-clad thigh.

Yes. She could feel the broad strength of his chest behind her now, and the faint sensation of his hair against her back.

Another adjusting squirm and she felt her bottom nudging his groin and his instant reaction to her wriggling nudity. Oh, yes, he could feel her, and she gave in to the temptation of tantalizing his elongated manhood with uninhibited little rippling movements of her hips, as if she were trying to find a comfortable place to settle the lush curve of her buttocks against his hard heat.

Every ravishing undulation aroused her still more. Just the feeling of him becoming hot and hard beneath her buttocks drove her excitement to a fevered pitch. She could hear his heart beating against her and his breathing accelerate. He felt her feverish response to his ramrod length; he felt her heat and her naked body writhing against him, seeking him.

She lifted her arms and encircled his head, pulling him forward over her shoulder, demanding his mouth, his tongue as her body demanded his hands and his potent male member.

And finally, as her buttocks wriggled tightly against his towering sex, he moved his hand ever so slowly over her hip and down toward her seductive sex, and simultaneously, he licked her waiting parted lips and entered her mouth as his hand entered her welcoming fold.

The contact was shattering. Her body arched upward, opening to his caress. Her left leg angled against his thigh, to ease his way. Her tongue dueled with his in a symbolic refusal to surrender when she had incited him to surrender to the seduction of her body, and his knowledgeable fingers probed lusciously deep within her just as she

222

yearned to have him do.

In the midst of his sensual seduction of her mouth and her womanly core, she felt him shift her body slightly and his right hand come around beneath her, and she almost swooned from the contact: his two hands on her satiny skin, feeling ever inch of her, cupping her straining, taut-nippled breasts, teasing the pleasure point of the nipple, first one and then the other, squeezing gently, just so those torrid streamers of sensation rolled through her body, wrapped around her the way his hands enfolded her. Both hands were between her legs now, stroking, caressing, delving into the heat of her satin sheath, threading through the golden tuft of hair that shielded no secrets. Both hands between her legs holding her, feeling all the lush heat of her body that beckoned to him and the lush heat of her tongue that devoured him.

Her provocative hips writhed in pleasure against the sensual exploration of his hands and mouth. It was almost enough, almost. Almost. In her carnal haze she never noticed when he removed a hand to unfasten his trousers. Instantly the right one replaced its seductive delving between her legs. A moment later, his left hand slid all over her body, up to the curve of her breast, and cupped it and held it.

His mouth moved a breath away from hers. "Sarianna?" His fingers grazed her tight nipple, and a spasm of glittery pleasure shot through her. "Such luscious nipples," he murmured into her ear. "So beautiful, Sarianna . . ." Her body twisted against him at his heated words and the sensations he evoked with his long fingers rubbing the turgid tip of her nipple so knowledgeably. And then she felt his rigid nakedness beneath her buttocks, nudging her, hard and seeking against the soft curve of her bottom. His hand caressed the hard softness of her breast while the one between her legs felt her moist heat, and his mouth covered hers, the firm tip of his tongue stroking her in the same sensational way as he stroked her body. Her sense of his carnal possession of her was absolute, and she surrendered to his hands and mouth, his words and, a long moment later, to the probing ridged tip of his masculinity as he shifted her upward and entered her from behind and below

The long hard satin slide of his granite maleness filled her with a thrilling sense of his power. He didn't move, once he was deep within her, and she felt that same sense of connection and oneness with him that needed no culmination to perfect the sense of his enslavement of her body.

He contained her totally with his mouth, his hands and his virility, his power shaped by the tight thrust of his elongated manhood deep within her wanton heat. She waited for the first thick movement of him within her, and he did not move. His left hand slid slowly down her hip to enfold her feminine mound, and his fingers found that lush little nub that gave her a tingling feeling of pleasure even when he touched it. Just that, and the gorgeous movement of his tongue in her mouth, the sense of his fingers barely encircling her lush nipple, and the fullness of his hard length nestled within her in that ravishing new way . . . she had waited all night for this—all her life, she thought—consumed with the erotic memory of what she knew would happen next.

He waited, and it became a lovemaking of the mind. Her body began its own insistent movement borne out of the rapturous memory of the feelings. She squirmed against him in voluptuous invitation, begging him to begin the lusty stroking that her body craved.

He lifted his hot mouth from hers for the barest instant. "Such a shameless Sarianna," he whispered against her lips. "So naked, so mine. Tell me, Sarianna. Tell me . . ."

Her tongue licked his hovering lips, and her body heaved against his with a frantic life of its own. All she could feel was his enveloping heat and the thick filling length of him. "I'm yours," she breathed, reaching for his mouth. She bit his lip as her body quivered at his fingers moving lightly between her legs. "Yes . . . more, please—" as his fingers stroked with sure knowledge of what she wanted. "Cade—" she felt a desperation in her, and she moaned his name and frantically reached for his mouth again. He moved, he moved, his body began the short turgid thrusts that shook her to the core. Her body moved with him at first, and then in ferocious counter gyration to his thrusts.

Everything became one: the pistonlike stroking of his torrid sex, his hands working creamy magic on her breasts and the sweet spot between her legs, his tongue thrusting against her mouth as he whispered love words on her lips—"Sarianna, Sarianna, naked in my hands, all mine, Sarianna. No one else can have your nakedness, *no one.* . . ." She tasted his words and his fervor, his fever to envelop her totally so she could never escape him, and it all became one—the words, the wetness, the heat, . . . the devouring of her mouth and

224

Get a Free
Zebra
Historical
Romance

*a $3.95
value*

Affix
stamp
here

ZEBRA HOME SUBSCRIPTION SERVICES, INC.
P.O. BOX 5214
120 BRIGHTON ROAD
CLIFTON, NEW JERSEY 07015-5214

B O O K C E R T I F I C A T E

— F R E E —

ZEBRA HOME SUBSCRIPTION SERVICE, INC.

YES! Please start my subscription to Zebra Historical Romances and send me my free Zebra Novel along with my first month's Romances. I understand that I may preview these four new Zebra Historical Romances Free for 10 days. If I'm not satisfied with them I may return the four books within 10 days and owe nothing. Otherwise I will pay just $3.50 each; a total of $14.00 (a $15.80 value—I save $1.80). Then each month I will receive the 4 newest titles as soon as they come off the press for the same 10 day Free preview and low price. I may return any shipment and I may cancel this arrangement at any time. There is no minimum number of books to buy and there are no shipping, handling or postage charges. Regardless of what I do, the FREE book is mine to keep.

Name _____
(Please Print)

Address _____ Apt. # _____

City _____ State _____ Zip _____

Telephone ( ) _____

Signature _____
(if under 18, parent or guardian must sign)

Terms and offer subject to change without notice.

5-89

MAIL IN THE COUPON BELOW TODAY

To get your Free **ZEBRA HISTORICAL ROMANCE** fill out the coupon below and send it in today. As soon as we receive the coupon, we'll send your first month's books to preview Free for 10 days along with your **FREE NOVEL.**

GET YOUR FREE GIFT

No Obligation!

a $3.95 value

FREE

IF YOU ENJOYED READING THIS BOOK, WE'LL SEND YOU ANOTHER ONE

Make This Special Offer...

Zebra Historical Romances

—Zebra Historical Romances
Burn With The Fire Of History—

body by the essence of his into a cataclysm
sensation, pure radiant lightning crackling t
body.

Her release thundered through him as h
writhing voluptuous pleasure. *Oh, God, So
anything tie you closer to me than this,* he thoug
rippling responses. It would take nothing to re
he wanted to prolong it, just to hold her a mome
just one more time, to caress her incredibly
to . . . thrust to the final . . . penetrating . . . spe
and he murmured her name in the throes of his

She could hardly bear to look at him over the bre
the memory of their lovemaking so close withi
wondered what he would think if she told him she wan
him. It wasn't possible, she thought, not this morning
tumultuous completion—not so soon. But her hot ga
hands as he buttered a biscuit or lifted his cup to his m
body remembered every touch of that hand.

"You are spoiling me," she said at last, having spent
minutes looking for an opening to say something—anyt

He smiled at her, a particularly sweet smile, one that de
lines around his eyes and mouth and made him look kind. '

She sent him a wry look. "Well, Mr. Rensell—" his
quirked at the formality as she knew they would—"you've
from degradation and humiliation, plunked me down in thi
town house in the middle of a fascinating city, provided m
clothes and—entertainment—and I find myself feeling u
useless and desperate for something to do."

"Surely you have *some* fulfilling—activities," Cade provoked
ignoring the flare of light in her eyes in favor of taking anot
biscuit. When he looked at her again, however, her face was con
posed, and she was waiting for his response. "You still need time
Sarianna. The hurt hasn't gone away."

"I may do, but I can't only play the guitar all day while you manage
a cotton plantation in some godforsaken wilderness."

"I assure you, you will get there soon enough," Cade said. "But tell
me then, *Mrs.* Rensell—what did you have in mind?"

ACCEPT YOUR FREE GIFT
AND EXPERIENCE MORE OF
THE PASSION AND ADVENTURE
YOU LIKE IN A
HISTORICAL ROMANCE

Zebra Romances are the finest novels of their kind and are written with the adult woman in mind. All of our books are written by authors who really know how to weave tales of romantic adventure in the historical settings you love.

Because our readers tell us these books sell out very fast in the stores, Zebra has made arrangements for you to receive at home the four newest titles published each month. You'll never miss a title and home delivery is so convenient. With your first shipment we'll even send you a FREE Zebra Historical Romance as our gift just for trying our home subscription service. No obligation.

BIG SAVINGS AND FREE HOME DELIVERY

Each month, the Zebra Home Subscription Service will send you the four newest titles as they are published. (We ship these books to our subscribers even before we send them to the stores.) You may preview them *Free for 10 days.* If you like them as much as we think you will, you'll pay just *$3.50 each and save $1.80 each month off the cover price. AND you'll also get FREE HOME DELIVERY.* There is never a charge for shipping, handling or postage and there is no minimum you must buy. If you decide not to keep any shipment, simply return it within 10 days, no questions asked, and owe nothing.

---

arky smile played across her slightly swollen lips. "I'm not ll you the truth." But she knew what she wanted to say; she have a protracted time alone with him, and she wanted to e with him every moment, every day. The urgency of it was ering, and she wondered if he felt the same sumptuous desire. a desperate need to come together with him again that was not d by the fact she had only just left his arms an hour before. s hard to concentrate on what he was saying, insanely difficult nink of all that molten emotion building in her as she watched th and hands, impossible not to think of him touching her in ys, new places.

ybe I should tell you what *I* have in mind," Cade murmured, s resting on that elusive smile that hovered on her lips. It was t as though he could not help the suggestive inference of his . Her very look invited it; her sapphire eyes flared with erotic st as she leaned forward slightly and her lips formed the word " He couldn't resist that blatant temptation. He kissed her eager gain and again until he had to push her away. Her glazed look e him smile.

t *is* time to talk, Sarianna," he said gently, reaching for her hand, dering if she felt that he had rejected her. But who could turn y Sarianna? How glorious she was, how utterly beguiling in his s in the morning, so beautiful, so overwhelmingly responsive, redibly fetching over a breakfast table in a simple, white muslin wn with her hair in tumultuous disarray and her intense blue eyes nned to him and thinking other thoughts that had nothing to do th talking.

"All right," she said, removing her hand from his as if the contact ere too much for her. What wouldn't be too much for her if she felt his volcanic after two nights of lovemaking? she wondered. And he vanted to talk. She swallowed her lust and tried to listen. Not a successful effort either, she thought, because a moment later he stopped speaking and just looked at her.

"You have no curiosity about what comes next?" he asked mildly.

She cast about wildly in her mind to see if she *had* ever given a thought to what would happen beyond their coming to Savannah. She supposed not; he talked about going to Haverhill, but he had never said how long they would stay in the city, or when he would take her to the plantation. No, he had said nothing, and she hadn't, after their

precipitate removal from Bredwood, really cared. She had only been concerned with getting as far away from her father as possible.

She felt safe here, she thought, as she examined her feelings, safe and cared for—by Cade who had not tried to make her give anything that she wasn't ready to give; by Alzine who was a comforting, and increasing, presence from her past; and by Amanda who didn't intrude at all but looked at her with all-wise eyes that saw everything and knew how to keep her own counsel.

But curious about the future? No, she hadn't wanted to look beyond the comforting days of new surroundings, new responsibilities, new people who really cared about her, the sensual new world that Cade opened to her.

She sent him a flirtatious smile, utterly unaware of how distracting she was. "I don't think I was thinking at all about what comes next," she said honestly.

Cade met her smile, answering it for what it was, and went on: "I had kind of a vague idea when I bought this place that I would spend a great deal of time here, since Haverhill isn't a far piece from town. And I thought, if I were successful and brought back a wife to Savannah from Sawny—yes, Sarianna, *I* thought that far ahead—she might stay here while Haverhill was being prepared and *we* would stay here perhaps as much as we stayed at Haverhill. And I had this funny notion that since the house came furnished, that a wife might like to choose new furnishings, and arrange things to make it—our own. . . ."

"Truly?" she whispered. "I could do that? We could have friends and entertain, and I could arrange things to suit my taste?" She was awed at his generosity and thoughtfulness. She had never in her life imagined she might have a house of her own, let alone be allowed to pick and choose the things *she* wanted or decide *how* she wanted them.

He meant it; she could see in his eyes that he meant it, and that he wanted her to be happy—or as happy as she could be under the circumstances.

But she was happy, she thought. Just the fact of her response to his lovemaking made her happy. The distance from Bredwood made her happy, and being in the city with the freedom to roam, explore, shop or even do nothing. The sense of her disparity being meaningless in this context made her happy. She couldn't imagine anything beyond that. There *was* no beyond that.

"Within reason," Cade said wryly. "Pierce can take care of the arrangements—set up an account for you to draw upon, and direct you where you ought to go. You can do as much or as little as you want." He smiled at her. "I don't know much about things like that, and I expect you're going to have your work cut out for you once we reach Haverhill."

She went silent, and he felt a little jolt of apprehension. It was so hard to tell what she was thinking, so hard to know how deep her pain went, or how much it still hurt her. Everything, he thought, might be affected by that. She might never recover from the indignities she had suffered. But surely she knew by now that none of it was important: In a real world such a minor inconvenience as which hand she used was not considered a matter of ostracism.

He felt the familiar fury grip him; he wondered if *he* would ever get over it. "Sarianna?" he prodded, as her silence started to become unnerving.

She looked up at him and smiled. "That sounds wonderful, Cade, really it does."

"But? I hear a 'but,' Sarianna."

"I don't know," she said slowly. "I think—I can't wait for us finally to go to Haverhill. I think I still miss the good things about the life I had at Bredwood."

She hadn't expected to say that, but later, Sarianna realized it was true. She wanted the space all around her, and the other kind of freedom, the freedom to run her home the way she wanted it, and the freedom to have Cade with her all the time so she wouldn't be in a position of waiting for him.

The waiting was excruciating. The next day she contacted Pierce because she knew that Cade would be spending several nights at Haverhill, nights that promised to be horribly lonely for her. She was gratified to learn that Cade had already spoken to him, they had set up an allowance for her and Pierce had a list ready of the most prominent craftspeople in the whole of Savannah and beyond. It was his job to know that, he said. He knew about everything being the best.

Sometimes when he spoke to her, he wondered whether she had any reason to want to know anything about him. He thought he was falling in love with her, with her sad speaking eyes and that curious air of fragility and urgency that surrounded her. She was a misfit, he thought, not unlike him. He empathized with her, and he had no sympathy for Cade's practically stealing her away from Bredwood. She deserved more delicate treatment; she was like a piece of china, he thought, fragile and durable all at the same time. He made himself very much at her service.

"Yes," he said, "Cade very specifically said you could order anything that pleased you for the house. Two of everything if that is what you want at Haverhill as well. Everything is to be ordered to your taste, Sarianna, and you must not mind the expense. It's negligible."

Her quirky smile answered him one afternoon as she presented several proposals from upholsterers and carpenters to him. "How can it be negligible? Mr. Rensell's assets cannot be bottomless."

"No, of course not," Pierce agreed quickly, running a practiced eye over the estimations of the carpenters. "Not bottomless; let us say sufficient."

Sarianna was caught up short; she knew nothing about Cade's finances, still less about how he had made all this money that had set Vesta drooling a month before. She knew nothing, she realized, at all about Cade . . . no, she knew something; she knew his concern and his practicality, and his mouth and hands and what they could do to her, the tightness of him within her, and those things were terribly important to her. But his wealth . . . ! That hadn't been important until she began toting up the numbers from the estimates for refurbishing the house on Malverne Row. And *he* was talking about extending the largesse of that renovation to Haverhill!

"*How* sufficient?" she asked point blank.

"As sufficent as it can be for any businessman who perceived where the real money lay in California in '49," Pierce responded obliquely.

"And where was the real money, Mr. Darden?"

Pierce flashed her a quick smile. "Supplies, Miss Sarianna. Goods to be sold to desperate men, a lot of them, in a place where supplies weren't easy to get. Cade was right smart about that; he didn't care at all about gold. He wanted real substantial money. He was one damned angry young man when he came west."

Amazing that she had not known that, she thought, folding up the pieces of paper with the numbers, so many numbers that would translate into Cade's money at sometime very soon.

"And of course when California got too crowded, Cade smartly followed the strikes. Wherever a mine opened up, Cade was right there. He had a wagon and his own express people who weren't beholden to anyone else, and he didn't have to wait any longer than it took for them to restock a wagon and come on back to wherever he was; and he was damned smart to think of that, Miss Sarianna. Got him a nice reputation through all those years. They knew Rensell was reliable and charged fair prices—or as fair as things went when they weren't available—and he beat out the competition and made, Miss Sarianna, a damned whole lot of money."

"I see," Sarianna said, envisioning in her mind a younger, wilder Cade adrift in a wilderness of tents, mountains, trees, setting up his stores in the middle of a canvas city, as impermanent as the riches that were sought in the mountains beyond it. She could hardly see it at all. An angry young man. A man flying west on the heels of the death of the woman he had loved so hopelessly. Oh, yes—she had almost forgotten about that. All of it came back to Dona. It had been easy to forget about Dona in her frenzy to flee Bredwood, and in her rage to be possessed by Cade.

Her hands began to shake, and she held them tightly in her lap.

Pierce noticed immediately her mood had changed. "Cade never told you any of this," he surmised.

"No, but how could he? We've been so busy," she said, and her oblique reference did not escape him. Nor did he like the fact of picturing them together in any carnal way. But no—Sarianna could be lying to save face. He didn't think Cade had touched her; why would he, when his sole determination had been to take revenge on Rex Broydon? And that he had done right enough, Pierce thought. He could not have done any better than that if he had taken a gun to the man. Broydon was on the road to ruining himself, if his response to the truths Cade revealed was still as overwhelming as it had been the several days he had remained at Bredwood after the wedding.

It was not impossible to imagine Rex drinking himself into oblivion—and wouldn't that be a fitting end to Cade's vengeance.

Even Jeralee, Pierce thought, had been shocked when Cade had chosen to marry Sarianna after two days' residence at Bredwood. No, Jeralee after the wedding had been ready to commit mayhem.

Sarianna had bested her, and Cade had humiliated her in front of all her Sawny friends and neighbors; and Vesta perhaps had done too much boasting so that the embarrassment of it could not be covered up by mere words.

And here was Sarianna freely spending the money that Jeralee had hoped to have; he was amazed at the workings of fate.

"Cade will be at Haverhill for a few days, I understand," he said.

"Yes," Sarianna said shortly.

"I wonder if I may call then to see how you're getting on?" Pierce asked cautiously. He wasn't at all sure how Sarianna felt about him, except that she had an easy friendliness in his presence which he found very provocative because there was nothing in it explicitly aware of him as a man.

"That," Sarianna said, "will be lovely."

Yes, she liked having company, and entertaining even Pierce Darden, who called the night after her visit both to see her and assess the choices she was making about the house. She played for him, the little she had learned, and was gratified by his approbation. She loved the instrument and was prepared to be upset the day he decided to take it from her. But for now, he was a rapt audience sitting across from her in the parlor, and if Alzine didn't stop muttering behind the curtain, she thought, she might throttle her.

She missed Cade. Pierce's solid reassuring male presence was not exciting or even stimulating. She talked about Savannah and the dressmaker who had delivered still more things to fill her bulging closet. She talked about going to the theater, and Cade's plan to spend more time in Savannah when they had finally removed to Haverhill. She talked about the exigencies of learning to play the guitar—in effect—backward, and how much she enjoyed its solace.

She did not talk about Bredwood, nor did she speak about Cade, and when he left, Pierce had the distinct impression that she was very unhappy and yearned for the company of people her own age; and he meant to see that she got what she wanted.

Accordingly, two days later, he escorted her to a dinner party in the home of a socialite friend, and he was pleased to see Sarianna's hesitancy evaporated as she realized everything had been done for her comfort there, at his behest; and her eyes started to glow with interest and spirit as she began, in her easy unaffected way, to make new friends.

The thing that astonished her the most was the interest of the men, and if she hadn't maintained that faint air of aloofness, she thought she might have insulted her lady hostess altogether.

Nonetheless, everyone was interested in Cade, and she spent much time talking about him and their romantic marriage—or so she told everyone because Pierce had amplified the sketchy details into an extravagant fiction.

She found herself liking her first foray into society without the armor of a family shield. The stunning thing was she didn't need it; she had never needed it, and she closed the door resolutely on what that might mean to her. She was having too good a time, surrounded by attractive men, basking in Pierce's approval at the pretty picture she presented, both to him and her hosts, and her sweet manners that won everyone over instantly.

She did, she loved being the center of attention and feeling beautiful and wanted. She had missed so much of this, so many years she could have had the little successes that Jeralee somehow was entitled to and she wasn't. And she closed the door on that thought as well before the whole tenor of her musings got totally out of hand.

When Cade sent word he would still be staying on at Haverhill, she threw herself into making arrangements for the redecoration of the house. She wanted, she thought, a more intimate feeling to the parlor, more chairs, warmer colors, the lamps on the table rather than in brackets appended to the wall. She wanted fresh wallpaper and fresh air. She wanted some stamp of herself in the bedroom, but she didn't know quite what. She wanted tactile fabrics and satiny bedcovers.

She wanted so much. Too much, she wondered, for someone who had planned to be content with her lot a month ago. Too much, she feared, for someone who had married in haste and was not repining in leisure. Too much, she was deadly afraid, for someone who was her mother's daughter.

At night, alone in that big bed that seemed monstrously empty without Cade in it, she saw it all too clearly: Cade's generosity had nothing to do with her—it was Dona he was giving free rein. When he made love to her, it was Dona he had in his arms. When he was cool to her, as he had been the morning he left, he was regretting that *she* was the one on whom he had spent his passion.

How could it not be so? Everything that had happened to both her and Cade radiated from Dona. The secret was Dona. Maybe, she thought in the dark of the room, the only answer was for her to become as much like Dona as possible.

16

What *had* Dona been like? Sarianna wondered. The dark was good for ruminating on questions like this. In the dark she felt a closeness to the hazy memories of Dona, the Dona of the golden curls and sassy smile, the quick word and a kind pat for the daughter who was her double. And not much more, Sarianna thought. There really hadn't been much more. She had followed Dona around as much as Dona would let her. But her mother was often out paying calls, or over on the mainland, much to Rex's distress, spending money, visiting relatives or friends—or doing whatever it was that Dona did that put creases in Rex's forehead and caused him to finally have her followed.

After that, the arguments had started, and Dona cried a lot and spent time sobbing over Sarianna's golden curls. And she couldn't make it better. Not ever, not for her father or Dona.

Dona was beautiful, heedless, self-centered. Dona loved being the center of attention, and she never shone more than when Rex entertained and all the men hovered around her.

Just like last night, Sarianna thought with a chill. Just like me. I'm just like her. I loved it.

But what was wrong with loving it? Cade was away; she couldn't turn to him to assuage that awful yearning that consumed her as she lay in their empty bed.

She hadn't meant to encourage any of them, and she didn't think she had. Most of the men were married, and their wives were very pointedly at their sides for most of the time she engaged them in conversation. She didn't even want them. She just liked the idea that men were drawn to her after such a celibate existence as she had led.

And it was a confirmation that Cade did not pity her, that she was attractive to other men.

Yes, she loved it. She didn't want to be isolated ever again. She was just like Dona—and she was herself. She would never betray Cade the way Dona had Rex.

Haverhill, what there was of Haverhill, was haunted by his vision of Sarianna; she was everywhere, the impetus and the goal for which he rushed to reach a point in the rebuilding of Haverhill where she could join him permanently. He wanted nothing more than to have her by his side every day, and he thought often in those ensuing days as he rode the fields and worked with carpenters in the house, that if it were not for Sarianna, he would never have considered undertaking the renovation altogether.

He loved the life and hated it simultaneously. He would rather, he thought, have made his way back west with Sarianna than work in a stultified economy that was doomed to disaster.

But he owed it to his mother's memory to try; he owed to his father to make a success of the root crop that had cut him down.

He owed everybody everything, and what did he owe himself? He owed himself the freedom to love Sarianna. God, he could love her; he felt so insanely possessive of her that it made him wary. It was the same intensity he had felt about Dona, and it was scary that Sarianna aroused it in him.

But Sarianna aroused so much more in him. The perfection of her utter surrender was nothing short of a miracle. The memory of it was his companion in bed at nights; the radiance of it warmed his days as he tramped through muddy fields and tried to exercise discipline over recalcitrant field workers and an equally intractable overseer who had had everything his own way for far too long.

This was a stepping stone, he decided; when all the political rumblings between the North and the South coalesced into the frightening war he foresaw, he would be able to leave it and go on to something else—as long as Sarianna was by his side.

He was falling in love with Sarianna.

It had taken but a month, and not even a lifetime of loving Dona before her could have prepared him for Sarianna. Dona had been the prelude, the measure by which he could judge the depth of his feelings for Sarianna. He had never, in all his futile longing for Dona, imagined such an end and such a beginning. Sarianna *was* the beginning, he thought.

He didn't even know how he could stay away from her this long. Haverhill didn't require this kind of dedicated attention from him. He wasn't interested in turning it into a life's work; he wasn't sure exactly what would happen with it. He had only thought about it as far as it being a place to come to with Sarianna.

She might love it. If she loved it, he would stay, no matter what happened in Washington. And if she didn't, they would make a life somewhere else—together. He was making it perfect for Sarianna.

And everywhere he went on the property in the ensuing days, he was filled with the sense of her silken heat and the possibilities of the future.

Finally he broke, and with no reluctance at all, he headed back to Savannah.

In the space of those several days he had been away, much had changed. When he entered the parlor, he was not surprised to see Sarianna and Pierce in consultation in the middle of the room. The furniture was covered, what he could see of it, and the couch was suspiciously missing. Long swaths of wallpaper hung precariously from the walls in several colors and designs; and Sarianna had a swatch of material in her hand and she was arguing ferociously with Pierce.

He supposed he ought to have been grateful to hear Pierce defending his taste and preserving his capital, but he was discomfitted by the sight of Pierce so intimate with Sarianna.

Amanda came scurrying into the parlor ahead of him. "Miss Sarianna, Miss Sarianna—Mr. Cade done come!" and Sarianna whirled, her eyes blazing a welcome that came purely from her heart.

Her first urge was to run straight into his arms, to feel the reality of his grimy male frame, to beg his kisses—she would, she would, she wanted him so badly—but then a touch of sanity prevailed. Pierce was watching, and Cade looked so formidable standing there—and then, Dona would *never* have thrown herself into his arms.

He wondered why she held back, why she came toward him so sedately, reaching for his hand and pulling him into the room, not offering her lips, not giving him a moment to put his arms around her.

"You've come *just* in time," she said gaily, and there was a false note in her voice. "Pierce has been trying to convince me that you would hate a room papered in a blue and cream stripe. Tell me the truth, Cade—what do you think?"

He pretended to consider the long strip of paper, but his mind was on Sarianna. "I hate it," he said at length. "I need a wash up." He turned to Pierce. "My felicitations on your good taste, Pierce."

Pierce acknowledged the backhanded compliment. "It's time to take my leave, Miss Sarianna. Cade . . ."

She walked him to the door, feeling awkward and powerful both. She couldn't wait for Pierce to leave. He took way too long with his good-byes.

When she returned to the parlor, she found it empty, and she flew upstairs, thinking, Dona would have walked. Dona would not have been in such a rush—oh, damn her. Where *was* he? She burst into their bedroom and stopped short.

Cade stood naked in the middle of the room.

He was beautiful in the glowing lamplight, just beautiful. His hips were narrow and his legs long and firm. His upper torso was muscular, hardened, powerful. She wanted to touch him, to affirm her knowledge of what every part of that forceful male body could do to her.

The wonder was she could hold him; she could take all of that virile maleness into her hand and hold it and feel its living heat with that knowledge cupped in her hand and her heart.

She felt a breathless moment of fear, as though deep within her she thought he might repulse her. And then she realized he was waiting, and that hot molten yearning surged through her and obliterated everything else.

She moved into the room and closed the door behind her carefully. No one must interrupt. She had Cade all to herself now, and her turbulent need consumed her and propelled her forward into his arms.

"Is it too late to give you a proper welcome home?" she murmured, winding her arms around his neck, feeling the smooth, muscled bare skin beneath her trembling fingers.

"I rather thought I got a very *proper* welcome when I came in," Cade said whimsically, drawing her even closer to him, utterly aware of the texture of his nudity against the soft material of her dress. His body responded instantly to the closeness and the possibilities of her inviting mouth, her questing fingers, and her pulsating sensuality. This was why he had returned so precipitately: He wanted Sarianna in his arms again, naked and open to him, quivering with primitive passion. The Sarianna of his bedroom was not the proper lady of his parlor, and he reveled in the difference. He bent his head to graze her lips with his, and she answered it with the seeking heat of her tongue.

"Kiss me," she urged in a smoldering whisper against his lips. *"Really* kiss me . . ."

"Begging, my Sarianna?" he murmured triumphantly.

"Pleading, Cade," she sighed, feeling the long thrusts of his stiff male self pushing between her legs through the billowing folds of her dress. She felt his hand grasp her chin and position her head so that his mouth slanted across hers for a long breathless instant before the moist tip of his tongue touched her lips and began its ravenous exploration. Her lips parted so he could reach the sweet inner skin of her mouth and then slide heatedly within feeling for her tongue, delving deep into the sensual recesses of her willing mouth, probing every inch of it, dueling with her and finally taking her tongue deep into his own mouth and sucking its erotic wetness with a ferocity that aroused the surging need in her to a fevered pitch.

Her hands moved, splaying all over him, sliding down his back, all the way down, feeling the incredible smoothness of skin against the hard bone of his spine, and the sensual male curve of his back and buttocks. How extraordinary that his flesh was so sleek and silky against her hands, so firm, as her fingers grasped his naked buttocks and almost mindlessly pressed him harder against her hips. His heated skin was so touchable; her hands roamed where she could reach, all over his buttocks, between them, down the long flank of his hip and thigh and back up again to grip the hard muscles of his arm and hand that held her tight against his dominating mouth.

Yes—that and more—she felt herself smoothing her hands all over him, wriggling her fingers between them in their tight embrace to feel his solid hairy chest and taut male nipples. How odd and exciting that he was so much like her and so different, she thought incoherently, as her hands felt the firm muscles of his chest and tracked an erotic path down his flat stomach to his vociferous masculinity.

Her questing fingers encircled its thick ridged tip, and he almost convulsed into her hands. "Oh, God, Sarianna . . ." he groaned, wrenching his mouth away from hers for just the moment it took to utter her name before he claimed her tongue again, sucking on it with the same hard intensity with which her hands grasped his ramrod length.

He loved that, she thought, and she loved the feeling of holding him so contained between her two hands, of being able to feel every hard inch and know that all of it could be encompassed by her femininity.

He tore his mouth away as his body spasmed with a molten pang of pleasure at the sense of her touch *there*, feeling him all over to know all of his secrets, holding now all of his sex in her two ravenous hands. "You have me now," he whispered against her swollen lips. "Don't move . . ."

She sensed his movement, the shifting of his body to ease her way as she caressed the firm flesh between his legs with a knowing touch that heightened her excitement and almost sent her over the edge of surrender.

"Oh, no, Sarianna . . ." She heard his words from a distance and pulled herself back. He didn't even have to touch her; she needed only to explore his maleness, and the heat of her need for him rocketed her body toward culmination.

But even as she thought that, she yearned for the rest, the joining and the closeness, his hands all over her naked body feeling her, exciting her—and why was she still in her dress, she wondered hazily—and then she felt his tongue seeking hers again, his hand moving from her chin down her neck and still downward to feel for the taut peak of her beneath her bodice.

He touched it, and her body writhed in pleasure; the sensation of the material against the sensitized nipple magnified the feeling a hundredfold, and he touched it and pulled at it, and stroked it beneath the dress until she thought her legs would give out from the sheer enchantment of it. Everything enhanced the feelings: his hot mouth all over hers, his naked body holding her tightly, her right hand moving mindlessly responding to her pleasure all over his thick hard male length, her left hand groping gently and firmly between his legs; his knowing caressing fingers playing with her nipple as though there were no impediment to its taut heat.

And then suddenly, there wasn't. His hand worked into her bodice, pulling away buttons and hooks to find the creamy mound of her breast and her tight luscious nipple. Her *left* nipple, she thought hazily as his fingers took its taut tip, held it, squeezed it and pulled it gently until they both could not stand the molten urgency that possessed them.

His hands pulled at her clothes, ripping them away, stripping off her bodice and underclothes, baring her breasts to his hot hands and devouring eyes. He kissed each pointed nipple, licking and wetting the taut tip of each, sucking the pleasure point because he could not help himself while she still held all of his hardness so wantonly in her hands. And while he sucked one delectable nipple, his hands worked at the skirt of her dress, while her husky voice murmured and moaned encouragement in his ear: "God, that feels so good, Cade . . . Cade, I love holding you like this—hurry, I need to feel your hands on me, *Cade;* oh, yeeess, do that. Do that—" as he tore away the last of her undergarments and enveloped her lower torso in his hands, front and back, and began seeking her moist sultry heat.

Her skirts fell to her feet, and his hands delved deeply within her straining center. He guided her downward to the floor, laying her down on the bed of the soft muslin of her dress, whispering, "Hold me tight, Sarianna," as he poised over her and thrust into her, pure silver melting in her veins at the feeling of his heated hardness deep within her.

He held her that way, nuzzling her lips, letting her feel the powerful thickness of him, and the ramrod strength. He covered her so that her whole body was tightly centered beneath him, ready for the first virile thrusts. He rested within her for that heady first moment of joining, to revel in the sense of her body accommodating his so perfectly to hear her disjointed little cries of yearning, and to kiss them away.

And then he moved, as her legs wrapped tightly around him and her arms guided his mouth to hers, and there was nothing in the world but the two of them rocking together in tandem to a rhythm of their own, not willing to break the communion between them.

He was so hard, so hot, so thick within her. Her hips ground against him as he began his driving thrusts, slow and heated, fast and quick little movements, alternating strokes, driving her wild with the sensational motion of his body, and her consuming need to feel him deeply, deeply with each vigorous forceful plunge of his ravenous manhood.

240

Her tongue captured his this time, greedy for the taste of his kisses. She played with him, drawing his tongue against hers, licking it, surrounding it with her lips playfully, dueled with it, aroused it, all as her body gyrated tumultuously against that dark male center that enthralled her.

The torrid surging of her body filled him with a voluptuous heat that almost sent him spiraling out of control. He wanted more of her insatiable femininity, more of her erotically whirling hips that made him the very center of her being. More—more—was there ever more, or was there just the moment between the two of them when sensation built beyond control, beyond words, beyond any sense of individuality to explode into a glittering new whole.

More. Deeper, as if he could possess her very core. And harder, as if he felt the need to imprint himself on her and in her.

Her mouth enslaved him; there was no room for words between them as she possessed his lips in concert with his voracious possession of her body. Her hands found mobility, and they moved sensuously all over his back and buttocks, kneading the firm flesh there, exploring the contour, holding them in the age-old feminine guidance as if she could direct his potent driving strokes to her exact pulsating center.

"Sarianna," he groaned as his hips lunged wildly against her. Her body heaved against him frantically, as the lustrous sensation began building within her, all long and strong and molten gold. She felt it in every pore, the melting gold, the shimmering just tantalizingly out of reach. Soon . . . soon . . . his thrusts became more heated, more focused; he reached beneath her and cupped her buttocks to bring her even tighter against his hips so his thrusts penetrated deeper still.

Now she bore down on him with frenetic little jolting movements of her hips. Now she felt it, the ravishing tightness, the fluid glide of his body in its ancient cadence within her, the slow simmering feeling that was beyond description.

She undulated beneath him provocatively, straining against him, pliant and volatile all at once, almost there . . . she ripped her mouth away from his . . . almost there . . . she heard her voice urging him on. She felt the hot rivulets of sensation streaming through her veins, she felt a thick flow of opaqueness gathering within her, and her flexing fingers felt, as they bit into the flesh of his buttocks, that she was gathering the sensation directly into her hands.

And she felt—"Ahhhh, Cade . . .'"—the white-hot eruption of crystalline culmination wash over her in a crackle of incandescent light.

"Sarianna, Sarianna," he whispered, as her body cooled down under his cascading heat.

"Yes, Cade," she murmured, moving her hands again, feeling his slick sweaty skin now, aware of him and his need in the sweet calling of her name. This was the closeness she craved; this was everything. "Don't move."

"No," he agreed, rocking gently against her, but it couldn't be for long, he didn't know how long he could restrain his raging need for completion. But not yet, not yet. She seemed to love the thickness of him nestling within her. Her body squirmed beneath him with torrid little movements of accommodation to his length that provoked him to a keen urgency that was even more exciting because he had to suppress it. Not yet, not yet. Her writing body bore down on his hardness as if she wanted to feel him still deeper; her lips nipped at his, and her tongue claimed him, thrusting teasingly into his mouth and licking him wildly as she whispered against his lips, "So good. So filling. Cade . . ." He kissed her . . . "I never ever dreamed . . ."

"No," he said again, "Sarianna . . ."

"Yes," she murmured, bracing herself and lifting her body with the help of his hands beneath her buttocks, and he drove into her seductive sex with a ravening hunger for fulfillment with her. Her body moved with him, and he reveled in every tenuous thrust that met his powerful lunges. He felt a ferocious possession of her and all that sultry heat. Sarianna was his, the words reverberated through his body as it poised to take the one last potent plunge into a searing climax in her arms.

What she was coming to hate most was the aftermath. The aftermath meant the end of the honey-thick sensations that engulfed her. The aftermath meant falling asleep on the floor and waking up in the morning to Alzine's startled exclamation. And the aftermath meant facing Cade in the morning and yearning for an instant repetition of all the things he had done the night before and knowing it just wasn't possible. Not now—maybe not today.

She felt stupid; surely she was not the first woman who had

discovered the delights of sensual cohabitation. But this was Cade, and she was her mother's daughter, and the circumstances were such she still did not know what to think. If she could hold him by the golden chain of her desire, she thought, he might remain married to her forever.

But still, now that he was home, he wanted to know all about her plans for the house, and all the people she had met, and all she wanted to do was sit on his lap and feel him respond to her mouth and body.

Instead, they talked about wallpaper and Pierce's friends and how she had coped with going out in city society for the first time.

She didn't want to talk about anything except his gorgeous masculinity.

They went for a walk, and she liked striding briskly beside him and showing him her discoveries. They went down to the port and watched the activity for a while. The day was perfect, with a wafting little breeze coming up off of the water, and the shifting scene of colorful wharf workers shunting cargo this way and that, unloading here, selling a boatload of fresh fish there, loading on the first of the season's baled cotton still farther on down, a kaleidoscope of noise and smell and color.

None of it penetrated. She wanted Cade solely to herself and nothing else, and her agitation was quite evident; but Cade said nothing as he steered her back to Malverne Row. Inside, a gaggle of workmen awaited her orders, and she gave them briskly, which amused Cade who didn't give a damn what she did with the house as long as she was happy doing it.

She ordered the wallpaper that he professed to like, and set two of the carpenters to work removing moldings, and the others upstairs to work on segregating one of the upstairs rooms into two separate rooms.

Cade admired her composure and decisiveness, and she wished he would admire her eyes and tell her he wanted her still again.

He went out in the afternoon to confer with his factor in preparation for shipping the first bailing later on that month, and when he returned, he had tickets for the theater in his hand.

Here was a new experience for her. She sat enthralled through a performance of *Romeo and Juliet*, standard repertoire, as Cade well knew, but he enjoyed watching her response to the magic and make-believe and the tragedy of the lovers.

She felt it deeply and slept trustingly in his arms, the raging desire in her quenched by the calamitous outcome of the drama. She took it too much to heart, Cade thought, but her enchantment with the theater was not diminished by it.

In the morning, he suggested she come with him to Haverhill—just for the day. He was on his way back for another prolonged stay, and he desperately wanted her with him.

"You'll see," he cautioned her, "it's in such a state of disrepair that it isn't possible for you to stay. But you should see it now."

"I want to see it now," Sarianna said eagerly because she did not want him to leave her again. Another day, another short separation and soon, he promised, she could remove to Haverhill. He *promised*.

Then there was the thought of a lovely two hours alone with him in the carriage that Owen would be driving. They would leave early, very early so she could spend a good part of the day, and then Owen would take her home.

She liked the idea. She told her workmen not to come the following day, and she began to plan just what she would wear to roam the fields of Haverhill.

"You ain't goin' with Mr. Cade lookin' like no strumpet," Alzine said firmly as she brought out dress after dress for Sarianna, annoyed' that Sarianna refused to make a choice.

"Which one can I wear without that damned everlasting hoop?" Sarianna asked, eyeing Alzine's slightly bulging stomach with great curiosity. How different things were here! It had been a month now, perhaps a bit more, and all constraints were gone. Everyone knew Alzine was going to have a child, and they had all rallied around her in sympathy. Alzine had found a home here, Sarianna thought, and she would be coming with them to Haverhill where they would all be just one big happy family.

And what if she were to conceive a child? her smart-mouth little voice wondered as she held up another white lightweight dress to the light.

She might not. And this damned dress was not dark enough or made of strong enough material to wear while she was tramping around the marshy fields of a plantation in transition.

She wanted to go so desperately. Savannah expanded her horizons and constricted her both. She wanted the freedom of the country. She wanted Cade. "I can't wear white, Alzine; it stains too easily. I don't know what Cade has planned, but I want to be dressed as simply as possible. This isn't going to be a tea party, just a brief visit."

"You don' want to wear no hoop and it ain't right," Alzine said stubbornly, her tone expressing her complete disapproval. She had thought now that Miss Sarianna had access to a good dressmaker and the money to spend on a wardrobe, she would let go of all that nonsense about not wearing hoops. "We got—let me see now . . . we got one plain house dress fo' yo' mornings at home, Miss Sarianna, but dat ain't nearly good enough to be travelin' with Mr. Cade," she added as a protest.

"Let me see," Sarianna said. She didn't remember it at all. There were so many dresses . . . how lovely to think about it: so *many* dresses now, in a new life that was very much like, she thought suddenly, the life that Dona had led. Dona had had all the elegancies at her command, all the devotion of her adoring husband, all the servants she could want to cater to her every wish.

It was easy to envision Dona sitting languidly before her dressing table in a bedroom such as this one, picking up a brush—summoning a servant to wield a fan if she were too hot—and then giving over the chore of dressing her hair to still another servant.

And her hair would not have been nearly as tousled as her own, Sarianna thought, dredging up a thin memory of her mother dressed for a gala evening, and she would have loved the wide, sweeping, hoop-skirted dresses that enhanced a woman's waistline and swayed seductively when she walked so that a man would spend a night trying to envision the sensual body beneath the dress.

Yes, she thought, Dona would have liked that a lot, just as she was coming to like it a lot.

And she liked the dress Alzine pulled out from the sweet-smelling recess of the closet. It was a lightweight cambric muslin in her favorite shade of blue, open in front, heavily embroidered on either side of the opening and collarless with a demi-sleeve embroidered to match the front of the dress. Yes, that *was* simple enough, she decided, if she did not have to wear a chemisette beneath. "Can you alter this for me?" she questioned Alzine.

"No, I ain't gonna change dat old dress one bit," Alzine said.

"Yes you can, you can adjust the waistband so the skirt is one piece, and you can put hooks into the bodice so I don't need anything under it. I *know* you can do that, Alzine."

"I don' want to do dat, Miss Sarianna. It ain't gonna look right; it ain't made fo' a one-piece dress."

"And it's too hot to wear all those layers either. Please, Alzine. I know you'll fix it just right."

Alzine eyed her coaxing expression, and Sarianna turned away abruptly. Alzine knew her too well, she thought. Alzine knew just what she was about.

"I'll do it," she said at last, "but you gotta have proper petticoats under, Miss Sarianna."

Sarianna held up her hand. "I will," she agreed, putting that hand on the soft tactile material of the dress and running it down the swirling enbroidery to the hem. It was perfect—light, pliable, simple. Sarianna watched in fascination as Alzine picked up the garment and began making the alterations.

They left early the next morning after Cade had spent a long night with his books, and Sarianna lay awake for hours, fraught with the onslaught of that hellish yearning that kept her tossing and turning all night. But what had she expected? A never-ending night of ongoing pleasure? Why not? she thought, as she donned the remodeled dress the next morning; maybe only that would quell the ravening hunger in her.

Or maybe there was no way to subdue it. Maybe her fathomless need stemmed from all her years of neglect. Maybe she could never get enough of touching and lovemaking.

Maybe, she thought, she had better squelch the notion that Cade was some kind of machine that could turn on and off whenever she needed him.

Oh, no, Cade Rensell was very flesh and blood, with his own needs and his own motivations, and as he sat across from her in the close confines of the carriage, he looked as if he didn't have a care in the world.

His eyes feasted on her; she felt them skimming over the lines of her body in the thin blue dress. She felt them admiring the curve of her breast and come to rest on her lips while he talked of inconsequential things and the carriage passed briskly out of the city limits.

He talked about the fact he hadn't farmed cotton since he had departed Greenpoint, and now that he was forced back into it, he wasn't at all happy with the crop or the economy. "I hate the dependence on one cash crop and credit," he told her. "You have no notion of what living on credit does to a man: It sneaks up on him, that subservience to the fact of what he might be able to buy *if* his strike proves out, or his crop sells high. And then if it doesn't, what is he forced to but begging for the alms of friends and merchants to carry him through the next season—and the next. Damn . . ." He shook his head and looked out the window at the rolling scenery, feeling as if he were gabbling to avoid the real fact of the steamy heat rising between them in the close confines of the carriage. And he knew what was causing it: his damned uncontrollable response to her relentless sensuality. It positively radiated from her this morning as she sat reclining against a thick satin cushion in her beguiling blue dress and white demi-boots. She wore a ribbon in her hair and no other jewelry but the plain wedding band he had placed on her hand.

And yet something enticed him—something in her lustrous sapphire eyes, something in the elusive quirk of her lips as she listened to him intently.

All he could think of in the welter of words was stripping her naked and pulling her beneath him. The powerful spurt of elongation between his legs impelled him to do it.

So he talked, and he watched her mouth avidly as she answered him, or commented upon what he said; and he noted each slithering little shimmy as she tried to make herself more comfortable on the thickly padded seat as the carriage swayed this way and that.

The tension built between them. Idle talk was not possible in the sultry atmosphere. His eyes never left her; every alluring movement turned into something blatant and enticing, a torrid little show inviting only him to savor the delicacy.

Was she aware she was doing it? he wondered, but only for a moment as his stiffening manhood assured him she was very well aware of her effect on him: Her vixen look fixed on his groin and then moved knowingly back to his face.

She knew, she wanted it.

She moved her shoulders impatiently and ground her hips against the tufted seat in a covert little movement that thrust her breasts forward brazenly. She didn't know what else she could do but issue a brazen invitation for him to come and feel her. She had touched herself everywhere, and she knew he was avidly watching the sensual course of her hands. She didn't want to wait until they reached Haverhill; but he had not made a move toward her, and the air now was so thick with her craving and his obvious hard desire.

She licked her lips in perplexity, and his eyes flared with that ravening light. "Come kiss me, then," she whispered, her voice barely audible for the edgy tension in it, and he heard every word distinctly.

"Surely you're not begging me, Sarianna," he countered audaciously.

She sent him a considering look. "No," she murmured huskily, "you want to."

"Maybe I don't," he retorted. "Would you beg me, Sarianna?"

"Beg for your kisses, Cade?" she asked just a little archly, lifting her hand and brushing her fingers over her ripe mouth. "I think not."

His eyes kindled as he followed the path of her fingers with his gaze. "Maybe you will."

She rubbed her lower lip with her forefinger. "Or you?" she said suggestively, hardly able to stand the strain of this erotic banter when her body screamed for contact with his. She could see he felt it, too; the bulge between his legs was massive and rigid, temptingly touchable. And it was just the two of them; no one would know what went on this morning in this carriage on a long carnal ride to her future.

She leaned forward and stretched out her hand without thinking another minute about it, and covered as much of his rock-hard manhood as she could encompass in her palm, grasping it with her fingers.

He felt it as keenly as if he were naked. "You win, Sarianna," he whispered, moving off of his seat and kneeling before her with his legs slightly apart to give her the ease to feel him as much as she wanted. Her hand turned so that her fingers could easily slide between his legs, and he leaned forward into her hand and she murmured, "Kiss me now, Cade. Give me all of your kisses, I beg you. I want you to kiss me. I need your kisses. I'm begging for them." And he answered her by shifting his body upward, more tightly against her flexing hand, and pushing her against the satin cushion, surrounding her golden

248

head with his hands while settling his mouth on her lips lightly enough so that he could both taste their texture and whisper against them between each succeeding, inciting foray into her mouth, "You have my kisses, Sarianna. I never want to kiss anyone else but you. Give me *your* kisses, my Sarianna. Open your mouth and let me kiss you as deeply as I delve into your body."

She moaned and opened her mouth to him and waited for the hot exciting touch of his tongue. But he didn't reach for her all at once. He wet her lips with his tongue, feeling their shape as if he had never had them before, slicking them with his moisture, nibbling at them, biting at her lower lip to punish her for inciting him in that provoking way. Then he inserted his tongue into the honey sweet recess of her inner lips, playing with just her pliant upper lip, squeezing it between his, and then sucking it gently, transferring his attention to her lower lip in exactly the same way.

And then, only after he had thoroughly explored her yielding lips, only then did he begin seeking the nectar of her tongue.

The kiss went on and on; she would never let him go.

She loved the greedy way he devoured her; she couldn't get enough. "I love your kisses," she whispered in a moment when his mouth eased away from hers briefly. "Your kisses," she breathed against his mouth as he came for her. "I'll always beg for your kisses," she sighed as he possessed her once again.

His kisses were a joining with her, an endless incitement of taste and texture and moisture. Her languorous body molded itself to him, both of her hands still holding him. Her mouth opened to him again and again for him to take the sweet honey that she offered, and she wished she could strip away her clothes and offer him her nakedness. She lived in this momentary world of the scent and taste of him, and his ardent demanding kisses.

She was absolutely shocked when the carriage jolted to a halt and she heard Owen's voice and Cade's answer—something dismissing him—and she opened her reluctant eyes to a dazzling erotic darkness.

"Welcome to Haverhill," he murmured huskily. "We're in the carriage house, Sarianna, and all alone, you and I, and I'm not done kissing you."

"No," she breathed, offering her mouth to him again. The darkness was a provocation, her mouth and body moved voluptuously against him on the narrow tufted seat and he thrust into her mouth heatedly as his hands began a patient exploration of her clothed body.

And he found, as he moved his questing fingers downward, that her dress was so soft, inviting him to touch it, to smooth it away from her legs, so crushable as he pushed it upward toward her waist to discover that all she wore beneath it were the tantalizing drawers with the enticing opening between her legs.

"Here," he whispered, holding her quivering feminine mound, "is another place I want to kiss, Sarianna."

She drew in her breath sharply. "I would never deny you any kisses," she breathed, feeling his fingers separate the edges of her drawers and seek her feminine hair.

"Let me kiss you there, Sarianna."

His fingers began their erotic outward stroking as he awaited her answer. He could feel her savoring what he was doing, wondering how, in this little dark universe they had created, anything could be better than his long fingers inserting themselves into the very core of her moist, moist heat.

"Kiss me anywhere you want," she groaned as a lovely slithering feeling curled through her.

She felt him move away from her and center himself on the floor of the carriage between her legs. She had to relinquish her hold on his stiff, throbbing manhood, and she hated that. She waited with a kind of carnal curiosity to see what he would do and how it would feel. The darkness surrounded her; she could see nothing. She could only feel.

She felt him moving her legs, spreading them wider apart, and then pulling her forward slightly so that she was angled against the cushion with her bottom almost all the way off of the seat. And then he lifted her, to slide his cushion under her buttocks, and she felt cradled and comfortable and totally open to him.

She had nothing to hold on to but the sensations that engulfed her, all honeyed and thick, escalating as he seduced her with his succulent kisses. Her body knew what to do; her body slithered against him, the opulent feelings expanding wetly—another minute, another minute —and she surrendered to the tremendous explosion that filled her, stunned by the force of her passion.

A moment later, she felt the swollen ridged tip of his thick hard manhood nudging her spangling body, and she welcomed his long length deep into her feminine core.

He lay within her in the deep caressing darkness, and she felt at one with him, connected in a new way without the need for words or caresses. His galvanic excitement precipitated his ferocious release the moment he moved himself within her, and he remained there, quiescent, for a long intimate time, content to hold her in that deeply elemental way.

17

Everything at Haverhill wore an air of desolation, Sarianna thought, from the dilapidated carriage house to the rambling, one-story plantation house with its dusky brick and peeling paint. It felt ghostly, haunted. The gardens were a shambles; the smokehouse, the office and the pigeonnaire looked like tumbled-down shacks, beyond redemption. Well behind the house, lining two sides of the square that was planted with the kitchen gardens and orchards, sat a line of single-room cabins for the field hands. And attached to the house itself, as Sarianna could see as they walked around the front portico, by an ell corridor, were the kitchen and the quarters of the house servants.

Inside Haverhill was the surprise. She was accustomed to the high-ceilinged roominess of a two-story house; here, too, was an unexpected spaciousness, despite the closeness of the rooms. They entered the hallway through a Palladian-windowed door from the classically columned porch. Off of the hallway was the library, the parlor—to the rear—the dining room right next to it, adjacent to the kitchen, and a bedroom to the left of the hallway. A short corridor beside the parlor led to a flanking bedroom wing, and, as Cade showed her, through the library there was access to additional bedrooms and the ell to the servants' wing.

But the interior was dingy, grimy from years of misuse. The furniture, what little there was of it, was dilapidated, with the heavy lines of the style from thirty years before and shrouded in gray holland covers. The wallpaper was peeling, and sections of ceiling molding had fallen because of a leak through the roof. Dessicated carpets lay futilely on the brown varnished floors, and cheap framed lithographs hung crookedly on the walls.

They went through the library with its excellent, stained marble fireplace surrounded by mahogany bookcases full of yellow mildewed volumes into the kitchen hallway, and out into the garden at the rear of the house. This too was in disarray, a small intimate place that was enclosed by the kitchen wing on one side and an unused extension on the other that had housed servants in Cade's mother's youth. This had been the flower garden Cade's mother had tended as a child, and the remnants of it were still visible in the raised beds surrounding this piazza that now grew wild flowers and weeds. The sun poured in on it, and a little path led from it to the more formal kitchen garden beyond which was shielded from the main house by a stand of trees.

Cade felt a distinct sense of *déjà vu* as he led Sarianna around the grounds of Haverhill. It was not Sarianna who walked so sedately beside him; it was not twelve years later and it was not Haverhill. He had walked many times in just such a way with Dona, over the grounds of Greenpoint and the Wayte plantation both, in secret and in public; and for a moment out of time, he could easily believe that it was Dona beside him and time was precious, and there would never be enough of it to encompass his need of her.

But he hardly remembered Dona. Yet the sense of her in this little moment out of time was so sharp and clear, he felt a wrenching in his gut for the futility of the love he had borne her. It felt like yesterday suddenly. It felt like all of his tomorrows were stretched before him because she walked again beside him.

Everything seemed different. He didn't know if it were Dona or Sarianna, and if it made a difference since one was the other and they were both one. He couldn't shake the feeling that Dona walked beside him, quiet as she always had been and without Sarianna's tingling curiosity.

They skirted the edge of the fields, and there, Sarianna could see the men in the fields moving through the sea of cotton stalks. The overseer hailed them and came to meet them, and as he was introduced briefly to Sarianna, Cade wondered that he didn't stumble over her name.

He felt displaced, in some kind of netherworld where an old dream was becoming a roaring reality.

He didn't expect Sarianna to say, as they pulled chairs onto the porch to escape the steamy heat of the confining house, "Tell me about Dona."

He wondered if she were a witch. She had perfectly defined the odd permutation of his thoughts. Maybe she felt she was competing with them. Maybe, he thought, she was.

He shrugged. "There is nothing much to tell. I wonder why you thought of it."

"I don't know. There is a sense here of something from the past, and I think you feel it. It was like stepping back into Bredwood fifteen years ago. A timelessness, maybe, that calls up memories. You went," she added, looking over the curving front drive so she did not have to meet his eyes, "far away from me."

"It was my mother's childhood home. I thought it had passed to someone on that side of the family, but it turns out *they're* all gone and I'm the closest living kin. I don't really think I want it, but I can't let it molder away. Hell—it might just molder away any damn how if South Carolina secedes. I don't believe I was ever here with Mother but once when I was a child. I didn't remember it at all. I came back after Pierce contacted me and my father had drunk himself to death, and I came here once before I settled in at Malverne Row. I thought I might try to make a go of it—if I had a wife and maybe a family eventually to settle here and pass it all down to. That doesn't look likely now, Sarianna."

"Why is that?" she asked curiously, her heart heavy with all the things he could possibly mean by those words. She still couldn't look at him.

"All that rumpusing over state's rights—it's damn likely this region is spoiling for some kind of conflict to prove its right, and when it does, I'm selling up and going west."

"Just—leave?" she echoed hollowly. "All your memories and all you're rebuilding here?"

"Just like I did when Dona died," he said gravely, and her fear-shadowed eyes shot to his. "You asked," he answered her look abruptly.

A wash of pure dread engulfed her. She had thought—but what had she thought? She had known there was a possibility he had taken her from Bredwood because of her resemblance to Dona, and she had felt those little tendrils of likeness within herself; even as little as she had known her mother she knew what others said about her. She knew Vesta. And hadn't she thought she might try to be as like her as possible? She hadn't examined the reasons, but she knew now, sitting across from Cade in this little warp out of time. She knew. It was only to protect herself, from him and from what the future might bring. Maybe she had thought if she played Dona, she wouldn't be at his mercy if he decided to abandon her. Maybe she had thought he might fall in love with that persona. She didn't know now, here. It had been so easy to keep questions and suppositions at bay when her only concern had been what to wear the next day, and what color upholstery she should order for the sofa. Oh, really—she had spent a month coming out of the horror of her life at Bredwood, and weeks in an all-consuming physical need for Cade and loving their drenching carnality which had nothing to do with who she was and what ultimately was going to happen to her.

The reality had always been Dona, and now perhaps she would hear the truth.

"Am I very much like her?" she asked boldly, veering her eyes away again. She knew what the answer would be.

"Very much."

"So much you can't separate us?"

"I know who you are, Sarianna, I do."

"But do you know who you are making love to?" she demanded desperately, the one question she had not wanted to ask—ever.

"I make love to Sarianna," he answered harshly.

She didn't believe him. *Why* didn't she believe him? An hour ago she had succumbed to his mouth and his hot driving maleness, and she knew he was making love to *her*. And now, in this place that was redolent of another decade, another past, she didn't believe anything. And she had to ask the real question that haunted her, the only thing she desperately wanted to know.

"Did you make love to Dona?"

He looked away this time. How brave of her to ask, he thought; how damning would his answer be? He had been so young, it was impossible to imagine ever having been that young. What he imagined was being as old as he was now, with the young Dona by his side. This young Dona-face who was almost the age Dona had been when she died. What he had imagined had been sitting on a porch with her in just this way, growing old. In this far present, he couldn't conceive of what else he could have wanted.

"What is making love to her?" he exploded suddenly. "What *do* you mean, Sarianna? Do you mean did I kiss her? Yes, I did. Did I touch her? I did. Did I possess her the way I have possessed you? I think," he growled violently, "that's none of your business." But why did he stop there? he wondered. He had never made love to Dona, never felt for her cool passion a hundredth of what he felt for Sarianna and her wild surrender. Dona had been purely untouchable —the goddess above and beyond him, pledged to another man against his will, needing his adoration and his services.

Well, she had had that, he thought, and he knew he ought to have told Sarianna; but he didn't know what her memories were of Dona. He didn't want her to know his; something tainted them: Dona's devotion to Rex in spite of all reason. Dona's slightly sadistic use of him. She had that in her, he remembered, and she exploited it. Sarianna was nothing like her except in looks. Dona in her best moments of unrestrained ardor could never have equaled Sarianna's consuming sensuality. Dona in her best moments could never have held a reasonable conversation about anything except the latest fashions and how dull it was being a mother.

He had loved her uncritically and unremittingly for those seven years, and he didn't understand why.

Sarianna was silent, daunted by his outburst. She couldn't stand the thought that he had touched Dona at all, but how could she wipe away the past? Time had stood still here at Haverhill; of course she would be much on his mind. He could have had a future here with her, if she had taken that one bold reckless step that he had implored her to. The echo of his pleading reverberated in her mind. She had heard him so clearly and her mother's definitive rejection.

What more did she need to know? She was a pale imitation, and Dona would walk beside him in his dreams forever.

Nevertheless, she would give him what he wanted: She could be Dona—nothing simpler. She didn't need to hear more. She would come to Haverhill as wished and spend her affection and loyalty on him as Dona never could. He wouldn't be sorry, she thought; even if Dona shared their bed, she never could have wanted him with such a driving frenzy. That was the thing that was better; that was the thing that would make him stay.

How had Dona been was now a question that possessed her days

256

when she returned to Savannah, desolate and alone. She found it too easy to slip into a personality whose sole concern was what bath salts to select for her morning bath, what dress would look best, which ribbon would complement it; and which piece of furniture should be relegated to the guest room as the redecoration of the house on Malverne Row proceeded apace.

It was too easy to bask in Pierce's admiration as well and to allow him to escort her here and there. It was very easy to let him convince her that this was just what Cade would wish, that she was enjoying herself and going out, meeting people, attending concerts and otherwise partaking of the numerous diversions that town life offered.

It was also too easy to play the simpering self-centered belle. She felt like Jeralee, totally self-absorbed and rather petulant when things did not go her way. It took all of a week to bring her to this point, and she understood the power she had when her servants jumped to do her command and Pierce himself was abject at her feet for some imagined slight.

A man didn't make love to a wrong hand, she thought smugly one night as she sat surrounded yet again by an admiring covey of men, both married and bachelors. They couldn't care less what hand she used to lift her fork, she thought, watching them respond to her from a place outside herself that perceived everything with a stranger's eyes. All they cared about was that she looked beautiful and smiled prettily, deferred to their opinions and had petal soft skin and no observations of her own whatsoever.

So easy to do.

So boring after two weeks of it. And yet the ease with which she fit into the skin that she imagined had been occupied by Dona astonished her. Money paved the way for all luxuries, and any deviation was overlooked. She wondered how it had come about she had not known these things at Bredwood. Jeralee knew them, and she had taken great advantage of Rex's wealth and position as if it had been her own; and now Sarianna wondered by what right.

It was nicer this way. She was a wealthy young matron, beautiful and desired, and because of it, all men desired her as well. They fell over themselves to be of service to her, to sit by her side, to compliment her newest dress or the arrangement of her hair, or the fact that she had even condescended to join them at all.

They demanded nothing of her except that she look beautiful and express mundane sentiments.

It was so easy after all. And at the end of two weeks, when Cade had not yet returned from Haverhill, she put the finishing touches on the refurbishing of the town house, and finally, with Pierce's encouragement and cooperation, she felt she was ready to undertake returning the hospitality that she had been so generously shown.

Even that was easy. The young matron had only to hand over all the details to her housekeeper and staff, confer on the essentials such as the menu and what she would serve to drink, and the rest of her time could be consumed with the burning question of what she would wear. The housemaids would clean the house and pick up after the guests. Herod would see to dispensing the liquor and the service, Amanda would supervise the cook and lay in the stores, and thus Sarianna would accomplish the arduous task of planning a dinner party.

And this, she thought, was what Dona had had at her command. She reveled in it, and she felt dull-witted about it at the same time. How much she had given up by allowing Rex to isolate her like that. How much she had missed. And that didn't even speak to her feelings about Vesta and Jeralee. But Vesta had been born to expect such lavishness. Vesta had meant to exclude her from the very first.

She counted them lessons well learned, and when her guests entered her home—young married women like herself, a sprinkling of lighthearted bachelors, and of course, Pierce—she felt the particular power of a woman who knows she is beautiful, accepted and successful.

When Cade returned home that night quite unexpectedly, he found Sarianna in the newly remodeled parlor, seated on the curvy reupholstered sofa surrounded by men—and Pierce, he noted disdainfully—holding court to both the men and women who were her guests, looking impossibly beautiful dressed in a sapphire silk dress that bared her shoulders and heightened the color of her eyes, and the first horrifying thing he thought was that Dona had come back to life and was entertaining in his parlor.

He hated the self-possessed way she greeted him and collectedly introduced him to her guests, most of whom he did not know. He

258

excused himself to wash and change, and when he returned to the parlor, Sarianna was strumming her guitar and Pierce and three of the guests were singing some simple ballads. While he ate his dinner, the men retired to his office and the ladies kept company in the parlor, exclaiming over Sarianna's competence with the guitar and never noticing or commenting that she played it upside down. And when he was finally ready to join them, they were ready to leave.

And all he could think of was how much like Dona she was. And how conscientiously like Dona was she deliberately? It was as if time had stopped altogether, he was being drawn into the snare of believing it, and Sarianna was going to try her best to make the delusion become truth.

When she joined him in the parlor, she found him examining all the changes with a minute eye to detail.

"I hope you approve," she said with just a touch of uneasiness. She didn't know why she felt nervous about his reception of the changes. Dona would have gone full steam ahead and ignored his opinion altogether. But she waited, and after a few minutes he turned to her and nodded. "It's very nice, Sarianna. I especially like the seating arrangement by the fireplace. I gather," he added, swinging around so that he would not be looking at her, "that your first venture entertaining was a success."

"Yes," she concurred, "it was rather nice. And look—" she held up her left hand—"it came through unscathed."

He took her hand and kissed it, swamped by the eerie feeling it was not Sarianna's hand his lips touched but Dona's. She reacted like Sarianna, leaving her hand in his firm grip for another moment, searching his eyes as he lifted them to look at her face, and then finally she pulled her hand away and turned a little pirouette in front of him in almost the same motion that Dona used to.

"I hope you like my dress."

"I do," he said. "I like your dress."

She curtseyed, and then straightened up and became businesslike in a way he did not like either. "You've eaten? Yes? Well, you must be tired, Cade. Are you back for just this evening? No? Then we can talk in the morning? Good. I'd like to convey my appreciation to Amanda for the beautiful table she presented. The meal was extraordinary, don't you think?" And he watched as she wafted away from him in a sea of rustling blue silk, as out of reach as the ghost of Dona that had begun to haunt the substance of his life.

In the morning, calling cards arrived, and Alzine presented them to Sarianna at the breakfast table as she and Cade had their coffee.

"I don' like it," Alzine said, placing the silver salver beside Sarianna's plate.

"There's nothing not to like," Sarianna said, reaching for the topmost envelope which she knew already was an invitation to pay a morning call to one of her guests' social arbiter of a mother. "Yes"— she nodded in satisfaction—"this one we will do, naturally . . . Alzine —there's the doorbell. It's probably Pierce." She didn't look at Cade; what did he expect after all? This had been a normal part of her routine for the past two weeks. At first, she had been grateful for his presence and comfort, his assurances that Cade would never fault her for the money she was spending and things she commissioned.

Within a very short time, the visit had become something a little more than that and a little less. She found she liked his uncritical company and his covert admiration. She could look at him as her advisor with whom it was expedient to consult daily, and it made his visits much more creditable—in his eyes, and her own. He could not be censured for seeing to her comfort as her husband's lawyer; she could not be rebuked for allowing a wiser and more knowledgeable man to see to her affairs while her husband was away.

But always beneath that socially respectable banner lurked the other thing: His awareness of her as a desirable woman, and his sojourn at Bredwood—which he never spoke about again—had not mitigated any of his feelings about her one bit. If anything, he was inordinately proud that she had adjusted so superbly to her new situation and the exigencies of being married to a man like Cade.

"I don' like dat neither," Alzine said stolidly as she turned to see to the door. And she had told Miss Sarianna not once but twenty times how much she did not like Mr. Pierce's morning visits, and coddling afternoon visits, and almost every night visits, and she thought if Mr. Cade found out, Miss Sarianna was going to be in deep trouble. It was enough to see his scowl as she passed by him on her way out of the dining room.

260

But it was worse to see it still in place as she escorted Pierce into the room. He, as always, was jovial as he seated himself and nodded yes to Sarianna's offer of coffee. "I reckon you're going to want an accounting," he said cheerfully to Cade, and delved into the inside pocket of his coat and pulled forth a folded piece of paper.

Cade waved it away. "I don't particularly want to talk money my first day home from that cauldron of a piece of property I am stuck with. You know I brought in the first forty bales of cotton, Pierce, and there's enough to press another twenty-five to thirty, except the damned gin broke down. Collard's got the haul, and I expect to see you later with names of places I can get parts."

"I am at your service," Pierce said instantly. "Now let me congratulate Sarianna on her triumph last night. What compliments we heard on the drive home. Cade—I wish you could have heard; you'd have burst your buttons at how successfully Sarianna has conquered Savannah."

"Oh, really, Pierce. A half dozen of your friends cannot constitute the whole of Savannah," Sarianna said coyly, and Pierce raised his hands in a gesture of deferring to her.

"Nevertheless, Sarianna, you were a superlative hostess." He lifted his coffee cup. "I salute you." He sipped and put it down again. "And now I must be off. Cade. Sarianna." He removed himself quickly and gracefully from the dining table, and Alzine led him with dispatch to the front door. He never saw Sarianna hiding a smile in her coffee cup, or Cade's look of extreme exasperation.

"Mr. Darden is too punctilious," Sarianna said, picking up a muffin and crumbling it in her fingers.

"It's one of his best qualities," Cade said, "his obvious and genuine concern for your welfare."

"How nice of you to notice," Sarianna said. "It's a trait I value."

"It's a lot of damned hogwash, Sarianna." Cade threw down his napkin impatiently. "What the devil's going on with you?"

Sarianna shrugged. "Nothing in particular. I've been occupying myself, and I'm pleased about this little party, and the next thing on my agenda is a nice long soothing bath." She sent him a guileless blue look. "I had supposed that would please you. I *am* trying to please you."

He stood up abruptly. "I can see that; I just wonder if I *am* pleased."

"You have only to tell me what you would like changed and I will do it," Sarianna said helpfully. "But I'm afraid now I have to plan my round of morning visits. Do excuse me, Cade." She rose gracefully and patted his hand as he stood there nonplussed, and as he watched her graceful exit into the hallway, he couldn't help thinking, *Just like Dona, damn it—incredibly like Dona, damn her face.*

And he couldn't in the following days make a dent in that bright, helpful, faintly patronizing attitude she had seemed to have developed since she left Haverhill. She became fastidious in bed, not allowing herself to give rein to her sensual urges, and there were nights he felt as if he were making love to a china doll. Like Dona, he thought, he felt deep inside himself. Dona at the root of everything. Dona would have been exactly the same with him in bed. Dona would never have begged for his kisses, but neither did Sarianna any more.

The fleshy body that had responded to his carnal kiss had been buried in petticoats, crinoline cages and corsets. Tactile silk shrouded the taut tips of her breasts that no longer yearned for his touch. The burning need for fusion between them was gone. She was there for him now, an accommodating body who enjoyed in an aloof kind of way his uncontrollable lust for her and her own constrained release.

It wasn't the same, and it wasn't what he wanted.

But maybe he hadn't known what he wanted. Maybe this Sarianna was the foreordained end result of all his machinations.

He decided to remain in Savannah to observe her, and Pierce was not very happy to find him the next day right in his accustomed spot at breakfast. Neither was Cade pleased to see Pierce.

"Is he here every day?" he demanded of Sarianna, and she shrugged. "I guess he is. I never thought about it, Cade."

Her tepid response made him feel murderous. But it wasn't only Pierce, he discovered. There was a small covey of gallants who called on Sarianna at any given time of the afternoon or evening. They were friends of Pierce's, or the university student sons of planter clients of Pierce's, and they all, in the several weeks that he had been away off and on, had sworn their vapid allegiance to Sarianna's welfare. It was comical—and distressing—and he didn't know quite what to do with

262

all that relentless adoration sitting in his front parlor.

"Sarianna, this is insane," he protested at one point.

"How so when I'm enjoying it so much?" she asked prettily, knowing already that her inexorable feminine guile was exacerbating his temper while it was feeding her conceit. She loved all the blatant adoration that demanded nothing more from her than a smile. And she loved the latent possibility of it becoming something more—but only if she desired it. How seductive all that unearned devotion was! It was almost too easy to begin to take it all for granted. She even felt a little contempt for how easily her admirers could be manipulated.

Of course, not Cade, and her fatuous words fell on deaf ears. He plainly didn't believe her assertion, and his expression showed it.

"Are you?" he questioned dryly.

"Look at all those lovely men awaiting their first glimpse of me," Sarianna said, and swept into the parlor. Instantly they surrounded her, and he watched her faintly disdainful maneuvering among them as if he were watching a play. They liked her haughty air, he thought in amazement, and they waited breathlessly for the one moment she would drop it altogether and favor one of them so as to single him out. They wanted her to be untouchable, aloof. Yet one of them wanted to be the one who would thaw her, and all of them wanted her to be the one to choose.

And when they were not there—and sometimes even when they were—Pierce danced attendance on her, with an ease of manner that proclaimed to everyone else that he stood on more familiar terms with her than all of her professed cavaliers.

Like him. Like Dona. She had loved Cade better than the rest—she had said—and he had agonized everytime he lost her in a crowd of sycophantic men. Agonized wasn't the word for it. And it didn't nearly approach what he was feeling now as he watched Sarianna in a scene that could have been a reprise of the past; with himself in the parlor at Greenpoint, or some other Sawny Island home, awaiting Dona's arrival impatiently, only to see her disappear into a crowd of anxious bucks who only sought the same thing from her that he did: the assuaging word and the lover's touch.

They continued on this way for the succeeding month, and Cade's patience stretched to the breaking point, while Sarianna became more placid in her acceptance of her role and her changing guard of men friends, and a shade too fatuous about the whole thing to suit his taste. The only constant was Pierce, and damn it, Pierce was too constant, Cade thought. It was obvious he, too, was hard put to keep away from Sarianna, and he had had to cut his visits from three times a day to one—and sometimes two when he could not stand being parted from her another minute.

There were times that Cade thought he was going crazy just listening to their honeyed conversation. There was nothing about this Sarianna that was even remotely lovable, and Pierce hung on her every word.

"I must have sensed somehow you were coming tonight," Sarianna would say as she entered the room and allowed Pierce to grasp her hands too tightly in his own.

"I hope you felt my need to see you," Pierce would answer. "But why do you say that, Sarianna? You could not have known."

"I just had this feeling I ought to change my dress because something special was going to happen tonight," Sarianna would tell him.

"I knew you looked especially delectable tonight," Pierce's response would come instantly. He didn't know whether she *had* changed—Cade knew damned well she hadn't—but he was flattered by the fact she had consciously thought of him at all, and never questioned the truth of any statement she made. He thought he was special to her, her glowing sapphire eyes seemed to tell him he was, and he was content for the moment with that and his open door entree to Cade's house.

And sometimes Pierce would say, "Your eyes are so beautiful, Sarianna. Has anyone ever told you how deep and blue and trusting they are?"

And she would push him away with words. "Don't be silly, Pierce; of course my eyes are blue, but who cares whether they are trusting or not. I wouldn't—actually—think they are."

Or he would say, "You *are* an opulent creature, Sarianna. Who would have guessed two months ago that you would turn into this bewitchingly proper lady who crooks a finger and steals every man's heart."

"Not I," Sarianna would say, knowing the irony was totally lost on him.

"No one could have known—least of all you," he would go on. "But you are such perfection that it is impossible for a man not to fall in love with you instantly."

"Do you think every man I meet does?" she would ask innocently.

"I believe they can't help it, Sarianna. But I also think you haven't given your heart to anyone yet, not even Cade."

Then Sarianna would remember Cade's mind-shattering carnal kiss, and she would think that indeed if she could give her heart to someone it would be the man who dared to beg to kiss her there. But he didn't exist any more than she did. They were both figments of circumstance, and it had been naive of her to think otherwise.

"My heart is here," she would tell Pierce, and touch her breast in the most seductively innocuous way possible, and it would make him catch his breath in his throat to think of all the delights of her body and who would be privileged to awaken those deeply trusting eyes. "I'm sure you have a piece of it," she would add, playing to his avid gaze that followed her hands with no attempt to hide his interest.

"If only I could ask you which piece," Pierce would importune—but even that was enough for one night with him. If she gave too much it might spoil the game; it was enough to know, as always, that she thought of him.

And so, in order to forestall any more of this sickening nonsense, Cade began escorting Sarianna around town, to a concert here, a recital there, an opera, the theater, a party at the home of friends of *his* where they ran into more chivalrous fervor from a new set of gentlemen meeting Sarianna for the first time.

Cade felt as if he were in a bad drama detailing scenes from his very own life. Sarianna was beautiful and Sarianna was kind. Sarianna was his, and she spent the most inordinate amount of time playing up to the frailties of men who were instantly smitten with her.

One night, when they came home from dining out at eleven o'clock at night, and they found a frantic Pierce waiting on their doorstep, Cade decided enough was enough. It was time to seclude Sarianna at Haverhill where he had had men working on the house for the past month.

And then he felt a resonating chill; he was actually thinking in terms of immuring her at Haverhill where she would see no one and no one could see her.

Insanity. Pierce would come willy-nilly, and he could not keep everyone away.

But the thing that terrified him most was that he had thought of the notion in those terms at all. He was no better than Rex Broydon, and maybe Rex had felt the same desperation as well. He had something in common with his enemy—the man who had set out to destroy Sarianna in the first place.

18

Haverhill, he thought, could manage without him being there full time. The next week Cade went back there, reluctantly, on a daily basis, with the fulminating feeling he shouldn't leave Sarianna alone even for those few hours.

He hated leave-takings. He hated parting from Sarianna. But he could not tell, from her attitude, how she felt. She gave him a chaste kiss on the lips and, unbeknownst to him, watched his departure from the parlor window.

But now, she thought, she would have yet another whole delicious day to do whatever she wanted. She wasn't sure what she wanted.

Alzine huffed into the room and demanded she attend to her breakfast. Amanda came in to consult her about the evening's menu and whether Cade would be home to dinner. Afterward, she admitted the workmen who were going to finish the construction on the uppermost floor, and she looked through the pile of invitations and mail that had arrived subsequent to breakfast.

These were easy to sort; she had become selective, perhaps too selective, but it seemed to her that she did not want to go about as much as she had before. Well, maybe not quite as much. But surely there was something of interest to do this morning, some brief visit she could pay that would relieve the boredom of staying home and listening to Alzine's mutterings about how she had become too fancy and too particular—which she had *not*—and how she was playing a dangerous game with Mr. Cade that might well backfire.

Sarianna reprimanded her in her best Dona voice. Alzine had changed as much as she, she reflected, now that she didn't have to scuttle about between the capricious whims of Jeralee and her own minimal requirements. Alzine had always cared about her, but here, away from the oppression of Bredwood, she really was overstepping her bounds.

"You think you is some big lady now," Alzine said stubbornly. "And you gonna be goin' to Mr. Cade's big house soon, and dere you is gonna be Miss Sarianna all over again how you should be. I don't like it, Miss Sarianna, dat's all I got to say."

"Which is more than enough," Sarianna retorted. "It's not your place to criticize how I choose to live my life."

"No, it ain't; but I be seein' how you treatin' Mr. Cade after all he done fo' you, and you got no shame about it neither. You done changed de minute you come back from de big house, and I'm tellin' you, Miss Sarianna, I don' like it; and I don' like dat Mr. Pierce oilin' his way 'round here all de time neither."

"That's *enough*," Sarianna said, but her reproof was mild. She wasn't sure she much liked it herself. But the adulation was seductive: all that perfection rooted in someone else's perception which had nothing to do with who she was at all. On the other hand, she was not Dona either, and she had the uneasy feeling that all her infatuated gentlemen friends were responding to *that* aspect of her, and that was frightening.

"My bath," Sarianna said, cutting off Alzine's next words.

"Yas'm," Alzine said, shooting her a baleful look. She knew just what Sarianna was about. She would spend the next half hour or so in a leisurely bath, and choose a new fashionable outfit to wear to whichever of the dozen invitations that had arrived this morning appealed to her. She would go off for an hour, and return for lunch and her invariable mealtime companion, Pierce Darden. Pierce would leave; Sarianna would bathe once again and consider what she wanted to do for the evening. If Mr. Cade were home, he would elect the evening's diversion, and Alzine knew full well he had begun to get very tired of uninvited company.

She didn't understand herself what the attraction was for Miss Sarianna to run around like that in the company of people she didn't care about at all. Maybe, she thought, as she tested Sarianna's bath water later, Mr. Cade was letting her have a lot of rope. Maybe Mr. Cade had some plan in his mind to turn Miss Sarianna off the course she was traveling.

Miss Sarianna was getting too involved with her own self; she was getting too bossy and aloof. Miss Sarianna was reminding her more and more of Miss Vesta, Alzine thought dourly, and that troubled her mightily. She didn't think Miss Sarianna was even aware of it. Miss Sarianna wasn't seeing anything she didn't want to, and if Miss Sarianna didn't watch out, she would likely become more like Miss Vesta than Miss Vesta herself.

Sarianna was bored. She sat in the parlor of the Barre house on Lafayette Square and politely clapped as one of the Soames girls showed off her artistry on the harp, and the several admirers who had shown up for afternoon tea latched on to whichever lady piqued his fancy. Sarianna was not surprised either to see Pierce in attendance or that he approached her as Emma struck the last note on the harp.

Pierce sat down beside her. "I thought to see you at the historical society exhibition today."

"I decided not to go," Sarianna said, her eyes scanning the room for someone of interest to talk to. Pierce was fast pushing himself out of that category with her; lately all his talk had been centered on his admiration of her, and she wasn't sure she could stand much more of leading him around by his nose. What she really wanted, she thought, was to go to Haverhill and take up her duties there. But even that nebulous wish was a little frightening: A sense of the past was so firmly entrenched there, she didn't know how she could compete with it. Here, it was easy. Here, the Pierces of their cloistered little set took matters totally out of her hands and made it simple.

She missed Cade—already—and there was a little niggling voice in her that derided the course she had taken which denied her the complete fulfillment he could give her. She had been a lady in bed, and she knew he did not like this new manifestation of her rebirth in Savannah. He didn't like Pierce's constant attention, and he didn't like how self-absorbed she had become.

What she didn't like was that he said nothing about it.

What she didn't want to explore was whether she was goading him to do it.

"Dear Sarianna, this round of appointments every day must tire you out terribly," Pierce said sympathetically, reaching for her hand.

She allowed him to take it, even allowed him to play with the ruffle of lace around her wrist. He bored her. His gestures, his words, his concern never changed from day to day. He never got angry with her or frustrated. He never demanded more than she gave. He never tried to divine the nature of the relationship between her and Cade. Sometimes she wondered just what he wanted of her because he didn't seem to want what a lot of the other men were not shy of asking.

Some of them were downright bold.

"What else do I have to do?" Sarianna wondered, more to herself than to him.

"It's true," he agreed. "You were much busier at Bredwood, but I wager you don't wish you were back there now."

"No," she said, surprised at his oblique reference to what she was coming to think of as her other life, "I wish we were ready to move to Haverhill."

"Sarianna!" He sounded honestly shocked. "So far away . . . from town—" He broke off abruptly, and she knew what he had not said— "from me"—and she thought that perhaps she couldn't wait to get away from him. He was too possessive and too blank altogether.

"Not so far from town," she contradicted as Emma Soames approached her to say a word, and rapped her fan flirtatiously against Pierce's shoulder.

It was more interesting, Sarianna thought, to watch women's responses to Pierce and the other eligible bachelors who put in an appearance for which they would be repaid with good food, witty conversation and perhaps the opportunity to put themselves forward with a promising young woman with whom they were only marginally acquainted.

Emma Soames didn't know Pierce at all except by reputation, but it was obvious she wanted to get to know him better in this socially acceptable circumstance where her mother hovered just by the music room door overseeing that everything was exactly as it should be.

Sarianna ignored Pierce's imploring look and graciously offered Emma her seat, hiding a smile as Emma jumped into it with unseemly alacrity. Emma was passingly pretty with slender hands and a heavy face. Pierce was discomfitted by her interest, and his darkening gaze followed Sarianna as she moved away in a total breach of good manners. Emma never noticed; he responded so reassuringly and interestedly to her comments.

Sarianna helped herself to some cakes and tea from the tea table, reflecting on how different this scene was from the last time she had been in company at Bredwood.

Amazing how Bredwood kept sliding insidiously into her thoughts. Everything *was* different now; she could hold her own with anyone, and she knew now she had always been able to do so. There was no need to make comparisons or have regrets. She was just weary of this go-round of meaningless events. Nothing made it clearer to her than the sight of Pierce squirming under the excessive enthusiasm of Emma Soames, who wouldn't let him utter one banal excuse to escape her earnest attempt to keep him by her side.

She put down her cup and plate and made her way toward her hostess to make her excuses. She left Pierce in a welter of frustrated fury as Emma Soames got a grip on his coat sleeve and wouldn't let him follow Sarianna out the door.

"That was damned unkind of you," Pierce told her heatedly at dinner. In point of fact, he thought it was more than unkind; it was downright sadistic of her to leave him in Emma Soames' clutches. He had even stewed about it for several hours, hoping to punish her for her abuse.

But she didn't seem in the least perturbed by his agitation. Nothing he said ruffled her composure as she invited him to stay to a dinner of *daube glacé* and a cheese soufflé. Two glasses of wine did nothing to calm him. He couldn't understand how she could just sit there placidly eating, totally untouched by his vexation.

"I thought it was very kind," Sarianna said. "Emma had your undivided attention, and that was only right."

He sputtered into his wineglass. "Sarianna—really? Emma is a dead bore, and her mother is trying desperately to marry her off."

"But we all know that," Sarianna pointed out. "But when you accept an invitation to the Soames', you tacitly agree to play the game, don't you think? I'm not the eligible bachelor, you know."

"I wish you were," he said fervently. "And the rest is neither here nor there."

"I'm afraid," Sarianna said regretfully, "that it is very much *here*; Cade plans to return here every night from now on."

"Fine. *Let* him." Pierce felt very close to violence. He couldn't get through to her. How could he conceive of becoming involved with

271

another woman when there was Sarianna? How could she not know it?

She rang a little bell to summon Alzine to clear the table. Alzine frowned at her and totally ignored Pierce, who resorted to pouring and sipping still another glass of wine while all this obvious hostility flared around him.

"We have a light lemon pudding for dessert," Sarianna said serenely. "We had an abbreviated dinner tonight of course because we didn't know when Cade would return."

She was so elegant, Pierce thought, as Alzine jostled him covertly; no wonder Alzine felt so protective of her. But no one worshipped her more than he. He wondered when it had begun. When he had first met her at Bredwood, he had not considered her very prepossessing. He had felt sorry for her; he had wanted to ease her burden as much as possible. But this intense devotion he felt . . . that had started when she and Cade were finally in Savannah. When, he thought with a rare flash of insight, she had come into her own, unhampered by the constraints her family had imposed on her. When, in fact, she had become Mrs. Cade Rensell.

The notion interested him for all of a moment: Sarianna had become desirable because another man desired her. He didn't know where to take that thought. He certainly would not have pursued her so ardently had she stayed at Bredwood (but then there was all that formidable opposition), and he certainly intended to follow her to Haverhill. The oddity of it did not strike him. In Savannah, she was Sarianna—*his* Sarianna. What she had been at Bredwood, he could not define at all.

But because he was recalling her days at Bredwood, he suddenly noticed that she handed him his dessert plate with her left hand, served his coffee with that same hand, used her fork with that hand, and rang the bell which sat to her left and thus close by him which suddenly made it jangle annoyingly in his ears.

Well, there was that; but he hardly paid attention to it any more. No one noticed it at all, and now that he thought about it, he perceived that she handled her wrong-handedness very unobtrusively in company.

He felt a rush of tenderness for her delicacy and covered it by lifting a spoonful of pudding to his mouth just as the doorbell rang.

He almost choked when Alzine came rushing into the room, almost incoherent with her announcement. "Oh, Miss Sarianna, Miss Sarianna. Miss Vesta done come, Miss Vesta done come! Her and Miss Jeralee is in the parlor and dey ain't goin' nowhere; dey done come to stay!"

Sarianna froze. Vesta here! The gall! For one frenetic moment she did not know what to do. The invasive presence of Vesta in her house paralyzed her, and she felt a long heated wash of helplessness. *Why* wasn't Cade here by now? she wondered frantically. How could she deal with Vesta's totally unwarranted visit? How could she deal with Vesta altogether—*and* Jeralee?

And then the question of going in to greet Vesta was removed from her hands as Vesta swept into the dining room and surveyed them both with that habitual snide look of hers.

"That stupid Alzine is moving so slow these days—imagine her leaving me and Jeralee in the parlor as if we were some unexpected strangers."

Sarianna lifted her golden head and her panic disappeared. "Hello, Vesta, have some lemon pudding," she said collectedly, helping herself to a second plateful.

"How can you talk about lemon pudding after the disastrous trip we have had from Bredwood? Honestly, Sarianna, your manners are still lacking. Where are your servants? We need help with our trunks and some money to pay the carriage man."

Sarianna shrugged. "I have no money. Are you saying you expect to stay here while you look for accommodations in Savannah?" She felt a trill of pure catty triumph as Vesta seemed taken aback.

"My dear girl, we expect to stay with you. *Everyone* expects us to stay with you. Where else would we go when we come in to Savannah? Your wits are addled, Sarianna. You do not send your kin to a hotel."

Sarianna stood up. Now, she thought, was the time to take control or Vesta would wrest it from her with the dirtiest tactics. She had already started, and Sarianna could not afford to let her get more than a toehold in the battle of wits between them. "*Kin,*" she said pointedly, "would have been sensitive to the fact that Cade and I are newlyweds and would not have intruded on our privacy."

Vesta sent a searing look in Pierce's direction. "And lawyers are known for their sensitivity," she snapped, a little put out by

Sarianna's cavalier dismissal of her claim.

"Mr. Darden is here to discuss business," Sarianna said, daring Vesta to dispute that. Vesta looked just as if she wanted to contradict her, but she had no weapons: Pierce was formally dressed, the hour was early, Cade did not seem to be around, which only meant there was some degree of propriety in Pierce's bearing her company until his return.

"I suppose," Vesta said, "that is Cade's business, not mine, but I tell you there are ten trunks outside on your stoop and a very impatient young man who is waiting to be paid, and I would appreciate your doing something about it."

"Surely you could have thought of that before you even left Bredwood," Sarianna said politely, seating herself again and attacking her lemon pudding with all the anger with which she would have liked to attack Vesta.

Vesta didn't like being ignored; worse, she didn't like being stepped on by this upstart of a Sarianna and her exquisite dismissing politeness. She expected to stay in the house on Malverne Row, and nothing was going to prevent it. She turned to Pierce. "Mr. Darden, you can see how impossible this is."

"I think the simplest solution would be for you to go right back to Bredwood," Sarianna said complacently, resolutely keeping her eyes on her food so she didn't have to confront Vesta's furious face.

"My dear girl, I'm embarrassed to death by your obtuseness," Vesta said, striving for an even tone of voice. "You cannot leave us standing on your steps all night."

"I'm sure you were counting on that," Sarianna said composedly.

"You *will not* embarrass me like this!"

"I'm afraid you're doing it very well yourself," Sarianna said, and lifted her little bell to summon Alzine.

Alzine scuttled in, scooped up the two plates from the table and disappeared fast. The hostility in the room was thick and corrosive, and she had been listening at the door, rooting for Miss Sarianna. But she couldn't imagine Miss Sarianna actually sending Miss Vesta away again. Not this late, this night.

"Sarianna," Pierce broke into the stalemate.

"Yes, Pierce?" she asked deferentially—too deferentially, he thought, and he felt shaken. Of course she should take his advice, and she should be a little more charitable toward Vesta's miscalculation of her reception. Of course after the wedding, Vesta had had a lot to say; indeed, she had shifted all blame to Sarianna's heedless shoulders. Pierce didn't care to debate the truth of her version of events or Sarianna's. After all, he had seen first hand how they had ignored her and disparaged her.

However, she had the upper hand now, and she could afford to be generous. But she didn't look as if she felt like being generous. She looked unruffled and perfectly at ease and very much as if she would not welcome his interference.

He had to try. "*I* will pay the driver," he said firmly, "and I believe that Owen should bring in the trunks. Perhaps you could leave them in the morning parlor until Cade returns. It isn't as if you don't have the accommodations, Sarianna."

Sarianna flashed him an exasperated look. "I do not wish to entertain Vesta in this house," she said painstakingly, speaking solely to Pierce.

"Well, you needn't *entertain* us," Vesta interpolated. "We merely need a place to stay while we pursue various activities in the city. What could be simpler than that? You would never know we are here."

Sarianna made a moue of disgust. "You have a most extraordinary way of interpreting the facts, Vesta. You always have." She wondered why Vesta and Jeralee had slithered away from Bredwood to arrive in the city in the dark of the night. She wondered a lot of things, not the least of which was whether Vesta had something else in mind with this precipitate visit.

"And you have the most irritating way of ignoring them," Vesta retorted. "This is getting us nowhere. Jeralee and I are here and we can't—nor do we want to—leave. Alzine, I'm sure, would be happy to show us to the guest rooms. Do what you will with our trunks, Sarianna. *I'm* going to bed." She turned and flounced out of the room, calling, "Alzine! *Alzine!* Where *is* that stupid girl? *Alzine!*"

Alzine peered around the door into the dining room. "I ain't goin' nowhere near dat lady less'n you say so, Miss Sarianna. She gonna kill someone, she is. Dat Miss Jeralee is just settin' dere in de parlor and waitin' fo' someone to come waitin' on her."

"Let them wait," Sarianna said. "You go back to the kitchen and ask Amanda to come in here. We will deal with Miss Vesta the best way we can. Although I'm not quite sure—" she slanted a baleful look at Pierce—"exactly what that way will be."

Pierce paid their carriage driver, and he and Owen brought the trunks up into the hallway while Sarianna conferred with Amanda. Amanda was a treasure, old and wise and very perceptive. "You must take in Miss Vesta," she pronounced. "There is no other way." Her gleaming dark eyes took in everything—Sarianna's hostility particularly.

"I know that; I just do not want her to become too comfortable."

"We treat our guests very well in Mr. Cade's house," Amanda said slowly, "but of course there can be times when the available accommodations might not be quite what we would wish for our guests—for one reason or another."

Sarianna considered for a moment. "Oh, yes? Yes, you are right. Work is proceeding as fast as it can be arranged on the third floor. It's truly a shame we must house them on the top floor . . ."

"Yes?" Amanda said softly.

". . . but of course they wouldn't want to sleep in rooms that are in disarray because of painting and plastering," Sarianna finished in perfect accord with Amanda's thinking.

"I will attend to it," Amanda said, and left Sarianna to return to the parlor where Vesta paced the floor fuming and Jeralee sat unconcerned trying to engage in conversation with a very exacerbated Pierce who awaited Sarianna's decision as if his very adoration of her hung in the balance.

Sarianna entered the room quietly and with a definite air of being in charge. She nodded at Jeralee and seated herself on the sofa opposite her. "Well, I have to say that under other circumstances I would have been very happy to welcome you, Vesta, and Jeralee, for an extended stay with us. But apart from the fact that Cade and I are still not formally receiving or entertaining, there is another reason that a surprise visit was not politic at this time: We are refurbishing the guest room floor, Vesta, and everything is totally pulled apart, the furniture has either been sent out or has been packed away so it doesn't get stained. So I'm not in the position of offering you our usual guest arrangements. However, there is no question that you are welcome to stay."

Vesta stopped her pacing. "I don't believe you."

Sarianna hid a smile. "I beg your pardon?"

"I said I don't believe you," Vesta repeated grittily.

"Vesta, this is really outside of enough. If you *need* an explanation, I may tell you that Cade has given me free rein to redecorate the house, and I have been doing so in stages so as to disrupt as little as possible. I did not take into account that we would be having unexpected guests of course, but if you really must have proof, you certainly are welcome to go upstairs and see for yourself."

Vesta stopped short, taken aback. Redecorate the house? Her mind immediately conjured up a bottom line figure on what that was going to cost Cade, as well as the money he would have to sink into Haverhill. The sum was staggering to her, and Sarianna's smugness about it didn't help her temper either. She still didn't put it past Sarianna to try any ploy to make them leave, and she was just as determined to stay no matter what they had to put up with. She didn't have a fair hope of interesting Cade in Jeralee with the hope of displacing Sarianna, but she still thought it was a shame that Sarianna had the run of all that lovely money and Jeralee had nothing.

More than that, she had a score to settle with Sarianna, and though she didn't know quite how she was going to do it, she had been quite sure she could accomplish nothing staying at Bredwood with Rex drowning himself in whiskey.

"Yes," she said finally, knowing that good manners required that she back down at this point, "I would like to see for myself."

Pierce looked aghast, and Jeralee looked utterly bored. "Must I climb all those stairs?" she asked.

"I'm afraid you will have to get used to it if you intend to stay," Sarianna said, and led the way up the stairs with Vesta and Pierce close behind her.

What miracle had Amanda been able to accomplish in these ten minutes, she wondered as they approached the first doorway on the third floor. Vesta flung it open, and the smell of paint assaulted their senses.

Sarianna took the lamp from its hallway bracket and led the way within the room. "Well," she said, turning around, as much surprised at what they found as Vesta and Pierce. The furniture was draped and tacked in a way that made it look like huge wrapped presents. Buckets lined the floor, and obviously, she thought, someone had smeared a lot of paint over the walls; the odor was overpowering. The bed was buried, and the room looked stark and uninviting. The second bedroom was in comparatively the same state, and the little hallway room at the front of the house was stuffed with odds and ends and pictures, end tables and one narrow bed, the foot of which could be seen in the lamplight.

"This is abominable," Vesta said heatedly.

"It can't be rectified tonight, certainly," Sarianna told her. "And perhaps not tomorrow, since the workmen are not expected back this week. There had been some plan," she lied audaciously, "of my staying the rest of the week with Cade at Haverhill." She ignored Pierce's look and replaced the hallway lamp in its bracket. "Well, the top floor rooms, while they are smaller, are just as comfortable, Vesta, I assure you."

"Two rooms on half the floor! Really, Sarianna, *how* comfortable could that be?" Vesta snorted.

"It's the best I can do on short notice," Sarianna said, reining in her temper. "Perhaps tomorrow you can relocate, if you find things are inconvenient for you here."

Vesta pulled back on her annoyance. She was not leaving Malverne Row—no matter what obstacles Sarianna threw in her path. She felt as if it were a fight to the death. Only one of them could win, and she meant to finish what she set out to do at Bredwood: destroy Sarianna.

It was like looking at Dona seated across the table from her in the morning. Vesta closed her eyes and opened them again, and the Dona-vision was still there.

Except it was Sarianna, expensively dressed, utterly composed and handling the silver coffee pot which Alzine had just set on the table. Delicate china plates were stacked to one side of Sarianna's place, and within five minutes, Herod appeared wheeling a service cart full of covered dishes, all hot and fragrant from the oven.

Vesta simmered with hate as she avidly watched Sarianna serve—first Pierce who had joined them for breakfast this morning when they learned that Cade did not expect to return home that night; then Jeralee and Vesta herself who demanded as much as her plate would hold, with the exhilarating feeling that she was taking from Sarianna, taking from Dona as Sarianna handed her a heaping plate of eggs, biscuits, ham and griddle cakes.

Sarianna poured the coffee, all with her awkward hand, Vesta thought with some satisfaction, and passed each cup around the table. For herself she took a biscuit and some ham and regarded Vesta across the table with the face of a concerned hostess.

"I hope you were comfortable last night," she said, as she took a sip of coffee. She had no appetite this morning, none at all. The thought of facing Vesta, Jeralee *and* Pierce across a breakfast table was daunting. Vesta did not look happy—she looked greedy, vindictive, and hollow-eyed, as if she had lain awake all night, just to prove the point of how inhospitable Sarianna had been.

But of course, Sarianna thought, there was no one to whom she could air her complaints.

"I don't like climbing all those stairs," Jeralee said pettishly.

"The beds weren't terribly comfortable," Vesta added, shoving a fork into her eggs vehemently. "There's hardly any wardrobe space and the rooms are so small there is nowhere at all to reasonably get dressed. You must remedy this, Sarianna."

"Why couldn't we use your rooms?" Jeralee asked, focusing her melty chocolate gaze on Pierce.

"I'm afraid you would have given Cade quite a shock if he had wound up in our bed with you and Vesta," Sarianna said lightly, but she was aghast at the interested expression that crossed Jeralee's face, almost as if Jeralee had not pursued that selfish idea to its ultimate conclusion. She would have liked that, Sarianna thought, utterly bedazzled by the depth of Jeralee's grasping selfishness, as well as the implication that Cade might have found that situation more to his liking as well.

But perhaps her jesting words had given Jeralee an opening she had not intended. "Of course," Sarianna added, with just the right touch of unconcerned disdain, "he would have noticed the difference immediately and torn down the house until he found me. No, Jeralee, I'm afraid you can't use our bedroom. Nor Cade's office which is not equipped for overnight guests."

"Well you must call your workmen and have them finish," Vesta commanded.

"I certainly will do that," Sarianna said agreeably, but she knew already what she would tell Vesta. "And that is as much as I *can* do today." She looked up at Alzine as she approached with the salver of mail. "Thank you, Alzine." The pile of envelopes looked particularly inviting, and rather than open them, she let them sit in the silver tray by her elbow, as she saw both Vesta's and Jeralee's covert glances resting there from time to time.

What must they think? she wondered, as she tried to draw Pierce into the inconsequential conversation. Were they surprised? Stunned? Envious? She hoped they were envious; she hoped they were stewing in jealousy that Jeralee could have as much were it not for her mean-spirited nature.

She had the feeling that Vesta was back in Savannah to search for a husband for Jeralee, and that she wanted to scout out how much Sarianna had in order not to accept less for her own daughter. It was too ugly, and the calculation of it was amplified by Pierce's pained expression as his loyalty was divided between his devotion to *her*, and his finely honed notions of what was right and due to relatives.

"Pierce, you are looking particularly put out." She approached him when Vesta had excused herself to finish her morning toilette after dictatorially ordering a bath at the instant.

"They should not be housed in what is essentially the attic of this house," Pierce said forcefully.

"Perhaps *you* could put them up," Sarianna suggested coolly. "And tell *me*, by the way, *why* I should want to put them up, or put up with them at all for that matter?"

"She's your aunt. You owe her that respect."

She was totally turned around by his surety. "I owe her *nothing* after all the years she abused me," she said, her voice dangerously calm.

"Then *we* have nothing to talk about until you do all you can to remedy the situation," Pierce said righteously. "In point of fact, you could have given over your room."

"So could you," she retorted, out of all patience with him. "I will be very interested to hear what Cade thinks we ought to have done in *his* house—won't you?"

"He'll agree with me," Pierce said with utter conviction.

She sputtered as she let him out the door. She hoped he didn't come around again for months, years. The arrogance of him!

She filed all her invitations in the wastebasket. She had the sudden feeling she ought not leave the house just in case Vesta took it on herself to rearrange things the way *she* wanted.

She made a show of sending Owen to deliver a note to the craftsman who was directing the work on the third floor, and a bigger show of receiving his answer when Owen returned. Vesta hung over her shoulder as she read the response. "This *is* bad news," she told her. "Since I had been going to Haverhill, and they expected to have a hiatus of five or six days, they undertook another commission which they will not be able to relinquish to come back to finish this contract. They of course have done everything to the letter; it is only *my* plans which have changed. Well—they cannot return here until late next week, Vesta."

"That's insane! Surely Cade could pay them the commission they would be giving up so they can come here faster."

"You're so free with Cade's money, Vesta, but please remember that *your* untimely visit is causing all this inconvenience."

"A good hostess is always ready to receive guests," Vesta said sententiously. "I would think from all your years at Bredwood, you would have known that would be the first order of business in your new home—to see that any surprise visitor would be accommodated as comfortably as you yourself."

"Certainly—after our month of privacy had been observed. Which is not to say that we haven't entertained. However, we did not expect to be housing our kin much sooner than that, and Cade thought it would be an ideal time to redecorate the guests' rooms more to our taste," Sarianna rejoined quickly. She had to have an answer for everything; it almost didn't matter what she said, just that she had something to counter Vesta's seemingly endless flow of words. Vesta wanted to run her into a corner so tightly, she couldn't fight her way out.

Vesta wanted to incapacitate her with words and allusions to the past, to try to diminish her status in her own home by imposing her own impossible strictures. She understood Vesta completely now; but the worst thing about her was that she would not listen, and that would be the hardest thing to combat.

"Well, Cade miscalculated," Vesta tossed back quickly. "Something must be done, and sooner than next week."

Sarianna tucked away the letter which she herself had fabricated. "When Cade returns, we will see what we can do." She started to walk away and then she turned back. "I expect you have considered the fact that I and the servants might not have been here when you arrived, Vesta, given our tentative plans. I marvel you didn't have an alternative arrangement to fall back on."

Vesta did not take the bait. "We were most fortunate," she answered ungraciously, and watched with consuming malevolence as Sarianna withdrew from the parlor without another word. She never thought to be in this position with Sarianna—Sarianna was not the one who was supposed to have married well, let alone marry wealth; Sarianna was not the one who was supposed to have had the running of two luxurious homes; Sarianna was not the one who was supposed to have had all that money at her disposal for gowns and refurbishings and who knew what else.

Sarianna had stolen all of that away from Jeralee—the way, Vesta thought viciously, Dona had taken Rex Broydon and Bredwood away from *her*. It was amazing how history repeated itself, amazing that such a graceless, gauche, mouthy person as Sarianna, who had no skills whatsoever in the art of attracting a man, should have been able to encroach on Jeralee and come away the victor.

Sarianna would not come out the victor in this contest. Sarianna's defection had cost her a husband for Jeralee, and the solace of Bredwood. Rex was riding a downhill path that could only lead to the devastation of his estates, and she herself was growing too old to combat the ghost of Dona.

But Dona was present in this house, laughing at what she had come to. Dona's perfect double mocked her, daring her to combat the nemesis who had risen in her place.

19

So Vesta had come.

Cade paused in the doorway as Herod took his bag and his hat, and listened to the bald recitation of the fact of Vesta's arrival, Vesta's turning the house upside down with her demands.

Oh, but that was Vesta, he thought, and how clever of Sarianna to circumvent her. He strode through the rooms, looking for Sarianna. No one was about except Alzine, who looked at him with speaking fearful eyes. He could see very well the imprint of Vesta in his house, and he didn't like it one bit.

The only consolation was, Pierce wasn't around, and he was going to make sure Pierce would continue not being around for a long time. It was one of many decisions he had made overnight, and though Vesta's arrival put a crimp in his desire to spirit Sarianna away to Haverhill, he was willing to wait, willing to pay Vesta back for all she had done. He was even looking forward, as he thought about it, to willfully spending all the money he had to in order to show Vesta what Sarianna had gotten that Jeralee could never hope to replicate.

It would give him great pleasure, he thought venomously, making his way upstairs. He would show Vesta. He would spend that money and make love to Sarianna in the front parlor; he would disgust the hell out of her and get her out of his house, and then he would carry Sarianna away forever to a place where they both could be happy.

Just like a child, he thought, pushing his way into the bedroom. No one there. He took the steps two at a time to the third floor and poked his head into the two guest bedrooms. Such guile, he thought proudly, shoving a bucket full of paint with his foot. Wonderful.

And then to the attic floor, where he was pleased to see Vesta's and Jeralee's trunks piled up in the hallway—easier to remove, he reflected—they had not fully unpacked yet. Good.

The rooms themselves were of a reasonable size, but not nearly as expansive as downstairs, nor high ceilinged. They were perfect for containing Vesta's evil intent.

And when he came downstairs, he found Vesta waiting for him in the hall, having just arrived in a whirlwind of boxes and a flurry of skirts.

"There you are, Cade. You're home later than anyone expected. I hope you're going to do something about our rooms."

"Hello, Vesta," he said mildly. "Nice to see you. How are you? Did you have a pleasant journey into Savannah?"

"Everything was lovely until we got here and Sarianna had to put us on the top floor. You must *do* something about those guest rooms. This is unconscionable."

"What is?" Cade asked, pretending to misunderstand. He didn't know what he liked about the picture of Vesta's perturbation— perhaps the fact that she wasn't going to get her way for once.

"The state of your guest rooms, of course." Vesta had begun removing her hat and gloves and ringing the bellpull beside the door for someone to come and see to her purchases.

"But we weren't expecting guests," Cade returned easily. "I don't understand your problem, Vesta. The rooms are being replastered and painted."

"I want you to make your workmen come and finish so Jeralee and I can be more comfortable."

"I assure you, Vesta, the attic rooms are extremely comfortable."

"Well, I can't sleep, and Jeralee can't possibly climb all those stairs two and three times a day to change clothes. What you ought to do is give over your own rooms to your guests," Vesta said, brusquely handing her boxes to Alzine and Owen and motioning them to take the things up to her room. "Thank goodness, I don't have to climb the stairs right now. Cade, you must consider our feelings."

He almost burst out laughing. "I am, Vesta, believe me, I am." He was just a little put out by both her insistence on his doing something and her notion he would be willing to give up his bedroom, but the whole of it was actually quite amusing. *Her* expectation was absurd, funnier because she was deadly serious about it.

"Well, you should hire someone else to finish the job," she tacked on rambunctiously. "You wouldn't want people to talk about how you're treating us."

"How would they know?" he wondered guilelessly. "And if it really is such an inconvenience for you, I would be happy to make reservations at a hotel, or perhaps there is a friend you'd like me to contact . . . ?" He paused delicately, knowing full well there was no one.

"Don't be outrageous, Cade. Everyone would talk if Jeralee and I put up in a hotel with you and Sarianna not a half mile away. What *can* you be thinking of?"

"Why—your comfort," Cade murmured, escorting her into the dining room where Alzine was laying the covers for afternoon tea.

"I would be a lot more comfortable if you would pay someone to come in and finish that work," Vesta snapped, seating herself and taking, with virtually both hands, a healthy helping of the small tea cakes that Alzine had set on the table.

"Someone *has* been paid to come in and do the work," Cade said noncommittally, feeling his way through that complication. What *had* Sarianna told her about that?

"Well, apparently they've taken on some other job because Sarianna was supposed to have gone to Haverhill with you. Or at least that is what Sarianna tells me," Vesta implied, looking at him closely, trying to find evidence of the lie in his eyes.

He stared back, his face taking on the lion-look that was a little formidable. "That was so," he agreed easily. "However, we were able to change our plans with very little trouble at all, fortunately."

"You could hire someone else to come in," Vesta suggested tentatively.

"I wouldn't dream of it," Cade returned smoothly. "Is there anything else, Vesta?"

"I—" she began, and thought the better of it. Cade could not be pushed. He had to be manipulated just like any other man. She pulled back a little. "No. It's so very nice to be here. These cakes are lovely. Your cook—?"

"Gwen," he supplied.

"Lovely."

"Mother-r-r . . . !"

"Ahhh, Jeralee—in the dining room, my dear!"

Jeralee flounced in, looking petulant. "Sarianna refused to take me to the Jewetts', Mother. You must speak with her."

"Well, I will. What bad manners not including your guests in your round of visits." Vesta turned to Cade. "I didn't know the Jewetts were friends of yours."

"Friends of Sarianna's, I believe," Cade said smoothly. "And Pierce's, too."

"Everyone is going to be there today. Sarianna told me, and she said she couldn't foist me—foist me, Mother!—on them without having asked whether I could come! She could have written them a note this morning. She could have thought to do that. I spent an awful afternoon, shopping, with only Owen for a chaperone. It was too awful. And now I have to walk up *all* those awful stairs."

"Have a cup of tea," Vesta consoled her. "These cakes are heavenly. Do sit down, Jeralee. Your agitation is understandable; but all we have to do is explain to Sarianna that she can write a note in the morning, and the next time you'll accompany her. As simple as that. Sarianna probably didn't know the proper form."

"I beg your pardon?" Cade said sharply.

"Well, Sarianna never—" Vesta began.

"Sarianna's manners are never lacking," Cade interrupted aggressively.

Vesta smiled patronizingly. "But there is the fact that Jeralee was left behind today."

"Perhaps," Cade suggested, "Sarianna did not want her company."

Vesta didn't like that. "Perhaps she didn't, if she were planning an assignation with Pierce Darden," she threw out, seizing the first thing that came to mind.

"Or perhaps Jeralee was hoping she could trip him up, render him unconscious, and perhaps con him into marrying her," Cade shot back.

Vesta bridled. "Jeralee is too well bred to do anything *obvious* like that," she said huffily. "This conversation is getting us nowhere. I'm sure if Sarianna is apprised of what she has to do, she will see to it that Jeralee is included in her various morning calls."

"But my dear Vesta," Sarianna's voice said intrusively as she came into the dining room, "you were at great pains to explain to me that you did not expect to be entertained while you were here."

"My dear Sarianna, how could you misunderstand? It *is* incumbent on you to make sure that Jeralee and I are included in your various invitations. But of course, how would you know that?"

Sarianna smiled grimly and turned to Cade. "I'm so glad you're back," she told him fervently.

He reached for her hand, his expression lightening at her faintly forlorn look. "Show me." He pulled her to him, and she came willingly, knowing Jeralee was watching avidly, feeling Vesta's eyes positively scorching her back. He slanted his mouth across hers and slowly lowered his head, and his mouth settled emphatically on hers. He didn't care one whit that they were watching. He wanted them to watch, and to be very sure that he would defend Sarianna against anything they threw at her. Anything. He crushed her in his arms, forcing her to hold him, forcing her lips, delving intently for her response, for her heat.

"This is disgusting," Vesta said loudly.

He pretended not to hear her, pulling Sarianna closer to him as she sought to pull away.

"I won't sit here and watch this display," Vesta said, her voice growing peevish.

Cade lifted his head long enough to say: "Then go away."

He thought he heard the scrape of chairs and receding footsteps, but by that time, he didn't care.

The next day, he fired Pierce.

Pierce was indignant, flabbergasted and terrified by turns. Cade's wealth formed the cornerstone of his newly thriving business. Without it, he would not be earning nearly the living he had become accustomed to in these last five or so months. Without it, he would lose prestige. Without it, he could not embellish his business overtures by mentioning Cade's name. Everyone knew Cade and Cade's money by now; he made sure to spread the word. Everyone in Savannah had a healthy respect for any kind of money, even if they did look down on those who used their hands to earn it.

And worst of all, he would have no excuse to see Sarianna.

Later, of course, when he thought about it, he saw that was exactly what Cade intended, and it became a point of honor for him to attend her anyway that night before dinner to insist that Cade's action had no bearing on their friendship.

Sarianna was as shocked as he. "He never said why?"

"He said he needed a lawyer and advisor who could undertake a larger scope of business than I was equipped to. Sheer hogwash, Sarianna. He is jealous of our friendship and wants to cut me out of your life."

She considered that notion for a moment, and then nodded her head. "You are probably right."

"But it won't affect our friendship, Sarianna. I won't let it.'

"Of course you won't," she came back automatically. "Neither will I," she added hastily after a pause in which he looked at her expectantly. "But there is nothing I can do about the loss of his business, Pierce. I hope you understand that."

"I do," he said, but privately he was thinking she ought to have offered; she ought to have at least said she would speak to him.

When he finally took his leave of her, Sarianna breathed a sigh of relief; he had gone not a moment too soon—Jeralee had been on her way up the steps and her noxious eyes said everything. "Doesn't he know he's wasting his time with *you?*" she asked snidely, as they entered the house together.

"Obviously not," Sarianna said. "I don't see him beating down the door to see *you.*" She wheeled and headed for the steps. It seemed to her these days that the only place she found peace and quiet was in her own bedroom.

"You think you're so clever," Jeralee spat, charging after her. "You think you're getting away with something, the way Pierce follows you around. You think you're some kind of goddess because you coerced Cade into marrying you, and all those men hang around you."

"I guess I *am* smart," Sarianna said calmly, turning around at the landing and facing Jeralee. "I'm waiting to hear exactly what you are getting at."

"Oh, I'm hearing about *you,*" Jeralee said insinuatingly. "Everybody talks about the gauche Sarianna Rensell and how everybody pities her so the men kind of gather round to protect her."

"You've heard all *that* so soon," Sarianna said wonderingly, thinking she was in the very position with Jeralee that Vesta had threatened her with all those months ago. She could just thrust out her wrong hand, and Jeralee would topple down those stairs like a house of cards.

Jeralee shrugged. "People talk."

"Or you do," Sarianna snapped. "Good-night, Jeralee." She stalked down the hallway, pushed in the door and slammed it behind her, and collapsed against it. How many more weeks of this? How many more mornings and evenings of this awful vituperation? It would never stop. They were grateful for nothing; they felt everything was their due, including their right to insult their hostess. She didn't know if she had the strength to play even the minimal scene she had just had with Jeralee for a prolonged period of time.

When Cade joined her, he found her seated in bed, her knees drawn up across her chest, with an air of deep contemplation. The lowered wick of the bracket lamp threw an eerie light over the bed alcove. She looked fragile sitting there in her thin nightgown, and a little sad.

"You heard about Pierce," he guessed as he seated himself at the foot of the bed in a fair imitation of her favorite position.

"Pierce told me about Pierce," she said. "Why?"

"I'm sure you can guess."

"Or everyone else can. It's meaningless nonsense, Cade."

"He follows you around like a puppy dog, Sarianna. How can I have that?"

"It's meaningless."

"He doesn't think so," Cade said, and she saw that he meant it. She felt a faint chill. How could she have misunderstood Pierce, and Cade have cut right to the matter? What did he see that she didn't? "Besides which, he's not a terribly astute manager, Sarianna. This new situation is much better, and it includes arrangements for you to be able to draw on funds rather than having to ask me or Pierce for permission. In fact, *he* advised against it, but you can see that put *him* in the position of having to give consent everytime *you* wished to buy something or pay your workers."

"I see," she said, her voice odd. She had not thought of that aspect of her relationship with Pierce. She hadn't asked him for very much as it was, but still, he had had to consent to payment; she was put in the position of asking.

How perceptive of Cade. "I see," she said again, because she didn't know what else to say, or even how to broach the problem of Vesta, whom they could now hear climbing the steps laboriously, perhaps acting a little for their benefit as she passed their room.

"*We*," Cade said, "will go to Haverhill. Soon." He paused as they

289

heard Vesta stumble on the steps above them, and he shook his head exasperatedly. "And *they* will stay here—if they must. They may not find it terribly convenient when they find out Amanda, Alzine, Owen and Gwen are coming with us."

"Perfect," Sarianna applauded.

"*You* are perfect," Cade said solemnly.

"They are doing their best to make me think I'm not."

"*Never* in my eyes," Cade swore. "Sarianna . . . ?" He held out his arms and she came into them. And still, it was not the same. The vixenish Sarianna had been buried somewhere, and he didn't know how to resurrect her.

"I wouldn't be surprised," he murmured at one point, "to find Jeralee listening at the door."

"It's the closest she will ever get to the real thing," Sarianna rejoined, pulling his mouth back against hers. "But why waste time talking about *her?*"

Dona, Dona, Dona. Vesta was obsessed by Dona. She saw her everywhere, in every movement Sarianna made, the way she dressed, talked, the way she so publicly displayed affection toward Cade, the way all the men were drawn to her like moths to a flame. She didn't see the strength in Sarianna's face, or the humor in her eyes. She didn't see the finely molded lips that did not have a drooping petulance to them. She never listened to Sarianna's musical voice to hear words of real conversation that others were interested in continuing.

The only thing she saw was Dona. Dona had had just that expression on her face when she was bored. Dona had the peculiar pause in her step, almost as if she were maintaining her balance. Dona had that flashy insincere smile. Dona always gazed directly into everyone's eyes as if she were hanging on every word.

But of course she wasn't; how could she be? Nothing interested her except getting whatever she could, and taking everything away from Vesta.

"You're just like your mother," she would say snittily to Sarianna, who would then reply: "Why, thank you."

"She was no angel, Miss; I wouldn't be so quick to feel flattered."

Sarianna's face would close up. 'I don't know what you mean."

"I mean," Vesta might say viciously, "she was not very smart, and the only thing that interested her was herself and what new dress Father had purchased for her. And she liked men, lord knows—and they surely like you, don't they, Sarianna?"

"Yes, they do," Sarianna would say, gazing straight into her eyes with a deep blue searching gaze.

"Any man," Vesta would add insinuatingly. "Or did you think your father, or even Cade, was the love of her life?"

"I wouldn't know." Sarianna's face would go blank. She didn't want to know. Why should she know?

"She adored Cade because they grew up together," Vesta said another day.

"Of course she adored Cade."

"She liked keeping men hanging around," Vesta went on spitefully. "It might even have been she had a liaison with someone other than Cade."

"Or it may be she didn't," Sarianna shot back.

"Don't be naive."

"Don't be stupid, if you want to stay in *my* house a moment longer."

The atmosphere thickened between them. Vesta hated her and everyone knew it, and everyone stayed out of their way.

Cade took Sarianna to order furniture for Haverhill. "I burned all that old stuff."

"That was a little drastic, surely?"

"I was feeling drastic," Cade said. "Come, pick out what you want. Whatever you want."

Jeralee overheard them and told Vesta. "He gives her a free hand. He said for her to choose whatever she wanted as if the cost never counted."

"So like her mother," Vesta muttered. "Didn't she do just that to Rex when they were first married, demanding everything he could possibly give her and never even thinking of the end cost of it all?"

She accosted Sarianna after she returned. "So you bought furniture today?"

"One never knows when one will need to have the spare bedroom furnished," Sarianna said, holding on to the aura of calm that had permeated her soul as she and Cade, *together,* had planned their future home.

"Where did he take you?" Vesta couldn't help asking. She *couldn't.*

"Why is this your business?" Sarianna wanted to know. But she had a grim feeling she knew why. It had something to do with her mother. Her militant face dared Vesta to proceed further with anything about Dona.

Vesta faltered, and Sarianna turned on her heel.

"Dona was something to watch," she said another time, as she and Sarianna watched the rain pouring out the parlor window. "On a day like today, ten men would come calling just to see her. And this while she was already promised to Rex. It broke my heart because he never knew. She would just surround herself with all those admirers, and Rex would be back home at Bredwood, thinking she was as lonely as he on a day like this. And she was busy being the center of attention in her parlor. They hung on every word, too."

"And where were you?" Sarianna asked softly, wondering how much Vesta was telling her about Vesta as well.

"Oh, I was there, too," Vesta said airily. "I had my share of admirers."

She hated Sarianna for asking the question. She had had no admirers. She was hard in love with Rex Broydon herself, and she had had to stand by and watch Dona twist him this way and that—just as Sarianna was doing to Cade. Jeralee never would have betrayed him with Pierce, or anyone else for that matter. Jeralee would have been as fixed and constant as the stars.

Jeralee said, "Pierce's friends are so interesting."

"I'm glad he's introducing you around," Sarianna said generously.

"I think he's forgotten you already." Jeralee was happy to impart this news to Sarianna. It was rather disappointing that she did not seem in the least upset. "Anyway, *I'm* going to the Jewetts' tomorrow. Are you?"

Sarianna said, "No," even though she had the invitation on her desk. She was going nowhere that Jeralee was to be present. She was enjoying her autonomy, and having Cade around as a shield against them. Vesta's words couldn't hurt her when she lay in his arms at night and he soothed away her perturbation over all these direct attacks.

And on her return one evening from yet another elegant soiree, Jeralee said, "All they talk about is secession, secession and more secession and how they're all going to fight! Those stupid men! Who do they think will be left if they go off to fight? And they always ask where Sarianna is. None of them have forgotten Sarianna."

Of course, Vesta thought, wouldn't you know it. Her mother's daughter—that was just how it had been with Dona, and poor Rex sighing for love of her all those months before they were wed and she was still entertaining in her parlor and sneaking out to see Cade—and at least one more lover that Vesta was aware of.

She wondered about Sarianna's relationship with Pierce Darden. She didn't wonder why he was still coming around after Cade had dismissed his services; rather she wondered whether it was something she could somehow use to Sarianna's disadvantage.

"A letter from Charleston, Vesta?" Sarianna inquired casually, handing a thin envelope to Vesta as she came into the parlor one morning. "You intend to stay so indefinitely that you have forwarded this address to your acquaintances?"

"This is from my cousin, Sallie Gill Lundeen, I'll have you know," Vesta snapped, taking the envelope and ripping it open. "You know I've kept in close contact with her. See here, she writes Mary Lacey is to make her come-out later this year. I wonder . . . I wonder whether Rex might see fit to take a trip to Charleston. She says they are staying on after the summer. No, it isn't possible, not the way things are going. And Jeralee . . . no, they should not be competing with one another. It's too bad. Yes, that's your mother's cousin Sallie Gill, Sarianna. I wouldn't think you would remember her."

"I know of her," Sarianna said, seating herself at the small escritoire near the window to write some notes—or pretend to write some notes depending on how abrasive Vesta became. "Your father went to her after he sold up, I recollect."

"And she, thankfully, had the task of burying him when he died," Vesta added, tucking away the letter in its envelope. She looked up with a gleam in her eye. "Is Pierce due this afternoon?"

"How should I know that?" Sarianna murmured, seeing storm warnings and bending her head over a sheet of writing paper so she didn't need to look at Vesta.

"It's amazing that man has the time to pay all these social calls," Vesta said suggestively. "One would think he would be courting potential clients instead of his clients' wives."

"He has a wide circle of friends," Sarianna responded noncommittally, but in her heart of hearts she hoped that Pierce would not drop by this afternoon. She had nothing more to say to him, and Vesta's hints were becoming more and more outrageous. And then she had a thought. "It may be, of course, that Pierce has continued his visits for an entirely different reason," she added casually.

"My dear Sarianna, he is totally smitten with you. It's all of a piece. Your mother was the same way."

Sarianna heard a reedy thread of something emotional in her voice; it interested her, and she wondered how she could push it. Vesta had hated Dona, that much was obvious. But there was something else. Something else. "What are you saying, Vesta? That my mother deliberately encouraged other men? That everyone fell at her feet whether they wanted her or they wanted someone else? She was some kind of mythic figure who could enslave men by merely looking at them?"

"How you exaggerate," Vesta said dismissingly. "Your mother was nothing like that."

"Of course she wasn't," Sarianna agreed. "Neither am I. And," she added slyly, slanting a covert look at Vesta, "I have been feeling for the past several weeks that Pierce's main motivation for seeing me has nothing to do with him being so devoted to me that he would disregard Cade's subtle warning."

"*Was* it a warning?" Vesta asked, almost to herself. If such a blatant loss of business didn't mitigate his devotion, what would? she wondered. Or was there something else, as Sarianna was suggesting.

"Nothing less," Sarianna confirmed. She waited; she saw Vesta was much taken with the notion that Pierce had been warned away and that he was risking much to see Sarianna anyway.

"Stupid man," Vesta said at last.

"Impulsive," Sarianna said, hoping the idea would root, praying Pierce would not show up this afternoon. She folded up the paper on which she had been scribbling nonsensical words. "The actions of a man who might well be smitten—but *not* with someone he knows he can't have."

But when he did arrive at the town house in the late afternoon, Sarianna found herself wedged between Vesta's knowing derisive looks and Pierce's unfaltering desire to spend every moment with *her*. He never even looked at Jeralee when she returned and poked her head into the parlor to say hello, and he was respectful enough to

Vesta as she passed back and forth in the hallway all those many times she felt it was necessary; and all in all, Pierce's visit gave Vesta a nice barrelful of dinner table conversation that made Sarianna squirm.

"Pierce paid us a surprise visit this afternoon," Vesta said offhandedly, as she passed a dish of onion custard over to Cade, and she had the satisfaction of seeing his face darken as he spooned the creamy vegetable onto his plate next to a wedge of chicken pie.

"Pierce is full of surprises," Cade murmured, sending a heated look over to Sarianna.

She shrugged. "He was not invited."

"Perhaps he sees invitations where they are not intended," Vesta said, her chocolatey eyes on Cade rather than Sarianna to see his reaction to this surmise.

"Or his intentions may be different than any of us know," Sarianna threw back, digging viciously into her vegetable. Vesta was getting to her now, bringing this nonsense up in front of Cade and leaving her no defense with which to deflect her hatefulness.

"Well, of course, Cade—you must remember how Dona used to claim the very same thing," Vesta said complacently. "All those visitors—and not to see her! It's amazing how history repeats itself."

"It's obviouis this deceitfulness was bred into my bones," Sarianna said dramatically, hoping to distract Vesta altogether. But that wasn't possible, she saw instantly. Vesta believed it.

"Who knows but that it was?" she questioned in all seriousness. "What else does the aphorism mean: like father like son, or the sins of the *mother* in this case. The similarities are astonishing to anyone who ever knew Dona, isn't that right, Cade? Don't you see it?" She looked at him maliciously, her eyes muddying in a kind of low of satisfaction that he was not liking what he was hearing.

But Jeralee prevented him from answering. She threw her napkin down in a petulant motion. "Oh, Sarianna, Sarianna—I am sick to death of hearing about Sarianna, and who comes to see Sarianna, and who misses Sarianna when she isn't there. You're all so stupid. Sarianna isn't the sun, moon and stars around whom everyone else revolves. Sarianna is married and not available, and it's perfectly obvious to everyone what is going on with Pierce. He is making himself indispensable to Sarianna because it's the only way he can get to see me. Why, we're not invited to half the same homes any more; he could never aspire entree to the Jewetts', for example, and he probably feels that Mother and Rex would never approve because of his profession.

"So you see—" she looked around ingenuously—" it has *nothing* to do with Sarianna, and everything to do with *me!*"

Wasn't it just like Jeralee to turn everything around to reflect on *her?* Sarianna mused. It was so delightful that Jeralee had come to the very conclusion that she had wanted Vesta to infer. And it was very much like Jeralee to be thinking that way in the first place. Her naive statement lightened the atmosphere around the table, but Vesta's biblical castigation positively hovered over her as she made her way upstairs later that evening.

She felt exhausted, emotionally drained, physically tired and utterly bored, and heavy with the burden of dealing with Vesta continually day after day with no cessation of hostilities in sight.

Alzine was turning down the bed when she entered, and she stood watching her for a moment. Alzine looked bulky in the dim light, her middle more expansive under the loose tunic she wore over her dress which was supposed to conceal her increasing belly. Alzine looked more tired than she, and had no hope of respite unless she granted it to her. There were only a couple more months until she would give birth, Sarianna thought, and she wondered whether Alzine were scared—or resigned. What did she know? How much more would she increase in size? Would it hurt?

No—she rubbed her hand over her forehead; she didn't want to know any of those things. But she found herself watching Alzine closely in the following days, too closely, as if something personal depended on it.

Did it? Because she was feeling so tired, and just a bit faint sometimes? Her stomach had begun to feel increasingly queasy, and her clothing felt just a bit tight.

It was nothing.

She watched Alzine lumber around the house, slowly climbing the stairs at Vesta's whim, and hanging on to the banister as if her life depended on it.

The weight of the baby made Alzine's movements unwieldy— clumsy. "She shouldn't even be waiting on them," Sarianna told Cade stubbornly, and he immediately hired a younger, stronger girl to relieve Alzine of those onerous duties. He didn't tell her; Marvela simply appeared, and Alzine's work load diminished.

It was such a kind act, she could have loved him for it. But he smothered her gratitude by asking if Pierce had come by yet—that day.

She sent word to Pierce she did not want to see him, and when he appeared anyway, she sent Jeralee to entertain him; and some small part of her was moderately gratified when she saw him leaving the house immediately afterward.

She kept a strong eye on Alzine. Alzine's lower back had begun to ache if she were on her feet too long. Sarianna told Cade, and he procured an upholstered rocking chair for her.

"How does it hurt?" Sarianna wanted to know.

"It just be dere. De baby is dere and dat old feeling is dere," Alzine described it, and it told Sarianna nothing.

"How shall I know what to do for you?" she demanded.

"You don' do nothin' fo' me, Miss Sarianna. Dat Amanda, she gonna take care of Alzine."

"*I* will take care of you," Sarianna insisted. "Are you so very tired?"

"I is tired. De baby make me mo' tired 'cause I didn't want no baby, Miss Sarianna, and I don't know what gonna happen with dis child."

"We'll figure something out," Sarianna promised. "We'll . . . make some kind of arrangement—whatever you want. . . ."

But they were such weak words to say when Alzine's child would be owned by her and Cade, a piece of property to be bartered however they would.

What if it were her child?

Unthinkable!

To bear a child in such a way, with such shame, and then not to be allowed to be a family—it was inconceivable.

Too conceivable now that Alzine's time was coming near. Alzine would come to Haverhill; her child would be one of the slaves on Haverhill. There was no other way.

"And when," Vesta asked disagreeably, "will our guest rooms finally be ready?"

Cade smiled, but the humor never reached his eyes. It had been—

what—two weeks since their arrival, and he had delayed and delayed to the point where Vesta was very close to stamping her foot each time he put her off. But the time to leave for Haverhill was coming soon, and he did not want Vesta taking over his bedroom. "I believe they will return early next week, Vesta. I hope that suits your plans."

"It can't be soon enough," Vesta snapped. "How many hems I have torn going up and down those stairs, I can't tell you."

"But Marvela is magical with a needle, Vesta. I made particularly sure that your new maid should be a skilled seamstress."

"She'll do," Vesta said ungraciously.

"I'm pleased," Cade answered in kind. Two more weeks, he thought, and he would leave them all behind. He was almost ready to give Vesta the town house just to be rid of her, but he knew the folly of that. Easier to hire on new servants and pay for their loyalty; Vesta would get away with nothing, and he might gain some ammunition to use against her. Sarianna was edgy and in an ongoing foul mood, and all of it he attributed to Vesta.

Maybe, he thought, it was too much to depend on removing to Haverhill to remedy things. Or maybe it would change things forever.

"I hate the smell of paint!" Jeralee fussed as she flew downstairs. "Is my carriage waiting? Sarianna, what is wrong with you? Didn't you have Owen bring round the carriage? I'm due at the Faberleighs' any moment."

"I beg your pardon?" Sarianna said politely. She was feeling particularly testy this morning, and having workmen tramping up and down the stairs disrupting everything did not help her mood.

"*Pierce* is going to be at the Faberleighs'! Didn't Marvela tell you? Where *is* Owen?" Jeralee danced before the front door, peeking out of the curtain and then turning back to Sarianna. "It's your house. You give the orders," she said defensively, as she caught the militant look in Sarianna's hard blue gaze.

"You'll have to excuse me if your whims are not the foremost things on my mind," Sarianna said, turning away.

"Oh, you're just jealous!" Jeralee shouted after her. "I told Pierce I knew what he was about, and he didn't deny it, Sarianna; and you're as green as that dress you're wearing today. You just knew I was going to meet him today, and you wanted to prevent it. I know you. You can't stand it if anyone interferes in your little liaisons. Not even if you're married. You just want to keep Pierce all for yourself, just like your mother did Cade—until *he* got wise."

Oh, but did he? Sarianna wondered, as Jeralee's high-pitched voice followed her down the hallway, or was it that his father made him wise? Would he not have hung on to Dona, even after she sent him away, if his father hadn't made him leave?

What difference did it make now anyway? *She* was the threat to Jeralee, not an episode out of her mother's past. She was the one Jeralee hated, envied, the one whom Jeralee wished to steal from, invade.

"Pierce is handsome. He's a gentleman in spite of the fact he's in the law; he makes me laugh," Jeralee said behind her, her voice growing shrill as Sarianna did not react to her words. "You're not going to stand in my way with him the way you did with Cade."

"Believe me, that is the last thing on my mind," Sarianna cut in to stop the heated flow of words. She reached for a bellpull at the entrance to the morning parlor, and Herod instantly appeared. "Were we aware that Miss Jeralee wished to go out this morning?" she asked him.

"No, ma'am. I shall summon Owen immediately," Herod said gravely.

"Thank you, Herod." Sarianna turned to Jeralee. "You had only to ask."

"They don't do what I tell them," Jeralee said defensively, pacing her way back into the hallway.

"Small wonder," Sarianna muttered, turning in the opposite direction. And where was Alzine this morning? she wondered fretfully. She was worried about Alzine. Alzine seemed to be expanding and shrinking before her very eyes, and she could not do a thing for Alzine.

"How will you know when the baby is to be born?" she asked idly, as she sat with Alzine that afternoon during her afternoon check to be sure that Alzine was feeling well.

'Dere is a feelin', deep down low, Miss Sarianna. It come first like a squeezin', like when you has yo' flow, and it get harder and harder, and soon enough, de baby comes."

"It sounds awful, painful," Sarianna said. It sounded worse than that, and her heart contracted in sympathy for Alzine, who knew how and what her baby must be born to.

"It hurt," Alzine said, "but when you finished, you got de baby and dat make it all worth it."

"Even this baby?" Sarianna questioned carefully.

Alzine didn't answer immediately, and then she said heavily, "I don' know, Miss Sarianna. I just don' know."

But the one thing that was going on schedule and with dispatch was the renovation of the guest rooms. Daily Vesta stopped to watch the progress and came away pleased and furious both. It could have been taken care of weeks ago. She and Jeralee could have had this lovely luxurious suite of rooms to themselves much earlier on had Cade insisted and laid out a little additional money to hire another crew of workmen to complete it.

Nevertheless, within the week they would be able to move right in and make themselves comfortable for a nice lengthy stay.

"How do you even know if you are going to have a baby?" Sarianna asked, her voice low as if she were ashamed of even having to ask the question.

Alzine's sharp eyes pinned her. "Dere is a stoppin' of yo' flow. It makes two or three months dat you been carryin' de child." She stopped abruptly; who was she to be telling the mistress this? But Miss Sarianna looked shocked—more than shocked. "Is you carryin' Mr. Cade's child?" she asked boldly. But she didn't need an affirmation.

It was there in Sarianna's questions, and in her troubled expression, and deep in her anguished blue eyes.

20

"This is positively indecent," Vesta protested for the one hundredth time.

"It makes eminent sense," Cade countered calmly yet another time in answer. "You want the season in Savannah and we don't. What is simpler than to give over the house to you, with servants of your own choosing, and leave you to your own devices. I rather thought I was exceeding the duties of the host by removing myself altogether. I tell you, Vesta—there is no pleasing you." He waved at Herod as two post-boys preceded him down the steps with one of Sarianna's trunks.

Vesta was silent. In truth, she was mentally rubbing her hands together. Such parties she would give. She would gather the elite of the city around her and present them on a platter to Jeralee. She would live like a queen without having to answer to Rex, and Cade Rensell would foot the bill. It was delicious, utterly decadent. Of course she had to do all she could to challenge his taking Sarianna to Haverhill just *now*. It would reflect badly on her if anyone thought that her presence had chased him out of his own home. Apart from that, she wanted his gratitude that she was willing to stay even if he and Sarianna elected to rusticate on a moldering plantation in the middle of nowhere.

"I'm grateful," she said at last, and the words came hard to her. She had never said them to anyone, and there was a part of her that wondered at this heedless generosity.

Cade looked at her for a long moment. "I believe we understand each other," he said finally. He turned to Amanda, who was just helping Alzine down the stairs, and went to help her.

Vesta watched expressionlessly. Alzine was very, very pregnant and very exhausted. She still wondered why Rex had given her up in spite of her pregnancy. She had wanted him to send her away—but perhaps to Greenpoint for the duration; she hadn't expected he would ship her off altogether in Sarianna's possession. All she had said was she wouldn't have Alzine in the house while she was carrying, but she didn't tell him she had a very good guess who the father was. One didn't speak of those things; one pretended they did not exist, and that it had only been the one time, the one slip—and the fault was never laid where it so obviously belonged.

Alzine did not look at her; Alzine knew already that Vesta had eked out her punishment in the only way she knew how. She didn't need any acknowledgement of what Vesta knew or did not know. She was not Vesta's property any more. Her child would never see Bredwood where it was conceived.

Jeralee came flying down the stairs, followed slowly by Sarianna, who was dressed all in blue today. She looked pale and drawn, but only Cade noticed.

Her eyes blazed as she looked at Vesta. Vesta took her hand and patted it. Sarianna pulled it away.

"I'm ready," she said to Cade, and he opened the door of their waiting carriage. It would be a far different ride, he reflected as he helped her in, than the last time he had taken her to Haverhill. The sensual awareness between them was as slack as a piece of stretched out elastic. She looked sad today, and frail. He wondered if they had finally beaten her down and she had not been aware of it. It was like handling a shell, delicate, fragile—breakable.

Her wan smile thanked him as he climbed in beside Alzine.

His fists clenched. God, if Vesta's smears had shattered her spirit altogether . . . Vesta would have a lot to answer for, he swore. If he couldn't bring her back to life at Haverhill . . . Vesta would pay.

Haverhill.

Their carriage swept through a double column of stately oak trees up a long dirt drive that arced into a curve in front of the house and turned back upon itself, branching off into separate byways to the stables, carriage house, the storehouse and the servants' quarters.

"Ohhh, dis be grand, Miss Sarianna," Alzine breathed, taking the

302

first interest in anything during the entire trip which had been traveled at half-speed to accommodate her discomfiture.

Sarianna smiled, a real smile. "It looks very different from the first time I saw it," she agreed. It looked more than different, she thought, changed—completely changed. Cade had waved his magic money wand, and everything had taken on a totally new cast.

That was good, she reflected. A gardener had worked on the lawn and cut back the trees. Freshly planted flowers and shrubs framed the small front porch, and the wooden trim had been scraped and freshly painted a pristine white. The windows shone, and the shutters had been replaced or repaired and painted a deep cheerful green. The brick had been scrubbed to a mellow pink that was welcoming, inviting. An air of prosperity pervaded the house now; the desolation had been banished, and the matte sense of the encroaching past.

Servants swarmed from the house and began removing trunks and aiding Amanda and Gwen, while Herod immediately came to Alzine's carriage to offer his help to her.

Sarianna waited for Cade to come for her, and in a moment, he appeared by the carriage door. "Welcome home, Sarianna." He held out his hand. "This *is* your home."

She slid across the seat and gave herself to his arms as he lifted her out and set her down on the fragrant lawn of Haverhill.

His power was astonishing; it radiated from his hands and it worked magic all around her. For a heady moment, she really felt that she had come home.

He took her hand and led her to the house, up the porch and into the front hallway and the faint smell of fresh paint.

All the doors to all the rooms branching from this central hall were wide open, and the sun drenched it with a warm welcome.

Here lay the narrow Brussels carpets they had chosen for the long narrow hall; there, the console table and a walnut-framed beveled glass miror. In the library, new shelves held the old volumes and more—a selection of books that were chosen to Cade's taste—and surrounding the fireplace were deep chairs and a tufted sofa. In the spotless dining room, wainscoting had been replaced and polished to a high gloss. In the center of the room, the long simple table they had chosen sat surrounded by a half dozen upholstered walnut, balloon-backed chairs. A sideboard was centered on one wall, its shelves filled with serving pieces to the extensive dinnerware that Sarianna had selected. Two additional chairs flanked this piece, and two others sat on either side of a narrow, drop-leaf table which would serve several functions in the room as needed.

The parlor was elegant and comfortable with its pair of serpentine-backed sofas opposite the fireplace, and the comfortable upholstered, tufted rocking chairs and several lady and gentleman chairs scattered throughout the room. A parlor stand sat by the side of each chair, and there was an overall feeling in the room of a welcoming coziness that was enhanced by the rich carpet underfoot.

And finally, in the bedroom, she found the same kind of tall, gleaming walnut bedstead as had furnished the bedroom in Malverne Row, with its matching washstand bureaus, a massive wardrobe and pier mirrored, marble-topped dressing case, and a taller dresser with two decks and smaller mirror obviously meant to be Cade's.

In a corner by the window was a tufted chaise longue, and Sarianna sank into it gratefully. "I didn't know about this piece either," she said chidingly.

"There may be a lot you don't know," Cade said roughly.

She looked up at him startled. *Or you,* she found herself thinking, and was hard put not to touch her stomach. And when *was* she going to tell him? she wondered. *How* could she tell him? The ineffable changes had changed her, too. She didn't know how she was going to reclaim the Sarianna who had married Cade Rensell.

In the morning, Sarianna met the servants, and an hour later, she could barely remember any of their names. "I must rely on Amanda to help me," she said to Amanda, who nodded graciously to say she would. A dozen strange faces scurried out of sight to attend to tasks of the day. Sarianna turned to Amanda. "How does Alzine feel today?"

"She is weary, Miss Sarianna; she is hankering for this baby to come."

"Yes," Sarianna murmured, and resisted the urge to touch herself. Would she feel like this? Would she feel as utterly drained and enervated as she did at this very moment as she progressed in her own pregnancy?

Her knees weakened, and she groped for a chair. "What must we attend to this morning, Amanda?" she asked, even as she sank into its comfortable depths.

"Everything is well taken care of, Miss Sarianna. We must of course start cutting the winter clothing, but that can wait a few days. We will check the stores and see what is needed. We must be sure that we have the medicaments we need. And perhaps we might have Mr. Cade inquire about a doctor or midwife."

"Yes, of course; I would feel better about that," Sarianna said, but when Amanda left her, she wondered for whose information the inquiry was intended. It wearied her to conjecture. She needed to check the kitchen and make out the menus for the week—nothing elaborate since it was only herself and Cade—and she wanted to see what further had been done to the house.

She wanted so many things, and all in a hurry. It took long reflective moments to restrain herself and realize that there was no hurry, that time had slowed down. She was going nowhere now. She was supposed to settle in at Haverhill.

So why did she feel frantic?

She might feel better if she took a walk, she decided finally, and she went out into the connecting hall that led to the servants' quarters and one of the rear exits to the piazza garden.

A dazzling display of flowers met her eyes. The whole square had been replanted, and the flowerbeds were rampant with fragrant blooms. Trees shaded the garden on either side, and a brick path led to the kitchen garden square and the cabins of the field hands.

Everywhere, everything was pristine, neat, cared for. The gloom had been banished, and the sense of ghosts hovering. In the kitchen garden a young slave was pulling weeds. Deely, she seemed to remember her name was. Down the two long avenues on either side of the garden square, two burly men were washing down the cabins, which had obviously been rebuilt and painted.

Far and beyond that lay the acres of fields that comprised Haverhill's wealth, and the gin house and balers, all of which groaned now with overwhelming noise to where Sarianna stood. She thought she could just make out Cade in the distance and a cadre of field hands cutting down the bolls for the second baling.

Wife.

The word entered her mind like a gunshot. Standing in the fields like this, she felt an echo of the past, a mocking of the things that Cade had said to her. But now there was a child to be; now she was not a Dona replication. She was Sarianna, so much changed, a mistress in her own right, companion to her own husband on her own plantation.

She didn't know *what* she had been doing for the past two months.

They should have come here sooner. She would have gotten this strong sense of herself and her future much sooner had they come to Haverhill long before this. She wondered if it were too late to start over again.

"Miss Sarianna—Deely don' feel too good. She got to spend de day in bed."

"Oh, Miss Sarianna, we ain't got no soap fo' to do de laundry. We got to have some from de stores."

"Miss Sarianna, we must begin to order the material for the winter clothes. It will take three months to cut and sew."

"And Alzine?"

"Alzine feels poorly; she wishes to stay in bed today."

"A cold soup tonight then, Gwen. Our cook at Bredwood used to make some delicious ones that were so refreshing on a hot night like tonight. Something light for dinner, please—what would you recommend for the main course? Is there fruit?" She loved planning the menus.

She loved to walk through the house after it had been spotlessly cleaned and smelling the scent of lemon and beeswax.

She loved the fact that all of it was *hers,* and though it was not nearly as big as Bredwood, it still required her managerial skills.

She spent an hour going through the storehouse making a list, including the notation that more soap must be made, and so many yards of woolen and cotton must be ordered, so many pieces of leather, for shoes, so many lamp wicks and containers of kerosene. So much of everything: She would order rice and beans, the meats they would not butcher for themselves; she could order needles and thread, and a good new pair of scissors. She could order yarn and hope that Alzine would be well enough to knit socks because she could not do that herself, and it too had to be done before winter. She would order stationery and pens, flour and cornmeal, an accounting book to keep her ledger, and a piece of lace for her hair.

She would write a letter to Cade and have it mailed from Savannah: Dear Cade, we are having a baby and I think I am happy about it.

As she immersed herself in her duties at Haverhill, she felt a curious contentment that was not marred by anyone saying any one wrong thing to her. Even Cade respected her silences, her distance. He worked himself to a frazzle every day and deliberately did not try to touch her.

Gradually, as the days lengthened into the second week, she began to want him to touch her.

And it was a different kind of want, born of her exhilaration of being in control and in command, of her growing joy at the sense of freedom she was finding at Haverhill, and the precious burden she carried.

All of that coalesced into a kind of yearning for the one who had given her this gift and as much affection as she had ever had in her life.

She wanted him suddenly, with an explosive need that had no basis in gratitude. It was as if her body had a memory of its own, long suppressed, and operating on some level that had nothing to do with her suffocating notion of giving Cade the Dona he never had. This was different—this was a reality that was tied solely to her response to him in the deepest part of her heart. This was the part she had given him glimpses of in her passion and her demands.

This, if only she knew it, was the part he desperately wanted back, and this, too, was the Sarianna who could work up the courage to tell him she was pregnant.

She waited for him that night, late into the night, as it had been his habit to retire long after she was asleep. The darkness surrounded her, a comfort, because she did not know how to approach him. When she heard the door open, her body began trembling, and she could hardly breathe.

He wasn't aware of anything. It was a night like any other; he was bone tired and damned proud. He wasn't a man to sit idly by and let others do the work alone: He had been too many years on the frontier to become accustomed to the idea of slaves assuming his responsibilities. Nonetheless, it still wasn't easy. His overseer as much as hinted he would lose respect by this stance, and he himself could see the unease in his workers' eyes as he prowled the fields with them. Yes, he was tired, and emotionally exhausted, too.

He managed a fast wash up, in the dark, and crawled between the cool sheets.

Immediately he sensed something was different. Sarianna was too still, breathing too deliberately. There was a scent in the air, and he couldn't define it. As he settled against his pillow, he was disturbingly aware of Sarianna in a way that he had not experienced since their first weeks in Savannah.

His mind flamed with memories, and the intensity of them left him shaken. He thought he had buried all that, for Sarianna's sake. He thought he could gradually unearth each passionate treasure and slowly, bit by bit, win back the Sarianna who had enslaved him. He thought he had the patience to wait until she was ready, but his imagination ran riot with just the faintest hint of a possibility that Sarianna might be awake and waiting for him.

But how? She had been so removed from carnal concerns for these many weeks now. She had allowed him to love her, and she had remained so cool and aloof beneath him. And then Pierce's continual presence disarmed him, and Vesta's unanticipated visit stultified the atmosphere altogether and left him with the additional burden of deflecting her barbs and protecting Sarianna.

On the other hand, he reflected, she had handled herself very well with Vesta. She had broken—perhaps once—and she had needed him, really needed him. The mortifying thing had been that Pierce was always there, whether she needed him or not. But he wouldn't think about that. Pierce had obviously fallen hard in love with Sarianna, and there was nothing he could do about it. Sarianna had not wanted Pierce, he was sure of it, and if *he* thought they spent a great deal too much time together, he did not make an issue of it with Sarianna.

And he knew why: He was taking Sarianna to Haverhill, and he was going to try to recapture a nebulous beginning that had held such promises.

But how did one resurrect fierce, consuming desire?

He felt it, he felt it all the time, and he had clamped down on it and watched Sarianna move away from him in some indefinable way that—were he to admit it—scared him. He couldn't touch the reasons why, and as the days went by quickly, too quickly, he didn't feel he could touch Sarianna with that heady passion that made him want to devour her.

The scent of it was in the air this night. He didn't know why he knew it—he just knew it. Sarianna's body curved tellingly near his, not touching him, but close, so close. He shifted his body slightly, turning toward her and bracing his left hand against the mattress.

The silence was dark, portentous. A chord sounded deep within him as he sensed each of her incremental little movements. Her reckless need was tangible, feverish. The air tingled with it; Sarianna's body was taut with it.

He could just reach out and touch her; one slide of his hand down the inviting curve of her cambric-clad hip, and she would turn into his arms, he was sure of it. But was it what *she* wanted? His intuition checked his hand, and he waited, wondering what Sarianna wanted.

His body was already screaming its response to just the possibility of caressing and kissing her. He didn't know how much more he could stand of feeling her heat and not touching her.

"Sarianna . . ." His voice was a breath between them, a mating call, but he did not touch her as he felt the powerful stretch of her body responding to his voice. "Come to me, Sarianna." She sighed and twisted herself to face him, and he heard the hard swallow as she extended her hands and touched his bare chest, and wound her fingers through the wiry hair.

Her whole body heaved as she touched his smooth heated skin, and he pulled her closer until he could stroke her face, feeling it like a blind man would, memorizing her features through his fingertips from the springy golden curls that wisped onto her forehead, to the straight bridge of her nose and down to the lush curve of her firm lips.

Her mouth fascinated him, she knew it. She felt him defining its shape just with his fingers, and crushing its softness, and invading its tender interior to feel its wetness.

She flicked his fingers with her tongue, and instantly he replaced them with his hungry mouth. How he had wanted those kisses, those uninhibited-seeking kisses that were the very essence of Sarianna's wanton mouth. He grasped her chin and held her immobile, probing and exploring deeply, as if it were the first time, the only time ever he had tasted her.

She melted against him voluptuously, her body a sheen of molten sensation. Nothing existed outside this cocoon of tactile excitement deep in the dark where no one could see them.

In the dark all bold explorations were possible. Her hands moved, quivering down his chest to the flat of his stomach and the enticing male hair that led ever downward. Her fingers constricted against his skin, and then slowly, awkwardly because she approached him from her wrong side, hesitantly, she worked her fingers into the waistband of his trousers, solely compelled by her overpowering need to touch him.

Her breath caught as she felt his hard pulsating staff nudge her fingers. She wanted that, thick and throbbing in her hand, naked to her touch. Her fingers pulled at the confining buttons, ripping them apart heedlessly in her reckless need until she could capture his living heat in the palm of her hand.

He pulled her tightly against him as he felt her greedy fingers grasp him, and he wondered hazily what had changed so drastically that she desired him with such intensity. And then he couldn't think at all as she began a tentative exploration of the very tip of his elongated length with all the sweet innocence of a virgin.

"Don't stop," he breathed against her lips as she shifted her hand at one breathtaking point.

"I need," she whispered, her fingers tightening convulsively around him, "I—you . . ." He felt her distress through his thickening cloud of pleasure and somehow, some way divined he needed to shift over so she could lie to his left to free the use of her hand. Gently, he clasped her to the length of his body and rolled her over onto the opposite side.

She sighed against his mouth and pulled at his trousers once again to release his massive manhood into her hand. He felt her shudder as her hand began its radiant exploration of the entire length of him. The perfection of him struck something primitive in her, a pure female thrill of possession of that which was so elementally male and *made* for her.

He was totally captivated by her sentient caresses and his own arousing exploration of her body. He felt suspended in molten space, hot and heavy in her hand, lulled by the rhythmic caress and incited by it at the same time. His nerve endings prickled at each firm stroke and his body began a tenuous thrusting motion, in the ultimate surrender to her passion.

"Dey is bringin' de sheep dis mornin', Miss Sarianna," Alzine told her from her comfortable position on the front porch. She was feeling so much better today, thank you, and everyone had rushed out to see the wagon load of woolly sheep before they were brought out to the pasture; and Alzine had come, too, as evidence that her aches had

310

eased and her heaviness was no longer a burden.

Sarianna didn't quite believe it, but the arrival of sheep sent visions of mutton dishes dancing in her head, something to vary their dinner table in the not so far distant future.

She could not really think about mutton at this moment; she could only think about Cade and his strength and prowess that he had put in her hand the previous night, and how, because she had refused equal release, she was now feeling utterly predatory as she gazed at him with a fierce longing that magnified the heat of her feelings the night before.

The animals were noisy, their b-a-a-a's and w-a-a-a's like sharp little knives in the air, intrusive to the point where conversation was almost impossible close by.

"We gonna breed dem," Alzine said, "and you is gonna have mutton on de table by winter, Miss Sarianna, and dat sound good to me."

Sarianna smiled and pushed back her wildly curling hair. She didn't feel the oppressive heat—she felt the radiance in herself, the streamers of desire curling through her veins, the white-hot yearning that possessed her even in this most public place, among her slaves and the workers, that could only be assuaged in one way.

Cade signaled to the driver to move the wagon down the track to the pasture. Sarianna's eyes flickered over his tall frame. He was dressed in doeskin trousers and a white shirt with the sleeves rolled up, over which was a well-worn leather vest. She could see the curve of his buttocks and the molded muscularity of his thighs, and were he to turn to her, she would know the secrets of his body that were contained in his everyday apparel.

Her whole body quivered at the thought of it; she wanted him instantly, right there, naked in the sun. Her fantasies crowded in her mind, one on top of the other, each more delicious than the rest.

"Miss Sarianna, we need clean linen."

The applications began. "Miss Sarianna, is time fo' you to dole out de rice and flour ration."

"Miss Sarianna, we got to start makin' de baby layettes—it seem like Deely's expectin' too," and Sarianna groaned because it was the last thing she thought would happen, all these simultaneous pregnancies.

"Oh, Miss Sarianna, I is too sick to go in de field today."

"Miss Sarianna, we got to go to the storehouse and choose up de day's food."

"Miss Sarianna, we got to pick de first plums."

"And who, Miss Sarianna, gonna be feedin' dem chickens dis mornin' if Alzine be sick again?"

Cade pushed his way through the small crowd of female servants crowding around Sarianna. "Come for a walk, Sarianna. We'll see the sheep to pasture, and you and I will feed the chickens. The rest can wait."

Sarianna took his hand and stepped over the kneeling figures and dismised them with a wave of her hand. "We need to churn butter today, too. I still haven't got a routine—everything seems to be coming at once. And I'm worried about Alzine, and then along comes Deely, same problem."

"Well—almost. Deely's man, Frank, works the fields. Don't worry about her, Sarianna. She'll be fine." He smiled at her as they walked down the branching track from the driveway out to the west of the verdant, white bolled fields where the barnyard and pasture had been laid out and fenced in.

The wagon was parked there and emptied of its cargo long before they arrived, and they leaned against the fence and watched the animals rooting around the field aimlessly as though they had been there for years.

They walked beyond the pasture behind the barn where the chicken house had been built, to find the barrel of feed which was scrupulously filled every evening before the dairy workers retired.

Cade took a large-sized dipper, filled it, and began cawing as he scattered the seed all over the feeding lot. Sarianna followed suit, clucking and banging against the side wall of the coop to rouse the chickens from their perches. A moment later, she was surrounded by a flurry of wings.

They watched them feeding for a while and then wandered into the barn to see to the cows, of which there were eight in the stall, all of which had already given milk.

The barn was empty except for the animals, and the heavy sense of their presence and their fecundity.

There was something about the barn, with its earthy smells and the closeness of it, that arrested Sarianna.

Her breath caught as her mind ran an unruly course through her extravagant imaginings. She couldn't look at Cade; she knew he would see it in her eyes. She felt inane, out of her head, unbalanced by a heady desire to have him *there,* that moment, undressing her and feeling her. She wanted his mouth and the scent of the earth beneath her nakedness and the final culmination that she had denied herself last night. She felt mad with wanting him, with this whole new experience of the demand of her desire.

Her excitement was palpable; her whole body shuddered with the voluptuous thoughts that swirled in her head. It had to be here; it had to be *now.*

She leaned her body against the door of the barn and waited for him as he checked out the stalls and ascertained each cow had been milked. She knew how she would look to him, with the long line of her body limned in the bright morning light that streamed into the entrance, and the sun dipping in and out of the uncorseted hollows of her body.

She had the unholy urge to bare her breasts to the sunlight—his light; no one was around, no one would see. The wagon had rumbled away fifteen minues before. . . . She ran her hands nervily down the length of her body. Her limbs felt heavy, yielding. She waited for him to notice, to come to her, and the waiting was unbearable.

Her body stiffened and stretched languorously as the desire thickened within her. And she knew he looked up and saw her. What now, what would he do? She willed him to hear the siren's call of her body, to feel the heat of her urgent need.

When he came for her, his eyes were in shadow and she couldn't see; she couldn't tell if he were as shaken by the ferocity of her convulsive yearning as she.

She wasn't aware of reaching out for him, or maybe he reached out for her, digging his fingers into the soft flesh of her shoulders, sliding them upward to tangle in her hair as his mouth crushed hers tempestuously, blindly, with a ravenous hunger for continuity and another kind of completion.

He felt what she felt, more perhaps; the sensation of her hand cupping him, learning him, was as keen on his body as it had been last night, provoking a resurgence of his checked-in desire as he felt the radiance of her longing.

Her hands slid under his shirt greedily, avid for the feel of flesh and muscle, pulling and tearing, finding his burning skin, his hair roughened chest, wrapping her arms around him to tighten the length of him against her, to feel the thrust of his whole hard erection against her hips, to slide her hands sensuously all over the smooth skin of his back.

"Sarianna, Sarianna," he murmured as he moved his mouth away from hers to nip at the corner of her mouth, "I love how you touch me. *Don't*—" as the tentative exploration of her fingers brought them just under the waistband of his trousers at the small of his back— "stop; keep going, don't be afraid to touch me there. Sarianna . . ." His mouth hovered over hers, goading her with quick, delving little kisses that left her breathless and fraught with the tension of wanting more.

Don't be afraid . . . her fingers slipped farther downward, seeking his bare skin and a place to settle, to stroke, to learn.

He thrust himself against her as if he could join them through their clothes. His kiss deepened, and his hands moved from her hair downward, to touch her ears and caress her neck and to align her mouth more tightly against his before he sought the luscious softness of her breasts.

He rubbed his fingers tantalizingly against the curved underside of its contour, emboldened by her very distinct response to the rhythmic movement; her fingers constricted against the firm naked curve of his buttocks, and she ceased movement, poised, waiting for him to continue the torrid motion of his fingers, leaning into him as she subtly begged for his caresses.

She had never felt a greater excitement possess her. The taste of his tongue, the primal scent enveloping them, and the sensuous play of his fingers on her breasts—deliberately avoiding the taut peaks of her nipples—all aroused her to a fevered pitch, swamping her with erotic need, drenching her with the liquid of her passion.

Her own hands began stripping away the confining material of her dress, and he moved his hands to help her, taking his mouth from hers, looking deep into her passion-hungry eyes as he efficiently helped her remove her dress and then ripped away the thin, plain, cotton chemise that covered her quivering breasts and bared them to his heated gaze.

He didn't touch them. His mouth centered on hers again and took it, his violent need escalating at the touch of her tongue and the brush of her naked taut nipples against the bare skin of his chest. Her hands demanded he caress them, pushing until his palms cupped the weight of her breasts and his raging need did the rest. His fingers stroked upward and caught the thrusting point of pleasure, and he felt around its taut tip. Her body shuddered helplessly as his fingers explored each naked peak, simultaneously and differently, squeezing and sliding around the tight nub until she was almost over the edge.

She grabbed for him mindlessly, her fierce need to touch him compelling her hands until she released his turgid length into her waiting hand.

He felt her take his hardness, and he squeezed her lush nipples gently as her fingers began their erotic play over the hard ridged tip of his manhood.

He couldn't last much longer now; her torrid hands and white-hot kisses incited him almost beyond endurance. He felt for her center with the thrust of his maleness, prodding, nudging her, demanding, "Help me, Sarianna, let me inside you, let me love you," and she heard him, somewhere in the thickening haze of molten cloud that supported her. Her hands moved, her body shifted and they were just inside the doorway; then his long hard length thrust easily between her legs into the heart of her femininity.

"Yes," she murmured, pulling his lips down to hers again; completion, hard hot possession, the oneness, God, how could she have denied him last night! She felt him lift her, sliding his hands under her underwear-clad buttocks with the lovely divided center that gave him such easy access to her womanly core. She felt the long thick slide of him within her, and then he settled her back on her feet, against the inside door that braced her back and allowed him the purchase to thrust.

It was perfect: the earthiness, the scent, his tongue, her nakedness, her hands finding all kinds of little places to feel and squeeze with the same intensity he had caressed her nipples; his power and strength, his driving lunges that filled her with his hard virility. In the shadows they were one, and the scent of the earth became the scent of their union.

This was the fusion she sought, the ultimate joining, where she could not differentiate between their bodies and the only thing she felt was the thick pistonlike thrusting of his lusty manhood.

Her body wedged tightly against him, feeling every long inch of him as he possessed her in this elemental male way. His forceful heat enthralled her as the cadence of his stroking began building into

315

something rich and molten that shimmered silkily through her veins. His body churned against hers, wringing each opulent spasm from her with harder and harder thrusts—two, three, four—and he heard her moaning in rhythm with her convulsive pleasure—and one more—five—no more, he heard her sigh against his lips.

No more—but was it enough? Six . . . and then, with one more reaching long lunge of his his body, he catapulted unexpectedly over the edge into a powerful drenching release.

She lay naked now on a pallet of hay and clothing, crushed in his arms, in the silence and primal scent of their lovemaking. If she reached out her hand, she could grasp his quiescent maleness, the root of her galvanic pleasure. She wanted to touch him, and to let him feel her nakedness in this idle, teasing way so that perhaps—just perhaps—something would happen again.

She wondered, as she tentatively reached for him, when—and where—she was going to tell him about the child.

She felt him respond to her questing fingers, and she lifted her face to his. He smiled and cupped her chin. "Beautiful Sarianna," he murmured, ignoring her fingers that already had provoked an erection just by her touching him. "Kiss me, Sarianna," he whispered, and she arched her body upward so she could touch his lips.

She marveled at how new and different each kiss seemed, how utterly individual each joining had been. His leisurely exploration of her mouth began to arouse her, and her body craved more. The craving, she thought, might kill her if he ever left her. Who would ever feel her breasts in such a way; who would ever tempt her nipples so gently and arouse her so thoroughly with just those few simple caresses? She felt as if she wanted to stay right there with him forever, a slave to his hands and mouth, and the burgeoning heat of his erection.

His erotic caresses deepened as he sensed her rising excitement that fueled his own. "Tell me what to do," he whispered as his hands sought every inch of her silken nakedness. "Tell me what feels good."

"Everything," she moaned, holding on tight to the thickening length of his manhood and reveling in its independent movement in her hand. A storm of ravening desire possessed her, as if their first joining had been a prelude to something more, and not nearly enough—ever.

"Sarianna!" He moved his hands all over her, whispering her name, demanding her kisses, and she floated on a honey-thick cloud of tumultuous yearning, not even wondering how it could be after the first shattering climax. It just was, and it was Cade, with his kisses and his hands and his massive male member that aroused this wanton desire, and nothing less.

"I didn't think . . ." she murmured as her hands stroked his towering manhood, the only part of him that was not clothed; he felt so sensual against her, all texture and subtle secrets, with the one torrid part of him naked to her touch.

He nipped her lower lip. "You excite me."

"I love touching you."

"Don't stop, then."

"I couldn't."

"Neither can I."

Her body squirmed as he played with her turgid nipples. "I love that," she whispered, running her fingers around the hard ridged tip of his tumescence.

"I love it, too," he murmured. "Let me kiss your nipples, Sarianna."

"Yes," she breathed, and he shifted his body so he could bend over her and comfortably settle his mouth on her left breast, at the very tip, and surround it with his lips. His hot tongue probed the shape of its taut point, and he began sucking it wildly, as if he couldn't help his response and his greed.

She groaned as she felt the heat of his mouth possess her nipple; her fingers grasped his elongated maleness convulsively with each sensual pull of his mouth on her nipple. His ear was so close to her lips. She heard herself murmuring things to him, intimate things, letting him hear her total enslavement to the sucking motion of his lips and tongue. Thinking or not thinking—she didn't know later—as her body moved against the cadence of his sucking that soon, very soon, there would be a baby at her breast.

"Oh, Cade, oh, yes, that, just that way. Cade!" She pushed at him with her shoulder. "Cade . . ."

"Sarianna, oh, God, Sarianna—what?"

She felt the warm air cooling on her heated breast. "We're going to have a baby," she whispered, the words almost torn out of her by the thought that a baby would replace this torrential succulent love-play—and would he care?

His body tensed. "Sarianna?" His voice was gentle, encouraging.

She took a deep breath. "There is going to be a baby."

"Truly?"

"Really."

She held her breath; what would he think? She had never stopped to consider that, nor had she even planned for the moment of revelation. Her body cooled as she waited tensely for his reaction, cooled and drained of the powerful sensuality that had enveloped her.

"Oh, my God," he murmured, "that is by all that's holy *wonderful!* Sarianna!" He grabbed for her exuberantly. *"Really?* Sarianna, you are wonderful." His lips grazed hers as he crushed her against him once more. His hand slid down her body to touch her stomach. "It's amazing, God, Sarianna—my beautiful Sarianna—a baby . . ."

But he felt vigorous in her hand, his body tight with the joyousness of her news, never questioning why and where she had chosen to tell him, only that she had presented him with this precious gift.

His body spoke for him, tensing with want of her, in gratitude and love. She felt it, and a pang of memory assaulted her. Yes, she thought, like that; she moved into his kiss. Like that. His hand began a second meticulous exploration of her body, as if he knew she had pulled back in inhibition until she knew how he felt.

God, how he felt; there were no words to say how he felt. A baby—with Sarianna. A child. A son, from the heat of their union. From his sensual communion with the essence of her femininity. His hand encompassed her feminine mound; his fingers probed her gently, seeking entry.

"Let me in, Sarianna," he whispered. "You are so ready for me."

"Come then," she invited, wanting him now as the warmth of his response heated her.

He got to his knees and lifted her legs, bracing them against his shoulders. "Like this." And he entered her, poised over her in a way that she could feel him once again even more deeply—if that were possible.

She couldn't hold him in this position, or kiss him, but she could see his face as he began the churning thrusts that would lead to the final soaring completion.

She loved watching his expression as every long stroke caressed her

318

in a new and different way, and it reflected in her expression as he watched her.

It was the most provocative of all the ways he had made love to her, to see his eyes and the depth of emotion his possession of her produced in him. She could love that soft expression; perhaps she did love that expression, she thought in awe. A pulsating excitement engulfed her at the thought, and she lost herself in the opulent sensations.

And then, when she was least expecting it, she came to a turbulent, dazzling climax that shook her whole body in torrid paroxysms of ravishing pleasure that she perceived reflected in his eyes. A moment later, he followed her, spending his potent desire with a hoarse sigh of her name, and the loving benediction as he collapsed against her, "A baby . . ."

21

The following day Sarianna began to establish a routine. She
assigned the housekeeping tasks after making out a precise list of what
she wanted to have done on which day of which part of the month.
One servant would handle the bedmaking and sweeping of the
rooms, another the dusting, including a thorough, down-to-the-
books-and-penwipers cleaning once a month. The cook's assistant
would have to clean the copper once a month, and two of the women
would handle the laundry twice a week, and ironing on Saturdays.
One of the younger girls was assigned the dishwashing. All of the
women would help with the soapmaking and candle dipping, and that
was due to be done soon because Cade had not laid in an extensive
supply of candles or kerosene lamps.

Then, they still had some leeway until winter, but already Sarianna
was leery of the amount of sewing that would have to be done to
accommodate making winter clothing for the field hands and the
house servants. She made some notes on her list for Cade to take with
him on his next trip to Savannah. They would need to buy their cloth;
they hadn't the means or the servants to help her produce it, although
they might be able to salvage some wool from the sheep and harvest
enough to bulk out the knitting of the stockings whenever that would
begin.

She would have to find out through diligent questioning which of
the women was proficient at any of those chores. She had a feeling no
one was going to volunteer the information and that they were
very used to fending for themselves after having done so for these
many years.

She went to the storehouse now twice a day, once in the morning with Gwen to mete out the foodstuffs for the day's meals, and then in the evening to dole out stores to the servants.

"Oh, Miss Sarianna, I cain't do nothin' today; I is feelin' poorly."

"Well, how come dat Alzine gets to have dem days in her bed and we gots to do all her workin' too, Miss Sarianna?"

"Miss Sarianna, we got to pick dem strawberries today, and get dem in de cannin' jars as soon as might be."

"Deely cain't do no weedin' today, ma'am; she say it hurt her back."

Sarianna sighed. More problems, always little problems: The house servants were unaccustomed to such ongoing work, the garden needed weeding, this one didn't get enough corn; that one got too much rice and someone else was envious. Someone's shoes needed patching, another one needed a blanket. The chickens needed feeding, and someone had to milk the cows; they hated churning the butter, and she asssigned that chore on a rotating basis, thinking she wouldn't like it either.

"I'm going to Savannah at the end of the week," Cade said that evening, and her heart thumped to a sickening halt for a long heavy moment.

"Must you?" she said at last.

"The second twenty-five bales are ready to go. I'm sending word to Vesta in the morning to expect me for a week or more; I'll take your list and fill up the wagon for you," he said, reaching for her hand. "I'll be back before you know it."

"I'll miss you," she said tentatively, wondering how she would survive a night without lying in his arms. That didn't sound bold; it sounded wifely, and she liked the fact she had the freedom to express such things to him.

"I wish I didn't have to leave you," he responded, squeezing her hand. "I wish someone else could take the blasted cotton to market, but I don't trust any of them worth a damn. I'm going to change that—but I can't yet. So I have to go, Sarianna; I have to miss a night in your arms."

"We'll make up for it then—tonight, and tomorrow and . . ."

"Sweet Sarianna," he murmured, running his hand over her mouth. "Nothing ever can hurt us—here."

Jeralee loved Savannah and she had not expected to. She was used to being catered to, and to having everyone at her beck and call. She was used to young men swarming around her and to being the most beautiful of all the girls who lived on the tight little island of Sawny.

But now she was one of very many lovely wealthy young women who had thronged into the city accompanied by their mothers, a houseful of servants and a wardrobe that was almost a trousseau, and perhaps was meant to be.

Jeralee had competition, and she found very quickly that the way to cut a wide swath through the elegant silks and manners of the horde of avid young women seeking to make a connection in the city was to offer up something that no one else would: herself.

She knew already, from Gaff Gilmartin's tentative gropings, and Samuel Summers' more experienced secretive feels, that there was much more to this ingrained fear of sex than her mother alluded to. Her body told her there was much more than her mother would even admit, and a lot that was pleasurable. She had found that out when Samuel daringly exposed her breasts one afternoon as they toured Summerton, and caressed her quivering virginal nipples.

Only her mother's eagle-eyed vigilance put an end to that delicious exploration that left her avidly curious to know more.

When she arrived in Savannah, she saw she was in the ideal environment to pursue a greater knowledge of her own sensuality. She knew one thing the other girls didn't: She liked having her breasts touched, and she knew through oblique questioning that the other girls had nothing nearly as exciting to offer a potential beau.

She wasn't sure she liked kissing so much, but she rather thought that if she really loved the man who was kissing her, it would seem less slimy and disagreeable. She was willing, at any rate, to kiss anyone who wanted to kiss her because she knew the other girls wouldn't.

Vesta was gratified at how many young men crowded the Malverne Row parlor.

"I'm so proud of you, Jeralee," she said at one point. "We didn't need that old Cade when so many of these younger men seem to find you so attractive. And there's money in that room drinking our sherry—more money than Cade Rensell will ever know. I just wonder why I got so upset about him marrying Sarianna."

Jeralee could have told her, but she elected silence. To her, Cade was the ideal the others had to live up to. She wondered about his kisses, and how his hands would feel on her skin. She agonized over

Sarianna sharing a bed with him and spending his money profligately. She hated Sarianna. She couldn't imagine anything more desirable than being married to Cade Rensell.

And if that were so, and her ultimate goal was to somehow thrust herself intrusively into their marriage and spoil things for them, she was wasting her time with all these young bucks who drank their hard-bought liquor and ate the delicacies prepared in their kitchen with such careless abandon.

But on the other hand, there was no Cade to overwhelm her with his lovemaking. She couldn't keep herself isolated because of her fantastical dream of winning Cade back someday.

She needed to make the most of her time in Savannah, and to learn as much as possible so she could be prepared for the day that Cade came to sweep her off her feet.

So she chose Pierce Darden as his comparable substitute.

They shared a mutual bond: He hated Sarianna and Cade both now, and he said so plainly to whoever would listen.

Jeralee and Vesta listened.

"Of course you feel abandoned; so do we all," Vesta said comfortably. She had been spreading this very story: Cade had left them precipitately to take Sarianna out of harm's way as her little flirtations began to get out of hand. It excused her and Jeralee from the speculation that it was their presence that Cade sought to escape, and it made her feel good to malign Sarianna.

"The bastard took away everything, even Sarianna, and I'll never forgive him for it," Pierce vowed fervently as Jeralee devoured him with her sheeny chocolatey gaze.

Their hate bound them in a fine web of endless conversation about Sarianna's betrayal. "But she never gave you anything," Jeralee pointed out. "She never cared enough to show you her appreciation of your devotion."

He snorted. "This is true, and I can't tell you how used I feel."

"We were all used," Jeralee said. "Aren't you sorry you felt such sympathy for her when you came to Bredwood?"

"I wish I could take it all back," Pierce ground out. "I wish I had never met her."

"I wish," Jeralee said slowly, "that she had never existed."

And Vesta smiled, her mind hard upon the ways in which she could use Pierce and all his lovely connections to further Jeralee's social position in Savannah.

She had no inkling that Jeralee had other plans altogether. Jeralee wanted to conquer every man who had ever *looked* at Sarianna, and she was after Pierce with an underlying ferocity that matched his passion for revenge on Cade. Pierce would be the first; if he fell, he who had adored Sarianna, the others would be easy, and she meant to enslave them all, one by one, with her body and her kisses and any other way she had to in order to obliterate Sarianna's memory in their minds once and for all.

Pierce fell. He was hardly proof against someone of Jeralee's inbred charm, and Broydon wealth. She was beautiful, too, in her own way, and she hung on every word he said. She hated Sarianna, too, and he loved that about her as their relationship deepened right under Vesta's nose without her even being aware of it.

He came to Malverne Row at all hours, whenever Vesta was to be away; or when Jeralee was to be visiting or at a party, she wangled an invitation for him, and he met her there, and they spent hours hashing over the wrongs Sarianna had done them.

"Did you ever touch her?" Jeralee demanded, and more than once.

Pierce would cast her a sharp look. He wasn't stupid; he knew his stature with her would be enhanced if he admitted something, and in point of fact, he felt humiliated because there had been nothing. But Jeralee would never know, and somehow he sensed it was important for her to believe he *had* touched Sarianna.

"Jeralee—let us not talk about it."

"I have to know." Her eyes fixed on him intently as if she could draw the answer out of his mind. She liked his mouth and the shape of his hands, and she wanted to know, when everything came to fruition, that her charms were the equal of Sarianna's—and more.

"A gentleman doesn't tell," he murmured sententiously, liking the say she leaned forward to expose the tops of her breasts quite by accident—except she had done it several times, and nudged into him subtly on one or two other occasions.

"Oh, don't believe that!" Jeralee rapped his arm with her fan. "Ladies tell," she added suggestively.

"Do they now, Miss Jeralee. I'd like to hear more about that." His face came close to hers, and her heart began pounding wildly.

"Well, for example, if you were to kiss me now, Pierce Darden, I would keep it a secret to my grave; but there are some others who would run and tell every one of their friends—everyone who would listen," Jeralee told him, embellishing as she went along.

A flash of some nameless emotion shadowed his eyes. What if Sarianna had told *someone* there had been nothing, *nothing* in *all* those months! Jeralee's brazen invitation hardly registered for the shattering fear he felt that he had been diminished somehow in some neighbor's eyes by Sarianna's careless gossip.

And Jeralee began to learn that she could not even allude to Sarianna if she meant to make a conquest of him, because everything she was curious about reminded Pierce of *her,* and she saw that seducing him would be a lot harder than she had originally foreseen.

It took one evening, when Pierce happened to be at the same party as Jeralee, for him to understand that Jeralee was offering what Sarianna would not. And that happened because he was unintentionally eavesdropping and what he heard turned his bones to jelly and gave him a monumental erection.

Jeralee was in the library with some man while he was in the garden, and he heard her teasing voice. "Come *on,* Hamp. We'll be alone in the library. No one will see; there are no lamps lit. Hurry, hurry." The door closed, and Pierce heard the scuffling of feet and a demure grunting sound from Jeralee. "Kiss me now, Hamp." A silence followed, fraught with awkward smacking sounds, and then Jeralee, breathless. "Oh, Hamp—I would love that, but we have to be very careful. *Very* careful." Another kiss followed, long and wet, and Pierce could hear every nuance of it, and then Jeralee's voice, breathy and petulant. "Of course I liked your kisses, Hamp. I promise you I want you to do more . . . but—let me think. I mean, what if someone walked in here and found us like that? I would *die.*"

Pierce heard the phantom Hamp whispering in her ear.

"Oh, yes, yes. Perfect. Come . . ." More footsteps, a bump into a piece of furniture, and a scuffling, shuffling sound as their presence drew nearer to the window, and Jeralee giggled, her voice muffled suddenly as she and Hamp ducked under one of the wide, heavy velvet curtains.

Jeralee again: "I'm yours," and that kissing sound and a silence that was broken long minutes later by Jeralee's long drawn-out groan.

A whisper: "I wish I could see them."

Jeralee: "But you can feel them." An extended period of silence followed that was punctuated by Jeralee's sighs of pleasure. "More," she begged huskily. "More."

Hamp's rough voice answered her. "We can't do more here, Jeralee. We can't risk it. Button yourself up now while I put in an appearance in the drawing room."

"Hamp!" A rustle of curtains underpinned her protestation. "Damn." Her muffled whisper was fraught with frustration.

Without a moment's thought, Pierce slid through the connecting French doors and behind the curtain to assuage her need.

In the excitement of the dark and the ardor of her arousal, Jeralee did not care who had come to her. She pressed someone's hot male hands to her naked breasts and crushed a pair of willing male lips under her own. Everything else was billowing sensations, one on top of the other, until both bodies were drenched with sweat, straining for release.

"Jeralee, Jeralee—" Pierce tore his mouth from her ravenous kiss.

"Oh, my God," she groaned, "Pierce? *Pierce?*"

"Hang on honey, it's me," he rasped as he ran his hands over her taut tipped breasts once again. "It's me . . ."

Jeralee felt a walloping sense of gratitude; his hands were no different, or his needs. In the dark she could hardly tell the difference between him and Hamp, and she didn't care. She wrapped her arms around him and pulled him closer to whisper in his ear, "Keep doing what you're doing, Pierce darling. I'm very, very glad it's you."

How many curtains they had hidden behind for their furtive explorations in the ensuing weeks, Jeralee did not know. She didn't care. It was either Pierce or one of the many faceless men who had courted attendance on Sarianna, and either or both were fine with her. She was becoming addicted to this clandestine groping, hardly able to go a day without yearning for some kind of contact.

The best part was, Pierce was always around, and they had

progressed to the point where Jeralee was sure he had forgotten totally about Sarianna and her caresses.

Now they sought opportunities to be alone in the house where they could have the freedom to explore and push the boundaries that restricted them behind dark musty curtains and dark musty conventions.

Now they planned their meetings for nights when Vesta was sure to be out, and when she was sure Jeralee was occupied elsewhere. How she would explain her numerous absences from the various functions, Jeralee did not know, but she was sure she could slide through the excuses when the time came.

Nothing took precedence over the opaque exploration of her darkest desires. She didn't even care that the servants were privy to these secret meetings.

When he came, she would answer the door, dressed in her wrapper. "Oh, hurry, Pierce, I've been waiting all day."

"Where's Vesta?"

"At the Harmons' tonight; she thinks I'm with Fanny Jewett, but we don't have much time."

"In the parlor, Jeralee, hurry. I can't wait another minute." He pushed her into the parlor and closed the doors as Jeralee stripped off her wrapper and laid it on the floor. A moment later, Pierce pushed her onto it and fell on top of her.

Marvela was the one who answered the door an hour later, after five minutes of impatient ringing. "Oh, Mr. Cade!" She looked totally flustered. "Was Miss Vesta expectin' you?"

"I should think so." Cade strode into the hallway. "Where is everybody?"

"Oh, Mr. Cade . . ." Marvela faltered. "Miss Vesta is out fo' de evenin'. And she didn't leave no word about you-all comin' here tonight."

"Well, I'm here," Cade said brusquely, looking around, reassured by the fact that everything seemed pretty much the same. "Would you prepare my bed, Marvela, and see if I can get something to eat before I retire?"

"Oh, Mr. Cade," she said again, backing away hesitantly. "I don' know if I can do dat."

Cade's eyes darkened. "Why can't you? Where is Hector,

327

and Elvira?"

"Hector done gone to bed, Mr. Cade, and Elvira could be in de kitchen."

"Get them," he said tersely, swinging his bag into a corner and heading into the dining room. It was too quiet in the house, with no sense that anyone was about. There should have been at least two other servants in attendance. He had the bad feeling that he had been taken advantage of for all these weeks.

Elvira appeared at the kitchen door, her eyes downcast, her manner meek. "Mr. Cade?"

"What do you have left over from dinner?"

"Dey wasn't no dinner, Mr. Cade. Miss Vesta done et out with de Harmons tonight. And Miss Jeralee, I don' know where she is at."

"Get me something to eat," he ordered as Hector shuffled into the room. "What's going on here, Hector? Why weren't you in attendance here? Why is the house so quiet?"

Hector stared at him as if he were talking another language. How could he tell Mr. Cade that Miss Jeralee had sent him to his room early on this evening. "Miss Vesta say I can have de evening 'cause I wasn't feelin' no good, Mr. Cade. Miss Vesta didn't need me dis evenin', Mr. Cade. Marvela was waitin', and dat Opal, upstairs, fo' when she done come home. Wasn't no need fo' me when I was feelin' so poorly."

"All right, Hector." Disgusted, Cade turned on his heel as Elvira came into the room with a tray of cold chicken and marinated vegetables. "That will do. Where is Marvela? Marvela! You get that Opal, whoever she is, to turn down my damned bed, please, and you wait up and tell Vesta I have arrived."

"Yassir," Marvela muttered resentfully, and headed for the stairs.

Cade took several ravenous bites of the chicken and downed a tall glass of lemonade that Elvira had also provided. Damned Vesta, he thought, losing his appetite; she couldn't run a damned thing efficiently except her damned mouth.

God. The chicken tasted like dust. Maybe the cook she had chosen couldn't even cook. He tasted the vegetables. Vinegar. Elvira had drowned them in vinegar and sugar. Lord. He finished the lemonade and left the whole on the table.

He heard a scurrying over his head, and secretive little grunts and groans coming from the parlor.

He flung open the parlor doors on an impulse, and light from the hallway flooded the floor, revealing the naked writhing entwined bodies of Jeralee and Pierce.

"Well, he might tell Mother," Jeralee said the next morning as, sedately dressed, she admitted Pierce to the parlor once again. She couldn't bear to look at the spot on the floor where she had found such dark rapture. It was sullied by Cade's presence and by the fact he might reveal to Vesta all he surmised of Jeralee's activities.

"We just have to push through this morning as if everything were normal," Pierce said decisively, seating himself with familiarity on one of the two sofas opposite the fireplace. "We'll have to wait and see what Cade Rensell decides to do, and then counter it as best we can."

Jeralee flew into his arms. "I can't wait for tonight," she whispered in his ear. "I wish they were all gone; we could do it right now, right on the floor again, in the light where you can see everything."

She jumped as she heard Cade's sardonic drawl. "Good morning, Jeralee."

She scurried across the couch and sat sedately facing him. "Cade."

"Pierce." Cade could hardly stand to look at the man.

"Good morning, Cade," Pierce said with equanimity, but even he was searching for some sign of what Cade intended to do.

"Where's Vesta?"

"Mother must still be asleep," Jeralee said cautiously. "She must not know you're here."

"She knows," Cade said shortly.

Marvela intervened. "Breakfast is on de table, Mr. Cade."

And Vesta was waiting, just as if it were her house and she had the run of things. "Cade—so good to see you," she said smoothly. "Jeralee, my dear, how is Fanny? Did you have a good time with her last night? And Pierce, always welcome, my dear. Cade, sit to my right, and tell me all the news of Haverhill."

"Haverhill is fine, thank you," Cade murmured, picking up his coffee and sipping it so he would not have to talk.

"And dear Sarianna?"

"Sarianna is enjoying life at Haverhill," Cade said curtly, reaching for a muffin and the butter keeper. A lovely object, he thought, chosen by Sarianna, soiled by Vesta's hands. "I'll be here for about a week, maybe a few days more; I'm not sure yet. I promise I won't be an intrusive guest in my own house."

"Oh, Cade," Vesta said coquettishly. "I must, while we have you here, tell you how grateful we are for your giving us the use of your home. We are having a wonderful time in Savannah, aren't we, Jeralee?"

"A wonderful time," she echoed obediently, not looking at Cade or Pierce.

"I'm delighted," Cade said, biting into his biscuit. He let them make the small talk around the table, and he let Jeralee and Pierce squirm, wondering what, if anything, he was going to say about their public coupling on the parlor floor. His heart and mind were filled with Sarianna; he was hardly aware of where he was for thinking of her, he couldn't let Jeralee's sordid trysts or Vesta's coyness disturb the pure bright thought of her at Haverhill, tending to her chores, and thinking of him.

"Surely," Vesta interposed, "you can tell us of some of the changes at Haverhill, Cade. I know it was very rundown when you took over."

"Yes, it was. Now it's not," he answered quickly. "We're baling up as fast as we can; I've brought the second load in, and I have business to take care of before I return. In fact," he added, throwing down his napkin and sending a searing glance in Jeralee's direction, "I'm late for an appointment now." He pushed back his chair. "If you'll excuse me?"

Vesta nodded, and he left them to the mountain of food that Elvira had prepared. In truth, he had no meetings; he only wanted to be away from the cloying atmosphere that seemed to surround Vesta and Jeralee even in his own house.

Vesta said, "He's still as rough as ever."

"Yes," Jeralee agreed, not looking at Pierce, "and just as desirable."

He supposed later if he had thought about it, he could have predicted that Vesta would squeeze every bit of gossip out of Owen, who had accompanied him to Savannah. Thank God, Vesta had another evening out planned. It was bad enough having her rap his arm endlessly with her fan as she chided him for not telling her this, and omitting to mention that, and otherwise keeping *everything* from her—including, she added, throwing a sharp leering look at Pierce, the fact that Sarianna was possibly going to have a child.

"And who told you that?" he asked silkily over dinner as his eyes skewed to Pierce's shocked face, damned Pierce who was never absent from either Vesta's table or latterly from his own.

"Owen has been telling me *everything*," Vesta said suggestively, "but that is the most interesting news of all. *Why* didn't you tell us?"

Cade was still watching Pierce's reaction with a tight closed expression on his face. "It hasn't been confirmed yet," he answered abruptly, wondering at Pierce's absurd reaction.

"Sarianna *enceinte*," Vesta murmured lovingly as if the vision warmed her. "What possibilities. Congratulations, Cade. You work fast."

He hated the smarmy insinuations in her words. Worse, he hated Pierce's dawning awareness of what she meant by them, as if there were some other explanation for Sarianna's condition that had nothing to do with Cade.

Even Jeralee's mind was following along the same lines. Her mother's suggestive words hit home with her. It was an ideal opportunity—for something, but she didn't quite know what. She admired with detachment Pierce's varying expressions as Cade's eyes pinned him.

Again, there was an atmosphere in the room he did not understand, and he had just the faintest inkling that Pierce wanted to say something and didn't quite know how or what to say.

Jeralee pursed her mouth, her mind totally on the notion of Sarianna's impending confinement and how she could make use of it. Vesta kept looking at Cade speculatively as if she knew something he did not. And Pierce, after his shocked response, kept searching his face as if he would find some perception there that was not obvious to Cade himself.

He was disgusted with the lot of them. The news of Sarianna's delicate condition had turned them back into vultures again, and he couldn't begin to understand what they would do about it.

It was a relief to finally be able to excuse himself and leave them in the mire of their useless plots and schemes.

* * *

"*Did* you?" Jeralee demanded insistently.

"Did I what?" Pierce pretended to misunderstand her question.

"Pierce—don't be obtuse. Did you sleep with Sarianna?"

"Jeralee, you are by far—"

"I hope I am," Jeralee interrupted. "Tell me you slept with her and that baby could be yours."

"Jeralee . . ." He felt as if he were on a speeding train heading downhill to a massive crash that would entangle him in the wreckage. And there would be wreckage if Cade ever found out he was even trying to perpetrate a lie. But the provocation was so great, and Jeralee was so sure.

"God, you were with her all the damn time," Jeralee said exasperatedly. "Cade never knew half the time you were with her. How many dozen witnesses can bear that out, do you think? It will kill him, Pierce, don't you understand? Utterly destroy him to think that his precious Sarianna had been even that much unfaithful."

"I know. It's tempting to claim patrimony, Jeralee, but we don't know what had been between them since the wedding. It's perfectly possible the baby is Cade's." He thought that was rather clever, the way he phrased that. He had admitted possible culpability without actually saying anything.

"And very possible *not,* given the way you two were carrying on," Jeralee put in. She wasn't sure herself how she felt about this tacit confession. The thought of him with Sarianna doing with her the things he did . . . she swallowed bile and forced her mind back to the notion at hand: Cade's reaction to finding out the baby might not be his. Even if it weren't true, just a hint of it would have to have explosive repercussions.

She had known instantly the moment he threw open the door and saw her on the floor with Pierce that any hope she had nourished in his direction was doomed. Now the only thing that was possible was to punish Sarianna for taking him away, and what better scheme than to question her fidelity when Cade Rensell had the nerve to question her own activities.

Even Vesta had come to the same conclusion herself. "Can you imagine," she said later, "Cade Rensell's brat—another Sarianna—another Dona . . . oh, my God . . ." Her eyes stared into the distance, imagining a golden curled image of Sarianna, reproducing itself, mirror image, on into infinity. The thought made her shudder in horror, along with the notion that all of that could have been avoided if she could have contrived to get him married to Jeralee. She just couldn't forgive him for making the wrong choice. It seemed just that the child who might have been her own flesh and blood could be used to exact a punishment on him, and Sarianna, and perhaps come between them in a way that would free Cade for further pursuit and send Sarianna away forever.

She felt an urgency about it because they had very little time to work on Cade, and that was coupled with a different kind of fear—the urgency over the secession talk that was being promulgated hot and heavy at every social function she attended. She foresaw everything in one blinding flash: The conflict would come, the men would go off to war, and there would be no one left for Jeralee, no one left for *her*.

"We can't be blatant about it," she mused as she and Jeralee talked it over the rest of the evening. "We want him to disbelieve Sarianna very strongly when he leaves here. We don't even know if she can talk him out of thinking he is not the father. All we can do is plant the seed in his mind that things were going on that he might not have been aware of, and that might have been questionable if he looked at them closely. But he trusted Sarianna, after all."

Vesta smiled, an ugly, unpleasant smile. "Just like Rex trusted Dona. So you see—the fruit doesn't fall far from the tree, does it?"

"Anyway," Jeralee said, dismissing the reference which of course only applied to Sarianna and *her* mother, "*we* can't be the ones to tell him outright. So how can we be sure he understands how it was with Sarianna when she was running around all that time being social?"

"I'll think of a way," Vesta said thoughtfully. "Perhaps a little dinner—here? A hint dropped in the ear of a friend to make a reference . . . ? It could be very nice." Her smile deepened into one of pure malevolent delight. "Yes, I really think that is the way to do it. He'll be here a week, after all; he'll want to see some friends—his new lawyer perhaps . . . who is that anyway? I think . . . I really think we can manage it very nicely."

By midweek, Cade was feeling incredibly uncomfortable in the company of Vesta and Jeralee who, somehow, had rearranged their busy social schedule to be sure they were on hand to attend to all his needs while he was their guest in *his* house. Vesta was a marvel, he kept thinking. It was as if reality didn't exist for her; she made up her own and ignored what she didn't want to deal with. If he said he wanted to be alone, she would keep him company. If he told her she needn't bother arranging a special menu for his dinners, she planned five-course meals. When he told her he did *not* wish to go out socially, she immediately made sure he was invited everywhere.

Maybe, he thought, that was her secret: She made a person so tired that it became easier to acquiesce than to try to reason with her. She was like a cannon: heavyweight, pointed right at a person all the time, and rolling right over all objections with unanswerable firepower.

And underlying all of that was a smothering, encroaching, spurious concern for Sarianna—and for him—that was laced with a patronizing air of knowing something that he did not and would never know.

He hadn't thought it was possible to dislike her more than he did when he left Bredwood; now she was impossible, and he was counting the hours before he could leave, and planning ways to evict her from her obviously well-entrenched occupation of his house.

"But business shouldn't take up the *whole* week," Vesta protested the next morning as Cade prepared to visit his factor's office down by the docks.

"Vesta, you need not trouble yourself to think up things to fill up my day," Cade said, eyeing her warily. It was the typical breakfast scene with Pierce right in place in the exact same chair that he had occupied when he had visited Sarianna and him on similar mornings a month ago. He was troubled by that, and by Pierce's reaction to the news of Sarianna's pregnancy, just as he had been troubled by his everlasting presence in this house and in Sarianna's company.

"One little dinner," Vesta compromised quickly, sensing an anger about to erupt. "Here, so you do not even have to go out to attend it. Some friends, perhaps your new lawyer—pardon me, Pierce, but facts are facts—and his wife? Yes? I promise—nothing else. But everybody, I assure you, is quite anxious to know how Sarianna is doing. They ask us all the time. She made quite an impression the months you were here."

She slanted a brooding look at him, wondering if she had gone too far, or if she had even gone far enough.

She could see her words working on him; she could almost follow his thoughts: everyone anxious to know how Sarianna was doing? She made quite an impression?

"Hell," he exploded finally, "do what you want."

Only it was worse than he could have imagined. All those people, none of whom he knew, all of whom knew him, all of them had something to say about Sarianna until he finally began to think they were talking about some other Sarianna altogether.

"But she and Mr. Darden," Mrs. Soames said, "they used to come to our little musicales together. Well, you must know my Emma looked favorably on Mr. Darden, even if it was out of the question. Of course she wanted to flirt with him a little, but who could compete with Sarianna?"

"Sarianna," Emma Soames said. "You're Sarianna's husband. Every girl in Savannah absolutely hated her. She would walk into a room and draw everyone to her like a magnet. The men just loved her, and none of us could ever figure out why. And Mr. Darden just hung around her like a bee sniffing out honey; he never saw anyone else. How could you *stand* it?"

"How we miss Sarianna," Patrick Jewett rhapsodized. "A woman of superior understanding. A wonderful listener. A perfect companion, Rensell; you *are* the lucky one, and it makes me wonder what on earth you are doing *here?*"

Cade was beginning to wonder about that himself. He overheard Nerina Jewett talking to Vesta. "You mean he doesn't know?"

"Am I to be the one to spread gossip, Nerina, when I'm indebted to him for his generosity?"

"And yet you let Pierce have the run of the place, Vesta. How can you countenance that?"

"He knows interesting people. He took Sarianna all over town when she first arrived, and everyone took to her immediately."

"None more so than Pierce," Nerina Jewett said dryly. "I swear people were beginning to wonder what kind of *menage* occupied this house, with Pierce here morning and afternoon and at night. There was *such* talk, with her husband gone so much. And he never suspected a thing."

"I must say Sarianna, who is the spit of my sister—in *all* ways, I might add, if you remember Dona at all—"

"Yes, and it was amazing that she wound up with her mother's lover; don't think *that* wasn't talked about. . . ."

"Sarianna could convince anyone of anything. Look at how she wound up marrying him when he was dead set on proposing to my Jeralee. She's heartless, Sarianna, spoiled horribly by Rex, his absolute favorite. She thinks she can get away with anything, even the possibility of passing this child off as Cade's if it turns out it is *not*."

"Possibility. Honestly, Vesta, perhaps you are being too kind. They were together so much. I don't know how Cade dares show his face in town after all that went on this summer. No one knows what happened behind closed doors."

"It's too true; I'm only delighted I got here when I did. I suppose my arrival forced Cade to remove sooner, but maybe it was for the best with this news of a baby. You know how many men were enchanted with Sarianna. I don't think a pregnancy would have stopped . . ."

Cade felt sick. Damned biddies, he thought. Stupid women, gossiping like that about his Sarianna. Thank God Pierce was not here tonight; at that moment, he thought he could have torn him apart piece by piece.

Whatever they thought, it wasn't true—he knew it in his bones. He knew Sarianna.

He didn't see Vesta's surreptitious peeking around Nerina Jewett's shoulder and her nod of complete satisfaction that he had overheard exactly the little scenario she had intended. She nudged Nerina, and Nerina disappeared to find someone else to accost Cade with an account of Sarianna's social life.

The person she chose was Anthony Argyle, one of the many young men whom she knew had been smitten with Sarianna. He had an appealing ingenuousness and no malice in him whatsoever, and she and Vesta made sure an appreciable amount of time passed before Anthony even approached Cade, which he did with a diffident shyness that made him all the more believable.

"So pleased to meet Sarianna's husband," he said enthusiastically, pumping Cade's hand up and down. "What a treat she is. All of us kept saying how lucky her husband is, and here you are."

Cade didn't know what to think, or even say. But he didn't need to open his mouth. Argyle was perfectly willing to sing Sarianna's praises to the sky, in the nicest possible way. "She would listen to what a fellow had to say, you know? Never put herself forward too much, but always knew the right words, always interested. Never forward, never. Everyone loved having her. Not many women are both beautiful and reserved as your wife, Mr. Rensell. All of us men fell headlong in love. Oh, yes. No disrespect intended, Mr. Rensell, but of course we all wondered what—if anything—was going on with her and Mr. Darden."

Vesta watched Cade's face, from another part of the room, and she knew the exact moment when the idea took hold, as he was talking to Anthony Argyle. She did not need do anything more to convince him.

She sped across the room to find Nerina to tell her there would be no more pressure. Cade had taken the bait, and Sarianna was going to be a dead fish.

22

Thursday, Cade sent Owen back to Haverhill with passes and an overloaded wagon with supplies. He could not bring himself to think of going home until he thought further about this phenomenon of Sarianna the social butterfly who had apparently captivated the whole of the male population of Savannah.

He understood; she had been so deprived there was no other course but for her to jump headlong into such rigorous social activity. That she was such a success at it was gratifying. That so many men admired her was heartwarming. The rest—he didn't know. All he heard was Pierce's name coupled with hers, and the idea that Pierce had been so often present in company with Sarianna and then subsequently to be found in his own home sat very hard with him.

He didn't like the innuendo, the covert assumption that Sarianna would have allowed Pierce to overstep his bounds. He hated it and the inescapable conclusion that he had to draw: It surely would have been possible for something to have happened between them.

The thought was like a burning coal in the pit of his stomach. Sarianna and Pierce. Hell, she had more discrimination than that, he would think, but the notion couldn't go away; it burned and ate away at his vitals, sapping his pleasure at the idea of returning home. What if it were true?

It couldn't be true, that Sarianna had allowed Pierce to—

And he remembered her strange distance after they had arrived in Savannah, and her aloofness, as if her mind were somewhere else all the time. He remembered her measured response to him, and his thinking that she only needed time and then the vixen in her would

338

show its playful face.

And this happened during the time that he was working at Haverhill and Pierce was forever following her around.

By God. By damn and hell.

The clues fit—too well—including Sarianna's sudden emergence from her self-imposed restraint. Damn her.

It wasn't true. It could be.

Where was the line? He almost—almost believed it was.

The next day brought a note from Bredwood, written by—of all people, Vesta said harshly—Samuel Summers. Rex was summoning her home to discuss matters of a private nature. "How inconsiderate of him," Vesta muttered. "And I suppose I must go and go soon if he intends to spoil what is left of the rest of the season for Jeralee."

She cast a speculative look at Cade, wondering whether he would stay on another day, and she could begin spreading gossip that he and Jeralee had made the most of the time she had been away.

Cade, however, was not predisposed to fall in with those plans. "I'll take you there," he offered purely as a courtesy, but as he watched her expression as she considered his proposal, he had a jangling feeling that she did not want him to accompany her, and more that she might be hiding something—several things. She looked distinctly uncomfortable as if she were trying to think of one or more reasons she should not accept his very proper offer.

Finally she said, "There's no need for you to go all the way to Sawny, Cade."

No, he thought, she surely wouldn't want him there, and her temporizing piqued his interest to the point of shunting the questionable relationship of Sarianna and Pierce out of his head for the moment.

"That is probably true," he agreed after pretending to reflect on her statement. "I certainly wouldn't feel right unless I saw that you got as far as the ferry, Vesta. I'm planning to leave tomorrow myself, and of course, I'm concerned now that Jeralee will be alone in the house."

"Yes. Well. Jeralee will go to the Soames' while I am at Bredwood," Vesta said decisively, not knowing how to deflect Cade's appropriate attentiveness. "That's settled, and yes, I would be grateful for your company to the ferry," she added, because she thought it would be easier to accept than make a fuss that might raise his suspicions about anything concerning her and Rex.

But he was suspicious already; it was unlike any gentleman to summarily bring his wife home in the middle of the summer social season, more so perhaps for Rex who hadn't seemed to much care what Vesta and Jeralee did, if the way they treated Sarianna were anything to go by.

Of course he had known where they were staying, since the note had come right to them, and Cade wondered if Rex resented it. He had never, all those long years ago, ever leased a house in Savannah for the season, and as far as he knew, Dona had never gone away from Bredwood from the time she had married Rex. Certainly Rex would never have done for Vesta what he did not do for Dona. But he had sanctioned her journey to Savannah, even to the point of appropriating his rival's home. He didn't understand that, and he wondered what Rex could possibly want these two months later that made Vesta drop everything and run back to Sawny.

They left the next morning, with Jeralee's fulsome promises to take herself right over to Emma Soames' the moment she finished breakfast.

Cade waited with Vesta at the dock until the first ferry returned from Sawny and made sure she was safely aboard with carriage, driver and boarding pass. He waved to her as the boat moved off, and she waved right back as if everything were harmonious and they were the best of friends.

An hour later, he paid the succeeding supply boat to carry him and his mount over.

And in the house on Malverne Row, Jeralee welcomed Pierce into her arms and into the walnut bedstead in the room that Cade had occupied only hours before.

He felt like a stranger in the land of his childhood, so much more so than when he had arrived on the afternoon of Jeralee's birthday ball. That had been a lifetime ago, he thought, as he cantered down the turnpike that bisected the island. He had been another man, with other goals. He hadn't known about Sarianna.

Vesta was about an hour ahead of him, he calculated; the ferry had been scheduled to make several stops around the island before

Greenpoint, which was one of two access points for Bredwood. It was conceivable he might make Bredwood before Vesta.

He had one moment where he wavered, and he wondered what he was doing there and what he hoped to discover.

What if it had something to do with Sarianna?

He spurred his mount on. Bredwood was about a thirty-minute ride from the loading docks down at the Summerton store. His sense of urgency increased, coupled with that gnawing malaise about Sarianna.

Bredwood looked, as he approached it from the turnpike, faintly desolated, with drooping pines and evergreens shading the long, flower-bordered drive.

An air of neglect permeated the entrance drive: patches of burn in the sweeping lawn, unpruned hedges, deadheads in the flowering bushes. God, he knew every shrub and bush on this property, places to shelter a clandestine meeting that could only be arranged through whispers and secret notes. Things he had forgotten in the intervening years, and had not thought of when he returned to Bredwood with his mind so set on avenging himself on Rex.

He had done that, and now as he skulked in the shadows of the greenery, he marveled at the path his vengeance had taken—even to the point that Sarianna might have betrayed him with another man the same as Dona had betrayed Rex.

He had never thought to return to Sawny again. He hitched his horse deep in the woods behind the stables and approached the house on foot with all the care of a man who had been set upon only once in his life and never would let that mistake be repeated again.

It was deadly quiet on the grounds of Bredwood.

No one impeded his progress; it was as if the slaves had totally disappeared. No one challenged him, and he made it as far as the kitchen before there was any sign of life.

Sylvia came banging out of the door, muttering to herself. "Dat ole Miss Vesta done come and givin' orders like Mr. Rex cain't do nothin'. I ain't got de dash fo' makin' no big meal tonight. I got nothin'; I ain't even got dem vegetables no mo'. She don' listen, she *don'* do nothin' but go away and den come back and disrup' Mr. Rex. I don' like it, it ain't right . . ."

Cade slipped around to the kitchen door and into the ell. There was a hallway here that branched off going to the kitchen at one end, as far

341

from the house as could be reasonably built, and to the dining room at the other.

He slid into the dining room which was, thankfully, empty, and cautiously out the door and into the hallway off of which were the library and the parlor and the anteroom.

He flattened himself against the wall and listened. There were voices, servants' voices, low, emanating from the parlor, the dining room where the appointments for the afternoon meal were about to be set up. Damn. He inched his way across the hallway to the library door.

Here, in Rex's sanctum, he heard Vesta's voice.

". . . I won't! And if this is what you've dragged me back from Savannah to—"

"Take Jeralee to your cousin in Charleston, Vesta; I'm not footing the bill for this exorbitant season in Savannah. Let the Lundeens put up a fair share for your nonsense."

"That damned whiskey has addled your brain, Rex. Jeralee needs this summer in Savannah."

"Oh, stop being ridiculous, Vesta. As if anyone would take to that self-centered little slut."

"*Your* little slut," Vesta spat viciously.

"You can't prove she's my daughter. I have one daughter, Vesta, just one."

"One who is about to reproduce another golden-haired, wrong-handed brat to ruin someone else's life—"

"*WHAT?* Whose child?"

Vesta paused, and Cade's hands clenched.

"Whose do you think?" she asked maddeningly. "Another troublesome brat, just as I said."

"Not in the least like your Jeralee," Rex snarled, pouring himself another drink. "God, I rue the day I brought you both back with me to Bredwood."

"Everything would have worked out if Rensell hadn't changed my plans around," Vesta said defensively. "Rex, I must find a husband for Jeralee."

"I don't care. No more money, Vesta, not for her, not for you. And I want your damned bodies out of Rensell's town house. How damned brazen can you be?"

"Yes—but Sarianna . . ."

342

"Your stupidity lost me Sarianna—*forever*."

"Don't be insane, Rex; she was never yours to have."

"She would have stayed if you hadn't brought that damned Rensell to Bredwood," Rex snarled.

"He was coming anyway. I couldn't have stopped him. Maybe you shouldn't have cut Parker Rensell's feet out from under him quite so ruthlessly."

"I had my reasons," Rex said, his voice slurred now.

"This has a ring of inevitability to it. I wonder, dear Rex, what your reasons could possibly have been."

"I wonder you're so nosy, Vesta. Sarianna never asked questions. And Dona never cared what I did."

"You sure as hell cared what she did."

"She was good at spending money; that is a trait all the Waytes seem to have in common," Rex interpolated nastily.

"You *cannot* renege on that now."

"I can do what I damned well please, Vesta, and I'll have you know I'm that close to throwing you and that damned Jeralee out altogether. *Then* what would you do?"

"You won't do that," Vesta said with evil surety.

"You have no legal recourse, you know. No ceremony, no paper. Nothing, Vesta. You agreed to the terms when we made them, and I can withdraw them at any time. Any time."

"I suggest you don't try that, Rex, simply because past sins will come back to haunt you."

"Don't bluff, Vesta. It won't work."

There was a long pause, and then Vesta said, "People still talk about the way Dona died, you know. Now, I truly believe, Rex, that I'm about the only person who knows that Dona was pregnant when she died. There might be a lot of folks who would speculate whose baby it was if some rumor started going around."

"Oh, no," Rex disputed warily, "you're not pulling that trick on me. Rensell threatened me enough with exposure. I don't give a goddamn hell about it now. So Dona was pregnant, so what."

"I know *who* the father was."

Rex laughed, an ugly taunting laugh. "That's good, Vesta. Most excellent. As if Dona would tell you anything."

"I know," Vesta hissed, and something in her voice stopped his laughing, and he took another long reviving drink of whiskey.

"And who was it, my darling?" Rex asked silkily.

"I'll never tell," Vesta said coyly.

"You bitch. I swear, it would serve you right if I cut you and Jeralee out altogether, and made everything over to Sarianna when I die."

"That's a good threat, Rex; quite wonderful, in fact, but you won't do that. You couldn't stand to have Cade Rensell come back to Sawny again."

"Maybe, maybe not. Maybe you should test whether I had the nerve to do it or not," Rex taunted.

"Maybe *you* should test whether I know something you don't know," Vesta challenged him.

"You made the whole story up," Rex said condescendingly. "Dona was not pregnant when she died. The next thing I know, you'll be telling me you know who killed her."

"I know one of four people could have done it," Vesta retorted cryptically.

"You know so much, Vesta. I'm quite impressed. And all of these threats merely to save a hundred dollar a month spending spree that I wish to have you end. There are no lengths to which you won't go. I tell you what, you take Jeralee to Charleston, to those Lundeen cousins of yours, and let her find a husband there. Austin has more than enough room in the town house, and he has all those sons and all those friends. It's a golden opportunity, Vesta. I'd look into it if I were you."

"I'm staying in Savannah, Rex, my dear, and if you pull too hard on the purse-strings, I promise you, I will make trouble."

"Make away," Rex invited goadingly. "Tell everyone all our secrets. Tell them too if you will how you tried to cut Dona out and marry me yourself. Tell them how jealous you've been all your life of Dona. Tell you were maddened enough to kill her at any one moment since you were children. Add to that the mysterious baby and the unknown father. Create the scandal, Vesta. Do it."

There was a heavy, murderous pause, and then Rex gleefully continued, "You see? You might have killed her, and there was no baby, no father. Nothing, except your damned greed and overwhelming envy. Don't tell me, Vesta. I *know*."

"Damn you to hell, Rex Broydon. You stupid, stupid man, standing by while she annexed every male body on Sawny. Maybe you didn't know then, maybe you were strutting around all fine and feathered

344

that somehow you captivated Dona Wayte, and I had to stand by and watch you make a fool out of yourself. I watched while it got worse and worse, and she was sneaking around with everything in pants— and my darling Rex, your beloved Sarianna is *just* like her—everyone on the island, Rex; how do you like knowing *that* now? Everyone, and finally she got caught, she got well and truly caught, and I'll tell you who, Rex. I will *love* telling you who the father was."

"Go ahead, go ahead," he jeered, his voice thick with drink and the pain of her revelation. "Tell me, my know-it-all Vesta—*who?*"

Vesta didn't answer immediately. There was another heavy pause, and Cade could just imagine her standing there, looking down at Rex with that supercilious expression on her face, pushing him with her smug smile and her hint of deep secrets to be revealed. Maybe she knew them, he thought; maybe the whole family was cursed.

Rex's voice, goading again: "Bluffing, Vesta?"

"You sure you want to know?"

"I'm damned sure you *don't* know."

"Why then, I'll tell you," Vesta said pleasantly, and her next words contrasted harshly with the tone of her vocie. "The bitch was rutting in the bushes—right here at Bredwood—with Parker Rensell."

God, it made sense, it made so much sense.

Cade didn't know how he got out of that house without running in to anyone but the stately old Eon, who was just coming out of the dining room as he turned away from the hell-hole of revelations. He felt sick and edgy all at once, and he never saw Eon until he heard his startled whisper: "Mr. Cade—what you all doin' here?"

And he knew, damn him, that there had to be secrecy; he motioned Cade away from the library and into the rear door of the parlor toward the windows where he could get away quickly. "Mr. Cade, you got to go; if Mr. Rex ever saw you, he gonna kill you dead right where you stand. What you doin' here?"

"Sneaking around," Cade muttered angrily, "for Miss Sarianna's sake, Eon."

Eon nodded his comprehension. "You can't stay now, Mr. Cade. Miss Vesta is tearin' de place upside down fo' Mr. Rex's callin' her back from Savannah. Ain't no one gettin' in her way now if dey can help it. He be real bad, Mr. Rex. Don' know how long he gonna last like dis."

"I understand," Cade said quickly. "I promise, I will go now, and if I can do anything, I will."

Eon thrust open one of the French windows, and Cade slipped out, cursing himself for making a promise he might never be able to keep. But, by God, Rex had sounded awful, saturated, primed for violence. And stupid Vesta, provoking him, revealing secrets better left buried. God, his father and Dona.

He couldn't get away from Bredwood fast enough, but even as he drove his mount hard down the turnpike, visions of the haunted places he had courted Dona invaded his thoughts, all twisted around to include a new perspective, Parker Rensell.

Dona, so often at Greenpoint as a child. Dona, flirting with everyone in sight, including his father. Dona, on the bluff with him one day and who else the next. Parker, buried on the bluff, the most special place on the whole of Sawny to his son. And Parker, urging him to leave Sawny after Rex brought the news of Dona's death; he could hear the words in his mind as if it were yesterday. *"You* were the last one to see her, son. I don't know how Rex found out about it, but you're better gone than being accused of killing her in some kind of jealous rage. And that's what they'll all think if Rex Broydon pursues this. I'm willing to bet he will. You know how he felt about Dona. And you damn well know how he feels about you."

Goddamn. And now he knew, more than he wanted to and less than he should have all those years that he had kept running to escape the stigma of being labeled Dona's murderer. And in the end, Rex took his revenge on Parker anyway, whether he knew the truth or not. Parker was doomed because Dona had pursued Cade first and then his father, and there never was any stopping her.

And over and above that, there was Vesta's dangerous obsession and her long buried love for Rex—dangerous, dangerous. Rex was courting danger provoking her, and she was too stupid to understand. Her petty triumphs meant the most to her, and she must have felt an intense power as she stood over Rex, telling him all those things he might or might not have known. It didn't matter.

Vesta, he thought, was doomed.

And he was doomed if anyone saw him as he approached the ferry dock. They ran twice a day, along with one supply boat, making a circuit of the island on the trip from Savannah, with a rest stop of a half hour at the Summers' store, and then back to Savannah for the next boatload of either supplies or residents. If he were lucky, he would catch the same boat back. If not, he would have to risk being seen.

The ferry was just about to pull out as he galloped up, and he ran a quick judicious eye over the passengers, most of whom were guests returning to the mainland. But there, on the upper deck, he caught a glimpse of Samuel Summers, the most dangerous man of all to be seen by.

He traveled back to Savannah in the hold of the ferry, side by side with his horse.

Alzine began feeling pains the day that Cade was due back from Savannah. "It ain't nothin', Miss Sarianna. I'll get used to it. It gonna be one long time till dis baby be born."

Sarianna put her to bed above her protestations.

"It ain't right, Miss Sarianna; anybody else got to labor while dey work, and I ain't been doin' nothin' to help you since we come. Dese pains gonna pass. It ain't my time. I knows it."

Amanda came to sit with her. "She should not be feeling labor now. There is still another month." She shook her head and her expression terrified Sarianna.

"What can I do?"

"We can give her some laudanum—but not yet, Miss Sarianna. This baby comes early, not so early as some, but still—too early for the good of the baby or the mother. In another several hours we wil be able to see."

Sarianna didn't know what they would see. She felt frantic and incompetent. Five hours later, as the pain intensified, she administered the laudanum, which did not take the edge off the labor by much. Alzine was covered with perspiration, sleeping between contractions and waking up, in the ninth, tenth, eleventh hour as the pains overtook her sleep.

"I will experience this?" she demanded fretfully. It was awful, worse than she could have imagined.

"Not this. Your baby will remain within you until its term, Miss Sarianna. This baby comes early," Amanda repeated in her cultured way, "not as early as some, but too early for the good of the baby. We will have to see how it goes."

"I didn't know de pain was so bad," Alzine cried in the midst of a long hard contraction. They didn't know what to do for her. They massaged her stomach and urged her to push with the contraction. They gave her laudanum, and when the bleeding began, they sopped it up with every available towel and sheet.

What would save Alzine's baby?

"Maybe it be fo' de best," Alzine whispered in the heat of another pain. "Maybe dis baby wasn't never meant to be fo' how I done got him. Maybe—"

"Don't talk," Sarianna pleaded. She had to conserve her strength. She had to survive.

She and Amanda, Deely and another woman, Kate, stayed with Alzine all through the night, helping, helpful and helpless.

In the morning, the baby was stillborn, and Alzine was barely breathing for having lost so much blood to the point of exhaustion.

They buried the baby quickly because of the heat, in the graveyard below the fields. The marker would read, Alzine's boy.

When Cade finally returned to Haverhill, he was met with the sad news that Alzine had passed away as well.

Now Cade watched her. He didn't think he was doing it intentionally; but he caught himself several times just staring at her, and he knew she was conscious of it and wondering why he stared and what he was thinking.

What was he thinking?

More to the point, *what* was he seeing?

He told her she was mistaken, but in his heart he knew. He was seeing Sarianna as Dona and in the arms of his father—and in Pierce's bed. A double, wretched image that would not leave his mind. Dona and his father. Sarianna and Pierce.

"You must be extra careful," he told her as she went the next morning to the storehouse for the day's supplies.

"I'm scared to have this baby," Sarianna said, and she meant it. She could die. She would be in excruciating pain. It wasn't worth it. Sarianna and Pierce. It drummed in his head, a cadence that was underpinned by Dona's liaison with his father. He could believe—he could almost believe—that Sarianna bore the same characteristic if all

348

they had told him in Savannah was true; they attracted men, she and Dona. Men couldn't help themselves around Sarianna and Dona and that was the whole of it.

And there had been Pierce, every which where Sarianna had been in Savannah, and there had been his father lying in the bushes with Dona. It was all of a piece—if they were one and the same, cut from the same cloth—and whether it was true or not, he was beginning to hate Sarianna just because the thought was in his head and eating away at his vitals.

She looked terrible, too. Alzine's death threw her into a deep despair where he couldn't touch her. But then, he didn't want to; and somehow, in her grief, she knew something was wrong, but at that moment she didn't care.

"Why must it hurt so much to bring life into the world?" she would demand endlessly of the patient Amanda.

And Amanda would say, "It just *is*, Miss Sarianna."

She spent much time at Alzine's grave, wondering what kind of sense it made for Alzine to die bearing her father's mixed-breed child, and what sense it made that she could never tell Alzine when she was alive how much she cared about her. Nothing made sense. Alzine's death had changed her, and Cade had changed, too; and that had nothing to do with Alzine, and much—she intuited—to do with the trip to Savannah, and she dared not ask him specifics.

"So what happened in Savannah?" was all she could muster in conversation one evening during dinner.

"Not much," he said casually. "I heard quite a lot about the charming Sarianna Rensell who captivated every heart from Savannah to the Ogeechee and back again. I found Pierce Darden pretty much where we left him, dangling after Jeralee this time. And Vesta is the same as ever. I believe she thinks she owns the Malverne Row house now, but I mean to disabuse her of that notion fairly soon."

He watched her closely as he recited these lighthearted words to see if any mention of Pierce had an effect on her. She was such a good actress, he thought. It had to be bred in the bone.

Did he believe it? Sometimes he thought he was going crazy. If Vesta had confronted him and told him outright, he would not have even considered that the gossip had a grain of truth. But all those testimonials all at once to Sarianna's popularity and Pierce's constant attendance. It was too much. He had been over and over it in his mind, and he couldn't come up with anything conclusive.

By rights, of course, she ought to be yearning to see Pierce, and she wasn't. That ought to have counted in her favor; but everywhere now he saw a secret conspiracy to foist the child off as his, and then they would resume their liaison. How clever of them to feel they shouldn't make him suspicious. He would never have known if he had stayed at Haverhill.

And to think he had been falling in love with her, Sarianna, the image of the perfidious Dona who had seduced his own father while she was moaning words of unswerving love to *him*.

The work made it easier to bear. There was another cutting and baling to come, and he could lose himself in the purely physical work of it.

Sarianna meanwhile had begun making the layettes and planning the winter wardrobe. In addition, she and Deely started harvesting the vegetables and fruit and gave over their mornings to boiling jars and mixing up pickling spices as they started the annual pickling and preserving ritual. There was no time to think of Alzine now or Cade's strange behavior, or the fact he had not touched her in bed since his return, or that she did not want him to.

Work was the panacea, and the baby did not seem real. She sent word of Alzine's death to her father, and she knew he would not mourn.

Perhaps, she thought, that was what she was doing. She was in the barnyard that morning, feeding the chickens and checking the milk supply as Deely applied her facile fingers to each cow's udder. She scattered the feed, thinking of Alzine and the note her father would never read and the child he would never grieve. It had been a son, but she would never tell him that, and she was the only one who cared.

Tears started pouring from her eyes, and Deely pretended not to notice. "Kate come soon fo' de churnin', Miss Sarianna," Deely said as she applied her fingers rhythmically to the udder nearest her.

"That's fine," Sarianna said, wiping away her tears. She looked down at her stomach. Nothing was noticeable yet, not a bulge or a flutter to indicate anything within that could cause the devastation that Alzine had suffered. Nothing.

How strange, and unnerving. She would never forget it.

The weeks wore on. Summer was turning very fast into autumn and the final harvest. Cade grew more distant, hateful in a way, and she didn't quite know why. There was the faintest bulge now to her belly, and she patted it every so often as she became reconciled to the fact the baby would grow and would be born willy-nilly, and she would not be able to stop the physical force of it.

Only nature could do that, or fate. A whim.

Or Vesta, driving up in a coach accompanied by Pierce and Jeralee, barreling up the long driveway, heedless of Sarianna in her simple pinafore looking like a hired laundress or something worse, something dispensable, as the driver shouted for her to get out of the way. And Sarianna not seeing or hearing, deep in her own joy or pain, or combination of both, was knocked to one side by the careering carriage, and when they came to her, she lay bleeding and unconscious; and her dress was wet with another kind of fluid, another kind of blood.

What she wanted, in the oppressive recuperative days after she lost the baby, was sheer oblivion. She couldn't even mourn. The insanity of it was stunning: Vesta again, Vesta always, bringing with her disaster, bringing with her Pierce Darden.

Even Cade couldn't bear it. He saw it as some kind of omen. He made them leave immediately after the doctor arrived. Pierce was not to know whether the baby that might be his survived.

But *he* knew. His grief was bottomless, and he wasn't sure whether to blame Sarianna, Vesta or Pierce—or all of them. Had Sarianna summoned Pierce to her side finally? He would never know, but Vesta's visit otherwise was purely spur of the moment, so like her— and not. He couldn't fathom the truth of it, and Vesta would never own up to anything devious. The baby was gone, and he would never know the truth of that either.

But the anger snaked through him insidiously, and it blamed Sarianna: She had caused the crisis, she had summoned Pierce, she had been in the way.

He couldn't help it—there was no other way to lash out in his grief. His beautiful Sarianna with all the potential of her love and redemption of the past had turned the whole thing into a mockery.

Whatever the truth of it, he couldn't forgive her, and as she lay in bed, with Amanda assiduously nursing her, he drew further away from her, less in love and more in hate.

And she knew it. His visits were perfunctory, his questions issued in a monotone. He hated her. And it had all changed when he came back from Savannah.

Such a mystery; what had happened *there?* And ultimately, what did it matter? There was nothing she could do to change things. The baby, which might have brought them closer, became a symbol of their ill-starred marriage. There was nothing to save suddenly, nothing to work for.

The worst part was, she had nowhere to go. Where could she run if Cade did not want her, as he so obviously did not? Would her life now follow the typical pattern: Cade would go off to Savannah or wherever men went to do business, and she would remain on the plantation, carrying on in his absence, isolated, lonely, unloved. . . .

So he had rescued her from one fate to deliver her to another, and she was never to understand why.

Could a woman ever be free, she wondered, as she continually ran her hands over her stomach which was now strangely flat. How much she had thought possible with Cade. And now nothing was possible but the same fate that had awaited her at Bredwood. She had exchanged one prison for another—nothing more, nothing less.

A thought obsessed her as she began to heal: What would it have been like if she had never met him, never wanted him, never—in fact—been the child of her parents; if she had been, in effect, someone like Victoria Gray. What if she had never married a Cade Rensell? If she were unmarried, on her own away from Cade and Sawny and everything the past entailed. God, how wonderful to even contemplate the possibilities of it.

She could pretend: She could be Miss Broydon again; she could surround herself with men who wanted nothing more than to admire her. Forget she had been bored with that in Savannah. She needed it now, and she could stand it very nicely, thank you, to have a cadre of men thinking she was the most delightful, beautiful, elegant thing in the whole world.

In Savannah they had known she was married. Anywhere else, she would be free to flirt, to play. To find some joy, and maybe someone who could love her for herself and not some moldering memory of a dead love for her mother.

She would be answerable to no one, just as Cade was answerable to no one, not even her.

There had been awful arguments lately at the dinner table that left her in tears, and what sense it made she did not know. Her tears didn't move him, nor her silence. He began goading her, almost as if he enjoyed her emotion, fed on it, despised it. And when she realized that, she had turned mute. It was only a question of time: She would have to do something, and as she regained her strength and a touch of her spirit, she understood she had no choice.

She would have to do something to save herself. Cade hated her now; he would never tell her what happened in Savannah, and he was devasted by the loss of the baby—and in some skewed way, she felt, a little relieved. She would always bear the stigma of her mother, she thought, for Cade and her father and even Vesta, and the only thing to do was to leave. It was the only course.

Where, how, she did not know.

She waited, thinking, and she did not let him force her into a fight. He became wary then, as if he knew she were planning something. He thrived on her tears, on reducing her to helplessness once again. He wanted to punish her endlessly for her betrayal and the loss of the child.

When she turned to him one night in desperation, begging for his love, he pushed her away and said plainly, "I don't want you anymore."

She would never stop hearing those words. I don't want you anymore. Just like that, away and out of the blue. I don't want you, after what they had shared before he left for Savannah, and the joy of the news of the baby. I don't want you anymore.

Could she ever stop wanting him?

She had to. If she were crushed by his callousness, she would die altogether, and they could bury her alongside her baby and Alzine.

She would have had a son, too.

I don't want you anymore.

No more sons, no more love. No home together. Nothing, nothing. Dead space where emotion once existed. How did she murder her own desire?

It was still there, in spite of the miscarriage, in spite of his rejection of her, in spite of Savannah.

353

I don't want you anymore.

She put away the layette that had been intended for her son, and handed the rest over to Deely to complete while she and Amanda cut patterns for shirts and pants, measured their servants and slaves, and began cutting material for sewing. It kept her busy.

She and Gwen put up jars of pickles, strawberries, plums, onions, corn, sugar beets, snap beans and raspberries. She and Kate began working on a carpet for the front hallway, and collecting chicken feathers and begging goose feathers, via a neighbor who visited, to save to make up a new mattress.

The work kept her busy, and the refrain in her head never stopped: You could be free, alone, wanted for yourself, bury the past and leave it in Georgia.

Bury the past and *leave* it? What was she thinking, *really* thinking? Leave Georgia? With what money?

Leave her baby at Haverhill?

Leave Cade?

Really?

Why not?

At first the niggling thought scared her, but as the idea took hold, it was superseded by a more palatable notion: She wouldn't have to face Cade again; she would never have to hear again the words that stood like a wall between them. And she could do it. There was no reason she could not do it.

She needed money, and she needed a place to go.

A place to go. An aunt in Texas, a cousin once removed in Charleston. No friends, not of her family's, none of hers. What a barren life she had led if she could not summon help for herself when she most needed it, she thought savagely.

I don't want you anymore.

The words were a spur for her to find a solution, and quickly. The worst solution would be to walk away without a destination and settle somewhere alone and by herself.

I don't want you anymore.

There was a slim chance she could appeal to relatives: Hadn't Vesta said this Charlestonian cousin had a daughter coming out this summer? That meant she could be located, could be appealed to . . . such a slim thread. The woman, unknown to her, would get a

354

letter from a cousin she had never seen, begging her indulgence and an invitation because her own husband did not want her anymore.

It defied belief that a letter of that nature would assure her a warm welcome from this unknown cousin.

I don't want you anymore.

The aunt in Texas—another unknown commodity, older than the earth, and not a likely source of help. An ancient woman who probably did not have the patience to put up with the nonsense of a younger generation.

How limited were her choices. And wouldn't it be ironic if it turned out she had to throw herself on Vesta's mercy! She didn't have the nerve to contact a relative she had never met and beg for help. She just could not see herself doing it, but she could not envision herself remaining at Haverhill. Cade had become a pitiless stranger whose eyes looked through her every night at the dinner table, and whose words were calculated to maim.

"You are unusually calm tonight," he said one evening after she had fretted the whole day about the notion of leaving him and how she could accomplish it alone, with no one's help, and concluded it just was not possible.

"Am I?" She refused to be goaded in her anguish; she had dissolved into tears too many times already, and what satisfaction it must have given him to reduce her to pure emotion after his rejection of her. It proved she still had feelings even if he didn't. How hard he was now, and unforgiving—but unforgiving of what?

"I was looking forward to another evening of melodrama, replete with recriminations," Cade said, eyeing her narrowly. Something was different about her tonight, and he didn't like that. Somewhere within him he wanted her to suffer as much as he had been suffering, both for her possible infidelity with Pierce, and for his father's betrayal of *him*. He didn't know that—it was just a pulsating emotion within him. If he didn't ride her, he thought, he might kill her, for the loss of their baby and the total disintegration of his faith.

I don't want her anymore.

She looked into his eyes and read the message there once more. Her spine stiffened, even though she was perilously close to tears. She could not live like this for the rest of her life, not with him, after all he had done for her, and how he had shown her what mattered and what

355

didn't. It was inconceivable still that it meant nothing to him now, but perhaps, she thought venomously, refusing to try to understand it, that was the nature of men. Women were constant, and men were stupid; and they seemed to be willing to give up more to attain less.

"Tell me my lines," she retorted. "I can't seem to find any coherent reasoning in this play."

"Women don't need reason or lines," Cade spat. "Go *on*, Sarianna, an appreciative audience awaits."

"No," she said, pushing herself away from the table blindly, "this audience does *not* appreciate me at all. Excuse me, Cade. This is totally futile. Perhaps we should dine separately as well. Perhaps I should go away. Or maybe you want me to obliterate myself altogether, Cade. I don't know what you want. I don't know why you came back from Savannah and suddenly hated me. I don't know anything now except I don't care. I would just as soon take my meals separately. That way, we can pretend I don't exist at all."

She walked to the door to the accompaniment of his applause and hooting derision: "Bravo, Sarianna, bravo. What an actress! What a play. What a ploy. Very entertaining. Curtain call, Sarianna—come back, take your well-deserved encore. . . ."

That night, she drafted a letter to Sallie Gill Lundeen in Charleston.

Money. She became obsessed with money. It took many days before she realized there was money, not an amazing amount of it, but enough for her needs in the household account Cade had set up for her when he had dismissed Pierce as his manager. She was sure he had not closed out that account, that somewhere in the environs of Savannah there was a bank that held money in her name.

The relief she felt was incalculable. The obstacle of obtaining the money seemed like nothing next to the insurmountable task of getting to Savannah after she received some word from Sallie Lundeen. And writing that letter had been like climbing a wall where there were no footholds. How much to tell or not to tell? Should Sallie know everything, or nothing? She had a daughter about her own age. Would that be a problem? Hadn't Vesta said something about a come-out this season, and wasn't it almost the time of year when such festivities normally took place?

God, her timing was faulty and perhaps her logic. In the end, she could only claim she had no one else to turn to—a precipitate visit on any other grounds but the absolute truth would make no sense to a woman she had never met, never written a letter to before.

"Dear Cousin Sallie," she had written, "I am the daughter of Dona Wayte and Rex Broydon, second cousin to you, and now wife of Cade Rensell of Haverhill Plantation, and I am in trouble, with nowhere else to turn. . . ." That claim gave her pause. There was always Vesta; Sallie might question why she had not gotten in touch with Vesta. "I am asking only that I might come for a short visit to relieve an intolerable situation here and to make plans for the future. I cannot return to the house of my father, nor can I make demands of my aunt and stepmother, Vesta, who does not have the means to render me assistance at this time. It is most imperative that I leave Georgia and remove myself totally from my husband's presence, which I wish to do with the greatest discretion. I understand, too, from Vesta, that the exigencies of the upcoming season might preclude your responding favorably to my petition, but I am hoping that out of your deep affection for my mother that you might be able to accommodate a most unexpected, unpropitious guest who means not to be a burden to you either financially or socially."

It was enough. She spirited her missive out of Haverhill in Owen's hands, and only let Amanda in on the fact she was expecting an important letter in return.

The days went too slowly after that, but the sense of having taken some action buoyed her spirit. She ate her meals alone now and began secretively packing a trunk full of her fashionable Savannah clothes, so sure she was that Cousin Sallie would respond affirmatively.

The answer arrived two weeks later, and Owen brought it to her, trembling from head to toe. "Mr. Cade almos' done caught me, Miss Sarianna. I can't do nothin' like dat again," he told her shakily, boldly for him who always followed orders. "He done axed what was dat, and I tole him it were a piece of paper Miss Amanda done give me fo' takin' into Savannah; and he didn't question it no more, Miss Sarianna, but I can't do dat no mo'."

Sarianna was hardly listening; she ripped open the thin envelope with shaking hands. "My dear Sarianna," Sallie Gill wrote, "come when you can. I am so very happy to be of service to Dona's daughter in her time of need. One guest more or less during the Big Season will hardly interrupt any arrangements we have made. Send us word when your boat will arrive. I look forward to greeting my new cousin and lending her whatever assistance I can."

A wash of pure unfettered relief flooded her whole body. Now it was only a matter of time before this nightmare with Cade became another dark piece of her past.

23

"I do wish this indigent cousin were not coming," Mary Lacey Lundeen said for at least the hundredth time as she and her mother sat in the side verandah of their town house drinking lemonade in the late afternoon. "At least not for the next two weeks."

"But she is scheduled to arrive today," Sallie Gill answered inflexibly, ignoring her daughter's petulant tone altogether. Lacey wanted to be the center of attention always, and she would be, Sallie reflected, as she gazed at her daughter's pink and white loveliness. She didn't understand yet about family and how one never turned down any application from a family member in need. What Lacey was afraid of was that this unknown Sarianna would distract from Lacey for even one whole minute. She had no sisters to compete with her, and she was very much afraid of a strange unknown cousin who would require the kind of hospitality that just had to take time away from Lacey's season. Lacey would have to act as escort and take her visiting and to all the boring places that visitors seemed to like to visit and even *entertain* her. Lacey didn't want to exert one lily white hand in the direction of any duty except that to herself.

Sallie was not unaware of this, or Lacey's fear that she might well be outshone by this young, but mature, cousin who was to arrive so unfortuitously in their midst. Two more weeks and the whole season would have been over, and they could have taken this Sarianna with them to Arboretum. Lacey would not have minded that one little bit.

"*Mother.*" Lacey pouted, seeing her mother's attention was not on her. Her mother had told her very little about Cousin Sarianna. There was some secret, but when she had tried to find the letter, she discovered her mother had either hidden it or destroyed it. Her mother would always err on the side of discretion, Lacey knew, but it was frustrating not to know the whole story of why Mistress Cousin Sarianna must make this hurried visit to Charleston, and more, why she could not call on Vesta Wayte in her time of need. All these things she would know in good time, she thought, the sooner the better. Mother knew just how to drag the truth out of a person, and how to make someone feel guilty for having attempted a lie in the first place. Whatever this Sarianna's reason for her visit, she would soon be revealing the whole truth to her mother.

Sallie Gill turned a speculative blue look on her daughter, and then she smiled. "Everything will be as you wish, Lacey my dear. If you only had counted the guests we are to be housing for the next two weeks, you would see that one more makes no difference whatsoever. She needs our help and we will give it to her, and in spite of that, nothing will interfere with your pleasure, I do promise you."

But she wondered idly whether she could keep that promise. Dona had been much on her mind since she had received Sarianna's letter. Sarianna, according to the brief mentions in Vesta's letters, was no ugly spinster. She was awkward and graceless and just like Dona in every respect, a caveat which, on reflection, made Sallie Gill wonder just what she was taking on in issuing her invitation to Sarianna.

But she had sounded so desperate and forlorn, and something in the tone of the letter seemed to tell Sallie not to speak of her history to her family—yet. And in fact, Sallie was loath to do so until she had heard Sarianna's story from her very own lips.

Sarianna would arrive this afternoon, and she had sent Eban down to the steamboat landing with the carriage. Very soon now, all her questions would be answered, and the mystery of what Sarianna looked like would be revealed. She hoped fervently that her inherent kind nature was not borrowing more trouble than she could handle during their sojourn in Charleston.

Coincidentally, or by the ordinance of some benevolent fate, Cade was called away from Haverhill on the very day Sarianna planned to leave. He was going upriver to the Montfort Plantation to look over a band of field hands that Montfort wanted to sell. Montfort was in trouble already this growing season, extending his credit to the point where he had to sell off property and slaves, and Cade meant to take advantage of it, as much as he hated the system anyway.

But then Owen almost refused to take Sarianna into Savannah until she swore she would walk or ride and without any chaperone, and Amanda interceded for her and convinced Owen that it was necessary, trunk and all, and that the first place he must take her was to Cade's lawyer's office.

Two and one half hours later, she was seated in the anteroom of Mr. Baldwin's office, shaking from head to toe at her audacity, prepared to lie and cheat to get whatever money he held in her name. The ease with which she convinced him she was merely going shopping in town for the afternoon astounded her. Within minutes, the dollars lay crisp in her hand, and he never questioned why she needed so many hundreds of them. His orders had been to give her whatever she needed on her personal application, no questions asked.

By noon, she had purchased her ticket for the Charleston-bound steamboat, and had only to wait for it to refit and pull from shore. By the time Cade returned, she would be in Charleston, and she could predict no further than that.

She could not even have conceived of Cade's reaction when Herod handed him her note.

"What's this?" he demanded harshly; he was tired, it was late, and he was worn out from the niggling negotations that had acquired him five strapping field hands and one house servant, the wife of one of the five. Damn the man Montfort. He was desperate, but he was canny. He got his price, but Cade had gotten six workers for the price of five.

"Dis a note," Herod said stonily. He knew right well what the note contained, and he wanted to be as far away from him as possible when Mr. Cade read its contents.

Cade took the crisply folded paper. "Where the hell is everybody? See to it that those hands get the end cottages down by the garden, will you, Herod, and make sure Amanda takes care of the woman—I forget her name. Damn. I'm hungry. Bring something into the dining room—anything, I don't care what."

He set the note aside on the dining room table and went to wash himself first. He felt caked with dirt and futility. There was no purpose to the bargaining and acquisition of land and slaves if there were no reason to have them. He felt no impetus. He felt empty. The house felt empty.

When he returned from his bedroom, he found a bowl of steaming soup waiting for him along with a crusty loaf of bread and freshly churned butter.

"Where is Sarianna?" he demanded of Herod, even though he knew the answer. Sarianna would be out in the fields, or sitting in Alzine's room, mewling over the loss of her baby, Alzine's baby, her youth, her appeal. All of that and more. Or she would be out in the kitchen with Gwen and those everlasting preserving jars.

She had meant what she said; she was not going to dine with him again, and in spite of the fact he had used this only time of togetherness to inflict his verbal wounds, he began to miss her the moment she made good her promise.

Curiously, Herod did not answer his question. Rather he scuttled from the room with as much dignity as he could muster. Cade bent his head over the soup and let the warmth of it trickle through his weariness.

And then—the note. He picked it up and unfolded it.

"Cade—I fancy this will be the best news you will have had in these several months, and I am happy that I am the bearer of it. I'm leaving you—will be gone by the time you arrive home— and I do not intend to return. You cannot imagine the weight this takes off of my shoulders, the knowledge that I will be free of you and you of me. The situation between us has been intolerable and so easy to remedy. Perhaps you can think more kindly of me in the future."

It was signed, simply, "Sarianna."

He sat utterly still for one long quaking moment, unable to believe that Sarianna had even had the temerity to walk out of the house by herself. *How?* As if he didn't know how! With her and Amanda thick as thieves. And Herod . . .

"HEROD!"

Herod marched in, determined not to be bowled down by the consuming rage in Cade's eyes.

"Where is Miss Sarianna?"

"She done gone, Mr. Cade. Upped and left us."

"That's not good enough, Herod. *AMANDA!*"

"You need not shout, Mr. Cade. I'm here."

Cade pointed a furious finger at the note. "Where is Sarianna?"

"She has gone."

"Damn it to hell, will *no one* give me a straight answer?" Cade raged. "*Where* did she go and who the devil had the gall to even take her away from here? You tell me!" He jabbed a finger into Herod's massive old chest.

"We do what we told," Herod said impassively.

"*Amanda?*" He thrust his face belligerently into hers, looking into her eyes and seeing only sadness and sympathy and none of it for him. She knew exactly what and why, and he swore he would wring it out of her.

But she was prepared. "There is nothing you do not know, Mr. Cade. You have treated Miss Sarianna with little respect and no love, and she has gone. The blame does not lie with your servants who only follow orders as they are given."

The truth of that was inescapable, but in his fury he was not prepared to confront it. "How?" he growled, cursing Sarianna under his breath even as he listened with half an ear. "*Owen* drove her? *Owen* took on that responsibility without consulting *me?*"

Amanda grasped his arm as she saw him going out of control. "Mr. Cade, Mr. Cade . . . you have said Miss Sarianna was free to do as she pleased."

"Get that . . . in here, *now.*" He pushed Amanda away. "Damn it, I won't have it, I *won't.*"

"And what won't you have," Amanda asked gently, "someone to torment who is totally at your mercy, even as much as I am or Owen?"

Cade's fists balled up. He could see no reason. "*You*, Owen," he shouted as the quaking Owen appeared at the door. "Where did you take Miss Sarianna?"

"We done gone into Savannah, Mr. Cade. We made fo' Mr. Baldwin's place and den fo' de docks, and I done left Miss Sarianna dere."

"*You left her there?*" Oh, the words were deadly, murderous, underpinned by his anger and his futility that vented itself solely on Owen's stupidity at taking it on himself to drive her away from Haverhill and his witless assumption that it was proper for Miss Sarianna to travel abroad in such an underhanded way.

Owen took it stoically, muttering, "Yassir, I knows it," periodically until Cade had discharged his rage with one last fulminating threat:

"Get the hell out of here and don't let me see you for a week. Go in the fields, you imbecile, and you'll be lucky if I don't sell you downriver tomorrow."

Owen fled, and Amanda, who had borne witness to this tirade, said gently, "What are you going to do now, Mr. Cade?"

He looked at her blankly. "Why, nothing, Amanda. Just nothing."

But when Amanda finally withdrew, he sat staring at the note for a long, long time, and ultimately he crumpled it up and threw it at the fireplace. "The bitch, the utter complete bitch," he exploded. He knew, he knew where Sarianna had gone and with whom.

He reached for the bottle of whiskey on the sideboard. Amazing thing about Sarianna, he thought vitriolically as he poured himself a stiff drink. She drove everyone to the bottle. Everyone.

He didn't retrieve the note for a long time, and by then he was thoroughly drunk and totally convinced she had sought Pierce's protection if she had indeed gone to Savannah. "The lovely, lovely bitch, how I could have loved her," he murmured, stroking the note with her firm feminine handwriting. "Oh, my lady—all that desire, all that love . . . you threw it away, just like your mother. . . ."

Oh, he would not try to find her, not he. She could descend to whatever depths she wished, he thought. She had been well on the way to it all by herself. Dona to the core.

And he had ignored all the signs.

"A damned good ending to the play," he said out loud to the silent room. "A wonderful twist, Sarianna. If I ever run across you, I'll kill you."

Sallie Gill Lundeen, poised and elegant, looked over the table appointments for the afternoon repast. She had set back the hour to one-thirty in order to give Sarianna time to refresh herself after her long journey and in the heat. She had ordered a light luncheon for her sure-to-be weary guest, with a more filling supper at five-thirty in order that Lacey could have time to prepare for a party she was to attend later on in the evening.

Presently, she heard a carriage rumble down the street, the only such sound in the past hour. Lacey, who had been peering out of a second floor window, flew down the stairs. "I must greet her first," she cried as she ran to the front door.

"Of course you must," Sallie said indulgently; but Lacey never heard her, and she followed slowly as the carriage pulled up by the curb where she could just see Eban's hatted head as he jumped off of the driving perch.

She waited on the verandah as Lacey opened the gate to Eban's distinct instructions: "T'rough de gate, Miss. I take yo' things to de house. Miss Lacey be waitin'."

The woman who drifted through the ornate iron gate and into Lacey's arms was enveloped in black. Lacey gave her a quick welcoming hug and then turned to look at her mother, her expression one of extreme satisfaction. An ugly old crow, she thought, leading Sarianna up to the verandah. Even if I have to introduce her to my friends. Oh, lord.

"Mother—Sarianna. Sarianna, your cousin Sallie."

Sarianna came forward hesitantly and extended her hand to the woman who awaited her. Her hand shook even though she saw instantly she had no need to fear Sallie Gill Lundeen. This was a woman whose kindly lined face had confronted worse problems than the one Sarianna would present her. There was humor in her face, and a kind of comfortable assurance that instantly accepted anyone at value, without judgments.

And she had been a beauty once. Vestiges still remained in the deep-set pale blue eyes and the fading, graying blond of her thick hair which was pulled into an elegant chignon. Her whole presence radiated an air of tranquility, like bedrock, and an inborn graciousness that Sarianna instantly envied and admired all at once.

She was dressed expensively and stylishly in a manner that did not attempt to hide her matronly figure. Her finishing school posture made her seem taller and thinner, and once Sarianna was enveloped in her loving blue gaze, she thought of nothing else except that here was sanctuary.

And Sallie, who was every inch the mother not only to Lacey and her sons, but their friends as well, smiled with benevolent understanding, took Sarianna's hand and gazed into her huge speaking blue eyes, as Lacey pointedly removed the suffocating black cape. What was beneath was no better. Sarianna was outfitted in a dress of black bombazine, utterly unattractive, and sturdy black shoes. Her hair was pulled tightly back and crunched into the tightest bun imaginable, and covered with a black net from forehead to the nape of her neck. Her face was pale, white. She wore thick glasses, and she carried a hat of the same dreary black material as the dress. She wore gloves, in addition to all of that, and worst of all, she was perspiring profusely.

Lacey moved away disdainfully, and Sallie put her arms around Sarianna and whispered her words of welcome. That close, she could see the gray powder in Sarianna's hair and the white rice powder applied thickly to her face. Such machinations for a little two-day trip, she mused. What *must* her story be?

"Come, we must make sure you have rest and refreshment. Esther will prepare your bath and you will just soak yourself in it, and if there is anything you require, you have only to ask her. Come down when you've rested and you feel ready to eat, Sarianna. We are in no hurry here, and we are very happy to have you."

"I'm grateful," she whispered and followed Lacey blindly to the stairs where Esther met her and led the way to her room.

Lacey ran back to Sallie Gill. "She's horrible," she mourned.

"Is that better or worse than beautiful?" Sallie wondered with just a trace of humor in her tone. Lacey was so literal, it could be that she honestly hadn't thought through the consequences of Sarianna being either. But Sallie knew something Lacey did not: Sarianna was deeply troubled and in no shape at all to go through the rigors of a Charleston social season.

The only thing she feared was Lacey's shock when she finally got to see what Sarianna really looked like, and in fact, Sarianna did not put in an appearance until after Lacey had left for her party.

It was just as well, Sallie thought, as Sarianna presented herself, late, to the supper table, dressed in a voile dress of the lightest blue shade that had a square neckline, short, puffed sleeves, and a lace encrusted, tiered hem that was supported by a modified hoop. Here was the real Sarianna, with her deep blue eyes and creamy complexion now that the powder had been scrubbed away and that mop of golden curls that was purely Dona's legacy. Her smile was so sweet and wiped away any vestige of haughtiness in her expression; but still and all, there were smudges under her eyes and hollows in her cheeks, and her lovely dress hung on her slender frame even more than it should.

"Sit, my dear, and have your dinner, talk or not as you wish. Everyone is gone. Parties and more parties, I'm afraid, and I'm very willing to sit this crush out."

366

Sarianna pushed the food around on her plate and finally ate, feeling like an imposter against Sallie Gill's open-handed hospitality. Fear rode her; it was just possible Sallie Gill would not think her reasons for leaving Cade were valid. And so—then what? She talked, amusingly, of her trip, and her decision to travel under the guise of the hot, perspiring black crow of a seeming spinster. Anything could happen at a dock port, and it had seemed reasonable to assume that men who might be tempted by an attractive face and figure would certainly be put off by a hot perspiring ugly one. The ruse had been wonderfully successful. No one had bothered that single, unattractive older female during the whole of her two-day journey upriver, and she had been able to do some reading and get some much needed rest.

She made a good story of it, but Sallie noted the great sadness in her eyes as she recounted it.

After she had eaten all that she could, Sallie summoned Esther to remove the dishes, and drew Sarianna out onto the verandah where it was cooler and dark, intimate, a place made to reveal confidences. She settled her in one of the several comfortable chairs and waited until Esther had brought out a tall iced pitcher of lemonade and left them alone.

A long while later, Sarianna sighed. "I could just lie here forever," she murmured.

"Yes, there is a certain peace here, behind the stone walls and iron gates. The trees swoop down to enfold us, and later, the night. There is great comfort in the night here, because you know that you are not alone and isolated from everyone else. Neighbors will always help you," Sallie said, "and so will your kin."

"I've never known that," Sarianna said hesitantly, and Sallie saw it as her opening.

"Tell me why," she invited, and the warmth in her tone and the warmth of the night made it easier for Sarianna to tell Sallie everything, from her restricted life at Bredwood to the coming of Cade and the resurgence of feelings about Dona, to the final disastrous turn of their marriage. She left out nothing, not even Vesta's hand in things, and her sly vilifications and open hostility. Nothing, not even her desire to emulate Dona, if it had been what Cade wanted. But she never knew if she had done the right thing. And she told Sallie about Pierce, and Cade's abortive trip to Savannah which had precipitated the divisiveness between them.

Sallie Gill was awfully silent when Sarianna finished. Thank God it *was* dark, she thought; she almost couldn't bear to look at Sallie's face or hear her judgment of a story that now sounded woefully weak in her own ears, and full of damning self-justification. Even worse, she had not hesitated to crucify Vesta in her own best interests, even knowing Sallie Gill and she were close correspondents.

Sallie said not a word. She didn't know what to say. The Vesta she knew through her letters was not the Vesta that Sarianna painted as such a villainess. And she never would have believed it, except for one thing: Vesta's descriptions of Sarianna which were no nearer to the truth than Sarianna's clever disguise. And as she ruminated about the discrepancy, she could see no reason why Vesta *should* lie. Therefore, it held that Sarianna spoke the truth, and that seemed more monstrous than the seemingly intentional falsehood.

She couldn't begin to understand a household like that, dominated by the strength of one long-dead personality, and the others revolving around its sickening ever burning flame. Poor Sarianna. It was true: Her mother had been an all-consuming fire who had burned everyone in her wake. If Rex suffered, they all must have suffered, but their sin was inflicting it on Sarianna, the one innocent who could not help what she was or who she was. And then for Cade to abandon her . . . her heart wrenched as she could only imagine Sarianna's pain.

"Thank you for confiding in me," she said at last, and Sarianna let out her tensely held breath. "Tell me now, my dear, how I may help you."

And Sarianna did.

Overnight, she became transmogrified into Sarianna Broydon, on an extended visit from Savannah, the cherished daughter of a beloved cousin, and nothing more or less than that. She was given Garnet, a young slave girl, who was to wait on her and accompany her everywhere. *Everywhere*, Sallie cautioned. She was *not* in the Georgia backwoods now. Social strictures were very precise. A maid must be with her whenever she ventured outside the walls of the town house.

As for the rest, Sarianna found she had three boisterous male cousins, Mary Lacey's brothers, Cloyce, Noel and Sonny. There was the kindly Austin Lundeen, Sallie Gill's beneficent husband, and a host of good-humored friends and relatives who were either staying at the town house, or living in adjoining town houses and hotels. A dizzying array of people shook her hand, pleased to meet her, and Mary Lacey stood on the side watching, her face a storm of discontent.

"Why, she *fooled* us, Mother," she whispered fiercely to Sallie Gill. She was utterly dismayed by Sarianna's golden beauty and the funny little smile that hovered around her lips that seemed to entrance every man from her brothers right on down to FitzJohn Dubbs, her own special friend.

Sallie watched Sarianna through hooded eyes, unable to find one fault in her impeccable manners, and still the men drooled all over her. Dona to the teeth, she thought, feeling a sympathetic pang for her daughter. Sarianna had to be hidden away for these two weeks. She could not be allowed to be seen in public; she would snare every man from the Brighton Club to Savannah.

She had told Lacey nothing about Sarianna's history or the reason for her now extended visit. Sarianna would stay, and they would figure out what to do after Lacey's come-out. It was unfortunate that this was the time she could come, Sallie found herself consoling Lacey. But on the face of it, she was no more beautiful than any other young woman of Lacey's acquaintance.

"Yes, but—" Lacey said turbulently, "she is not *living* with them. Now I *have* to include her in all the get-togethers we have here, Mother."

"She'll beg off," Sallie suggested comfortably.

"But they've all *met* her now; don't you think everyone will question why she is so continually absent?"

"I suppose," Sallie said, watching with a keen eye as Sarianna effaced herself into the background of the guests crowding their parlor. It was so interesting: Sarianna didn't make one move to put herself forward, and still she was surrounded; and she could not see that Sarianna even volunteered one useful sentence of conversation, and yet later, all she heard were praises of Sarianna's congeniality. It was as if the less she tried to attract, the more she pulled. It was like being with a force of nature: Everyone was drawn to her, and she could no more help that than she could help breathing.

Cade Rensell was a fool, Sallie thought, and she was a bigger one. She had known Dona; she ought to have been able to predict what to expect. Except she hadn't expected Sarianna. And she couldn't predict what effect Sarianna's presence would have on Lacey. As beautiful and good as Sarianna was, she might still all unknowingly spoil Lacey's come-out week, if tonight were any indication of the impact Sarianna made in company. Lacey's happiness must come first, this of all times, and Sallie wondered if she already didn't have cause to regret her well-meant invitation.

He found no solace in drink, no consolation in work. The farm could go to hell for all he cared, and maybe he didn't care that much. He threw Vesta and Jeralee out of the town house with no compunction and moved back in so he could be near the source of liquor and the money he had to spend on it. Minus, of course, the money Sarianna had stolen.

Vesta and Jeralee went back to Bredwood, and he had the house cleaned from top to bottom and back again. The claustrophobic atmosphere remained, even after he brought Amanda back, and Herod and Gwen, and after much soul-searching, the poor blameless Owen who was deathly afraid of him now.

And he lashed himself with the pain of knowing that Pierce was in Savannah and could give him all the answers he wanted, all the answers he claimed he didn't want. But no, the bottle held all the answers. And the money. Haverhill could go. He sent Mr. Baldwin to find a buyer for the house he would never return to again, the house with Sarianna's touch, Sarianna's scent.

He would never be free of her, never, and he would never be free of the taint of his father's treachery. No wonder the bastard drank himself to death; he knew what he had done: He had made Cade the scapegoat for a conception and a murder, damn his soul to hell.

He would follow right in his father's footsteps; he would drink himself to hell and back, and maybe someday Sarianna's betrayal would seep out of his soul.

He found it was not so easy, either to kill himself with whiskey or forget Sarianna. He wondered how his father had managed so efficiently.

At the end of two weeks, he was damned tired of trying, and he was feeling desperate for some direction to take.

"But you know what you must do," Amanda said one evening,

noting with pleasure how much fuller the decanters stayed these last few days.

"I know nothing," Cade contradicted stormily.

"As you say, Mr. Cade."

"Damn it, Amanda, that kind of submissiveness doesn't become you."

"You will see," she said ominously and left him to his dinner.

But in the succeeding days, he felt useless, and he saw nothing. He refused to admit Sarianna into his heart.

But she crept in there without his being aware of it. The streets of Savannah were as filled with her presence as Haverhill, and the thick sense of Pierce somewhere in the background. He was half surprised that Pierce had not shown up for his customary invitation to breakfast.

But Pierce was nowhere in Savannah, and no one knew where he had gone. When Cade tried halfheartedly to trace Sarianna, no one remembered having seen her. She had disappeared—with Pierce or not, he would never know.

The crisis came when he realized finally he *had* to know, that in destroying her, he was killing himself. He didn't know quite when he comprehended it clearly, but it was after the drink, and after he learned that Pierce had been absent from Savannah three weeks or more.

For the first time since he had returned to Savannah, he sat down and thought about Sarianna.

The pain was like a knife, cutting into parts of him that he did not know could hurt. When he closed his eyes, he could see her clearly, with her vibrant body and quirky smile. That was his Sarianna. And he was killing her, so she left him. He had punished her because it had been so easy to believe the gossip; he had even allowed Vesta to feed it to him in his very own house.

He had known nothing of the social Sarianna in Savannah, and he hadn't cared to find out. He had let her have her head, and he had given Vesta the means with which to cut it off.

He would never be free of culpability. He had sworn to protect Sarianna from her family, and he had handed her right up to them, and lost her in the process.

He *had* to find her. As he began making further inquiries, his need

371

became an obsession. He was going to find Sarianna and make her whole again.

"I wish she had been married at least," Lacey muttered in an undertone to Sallie as they prepared for yet another party that Sallie was giving in Lacey's honor.

Sallie's nose quivered. She could not make the expected rejoinder; all she could do was murmur some commonplace observation that Sarianna was in no way trying to eclipse Lacey's season, and Lacey hardly believed that. She snorted disdainfully as Sarianna entered the room.

Immediately she took a deep breath. She didn't understand how Sarianna could dress with such simplicity and always look so spectacular. Her own bandbox prettiness paled beside the ivory cream silk that warmed Sarianna's skin and had not a single additional decoration it did not need.

Lacey herself wore white, as was traditional, trimmed in blue to match *her* eyes, but they, she had noted almost instantly, were pale beside the blazing sapphire of Sarianna's.

"Lacey, you look lovely," Sarianna said warmly, reaching her hand out to Sallie.

And Lacey hated her more because she always tried to say nice things all the time about everybody. She never entered a conversation unless someone addressed her; she never pushed herself into any *tête-à-tête;* she tried very hard, as Sallie often pointed out, to spend the time at the party talking with parents and with Austin or Sallie herself rather than sequestering herself with any of Lacey's friends. And Lacey appreciated that, she truly did. The problem was it just didn't help.

"Thank you," she said belatedly, realizing she was cataloguing everything about Sarianna's appearance, staring even, and that was rude. "Now, Sarianna, we must *not* look as if we have been sitting and *waiting.*"

"Of course not," Sarianna agreed. "Let me see, I could work at some embroidery—which I am very bad at, by the way, but no matter—or I could read. Or play the piano, except I don't play it. I don't suppose there is a guitar? I really can strum quite passably."

"Really?" Lacey breathed with the first show of interest Sarianna had yet seen. Immediately she felt suspicious, but Lacey went on, "I do believe Sonny has one, but it must be badly out of tune. What a lovely idea. And I can accompany you on the piano. If we can find it, would you play?" She loved the idea, just loved it, because Sarianna could not possibly look beautiful and arrange herself around an instrument like *that* at the same time.

She rang for a maid and sent her to look through Mr. Sonny's belongings in his room. Fifteen minutes later, a battered and dusty guitar was set in Sarianna's hands. She looked at it, struck the strings as someone handed her a handkerchief with which to wipe it, and rued her dress if the dirt smeared onto it. She begged a moment to tune it and practice, and took the object into the first floor library to do a hasty restringing and retuning.

Why had she allowed Lacey to talk her into this? she wondered, as she wiped down the body of the guitar and the strings once again. The damned cloth was black with dust. She pushed it into a vase and sat down to finger a chord.

Amazing—she still remembered everything. She crossed her leg and balanced the guitar on her knee. Her breasts fell naturally into the hollow of the body as she leaned forward into the playing of it.

A moment later, the library doors swept open, and Lacey and the family poured into the room. "Oh, look," she whispered to Sallie Gill, "she's playing it the wrong way!" She felt the faintest discomfort over the fact of how happy she was that Sarianna was not perfect, and her mother put a damper on it.

"I guess," Sallie Gill said sharply, "that for her, it's the right way." She did not like at all how much of Dona was present in Sarianna; she had noted the opposite hand at dinner and not thought much about it. But now, watching Sarianna play, she understood Vesta's veiled reference. And she understood Lacey's anger.

Sarianna made a damned pretty picture sitting there, and if she were allowed to continue, she would overshadow Lacey altogether.

The family sang with Sarianna several simple songs that every school child learned, and then Lacey spoke up. "Let's try it with me at the piano. I know some of the new songs, you know, and they're not all that hard." She led them back to the parlor where the grand piano sat in its own bay-windowed niche, thinking what a charming picture she and Sarianna would make when their guests finally arrived.

And indeed, they had timed it perfectly. They were stumbling through a waltz when Sarianna heard a name announced, and she looked up and into a pair of eyes as blue as her own in a lean arrogant face that was as different from Cade's as night was from day, who regarded her with the lively interest of a man who has discovered a great unexpected treasure.

24

She felt brilliant and young and free, her fingers liquid with music as she played with Lacey for the strangers who crowded around them, the one stranger whose eyes never left her face. The stranger who was not Cade, who looked at Sarianna Broydon and saw Sarianna Broydon.

But he was meant, she discovered, to see Mary Lacey Lundeen. Sallie made her instantly aware of it, very fast. She retired from the musicale, lost herself in the crowd, and latched on to Cloyce in a manner that might have embarrassed even her if she had not been so desperate to escape those hot blue eyes.

She watched them, for a good part of the evening, play over Mary Lacey's silky blond hair and pink and white skin that was virginally revealed by her not so innocent white dress. She watched him talk and laugh and slide into the family realm with great ease. She felt immediately outside the fringe of it, the interloper who was feeling an unholy attraction to a man who was not her husband and wanted by the one who considered her her worst rival.

It wasn't a fit scenario to cope with. She could not have him, could not even enjoy a harmless flirtation in the course of the evening. Her only recourse was to absent herself immediately and foreswear the temptation.

Oh, but he was big and brown and muscular, the kind of man who dominated the room when he walked in—totally different from Cade. This man wanted to be noticed, and did everything in his power to ensure he would be noticed.

She had the feeling as she fairly ran up to her room an hour and a half later, that his eyes followed her, and that he fully intended to find out who she was and why she had fled.

And the following afternoon was not too soon for him to call, though she had not expected it. It was the time of day when Lacey took an afternoon rest, and Sallie Gill made her afternoon calls. It was also the time of day that Sarianna became the most fretful because there was nothing for her to do but lie on the lounge on the verandah and hope that a carriage drove by. The city seemed to take a long, sequestered break at this hour, and she had been here two weeks and still wasn't used to it.

So she was almost startled out of her wits to look up when she heard the gate latch release, and see *him* standing there, all tall and brown and muscular as she had first perceived him the night before, a delicious stranger actively seeking *her*.

"Hello," he said, and his voice was as deep and mellow as she expected. He was so well-dressed, impeccably dressed in a dark suit and white shirt. He walked up to her and braced one leg on the verandah steps. "Who are you? Tell me now."

She didn't want to tell him anything. His question was a demand, made in a meltingly mellifluous voice that did not move her at all. She had no doubt he spoke to all the women of his acquaintance in this way, even Lacey. There was a charm in it, and she was not immune to those stunningly blue eyes that gazed into her own so deeply. He expected her, she thought suddenly, to play some kind of tantalizing game with him as Lacey might. A mistake with this kind of man. That was a game he knew well how to play.

Her lips quirked. "I'm Sarianna Broydon." She did not ask his name, and she saw immediately that this disconcerted him. He had no way to venture it without looking just a little pompous.

She felt very powerful, and the newness of the sensation was very pleasing to her. She marveled at the ease with which the name Broydon sprang to her lips. It was as if Rensell had been something she had invented and then discarded at the South Carolina border.

She felt his eyes leave hers for a moment and stray to her mouth. She imagined he could read the slight contempt in her smile; she was not a woman who jumped at the sight of a handsome—yes he was— eligible man, and perhaps he did not understand that. He seemed too aware of himself and sure of his welcome. His eyes jolted back to hers, and he sent her a smile to match her own.

"You are the cousin from Georgia?"

"I am," she concurred, offering no more information.

"Are you enjoying your stay with the Lundeens?" he wondered next.

"It has been quite delightful," she answered in kind, again volunteering no opinion, no comment. This tack, which had been ravishly successful in company, certainly left much to be desired face to face, she decided.

Her stranger waited for her to speak, and she waited for him to initiate a question. "Are either of the Misses Lundeen at home?"

"I think so," Sarianna said, and clapped for the maid, Vida, who came rushing out instantly. "Vida, please see if Lacey is receiving visitors this afternoon, and tell her who has come."

She turned back to the stranger triumphantly, pleased with herself for having cleverly circumvented the need to ask him his name.

Vida returned within a moment. "Miss Lacey, she sleeping," she told Sarianna in a loud whisper.

"Thank you," Sarianna said, and then to her guest, "I'm sorry."

"No need," he said brightly. "I will visit with you." His eyes, his cocksure smile dared her to brush him off.

"If you wish," she agreed. "Vida, some refreshment, please." Vida disappeared, and she turned to him. "Do sit down."

He stayed where he was.

"I collect you must be a very good friend of the family," she began conversationally, still amused.

"Tolerably good," he agreed, that smug smile still hovering on his lips.

Her brow furrowed for a moment, and then she went on in the same vein: "Lacey will be so pleased to hear you called."

"So I intended," he said sharply.

"I do admire such surety in a man. Something to drink?" she inquired as Vida set down the tray with two glasses, a pitcher and a small decanter full of some colorless liquid that was obviously intended to enhance *his* libation and not hers. She almost felt as if she needed it right now—the tension was rising, and he was not at all happy with her recalcitrant attitude.

"Yes," she went on as she poured the lemonade into one glass and added the additional fillip of the clear liquid to his, "I do admire a man who is sure of his welcome before he even arrives. One becomes so

377

practiced, I would imagine, honing the art of visitation to a fine degree to a point where you never doubt that your host would be glad to see you. I *have* been glad to see you," she added, setting aside her glass.

He did likewise, having only taken one sip from it. He was angry and she knew it. She gave him her hand. "I shall be counting the minutes until you feel you wish to honor us with your presence again," she told him, keeping her expression bland.

He locked her hand in a rough grip and pulled her close to him. "You'll be very glad to see me—when I choose to come," he growled, tilting her face up to his with his other hand. "It's in your eyes, my girl."

"And you," she interpolated boldly, "will be very glad to see *me*, won't you? When you come, that is."

He let go of her hand and face simultaneously. "I'll be back again soon, Miss Sarianna Broydon. Don't think you can hide."

She sent him one of her quirky little smiles. "I'll be enchanted to see you, naturally."

"Bitch," he hissed. He turned away, the set of his shoulders revealing his frustration. She waited until he had closed the gate behind him before she burst out laughing. And she knew he had heard.

The intoxicating sense of her femininity lasted for exactly an hour. When Lacey awoke and heard the details, she became distraught. "Do you *know* who that was?" she demanded of Sarianna. "*Do you?*"

Sarianna shrugged. "I'm afraid I never asked his name."

"Oh, God, what kind of manners were you brought up on?" Lacey screamed. "*Mother!*"

Sallie appeared, shooting a reproving look at Sarianna. Lacey threw herself on a sofa and moaned. "I'm sorry you ever came," she threw out at Sarianna.

"He didn't regard it, Lacey; it was a game."

"He'll never come back again," Lacey cried.

"Believe me, he'll be back," Sarianna said.

"To see *you*," Lacey accused petulantly, and finally Sallie stepped between them in disgust.

"All *right*, the two of you. This has gotten totally out of hand. Sarianna, you are not too old for me to reprimand. Lacey, I suggest you had your hair in papers, and you were sound asleep; and in no way were you prepared to receive a visitor. I suppose you thought to have Vida ask your caller to wait for you to dress and make yourself ready. Believe me, Lacey, he is not wasting away for love of you, and in no way would he have contained himself for the hour it usually takes you to get ready. Be that as it may, you also needed to conserve your strength for the things we must accomplish this afternoon. I suggest you make yourself ready for *that*.

"As for you, Sarianna," she said pointedly as Lacey fled the room, feeling utterly humiliated and chastised by her mother's good sense, "it appears to me you were downright rude."

"I didn't mean to be," Sarianna said, turning away to stare out of a window. "It is just as I said: a game. It intrigued him. I was playing. I didn't fall all over him, and it piqued his interest, that is all."

"You cannot play, Sarianna. Your behavior until now has been exemplary; but you are not free to play, my dear, and I wish you would remember that whenever you are tempted."

Sarianna felt an unaccustomed pang. *She* was not free to play, and Cade was doing God knew what back in Georgia. Her father had not been free to play and look at what happened. Men, obviously, were exempt from consequences. Always a woman was bound and constricted and suffered. She hated it, and she had tried so hard to behave and not to adore all the attention that was showered on her. It was so easy to forget in the gregarious company of the Lundeen family and friends that she still was Mrs. Cade Rensell. That was another person who had lived in another place, another life.

And the stranger was the only man who had fascinated her at all since she had come to Charleston. The *only* one.

"Who *is* he?" she asked idly, trying to disguise her interest.

Sallie was not fooled. "I believe I will let you find that out for yourself. Do ask him, Sarianna, when we see him tonight—in the nicest possible way, of course."

"Tell me again," Cade said patiently, pulling the shaking Owen into his office in the town house and sitting him down in the chair opposite his desk.

"I done tole you, Mr. Cade. Dey ain't no mo' to tell," Owen protested.

"There must be; there is something I don't understand," Cade growled, and Owen shrank back against the chair. "Dammit, man, I'm not going to kill you. Just tell me again." His frustration was high. He had spent two futile weeks trying to figure out where Sarianna had gone, and he had come up with nothing. No leads, no witnesses—she had disappeared into the clay soil of Georgia after Owen had taken her down to the docks and stored her trunk in a shipping office.

Where the damn hell could she have gone? He couldn't remember one thing she had ever told him about her relatives. She had none, hadn't she said? No, there was something, something in the back of his mind, and he couldn't quite dredge it up. Something when he had asked her if there had been no escape from Bredwood.

"We took de carriage, and I let Miss Sarianna off at Mr. Baldwin's office. She come out after some little while and tole me to take her down to de dock. She went into a place I don' know where, and when she come out again, she take de trunk and put it in de place, and den she send me home," Owen recited in a monotone.

The same story, as he had expected, and the damnable thing was that Owen could not identify whatever building it was that Sarianna had entered. They all looked alike to him after these two months; the momentum of his memory had been totally impaired by the time Cade had wasted. He couldn't be threatened now or bullied into choosing one of those imposing buildings.

"She meant to go *somewhere*," he mused out loud. "She had something in mind, had she not, Owen?"

"I don' know," Owen said, and it flashed in his mind that he had not mentioned that letter to Mr. Cade. And he wasn't going to do so now. Mr. Cade would skin him alive. Just have his hide. "Can I go?"

"Send in Amanda, please."

Amanda came in, stately and diminutive. "Yes, Mr. Cade?"

"I don't know," he said. "I can't find a damned thing. I don't know anything. No one saw her, or if they did, they don't remember now."

Amanda looked at him consideringly. She wondered if he didn't deserve to suffer this much, even though it was not her place to wonder anything at all. Owen had told her how he had forgotten the letter, and she thought it was best they pretended it did not exist at all. He would have to find her otherwise. He did not deserve that kind of help for the way he had treated her before.

"There must be a relative," she said finally, insistently.

"The only way to find that out would be to ask Vesta, and you can be damned well sure I won't do that."

"But Miss Vesta was writing to someone during her stay here," Amanda said suddenly. "Truly, I remember. Miss Sarianna even commented upon the fact that Miss Vesta must have intended to stay a good long while if she had arranged to receive mail here."

"It may have been just a friend," Cade said, and even then he thought he was being generous. Vesta was a woman who had no friends. Who could have been writing to Vesta?

Damn it. Damn it. Vesta's mail coming here. Sarianna disappearing into thin air after depositing her trunk somewhere down at the docks. No one had seen her, slender and beautiful and sad-eyed that day. Owen was too goddamned obedient.

He had inquired everywhere. The most likely clue had been the steamship that traveled up the Georgia coast and on to Charleston and the Carolina sea islands. But *where?* She had not appropriated enough money to buy herself a house, for God's sake. She hadn't intended to set up her own household; she had no servants, and she knew no one in South Carolina. She could not have intended to go back to Bredwood. She had no relatives . . . damn it—no, she *had* said something about that. Relatives, damn it, and he could not for the life of him pull it from his memory.

Whoever they were, she had never met them, he was sure of it. Damn it, he would go down to the steamship line once again and pore over the passenger list. He had to do something.

Vesta was not happy. Nothing was going her way. Rex poured himself into a drunken stupor every night, and that damnable Pierce Darden was practically living at Bredwood and courting Jeralee with outrageous brazenness right under her very nose.

Nothing had gone right since Cade had summarily demanded that she remove herself from Malverne Row and hadn't given a good goddamn where she wound up.

At that point, she could not persuade any of her so-called friends to take them in, and Cade was immovable on the point of a solitary man sharing his home with two such tempting women and how it would look to *their* friends. They had to go, and she had not even had time to send word to her several correspondents. That she had done on their return to Bredwood when she was singularly unsuccessful in convincing Rex to foot the bill for the rest of the season.

The jackass would rather spend it on liquor, she thought resentfully. The house and grounds, the whole plantation was going to hell for lack of management, and Rex didn't seem to give a damn. Well neither did she, she thought. When Rex drank himself to death—which surely would be soon—the whole thing would be hers, and she was willing to wager she would have an eager buyer somewhere on Sawny.

The devil of it was, she would have to wait.

But why *should* she have to wait, after all?

She spent many days mulling over that question.

"You again?" a good-natured voice greeted him as he entered the office of the steamboat line.

"Yet again," Cade agreed wryly. "I still can't give up. I still keep thinking this is the only thing that makes sense given that she had her trunk and she deposited it here—or at one of the offices along this row."

"Yes, yes. I know—slender with curly blond hair and a sweet smile, right? Liked to dress in blue. I tell you, man, there's been no one here like that, and believe me, we all would have remembered."

"Let me see the passenger list again," Cade said, battling his feeling of hopelessness. The clerk had said this to him a dozen times before, and he still couldn't—or did not want to—believe it. He took the sheaf of papers that represented the travelers for the previous month, and he sat down once again to peruse it.

Nothing different. Nothing recognizable.

When he had tried to contemplate what Sarianna might have done, he had concluded that at the very least she would have changed her name somehow to throw him off her track. But there was no Broydon here, no Wayte. He even tried Bredwood and Haverhill as substitute names that she might have faked, and he had come up disappointed.

He stared at the sheet, moving his fingers down the long listing of names that were all so much jumble to him. No Sarianna. Nothing.

He shuffled the sheaf of papers and clipped it together to return to the clerk.

"Sorry," the clerk said. "I wish I could help."

Cade put the papers down on the counter, almost unwilling, to relinquish the final possibility of his finding Sarianna, and his eye lit on a name that sounded familiar. None of the ones he had guessed. Nothing he ever would have thought of, he thought shakily, with a burst of admiration for Sarianna's thoroughness. She would have paid cash, so no one would have questioned her name. No one.

He looked again at the nondescript print. Not even her handwriting, he thought, just the name and the destination—Charleston. She had disguised herself totally, down to her shoes.

The name on the passenger list was S. Alzine.

When he returned to Malverne Row, Amanda awaited him, her expression fraught with excitement. "A letter has come, Mr. Cade. A letter for Miss Vesta," she added meaningfully.

"I found her," he said shakily, taking the envelope she held out to him. "I *found* her. She went to Charleston, Amanda; she went there, and we're leaving in the morning."

"The *letter*, Mr. Cade," Amanda prodded. "I will pack, but look at the letter."

He looked at the letter. It was addressed to Vesta in a thin spidery handwriting, and the return address was the Lundeens, in Charleston, South Carolina.

The morning he left, a brief notice appeared in the Savannah newspapers on the obituary page, announcing the unexpected death of Rex Broydon of Bredwood Plantation due to an accident.

Two weeks later, the newly widowed Vesta, poor as a church mouse, with Jeralee and Pierce in tow and newly married, set out for Charleston to pay her cousin Sallie Gill a much overdue bridal visit.

25

The season ran from May to October, and as the cool weather set in, the social activity was at its height. No less than twenty-five young women had planned their come-outs this year, each with her own coterie, and since all entertainments were private and intermingled various sets of families and friends, no stranger could enter the tightly knit communal society unless he knew someone.

There could be as many as four or five parties in one evening, and everyone vied to arranged the come-out ball at one of the huge Regency-style clubs that were the hallmark of how much money a father had to spend on displaying his daughter and his wealth to the world.

Lacey's party would be held at the Brighton Club, the biggest and most expensive of the halls, and she was right proud of it. The invitations had been sent even before she and her family had come to Charleston in May, and she and Sallie had spent the better part of the intervening months choosing decorations and menus, and ultimately, shopping for the perfect material to make into the perfect creation to crown the perfect evening.

And now there was Sarianna to contend with. She had withdrawn from several social engagements after the debacle over Lacey's would-be suitor, but she had no excuse to avoid going to Lacey's come-out party.

Sallie, in fact, was adamant that she have a new dress for the ball, and at that Sarianna demurred.

"It's an unnecessary expense for me—and for you," she said adamantly. "Lacey would just as soon I did not attend, and you know she is now rather scared of me, as if I had some power that she didn't. I don't want to ruin it for her."

"Nonsense," Sallie said briefly. "There is no question but that you are going, and I mean for you to make us proud, Sarianna. The cost is nothing in comparison to the whole."

Sarianna shook her head. Sallie was making life very easy for her. Too easy. They had been on a round of social visits, and attending the theater, musicales, concerts, lectures, visits to the library mainly to be seen by others visiting for the same purpose.

The Lundeens' circle of friends was enormous, not only Sallie Gill's and Austin's, but the peripheral circle of the friends of their sons and Lacey. Evenings were a merry-go-round of dressing, piling into carriages, entering some brightly lit place or another, greeting familiar but still unknown faces, making small talk and returning home exhausted and replete.

Lacey thrived on it, encouraged by the fact that Sarianna always looked pale and worn out the next morning.

"You can beg off," she suggested solicitously, "if it is becoming too much for you. Obviously Savannah can't compete with the social life here; you're not used to it."

"I must not be," Sarianna murmured. "I certainly could use an evening off." And an evening away from Patrick Bohan as well, she thought. All that stupid provoking had led to his latching on to her in order to get to know better the woman who wouldn't ask his name. But she knew it by then, and she didn't have to ask him.

What a tangled web, she thought wearily. He was too attracted to her, and she was too prone to succumb. An evening off would do her a world of good.

Sallie wasn't so sure, but there was a cadre of servants between Sarianna and any unexpected visitor. Sallie left her unwillingly, upset that Sarianna would be missing a most enjoyable evening.

Sarianna took to her bed, exhausted, after a long soaking lemon-scented bath. Nothing would revive her more than a cool evening and a deep sleep. She closed her eyes and just drifted off into a nether-world of pleasant dreams.

In the morning, Lacey's high-pitched chatter awakened her. "Sarianna, Sarianna—the most wonderful thing. Wake up and listen. There was someone new in the theater party last night, Sarianna, and he said he knew you. He came from Savannah—"

Sarianna shot up in her bed and grabbed Lacey's shoulders.

"I *knew* you'd be interested," Lacey said complacently. "His name is Cade Rensell, and he just arrived from Savannah."

Oh, God, the worst nightmare—facing Cade and having to make explanations to him. What had Sallie thought? What on earth had she told Cade?

Sarianna dressed rapidly and ran downstairs. Sallie was in the morning room just as calm as you please pouring her tea. "Good morning, Sarianna. Have some tea. Do you know, you should have come with us last night."

"Yes, indeed, so I hear," Sarianna said, warming her cold hands around the hot cup.

"Lacey is very excited at the notion that a beau might have followed you from home, and thus divert your attention from Patrick. It's perfectly natural. Of course *he* was there, too, listening with avid interest. So, my dear, my question is, what are you going to do?"

"Do I have to do anything?" Sarianna murmured, her mind seething with questions herself. "What did you tell him?"

"Nothing. He knew you were with us—I don't know how—and I invited him to call on you today, and we left it that if it were inconvenient you would send him a note."

Sarianna turned her head away. To see Cade after this many weeks when she had been basking in the freedom of this singular life that her cousin enjoyed—*what* would she say to him?

She didn't have to say anything; Lacey got to him first. She must have been watching from the parlor window, Sarianna thought in exasperation, but it gave her a moment to prepare, a moment to see him before he saw her and all the changes that her time away had wrought.

Damn, but he looked the same—more so. The lion-man had come to life again, the way she had seen him that first day at Bredwood, with his long hair and forbidding expression that unexpectedly wreathed into a smile at something Lacey said. He was dressed in black, and he looked, to her mind, utterly formidable.

Lacey came into the parlor. "Here is Mr. Rensell," she said brightly, looking from one to the other. Gracious Mr. Rensell was looking grim, and Sarianna looked as if she would just turn and walk out of the room. "Of course, you'll want a nice long visit," she added as she withdrew from the room. "I'll have Vida bring some refreshments."

"Do that," Sarianna said lightly. "Hello, Cade. Sit down, won't you?"

"I damn *won't*," he said testily, walking around her, surprising himself by his reaction when he was so outrageously glad to see her—and fuming mad that she looked so beautiful and desirable and not the least bit in mourning for her marriage or her life.

Vida entered with the ubiquitous tray and set it down. Cade felt like knocking it to the fire. Anything he thought he had wanted to say stuck in the back of his throat. Sarianna was perfectly all right without him.

He poured some coffee instead, and stood looking at her. Too beautiful, he thought, as she drifted to the window and began staring out of it. Too fragile, too haunting.

She had filled out, and her face no longer looked tragic. She wore another of her simple house gowns which draped over her figure and touched her womanly attributes with the skilled precision that only a fabulous dressmaker could imbue. Her hair, in its usual curly tangle, was piled on her head this morning and trailed tactile little tendrils down the nape of her neck.

"Have some coffee, Sarianna," he said. He didn't know what to say.

"Thank you." Neither did she. But when he handed her the cup, she said, "I didn't expect to see you again."

"I don't believe that."

"Believe it," she said stonily. "I didn't want to see you again. After this morning, I hope I never see you again."

"Sarianna!"

"No." She moved away as he set down his cup and began pacing toward her. "Let me read you your lines again, Cade. Maybe you forgot what scene we played in Savannah. I believe your cue is 'I don't want you anymore.'"

That stopped him in his tracks, she saw with satisfaction.

"I do want you," he said finally when he could get the hurtful sound of her words out of his mind. Had he really said that to her?

She lifted her chin. "Then I suggest you stand in line, Cade. Since I came to Charleston, I have been Sarianna Broydon, unencumbered, unmarried, and if you dare make public the fact we *are* married, you will cause a scandal that will reflect on Sallie Gill; and I wouldn't want to repay her kindness like that. I'm having a fine old time, Cade, with people who know nothing about Bredwood and nothing about my mother, and nothing about you, and I love it, do you hear me? I love not being married anymore. I could make it a permanent condition without any problem whatsoever. I don't need the torment a man can inflict. I do not need *you*, Cade. Just leave. Go back to Savannah, run your plantation, make your money, and marry someone else. I promise, I won't contest it. Pretend I never existed. *Don't* want me anymore."

He saw her determination and her pain. He didn't know how to get past it in one brief morning. And he knew he wouldn't let her go. He put down his cup.

"I'm here for the end of the season, Sarianna. I have my invitation to Lacey's ball, and I know a host of people in town. I'm sure we will be invited to the same functions, and I'll take my chances against anyone else who wants you. And I'll win, Sarianna." He walked over to her and tilted her unwilling chin up so he could look into her eyes. "But I'll play it your way—for now."

And he did. She saw him everywhere that she went with Sallie and her family. Everywhere. At the theater, he came to their box and dropped a caressing hand on her shoulder, while whispering in her ear, "Remember our first kiss, Sarianna?"

And she shook him off. I don't want you anymore was a statement that did not remember first kisses. It denied last kisses forever. She refused to listen.

At the assembly hall of the St. Cecelia Society where weekly dances were held, he begged her company which she could not refuse without being ungracious, and she held her head away so he could not whisper to her things that she did not want to hear.

"But I loved kissing you, Sarianna," he murmured, as he handed her back to Sallie Gill, and then saw her go off to waltz with Patrick Bohan and noted Lacey's crestfallen face.

At a lecture—an *improving* lecture, Sallie Gill hastened to add—she sat between Cade and Patrick Bohan and squirmed uncomfortably as each of them pressed his case. "You're so beautiful, Sarianna," Patrick whispered in her right ear.

"How tightly you held me," Cade breathed into her left.

"This cannot continue," she raged privately to Sallie Gill.

There was a private party, given by friends of Sallie Gill's and Austin's, for their own circle of acquaintances, and still, there was Cade, surrounded by a circle of fatuous women, lifting a glass to toast Sarianna's entrance.

"On the chair," he whispered as she passed him by one time.

"On the floor," he said the next time as she was sitting and conversing with Patrick Bohan.

"In the barn, Sarianna, *I* haven't forgotten."

"Stop it!"

"The man is a nuisance," Patrick commented belligerently. "I wish someone would just tell him he is not welcome."

Lacey's ball was the following weekend, and all energy turned toward making it the event of the season.

Sarianna wore a gown of deep sapphire blue with a deep lace encrusted décolleté, tiers of satin rising from the hem, and a puffed demi-sleeve gathered with matching lace. It was a ravishing dress, wide-hooped, and draped with a small train. She wore a matching blue satin ribbon entwined in her hair, and blue kid slippers and lace mittens.

Lacey wore white, traditional, and beguiling, all in satin and lace dripping over her shoulders and bosom, encrusted with pearls and overlying a glowing satin underdress. She wore white satin slippers, and a fabulous pearl necklace wound around her throat, her parents' gift on this momentous day.

Carriage after carriage drew up to the Lundeen town house to take them all to the Brighton Club, and when they arrived, it was all lit up like some magical palace.

Inside was a symphony of luminescence and flowers: white, blue, yellow, pink—camellias, tea roses; while cherry blossoms, azaleas and oleander interspersed with fragrant branches of evergreen that bedecked every flat surface on luxurious swaths of red velvet, and hung from the walls. Candles flickered warmly everywhere, reflecting in flower-filled brass and cut glass bowls that decorated burled wood, brass-tipped tables that stood beside elegant arrangements of satin upholstered sofas and chairs. All over the room, thick oriental rugs carpeted the parquet floor, surrounding a center area for dancing. Four additional chambers abutted the main ballroom: a ladies' dressing room, a library, a common room, and the service room that led to the kitchens.

"It is perfect," Lacey breathed as she wafted into the room. "Oh, Mother, Father. This is perfect."

They watched her dance around the perimeter of the room, touching the flowers and the satiny wood tables, and trip up onto the dais where the orchestra would play. "Perfect . . ." her voice echoed down the long alley of the room. "Just utterly perfect . . ."

The guests began to arrive promptly at eight. The music had begun, a soft background to the brilliant conversation as couples circulated, or drifted onto the dance floor to waltz, or into the common room where it was quieter and there was an ell where cards were available.

A hundred guests entered the Brighton Club that night and still did not fill it up.

Sarianna conscientiously waited inconspicuously by the Lundeens' side as they greeted their guests. Everyone knew her now, everyone had a pleasant word to say to her before they entered the ballroom, and she felt comfortable; and for the first time she did not feel that her presence was drawing any attention away from Lacey.

Lacey glowed. When Patrick Bohan strode in, she positively flamed.

He was a charming man, Sarianna thought, watching him. He knew just the right thing to say to her that made her extremely happy and committed him to nothing. He had eyes only for Sarianna, and Lacey was blissfully unaware of it. He spent the proper amount of time talking to her, and then gracefully excused himself with a meaningful glance at Sarianna, and made his charming way around the room, greeting mutual friends, and saying a humorous word to the women who were eager to make conversation with him.

Sarianna followed his progress around the room as he kept looking back at her while he was being detained by one or another of his friends. He wanted her to follow him, it was obvious, and relieve him of this onerous duty, and she had no intention of doing that. This was Lacey's night after all, and nothing should mar it, even the fact that Patrick Bohan had no interest in her whatsoever.

But someone was very interested in her, Sarianna. She felt Cade's presence even before he walked in the room, and even from afar, she knew he picked her right out of the crowd.

She felt an insane sense of having been here before; it was like

390

Jeralee's birthday ball, and she was hiding in the crowd again, anonymous to everyone but him.

The pull of his intent gaze was unavoidable; it was like a tangible thing, constant, physical. She could not run from it. And she would not acknowledge it.

Only when he passed her on the receiving line did she look at him, and then her eyes were blank and her expression bland, her tone civil as she greeted him.

"It won't work, Sarianna," he murmured, keeping her hand imprisoned in his own.

"You're quite right," she agreed, her composure slipping a little. "I'm glad you have come to that conclusion."

"I'll find you wherever you are," he assured her, relinquishing her hand. "I haven't forgotten a thing, Sarianna."

"I hope not. Neither have I. And since you don't want me anymore, please feel free to make the acquaintance of any and all of Lacey's friends. I'm sure there is someone here who could make you forget me in a moment."

"Not in a lifetime," he said calmly. "I remember everything."

"And you don't remember not wanting me. How convenient. Excuse me, won't you?"

She turned away from him, her emotions in a turmoil. Why would he pursue her like this after all that had happened? Now he forced her to seek out Patrick Bohan, and she didn't really want to do something like that—it would just bolster his firm sense of his desirability which had nothing at all to do with any emotion of his being engaged while he stalked this female and that.

She was an enigma to him, she understood; he sensed that mystery about her, and her air of worldliness which he hoped translated into a concrete sensuality that would not faint at the first caress. He was almost sure of it, and Sarianna knew it. She could not play the virginal debutante with him. They had gone too far past that point the day she had snubbed him in the garden.

Cade watched her as she merged with the guests on her discreet, well-mannered course to Patrick Bohan's side.

He had said that to her, he thought, and he could never take back the words; they would always be engraved in her heart. She had buried her feelings for him as deeply as she had buried their child. How much she had suffered at his hands. His callousness defied description; yet here, with Sallie Gill's affection and understanding, her spirit had risen again.

It was curious, he thought. No one knew her here. Here she was not Dona's child, and here she was not the odd, awkward misfit. Here she was Sarianna Broydon, a beautiful woman in her own right, and everyone responded to her. In this time and place, he reflected, this would have been her birthright had she had a mother and father as loving as Sallie Gill and Austin. All these years, she would have had Savannah at her feet if it had not been for Vesta and the living hatred of Dona's legacy.

She was wonderful to watch, graceful, restrained, refined, smiling gently as she said a word here, patted a hand there. Only he saw the great sadness in her as she progressed from guest to guest, and he knew none of her success in Charleston would wipe it away. The past would be ever with her, and the unnecessary death of their child. How deeply she had mourned, he did not know. He only knew his own pulsating grief still, at times, overwhelmed him. He needed to hold her and let her cry, and he knew none of this was possible until he had again won her heart.

"Ah, Sarianna . . ." Patrick, his great relief evident in his voice, held out his hand to her. "I hoped—"

"My dear Patrick, don't expect me to believe anything you say tonight," Sarianna said tartly. "This is Lacey's night, after all, her dream, and her fairy tale. And you are not going to ruin it with any kind of excess."

"Yes, ma'am," he said obediently, sending a crooked smile to the couple he had been conversing with. "But you will dance with me? Surely Lacey can have no objection to that?"

"Perhaps I do," Sarianna said severely, and she really felt she might; she didn't feel like dancing or trading words with anyone. She felt Cade's eyes on her all the time, as if he had just stepped back and decided that she was the one component of the whole scheme that he was going to concentrate on. It was unnerving, particularly because he still affected her, and she hadn't expected that. Cruel words, apparently, were not enough to beat down a hopeful heart. And all the lovely attention that had been showered on her here could not mitigate the fact that she was still married, and she was not free to respond to it. And the underlying double edge to that was, she didn't even think she really wanted to.

Her treacherous body knew what she wanted, and it wasn't Patrick Bohan. She wanted to reclaim the first golden weeks at Haverhill, and the sense of creating a new life and a new self. And yet here, in Charleston, she had found still another new self, a different one than the Sarianna who had unintentionally turned Savannah all topsy-turvy. Here, she hadn't intended anything like that at all, and she found the unrestrained admiration she had always sought for her own worth alone.

It astonished her; it was like opening up a present that was made up of boxes inside boxes, and as the larger whole was reduced to the smaller parts, the present became ever more meaningful, until the larger, more useless container could be totally discarded.

She had only to discover the ultimate interior box and the thing that was the most significant of all.

Patrick eyed her pensive expression warily. "It won't do for you to go around looking like that either," he chided her. "You look like you might cry."

"How could I when I'm the envy right now of every woman here?" Sarianna retorted. "My goodness, when I think of the reception you would receive in any one of those little knots of ladies who are watching us, my mind boggles at the thought you asked *me* to dance."

"And why is that, I wonder?" Patrick asked caustically.

"My dear Patrick, I'm hardly some sweet young thing on the verge of her debut," Sarianna began, and then stopped. She was on shaky ground here. She knew Patrick was trying to ferret out her secrets and the reason for her elusiveness. He still could not understand why she was not eager to claim him as her suitor, and she had put herself, with her wary awareness of Cade's intense observation, on dangerous ground with her idle words.

"Don't I know it," he said huskily, pulling her tighter against him and whirling her into a dizzying swoop in time to the music. "Tell me *what* you are, Sarianna," he added cagily, as the music wound to a resounding finish.

"Why, I'm Sarianna Broydon from Savannah and Bredwood Plantation," she answered lightly in her best debutante voice, curtseying in respect for his attempt to catch her unawares. "And now, of course, you'll excuse me. I should get back to Sallie Gill." She paused a moment and sent him a hard look. "Shouldn't I?"

"By all means," he said, and his tone had a shade of resentment in it. She was slipping away again, he thought, as he watched her glide through the crowd, and he didn't yet know quite how to detain her.

She however felt nothing but relief. She felt as if she were walking a thin line; she had no guarantees someone might not show up who had known her in Savannah, or had heard of her abortive marriage. And she knew just why she felt so tremulous: Cade was watching her with a speculative gleam in his hazel eyes, and she just wasn't sure what he himself might do.

She didn't want him to do anything. She just wanted him to go away. She felt as if he were stalking her, even though he had not moved an appeciable distance from the circle surrounding Sallie Gill and Austin. It was just his eyes, following her everywhere, assessing everything, probably making judgments, she thought wearily, never letting her alone. His coming was surely going to mar her enjoyment of her distinctive status in Charleston. His presence made everything real again, and she felt as if she could never bury all the pain deep enough.

But with it, without her wanting it, came the memories, and she didn't understand that. Surely those last turbulent weeks at Haverhill had been enough to utterly sever the fragile thread of their passion. That was all it had been: an exhilarating hunger that had been born of her need for affection. It could have been anyone, she thought, even Patrick Bohan, if he had come to her first.

But it hadn't; it had been Cade with his surety and his masterful kisses, and his long hard body and her voluptuous surrender. Her body remembered it just as intensely as he claimed he did.

The glittering evening encompassed many facets—the dancing, the dinner, the card games, the political discussions in the corners of the common room and in the smoke-filled library.

Sarianna watched as couples paired off right under her very eyes, debutantes and bachelors who had not hitherto even given each other a passing glance throughout the season.

More than one of these would-be suitors came after Sarianna this night, not in the least dissuaded by her aloofness. And as the evening progressed, she had to admit to herself that she enjoyed the attention and the fact that these disparate men were vying for the opportunity to honorably court her.

The irony of it was staggering, particularly with Cade on the sidelines taking in every minute of the jockeying for her favors. More than once her eyes clashed with his, daring him to step in and destroy her reputation, daring him to come claim her because she would deny it.

The incandescent glow of the evening became reflected in his eyes as he watched her every movement. *His* Sarianna.

"It's so romantic," Lacey whispered to her once during the evening.

"What is?" she asked curiously.

"The way Mr. Rensell watches you and just stands there and never takes his eyes off of you. . . ."

"You call that romantic?" Sarianna demanded in disbelief. "Try unnerving. Try disturbing."

"Oh, no," Lacey told her earnestly, "you have it all wrong. He's watching you so closely because . . . because—well, he wants you to notice him."

"I've noticed him," Sarianna said dryly.

"*I* think he followed you all the way here from Savannah," Lacey pronounced. "That must mean something."

"He probably had business in Charleston," Sarianna said.

Lacey made a face. "Well, I still think it's romantic. And he did say you knew each other in Savannah."

"Ah, but did he say how well we knew each other?" Sarianna asked facetiously.

Lacey considered this seriously. "Nooooo . . . he didn't. But I just looked in his eyes, and I knew!"

Romantic Lacey, Sarianna thought acerbically, as she sent her off in Patrick Bohan's reluctant arms to the dance floor. If she had instantly jumped to that conclusion, what must others be thinking?

But what did she care anyway?

Patrick came for her, too soon, and she knew it caused comment, but she allowed him to take her arm and lead her into the library.

395

"You keep doing this to me," he said, and there was a warning note in his voice. "I won't allow it, even if I have to tell Lacey point-blank that I do not and never have wanted her."

"You read too much into it," Sarianna responded abstractedly as she felt her heart jump because Cade had followed them into the crowded room.

"*You* are not reading what I am trying to tell you, Sarianna, and I damn well think you're doing it deliberately."

"You misunderstand me," she said frantically as she perceived that Cade was actually approaching them.

"I want you, Sarianna, can I be clearer than that? Above and beyond all the other gawking boys who keep hovering around you whom I know damned well you don't want, *I* want you, and I damn well want to know why you're holding back."

"This is not the place to discuss it," she hissed, just as Cade touched her arm, and she turned with a mendacious smile to greet him. "Hello, Mr. Rensell. So nice to see you."

"Delightful to see you *not* surrounded for a change," he responded smoothly.

"Yes, well. Patrick, this is Mr. Cade Rensell of Savannah; Cade, Mr. Patrick Bohan, of Charleston."

She watched them acknowledge the introduction with grim humor. They had nothing to say to each other. Rather, they stood there like two combatants, sizing each other up, and she could see already that Patrick had ten questions right at the tip of his tongue, starting with did she know Cade in Savannah.

"Lacey's party is a triumph," Cade said at last.

"Indeed it is. I trust you have danced with her?"

"Do you know, I have been remiss. I hadn't thought to put myself so far forward on such a short acquaintance."

She held his gaze, noting the faint smile on his lips and his predatory expression that just dared her to counter that very proper response.

"Dear Mr. Rensell, a word to Sallie Gill is all that is required," she said lightly. "Lacey would be so disappointed besides. She has some romantical notions about you. Perhaps you could confirm—or deny—her conclusions."

"I believe it would be even more proper if you presented me," Cade proposed easily, counteracting that evasion neatly. He was aware of Patrick fuming beside him, and that he had deliberately broken into what had seemed about to become a very heated exchange. It wouldn't do, he thought, looking into Sarianna's icy sapphire eyes, to let Sarianna think she could get away with playing this little game. Patrick obviously wanted more of her than she was willing to give, and she had looked mighty uncomfortable when he walked in the room.

She turned her gaze to Patrick whose own eyes were stormy with protest. "I suppose I must," she said ungraciously. "Excuse me, Patrick."

She knew, too, he was watching as she exited the room with Cade, and when they were out of his view, she turned on him furiously. "And what was *that* about?"

"I was saving you from yourself," Cade said calmly.

"I do not need saving. Nor do I need the good offices of a man who expressly made clear that he did not want me. Perhaps it needs to be made clear to you that other men do. That, for me, is enough for now. And you, Mr. Rensell, are *too* much."

"Sarianna, Sarianna . . ." He was almost tempted to chide her, to play games, to make light of the fact that he had suffered as well. "I'm coming after you, Sarianna, and no one is going to get in my way. You don't want to know anything now, and that's fine. As you said, this is not the place for it. But there are two more weeks that the Lundeens will be here, after which you must make some kind of decision. Oh, you didn't think I knew that? All right, play with this Patrick Bohan's feelings, Sarianna. The poor man will be wrecked when you finally reject him. I will see *you* tomorrow. And in the meantime, I will ask Lacey to dance."

His words totally spoiled the rest of the evening for her. But she would not let it show. She presented her most social self to his penetrating gaze until the end of the party, smiling, flirting—mainly with men she cared nothing about—with volatile concern for Patrick Bohan's well-being, always mindful that she did not mean to let him come further into her life. If only he would stay just the way he was tonight: aggressive, faintly romantic, just outside of actually handling her physically . . . admiring her with his eyes and a wellspring of unspoken words that she could see just ached to be released.

Cade's arrogant gaze was like a pointed barb—an affirmation of

397

his prediction.

She was unbelievably grateful when the party finally ended.

Sallie Gill was well-pleased. She bent her graying golden head over a slew of invitations that had arrived with the morning mail. Lacey was not even awake as she and Sarianna sat down to partake of the noon meal, and Sarianna was tense and overwrought. She held a note in her hand from Patrick Bohan. He planned to call on her this afternoon, too.

Sallie said, "Everything went extraordinarily well, did it not, Sarianna?"

"It did," she agreed, picking at a biscuit. She wasn't hungry. She was frantic. She didn't want to see Cade, and she wanted to see Patrick even less. Her eyes were smudged with lack of sleep, and her hand shook slightly as she lifted her coffee cup to her lips.

"Sarianna," Sallie murmured, noticing the signs. "What *are* you going to do?"

"I don't know what you mean."

"I mean, I saw the way Cade looked at you and came after you last night. To your credit, Sarianna, you did nothing to disrupt the party, despite Cade's provocation. I'm not very happy about that. Your disagreement *should* be discussed in private, and *you* handled that very well. But now—"

"Yes, now. And Patrick wishes to call this afternoon as well."

"You *must* see Cade," Sallie stressed gently.

"I must not. Why can't he just go away?"

"My dear, he came for you."

"He could not have. He was very precise: He did not want me anymore. His very words, Sallie, and I took them to heart."

"And Patrick seems to want you, and you cannot encourage him. So what sense does that make?"

"And it will break Lacey's heart as well."

"I'm happy you are sensible of that, but I will tell you in confidence that I'm certain they would not suit anyway. He is much too sophisticated for her, and he is used to being fawned over and invited everywhere. She would bore him in a week, and you and I know that. However, his response to you is an entirely different matter, and well you know it."

"Yes, and it *is* tempting to—pretend that I'm eligible and to puncture all that puffed self-esteem of his. I wish I could just spend the next two weeks playing and then go back to considering what I must do next."

"Indeed, and I suppose if Cade had not come, you could have allowed yourself the luxury of it. Since he has . . ."

Sarianna sighed. "I suppose . . ."

"You certainly must receive him, Sarianna, because you and I know the truth of the matter, and now he knows who possesses the information, too. Consider this as well: It is the proper thing to do, and I am ever known for doing the proper thing." She smiled at Sarianna to lessen the sting of her words. "Talk to him, Sarianna. Don't make the mistake of thinking he felt no pain or that his cruelty did not arise from that. Really *talk* to him, Sarianna."

But that was easier for Sallie to advise than for Sarianna to do. She sat in the parlor with her hands folded and her eyes down, and she would not allow him an opening.

He paced, like the lion-man he was, and the tension grew to the bursting point. And it was made worse by the fact that before either could say anything meaningful, Patrick Bohan was announced. He was none too pleased to see Cade, and the tension escalated.

Sarianna sat primly in the parlor with two desirable men, on either side of her, and no one could think of a word to say.

"Perhaps tomorrow," Patrick said, after thirty stilted minutes of staccato conversation about the weather and the success of Lacey's come-out.

"I would appreciate that," Sarianna said stiffly as she saw him out.

Sallie sent her a rueful look as she passed her on the way back to the parlor. She felt a great deal of sympathy for Sarianna, and perhaps some for Cade. Men were fools, she thought, all of them, except for her beloved Austin.

Sarianna stamped back into the parlor. "*That* was a pleasant interlude," she snapped. "Now would you please leave?"

"I will *not*. Sit down, Sarianna, and don't tell me you'd just like to follow that Bohan to hell and back."

399

"I do not want to sit. I want you to leave. Can I be plainer than that?"

He smiled then, his slow easy smile that definitely told her he was amused. "And how far and how fast do you think you can run, Sarianna?"

"Far enough to make a life for myself that doesn't include *you*," she snapped.

"That is not possible."

"Anything is possible."

"You are *im*possible, Sarianna, but I won't quibble on the wording with you."

"Neither will I. Let me quote: 'I do not want you anymore.' And I'm pleased to announce that neither do I want you. I think that nullifies the marriage, don't you? If neither partner wants the other?"

"Excuse me, perhaps you have forgotten, Sarianna. Or perhaps I did not make it plain enough—I still want you, and I still want our marriage. And *you* are lying."

"What? I can't decide suddenly that I don't want you, Cade? You give yourself too much credit."

"You're lying to yourself."

"No, you killed my desire with your cruelties and your words, Cade. *That* is the truth of it. I won't go through that hell again. I won't. I won't put myself in a position like that again, to let someone else be able to inflict such pain and for no reason that I could understand. No. That part is over, Cade. I will not allow myself to be a victim—and I marvel at your gall for even suggesting it."

"We are married, Sarianna, and nothing can change that."

"I *could* apply for a divorce. I'm told there is some possibility it might be granted."

"And just as much possibility it won't, along with the attendant scandal, and the negative reflection on Sallie. I don't think you want that."

"You're right. I just want you to go away."

"I am not going away, Sarianna."

"Fine, then leave this house and don't come back."

"I won't do that either."

"Well. I guess that finishes that discussion. Excuse me." She made for the parlor door, and Cade blocked her.

"We are *not* finished," he said grittily, feeling as if he wanted to shake her—no—take her in his arms. He took a step and she backed away. "You can bandy words back and forth with me all you want, and you can see Patrick Bohan as much as you think you want to; but I tell you, Sarianna, that I will have you and no one else."

The challenge was too much for her. He had a nerve thinking he could walk into Sallie's house and totally reorder her life after doing his best to destroy it. "Fine," she said antagonistically, "let's see if you do."

26

And then, for all his provoking words, Sarianna did not see Cade for the following three days. That was good. Perhaps he took her seriously that she meant not to succumb to him. She didn't know. She was too busy trying to fend off Patrick Bohan who, the next day, asked all the predictable questions.

"You knew this Rensell in Savannah?"

"Let us say we traveled in the same circles."

"I see." But he didn't want to see. Cade Rensell seemed too familiar with Sarianna, and she was too guarded with him. He knew nothing of her life prior to her unexpected visit to Sallie Gill, and the more he tried to find out, the less she would tell him.

Moreover, she did not beg for his company or ask when he was coming back to see her, and he found this disdain rather refreshing. But on his part, he wanted to know and direct everything, and she gave him no quarter on that.

"And your father, where is he?"

"Back on Bredwood, I expect. Sallie is my mother's cousin, you know."

"Right. Wilmot's daughter."

"Exactly."

"And they say you look remarkably like her."

"I don't remember her very well." And why, she fretted, did he have to drag Dona into it? The best part of her being in Charleston was that no one, save Sallie, had known Dona, and yet someone had spread the word.

"You are beautiful, Sarianna."

She waved the compliment away. She didn't want that from him, but she didn't know quite what she did want now that she had granted him the privilege of calling on her at the Lundeens'. "And you are quite handsome, Mr. Bohan."

"We make a very good-looking pair," he agreed with a trace of satisfaction. "Let me love you, Sarianna."

"Patrick!" She was shocked; she hadn't expected him to declare himself so boldly or so quickly.

"Sarianna," he answered in kind.

They stared at each other, and he shook his head. "You are something. You tell me you are not some innocent in the big bad city, you have this air of earthiness about you, and a mouth that just demands to be kissed, and all you do is hold me off and hold me off; and I have to wonder just how much you think I can stand?"

Her eyes turned cold blue. "As much as you have to, I would think," she said pointedly. "I'm sorry I haven't just jumped into your bed, Mr. Bohan, but as you have observed, that is not precisely my style. I don't hanker for you quite as much as you seem to desire me. Perhaps it would be better if you quenched your need by not seeing me altogether."

Now he was shocked; he had used a ploy that generally yielded some degree of capitulation on the part of the woman he was pursuing. Sarianna beat all bounds by her cool rejection of him. It made her all the more admirable in his eyes, and much more valued. Now he had to have her, and he knew he would stop at nothing to force her surrender.

Finally Cade came, and Sarianna didn't know whether she felt relieved or exasperated. He acted as if she had never told him to leave her alone. He proposed a walk, properly chaperoned, of course, a mere half hour of her time, and he asked her in front of Sallie, which she later thought was a good tactic because Sallie was damn well on *his* side for some reason; and he recruited her meaningful looks and reputation for propriety shamelessly.

She reluctantly agreed to go because she could not avoid Sallie's frowning eyebrows, and she sent Garnet to fetch her a hat and to prepare to accompany them on a short stroll.

Of course her intention was not to give him an opening for

conversation. However, it was going on noon, the streets were very quiet due to the ladies' rest hour, and the silence was deafening. Cade chose that moment to be infuriatingly conventional. "I trust," he said, "that your visit to Charleston has been rewarding."

She made a sound, but she suppressed the words that rose to her lips.

"Don't you find the weather lovely, Miss Broydon?" he went on in the same vein, his tone perfectly serious.

She made another noise but forebore to comment.

"And the company in town this year is most congenial," he finished. "I wonder I waited so long to visit."

"Dear God, Cade, what is *that* about?" she exploded.

"Conversation, my dear Miss Broydon. Do you have some?"

She looked away, irritated. She did not want to make conversation with him. She did not want to be with him at all, and she said so.

"Yet here you are," he pointed out gently.

"Out of sheer boredom," she retorted. "I had nothing else to do."

"You could have something else to do," he suggested.

"I have no idea what you mean," she said stiffly.

"Sarianna . . ."

"I won't listen."

"You are still my wife."

"You do not want a wife."

"I *beg* to differ with you."

"I *beg* your pardon, but we have differing views."

"They—and we—can be reconciled," Cade insisted. God, she was damned stubborn, Cade thought, as a negating silence fell between them. But he had not really expected much more at this stage. He fully intended to take his time with her, and to court her, as she had always deserved, as Miss Sarianna Broydon of Bredwood, for as long as it took, and no matter how many obstacles she threw his way.

"*I,*" Sarianna said, "am fully reconciled. I do not need you in my life. I do not want you. I am happier without you."

He came the next day, her rebuff notwithstanding, to escort her to an art exhibition.

"I know nothing about art," she said testily.

"A perfect reason to come with me then," he said reasonably; and before she knew it, she was in his carriage, Garnet by her side, and they were rolling down the quiet streets to the exhibition hall of the Art Association to view a selection of silhouettes and miniatures and portraits on loan for this particular showing.

Sarianna could not have cared less about art, but she was entranced by the perfection of the miniature portraits and landscapes, and the perception of the fine steady hand of the artist and his infinite eye.

They walked a little afterward, with their carriage following them, and Cade made knowledgeable references to the city about things she had not known he was aware of. When they passed a square of row houses that reminded her of Malverne Row, she broke her silence long enough to ask, "How does Amanda fare?"

He felt a glimmer of hope. "They are all well, and back in Savannah with me."

"Oh? But the harvest . . . ?"

"I sold it off."

"I see." But she did not see. If he were back in Savannah, where was Vesta, and if he had sold the harvest, what did he intend to do about Haverhill? But then, it was none of her business. But she was aching to know if Amanda had gotten in trouble over her defection, and she knew she could not ask him. Or had he intended to pass by this way deliberately to provoke some kind of question?

"I remember our first night in Savannah," he added, watching her face.

"*Don't.*" Her vehemence made him wince. Her memories were too tender, too intertwined with his rejection. She had to deflect him, and she uttered the first thing that came to mind. "Where *is* Vesta if she is not in Savannah?"

He sent her an odd look. "Back in Bredwood as far as I know."

Not in Savannah. How ironic, and futile. She had come to make trouble—maybe she had—and to snare another man for Jeralee, and she had wound up right back where she started. It served her right. Really it did. But there was no Alzine for her now, and no Rex, if the rumor of his drinking were to be believed. How glad she was she had gotten away.

But she would not have gotten away without Cade. Of anything, it was the one thing she owed him, and she hated the thought now. Her helplessness was real and would have existed without the artificial impediments Rex had placed on her. What would she have done were she still there, with the burden of Vesta and her father? Everything else could pale beside the question of what she would have become had she never left Bredwood.

She did not want to talk about it.

He did not want her anymore, and that—in fact—was the end of the story.

They sat on the verandah, a place where, two days later, Sarianna did not feel she needed to make conversation. She knew as well that behind closed doors Lacey was observing her, and Sallie Gill's well-meaning eye watched her.

Cade provided the running commentary. "This actually is much nicer than the garden in Savannah, don't you think, Sarianna? I would love to make love to you right on this verandah."

"I'll walk away if you continue one more word in that vein," Sarianna said.

"I still want you."

"No—no. You still want to humiliate me."

"And it isn't at all possible I want to make amends?" he asked carefully.

"For what?" she retorted. "I have no idea. But don't tell me now. I don't want to know."

"You're right," he agreed. "There is no reason why I should want to reveal to you the depth of my stupidity."

"Exactly," she said complacently. "Would you like some tea?"

They were invited to a garden party at a mansion just outside of Charleston; the daughter of the house was a friend of Lacey's.

Cade was in the lush garden when Lacey and Sarianna wandered in. "Sarianna," he said, holding out his hand, and she took it because it would have been churlish not to. "And Lacey. You look lovely."

Lacey flashed Sarianna a look. "I will leave you, if you don't mind. I think I see Patrick."

Oh, please, Lord, no, Sarianna prayed, as she let Cade lead her farther into the garden.

"The first time I kissed you, you were in the garden at Bredwood," Cade said.

"I don't remember," Sarianna said cuttingly. "Perhaps want and memory go hand in hand."

"Right. You don't want me," Cade reiterated. "Would you like me to disprove that?"

"Not particularly," Sarianna said, her eyes shifting around to see if Lacey were anywhere near.

Cade took a step closer. His hands reached out to touch the thin material of her voile gown, her arms, her shoulders, her mesmerized face. She had forgotten totally the magic of his hands. The words had wiped out all feeling, all the memory of the sensuous contact that would make her vulnerable again. And if she stood here one more moment, she would be utterly defenseless. One touch and she remembered everything, and worse—her body clamored for more. What insanity it was, the need for total capitulation that warred with the intense pain that still permeated her mind and soul.

Yet she didn't move. Perhaps one part of her wanted to prove that he couldn't reach her anymore. Perhaps she thought she could render herself immune to him if she just allowed him to have his way, and she could show him that nothing about him could affect her anymore.

"And so," Cade whispered, touching her lips once again with his fingers, "I will kiss you again in the garden," and his lips brushed gently where his fingers had stroked.

She was utterly still, and her whole body reverberated to the light, sizzling caress of his lips.

He let her go almost immediately, gratified by the faint tremor of her chin and the faint flick of her eyelids.

"It's enough," he murmured in satisfaction, sliding his fingers across her lips again before leaving her.

And Patrick Bohan watched from the shadows.

Sallie Gill hosted an evening musicale during which a number of Lacey's friends, as well as Lacey and Sarianna, performed on piano, harp and guitar. Several of the girls were well versed in light classical pieces, others played more current romantical selections—"Yes, I Have Dared to Love Thee," and "O Sing Once More That Melody"— while Lacey and Sarianna chose the more traditional backcountry ballads: "The House Carpenter," and "Sweet William," and rousing drinking songs with which everyone was familiar, and everyone joined in singing.

Within the crowd of guests, Cade watched proudly as Sarianna led the singing and played so sweetly. When the performers finally broke, everyone surrounded them, and Sallie led the way into the buffet for refreshments.

"Sarianna is wonderful," she said to Cade, her sharp blue eyes meeting his in a brazen question.

"Yes, her talents were much maligned and otherwise untapped before she came to Savannah and Charleston," he said gallantly; but it was true, he realized, and also, for some reason, he had said something that made Sallie nod her approval. "She has been hurt," he added, "in a hundred ways, and in my stupidity, I added to the burden."

"Yes," Sallie agreed tartly, "you *were* stupid."

He smiled ruefully. "Not any more."

"Good," she said emphatically, and left him to root out Sarianna from her admirers. Foremost among them, he discovered, as he reentered the parlor, was Patrick Bohan, who held her hands tightly and would not let her say one word.

It was hardly surprising she welcomed him so warmly as she saw him heading toward her. Patrick relinquished her hands immediately, and she held them out to Cade.

"Mr. Rensell," she murmured with some enthusiasm.

"Miss Broydon," he acknowledged, "how well I remember your hands."

She wrenched them away. "Don't *do* that.'

He ignored her, and took them back again to touch each finger with a light caressing stroke of his own fingers. "Such gentle fingers, and such a firm touch and grasp, Sarianna. Unforgettable."

"Cade . . ." she said warningly.

He lifted her hand to his mouth and kissed it. "Wonderful loving hands, Sarianna."

"*Stop* it!"

"I want those hands again, Sarianna."

"But you don't want me," she interpolated, pulling her hand away.

"I want you most of all," he repeated firmly.

"And I want you not at all," Sarianna said with all the firmness she could muster. In fact, he was muddling her thinking, with his words and his insistence.

In a crowd where he could get to her, or in the parlor, with Sallie's approval, he had all the advantage. They were married after all; she had very little recourse for all her protestations.

"Why do you let him do that?" Patrick Bohan demanded from behind her.

She whirled. "Do what, Patrick?"

"Talk to you like that? What is it about him? Your whole face changes, and your body, whenever he is near you, and in a way you do not react to me."

"You are imagining it," Sarianna said sharply, but in her heart she was not so sure. The only thing she knew was that she was not going to give over an inch. Cade had tormented her enough with his words and his rejection. There was no reason not to pay him back in his own coin.

Sallie arranged a massive picnic for a group of Lacey's and Sarianna's friends. Her sons had already left Charleston in pursuit of their varying activities: Cloyce back to Arboretum, their plantation upcountry; Noel to prepare for his grand tour, and Sonny back north to complete his schooling. There wasn't much more than another week or two left to the season, and as the weather cooled considerably, outdoor activities began to come to the fore as the primary entertainment; and picnics, which included a sturdy hike and lawn games, were a popular pastime.

Sallie engaged a dozen carriages to convey the food and servants and large assortment of guests. Cade coincidentally sat next to Sarianna in the carriage with Lacey and Patrick Bohan and two other of their friends.

"This reminds me," Cade said in an undertone, "of the first time I took you to Haverhill."

Sarianna's heart lurched. Didn't she remember that! No, in actuality, she had tried very hard not to think of it.

The man was diabolical, dredging up all the perfect memories and presenting them to her at times and in places she could hardly make much objection.

"I don't seem to recall that," she said aggressively, but the squirm of her body said differently.

"Think about it," Cade said. "I'm sure you'll remember."

She let a beat of a pause go by. "No, I have no memory of that day

409

whatsoever."

"*I* seem to recall something about a . . . kiss," Cade murmured. "Could you possibly conjure up something as fanciful as that?"

She could swear she was blushing, and she refused to back down.

"Well, *I* remember everything," Cade said complacently, because he knew very well she had not forgotten either.

"It must have been somebody else," Sarianna said. "It could not have been me."

The picnic was a huge success, barring the moment when Patrick Bohan cornered her away from the others.

"Sarianna," he began touchily, "tell me why you let that man kiss you, and you push *me* away?" He didn't even know if he expected an answer; he only knew his mind was consumed with the picture of Sarianna lifting her willing lips to Cade Rensell's when she denied him kisses everytime he asked her.

"I don't know what you're talking about," Sarianna said defensively, while inside she groaned. Cade was becoming more damned trouble, and trouble begot trouble, and here was Patrick Bohan to prove it.

"Do *not* hide behind the standard cowardly expressions of denial," he said sharply. "I know what I saw at the Anderburghs'. There you were, just as you are now with me, and you allowed him to kiss you. You certainly are no innocent, Sarianna, if you were permitting such liberties in public. What might you allow in private, I wonder?"

"*Don't* wonder," Sarianna snapped. "You have no cause to believe that I am in any way interested in you on that level."

"Please, Sarianna. What hogwash. I would accept that from Lacey, but certainly not from you, not now."

"Patrick . . ."

"You're so beautiful, Sarianna. There isn't a man in Charleston who isn't hungry for you. So why should this Rensell stranger have you, tell me that?"

"You sound like a little boy," Sarianna retorted, "a *spoiled* little boy who isn't going to get what he wants. I don't particularly want to kiss you, Patrick, that's why. Now let me go, please."

"Sarianna, I swear you drive me to excesses," Patrick growled, reaching for her.

"I surely know that feeling," Cade's voice said behind them.

"We are fine," Sarianna said tartly, because she did not want him interfering. Patrick looked ready to strangle her—and Cade come to that—and Cade was smiling, lounging against a tree while Patrick waited impatiently for him to depart.

"We are fine now, Cade, *thank you*," Sarianna said pointedly.

"So am I," Cade said amiably. "Nice scenery. Nice place for a little talk, don't you think, Bohan?"

Patrick made a strangled sound and threw a fulminating look at Sarianna before he stomped off.

"You didn't *look* fine," Cade offered as Sarianna bit her lip.

"Yes," she said, "but he *wanted* me."

Cade's expression darkened. "Did he kiss you?"

"No, but he *wanted* to."

"I see. And my wanting to doesn't count."

"No," Sarianna said, and she knew how dangerous it was to goad him. He came toward her intently, and she backed away and backed away to the tone of the menace in his voice.

"So you don't remember *my* kisses, Sarianna, not any, not ever, and now I can't want you but everybody else can, is that the story? Is it?" His hands reached for her. "How much patience am *I* supposed to have, Sarianna, when I am the only one who has a right to kiss you?" He pulled her against him. "When will you start remembering my kisses?" he demanded of her mute face. "Try *now*, my Sarianna. I intend to take what you seem to be so willing to give to someone else." His mouth crashed down on hers, and it was like an earthquake engulfing her. So many weeks without him, without *this*, this masterful domination of her femininity, this wet wild possession that cóuld never ever be duplicated by anyone else.

Oh, she had missed this, and she remembered every nuance of his mad exploration of her mouth. She felt her own hunger compel her response; he would find no unwillingness here despite her protests. She would find she remembered everything that had gone between them, and that her lips knew just how to caress his and reveal her total capitulation, her instant arousal. Her words became lies under the powerful caress of his tongue, and she wondered somewhere in the deep recesses of her mind, whether his words might have been lies as well.

Yes, he wanted her. She felt it in her very bones, and the truth was if she let herself believe his rejection had been the emotion of the moment, she might lie on the ground with him right there for the joy of having him caress her once again.

But that was insanity. She remembered, too, in the course of his galvanic exploration of her mouth all the weeks of verbal torture she had suffered, and the overwhelming anguish of her loss of the baby. Where were his kisses then? Where was the haven of his arms, and the sweet consoling words he was willing to murmur in her ear now.

She wrenched away from him as her own memories came flooding back into her mind to supersede the sweet pleasure he created with his mouth.

"Sarianna . . ."

"You cannot do this, Cade. You *can't*. You made everything perfectly clear at Haverhill. How can you even *think* your kisses could make up for the pain and anguish? You made your position plain, I believe. I don't imagine things can have changed appreciably since then. I won't let you seduce me with your kisses, damn it."

"And I know why, too," Cade said tartly. "You know I can do it, don't you, Sarianna? I was within inches of doing it right here—and you, my girl, were responding very nicely."

"Nonsense," Sarianna snapped. "No one would respond to such brutal tactics. You're an animal, Cade Rensell, and I don't think you have the right to use me this way."

"Sarianna—" he began exasperatedly, but he could see there was no talking to her, and he knew why. His kisses aroused her, just as they had done from the start, and she could not maintain her painful anger if she admitted it. But then, he thought, her pain was very real, and she had not yet mourned with *him* for their son and the lost impetus of their marriage. How could he condemn her, when he had been the one to set the whole disaster in motion? He ran a futile hand through his hair and looked at Sarianna's obdurate face. "I love your kisses, Sarianna, and I won't give them up willingly," he said at last.

"That is *not* the story I remember," she said grittily, "and isn't it damned convenient for you to change it now. Excuse me, won't you? I came here to eat and have a good time, and *not* to be mauled by you."

Oh, but Sarianna, he thought, watching her stiff postured figured retreat back into the trees, *how you do protest.* She was not immune to his kisses, he thought. The problem was, she wanted them too much.

*　　*　　*

Sallie Gill had an interesting idea. "Cloyce and the boys are gone now," she said to Cade. "There is no reason for you to be putting up at the hotel when we have all this room."

"That may be pushing things just a bit much," Cade temporized.

"How silly. You will be my guest."

"Ma'am, you know nothing about me," Cade said.

"I know about Sarianna," Sallie told him stringently. "We can handle the likes of you, Mr. Rensell. You just mind your manners and behave yourself."

"I'll try," he said humbly, but he wondered what Sarianna would think of this contrary arrangement.

He could have predicted she wouldn't like it.

"What on earth are you doing *here?*" she demanded at breakfast the next morning when she and Sallie were the only ones down early. Sallie excused herself instantly, and Cade gave Sarianna a rueful smile.

"Miss Sallie invited me to stay here."

"Did she?" Sarianna murmured, beginning to feel surrounded on all sides. Oh, she knew Sallie thought she ought to make more of an effort with Cade, because in truth there was very little else she would be able to do, but Sallie was not being very subtle about shunting them together whether she wanted it or not. And she did not want it. Cade Rensell at the breakfast table was too reminiscent of Haverhill, and as she seated herself across from him, she felt that savage divisiveness about his rejection and his overtures.

"Don't you have business or something to attend to in Charleston?" she asked idly after a few moments as she realized once again her appetite was nonexistent in his troubling presence. Obviously, she could not fault Sallie Gill for inviting him to stay; Sallie's kindness was hardly in question. She liked happy endings, Sarianna thought; but this was no fairy tale, and Cade Rensell was hardly a prince, with that lion-look of his that now stared at her from across the table.

"I am now a man of leisure," Cade said, helping himself to more ham and biscuits.

"Oh, how so? You trust your overseer so much you can leave him alone for so long while you tarry in Charleston? You must have such confidence."

Cade looked at her thoughtfully, wondering how she would take his news. "I sold up Haverhill," he said finally.

413

"You *what?*"

"I sold up—don't *look* at me like that, Sarianna."

She looked stricken, sick; she could never have conceived of his doing that. "But . . . Alzine—the baby—"

"We moved the graveyard; I retain the land rights to that, Sarianna. It's ours."

She wanted to say, it's *yours,* but nothing would make her relinquish her right to visit her child. Baby boy Rensell, it said on the grave marker, just as Alzine's child had not been named either. She didn't know if that were better or worse than having bestowed the name and given him life through it. She didn't know anything about it. She wasn't even sure she had examined her grief. "Who . . . who bought it?" she managed to ask finally.

He made a self-deprecating motion with his hand. "Samuel Summers, of course. The first person we approached."

"And so you went back to Savannah," she concluded, "and that is why Vesta went back to Bredwood."

"Indeed, and I had had enough of her and her tricks and deceit," Cade said stonily. "I am not honor bound to offer her hospitality, and I pushed her out as fast as she could pack. I wish," he added darkly, "I had done it a damn sight sooner. I wish I had done a lot of things—sooner."

Sarianna turned her head away. "I won't listen to anything else, Cade. You made your feelings very plain. I don't see how they could have changed so abruptly in a few weeks' time."

She would never accept his explanations, he knew. Nothing could excuse his behavior, come to that. "I'm here," he said finally.

"Yes, and spreading money and good will, and making trouble. Excuse me, Cade, I think you should return to Savannah and find some other likely lady you can rescue and reject. You might make a career out of it. Don't marry her though; then you might get stuck, and we couldn't have that." She pushed herself away from the table, having eaten nothing, and he grasped at her as she pushed past him, and pulled her down onto his lap.

"Sarianna, Sarianna," he chided gently as she struggled against his hands and the sense of his hard body pressing against hers.

Would she always be susceptible to him in that way? she wondered frantically. Was it foreordained that reason went out the window the moment he touched her?

"*Sarianna*—listen to me," Cade commanded, grasping her writhing body tightly against him.

"Let me go."

"*Never*," he said emphatically, wrapping his arms around her midriff so that she could not easily pull away.

"That seems rather optimistic," she said sourly, pushing heavily at his arms. It would be so easy, she thought, to just relent and slide herself against him and forget the past and the weeks and weeks of pain. They all seemed curiously unfocused since she had come to Charleston, as if Sallie's common sense and understanding had been some kind of healing balm that had made the pain recede to a place where she could almost bury it—until Cade's arrival opened the wounds once again.

The thing she knew was he had the right to demand her back, and she—without some kind of independence—had no choice but to obey. There were no options for her; there was only capitulation.

He turned her face so that she was looking at him and not at the hallway hoping that Sallie would come and rescue her. "I love you, Sarianna," he said gently, speaking to her mutinous eyes, and the sweet stubborn curve of her lips.

She laughed. "That's wonderful, Cade. The ultimate insult, from the man who cannot make up his mind." Or maybe she was almost in tears, she didn't know. That declaration was totally unexpected, and it caught her off guard. It was the last thing she ever would have expected him to say, and the most deceitful.

His arms unfolded from around her waist. "Perhaps I am not the only one who cannot make up my mind, Sarianna. Maybe someone else in this room is practicing a greater deceit than I. You might be very sorry, Sarianna, if I finally decided I would let you get away with it."

She almost said, don't.

But that was crazy; the one thing she wanted was for him to leave her alone. Or did she? Why did she feel a rejection in the way he relinquished her and lifted her away from him? Why did she feel so confused?

There were no answers in the unvarying round of social calls that she was committed to make with Lacey this morning. It was too easy to sit in a corner, smoothing the wrinkles from the flowing silk skirt of her gown, and think of the morning's conversation, without having to concentrate very much on what was going on around her.

"Have it your way," Cade had said, as he stood up beside her. "For now, Sarianna. Just be aware that I have only so much patience."

But she knew that; it had gone totally out of control somewhere, somehow on a business trip to Savannah. How could she forget it?

How was it possible that he loved her?

How could he have given up Haverhill?

The questions nagged her, and a sense of her becoming out of control possessed her. The season was coming to a very polite and well-mannered end. The parties were over, and one by one the planters' families were packing to return home to an autumn of harvesting and fall planting. The Lundeens were leaving the week after next because Lacey was having such a fine time spreading her social wings and spending money on the finest imported fabrics to make up dresses for a non-existent trousseau. And Sallie Gill had said nothing at all to her about leaving, or even inquired what her plans would be. She must be very sure, Sarianna reflected, that Cade would succeed.

She did not even know how to express her gratitude to Sallie Gill and Austin. She had never met anyone in her whole life who had accepted her so completely and unconditionally, and with all warm feelings for her happiness. She loved Sallie Gill, and she supposed if Sallie thought it was best for her to return to Savannah with Cade, she might consent to doing so.

Ah, but that would put the decision on Sallie's shoulders, wouldn't it? her long-silent little inside voice asked now—her conscience perhaps—as she fretted her way through yet another boring morning call at yet another of Lacey's friends' homes. This family, too, was preparing to leave town, and Lacey would not see them all for probably three or four months because of the distance between their plantations. Lacey did all the talking, and Sarianna did not need to say anything at all. They were all so delighted to meet her, and they all invariably wished her well.

She didn't want to make the decision, she concluded, as she and Lacey finally made their way home late in the afternoon. One visit had lasted longer than planned, and Lacey had become morose at the thought that the season really *was* over, and the good times must be replaced by the reality of returning home. "Oh, when I am old enough, I will live right here in Charleston," she vowed. "There is nothing more interesting than living in a city. I don't know who would choose to spend her life closed away on a country plantation where you see no one for months, and you have to keep after your slaves to ever get anything done. Don't you agree, Sarianna?"

Sarianna thought about it a moment. The notion was like a blinding light illuminating a possible solution for her—and an unorthodox one. Sallie Gill would never approve, but surely she could lease a town house now that the season was ending and could remain by herself in Charleston. She still had much of the money she had taken from Savannah; it might be enough to last her the year, enough to give her some time so that she didn't have to make a decision about Cade. She could hire servants, a chaperone. She might even be able to coerce Amanda away from Cade . . . her mind flooded with ideas, loving the idea of independence and solitude.

Self-reliance on *Cade's* money? demanded her insouciant inner voice, forcing her to examine all the angles of this precipitate decision. What could he not demand of her then? It might just be easier to go back to Savannah with him, but her mind was very taken with the idea of staying in Charleston without him.

"Oh, look—*we* have company," Lacey cried, as Eban drew up to the town house. "No one *I* know," she added pointedly, as she opened the carriage door and let herself out before Eban could hop down to assist her.

Sarianna followed slowly, wondering how she could excuse herself from a dull afternoon of waiting on Sallie Gill's friends.

The last person she expected to see sitting in the parlor was Vesta.

"... but Sarianna is here," Sallie Gill said brightly just as Sarianna entered the parlor.

Vesta looked up, and indeed there was Sarianna; and they stared at each other as if each were the stuff of the other's nightmares.

"So my dear," Vesta murmured, "who would ever have guessed that you came to Sallie Gill?" She lowered her eyes because she knew the hatred she felt was blazing there; it was not Sarianna standing before her; it was Dona usurping the one thing she thought she had been able to count on—Sallie Gill's affection. Sarianna was about to have it all, she thought viciously, just like her mother, and there was no getting away from it. She wished she had known before she had announced the news of Rex's death to Sallie. Now there was no stopping events. She had been so sure ... if Sarianna were missing for any appreciable length of time, she would have been able to step in and claim the whole of Rex's estate. And if Sarianna had shown up afterward ... she had planned to take care of *that* as well.

And now look. Sarianna placed herself next to Sallie, almost as if the two of them were aligned against *her,* and Sallie was saying that Vesta had come with some very bad news and Sarianna must be prepared.

Ha! Vesta thought, all she had to do was prepare herself to spend the hundreds of thousands of dollars that Rex had left her. And she could not avoid discharging her duty—she had to be the one to tell her.

She lifted her head and took a monumental grip on her emotions. "Rex died unexpectedly several weeks ago."

"I see," Sarianna said, her voice neutral, her mind grappling with this statement from a long distance away. The announcement produced no pang of regret in her. It was unnatural that she felt nothing.

"He was drinking," Vesta went on dryly, "but I think you were aware of that. He shot himself one morning, quite by accident." Her gaze slid away from Sarianna and rested on Lacey's shocked face. "I assure you the authorities looked into it very thoroughly. There is no question but that it was an accident and caused in all probability because he had been drinking heavily just before."

"I'm so sorry," Sallie Gill murmured; how odious that Rex had died so ignominiously, she thought disgustedly.

"Well," Vesta said, "no one knew where to find you. Cade had left Savannah also, but perhaps you weren't aware of that?"

Sarianna said nothing.

Vesta peered edgily into the silence. The worst part was yet to come. "Rex made a will," she continued slowly, trying to keep the querulous resentment out of her voice, and not quite succeeding. "He liquidated his holdings, Sarianna, and kept a lifetime lease on Bredwood only. But the buyer got the land and the cotton, and Greenpoint and . . . well, it was Samuel Summers, who was, as you might imagine, a most anxious and accommodating buyer who was very happy to have Rex occupying Bredwood while he reaped the profits. At any rate, he left—" she almost choked on the words—"he left everything to you, Sarianna. A Mr. Honeywell is the trustee, and there seems to be quite a lot of money. He left me nothing, Sarianna. All of it—is yours."

Sarianna said, "Excuse me?" and sank into the nearest chair. Ten different sensations assaulted her: a passing feeling of grief, and guilt, elation, freedom, and from across the room, a vast comprehension of the depth of Vesta's hatred.

But she could spare no more than a thought for Vesta's problems. Rex had contrived to make amends in this wrong-handed way, and she would not question the means and method. She had money, unentailed money suddenly, and she could do whatever she wanted. Anything. Nobody would question the eccentric Sarianna and her money. A cleansing sensation of relief washed over her. She could refuse Cade with impunity now. It required only a letter and a transfer of funds. She never needed to go back to Savannah again.

"Well," Sallie said, "that does change the complexion of things,

419

doesn't it, Sarianna? Perhaps some additional good news is in order here. Vesta will be staying with us for the next two weeks, Sarianna, and I'm pleased to tell you that Jeralee and her husband will be visiting when they will. They're staying at the hotel, which is perfectly understandable, to insure some privacy, and they were married just before they left Savannah."

Vesta spent the remainder of the day following Sallie all over Charleston because she did not want to be alone—she didn't. If she had stayed at the town house, she might have said something or even done something to Sarianna that she might regret. As it was, she was on touchy ground with her inexplicably sudden unannounced visit, and she knew Sallie was not happy with it. It could have been excused on the grounds that she needed to contact Sarianna, but since she had not known Sarianna was in Charleston, she could not even try that specious reasoning.

Sallie herself was gracious as ever; but Sallie was absolutely certain she had informed Vesta in detail about Lacey's come-out, and she was equally sure that Vesta had assured her that she would never put their two daughters in direct competition. But then, Jeralee was married now, so it should make no difference.

But it did make a difference. Sallie was astonished at her perception that there was something very negative about Vesta. She criticized and carped all up and down the Battery and the streets where they shopped, and it didn't matter what was shown to her or pointed out to her. She criticized Sarianna, too, and Sallie just could not stand for that. Here, in the flesh, was the embodiment of how terribly Vesta had probably treated her. She did not like the affirmation that all Sarianna had told her was true, but her manners and her good sense held. This was not a propitious visit at all, but there was just no way she could get rid of Vesta.

And Vesta, for her part, simmered in a fine jealous rage against Sallie, with her devoted husband and adoring children, *and* Sarianna, who had made a place for herself in Sallie's heart so quickly.

Sarianna got everything, and she got nothing, and nothing ever went right for *her*, Vesta thought venomously. Right down to when she was a child, and Dona got everything as well. Dona had gotten Rex, and when she had done with him, and *he* was worth nothing, only then would he have Vesta. It wasn't fair. It just wasn't fair. There had been no love; he had only done what was expected of him for Dona's sister. He had picked her and Jeralee out of their poverty and brought them back to Bredwood and promised to marry her some day, and he had never kept his promise. And he had sworn, early in their years together, that if she helped him keep Sarianna immured at Bredwood, he would provide for her, and he had left her with nothing but ashes in her mouth.

All her plans and schemes had come to nothing, her elaborate hopes for Jeralee now contained in the persona of one handsome, good-natured, mediocre lawyer who might be able to provide a decent standard of living for Jeralee, but whose income would never encompass the ferocious wants and whims of his mother-in-law's lifetime.

Nothing short of Sarianna's death could repay her for that.

The thought was shocking, and it sizzled around in her brain like lightning, as if it always had been there, stabbing at her for recognition, and not crackling into fruition until every hope was gone.

And indeed, she had no idea where she would go and what would happen to her when Sallie closed up the town house. She was now the poor relative who must throw herself on the mercy of her kin to survive, and the thought was galling. She was but one step away from claiming that which Rex should have ceded to her in the first place, and how tempting it was to think of ridding herself forever of Sarianna and the ghost of Dona at one fell swoop.

The how and the why of it she did not know; she was content to have admitted the desire into her mind. The planning of it kept her occupied for the rest of the afternoon; her cavilling stopped, and she became almost quiescent which worried Sallie even more. It was as if something had plugged up Vesta's mouth, and it just wasn't likely that she would stop that way in mid-stream.

She was almost relieved to return home. Cade had returned, and the sight of him waiting provided a reassuringly solid male presence against the evanescence of Vesta's personality.

"Cade!" Sallie cried eagerly. "Have you heard the news?"

Vesta stopped in her tracks. Of course there would be a complication. Cade had left Savannah, and she assumed he had gone west again. She had even wondered who was occupying the town house, and whether she could just brazen her way back in there again. She would never have dreamed he would wind up here in Charleston, *and* a guest of Sallie Gill's. From all she had heard, he was through with Sarianna, and she had disappeared altogether. She hadn't expected him to come after Sarianna, and she wondered just what Sarianna had told Sallie.

Cade's cool hazel gaze sliced through Vesta, and she felt a chill. He knew what she had done, she thought, and she was terrified. He had no sympathy for *her*.

"What news?" he asked politely.

"Well—Vesta has come to visit us with the good news that Jeralee is married, did you know? And she and her husband are staying at the hotel, while Vesta will stay with us. A very nice arrangement. I must remember to send Eban over with an open invitation for Jeralee and her husband to dine with us for as long as we remain here. And the rest, I think, is for Sarianna to tell you. Come, Vesta," she said briskly as Sarianna appeared in the hallway, followed by a panting Garnet, who had barely been able to keep up with her on her furiously brisk walk.

Vesta could not resist the command. The enmity between Sarianna and Cade was evident even to her eyes, and she was satisfied that the trouble she had caused was still fermenting between them.

"Sarianna?" Cade said politely.

"Rex is dead," she said baldly. "And he apparently showed some conscience. He left me a lot of money, and I'm pleased to tell you that I need not be a burden on you anymore."

"Fine words, Sarianna. But the burden of your body on mine is a pleasure. And I know you haven't forgotten, either," he added, and turned away from her. Endless complications, he thought furiously. Vesta, here. Money for Sarianna. Was that better or worse? Would he rather she come to him of her own volition or because she was forced to, merely by virtue of the fact she was a woman, and his wife. And God—what would she do with the money? He could just intuit her thinking. She would be after a house, a place to stay because she would not want to return to Savannah. She would want to spike his plans every which way and make him suffer as much and more than she had.

They were equal now, he thought; he didn't have to respect her feelings anymore. He could go after her with a vengeance now, and he fully intended to win the war between them.

Vesta's presence cast a pall over the house.

"Who is that old crow?" Patrick demanded when he finally summoned up enough nerve to call on her again.

"That is Vesta," Sarianna said, "a distant relative of Sallie's." Vesta heard what she said and fumed in silence.

"Sarianna . . ." Patrick began, and reached to pull her into his arms. He thought she might forgive him; but she was looking impossibly fragile and desirable, and he could not keep his hands away from her.

"Who is this?" Vesta demanded, coming into the room just as he managed to slide his arms around her.

"Mr. Patrick Bohan, a friend, this is Vesta Wayte, another cousin of Sallie Gill's, from Georgia," Sarianna said stiffly. She didn't like the look in Vesta's eyes one bit.

"Pleased to meet you," Vesta said, and promptly exited the room, closing the door behind her.

"Damn," Sarianna exploded. "Patrick, will you never listen?'

"Never. The minute I saw you this morning, Sarianna, I knew I must have you."

"God, it cannot be that you talk this way to all the women of your acquaintance," Sarianna said dourly. "I have said about all I am going to say to you."

"It's that damned Rensell who has been hanging around then, isn't it? The man just walked in and cut me right out with you," Patrick lashed out. "Tell me why, Sarianna. Tell me what is so appealing about him, why you'd choose him over me.'

"I don't owe you explanations."

"Hell. You owe me something, Sarianna."

"Good manners, perhaps," she agreed tightly. "This gets us nowhere, Patrick. I never evinced the kind of interest that would lead you to believe I would be interested in your pursuit. I wish you would believe that."

"Women never say what the hell they mean," he shot at her. "You don't mean that."

"I mean it."

"Has Rensell proposed?"

She gave a short harsh laugh. "Not likely, Patrick."

"So you're still not encumbered," he muttered, which was some little sense of satisfaction to him.

"I wouldn't say that either," Sarianna interposed. "Don't assume anything, Patrick, and just listen to what I say: I am not interested in anything more than friendship."

"Lying lips," Patrick said succinctly, coming after her again.

"You can stop right there," Sarianna said, and her hard voice and balled fists told him she was serious. "If you leave now, I won't hold this unmanly behavior against you. If you come after me again, I will scream the house down, and I do believe Cade is home, and Sallie. I think you must choose now, Patrick, between selfishness and good manners. I presume you are gentleman enough to do the right thing."

She turned her back on him then, brazen to the core, he thought, as he wheeled away from her and strode to the door. "Good-bye, Sarianna. I won't presume on your time again. You will have to come begging to me."

She whirled as the door closed behind him. Where had she heard those words before? And why the devil had she let herself in for them again?

Outside, beyond the hallway, Vesta, who had been avidly listening to the raised voices, rubbed her hands in glee.

She began a new tack. "Rex left you so much money, Sarianna, I don't see why you can't make some of it over to me."

"Why on earth would I do that?" Sarianna wondered; instantly, she was wary. They had only just sent off the papers which contained letters of verification as to her identity and a request to transfer the funds to a bank in Charleston, and it would be another week before that was accomplished. She had thought, however, she might begin making inquiries about leasing a house. The thought of that drove everything else from her mind, and Vesta's insidious request took her quite by surprise.

"I do feel that you owe me something, Sarianna, and so does Rex. All those years I raised you and took care of you . . ."

"Humph," Sarianna snorted, amazed at the depth to which Vesta could delude herself.

"All the hardships of life on Bredwood," Vesta sighed. "And of course," she added knowingly, "the little fact that apparently no one seems to know that you and Cade are married, if I heard that little scene aright this afternoon."

Sarianna almost laughed in her face, and then thought the better of it. "I see," she said slowly. "You're blackmailing me. You've heard enough to know that I've made a nice life here in Charleston and that to all intents and purposes no one is aware of my marriage to Cade, is that right? And you will keep my secret for a modest recompense?"

"A perfect summary," Vesta agreed.

"You must let me think about it," Sarianna said, and then she was dismayed because she had not turned Vesta down outright. No, that would be too kind, she thought. She felt such animosity toward Vesta, and she could not shake it. The woman was amoral, not of her flesh. In the intervening months between her marriage and Vesta's arrival here, Vesta had aged and thickened and she bore no resemblance to Dona anymore. Sarianna wondered if Vesta even looked in the mirror or noticed that the minute vestiges of beauty and similarity to Dona had totally disappeared. She was raddled, ugly and old, and she deserved some kind of retribution; but Sarianna did not quite know what it would be.

She saw Vesta's eyes fasten on her greedily at the dinner table, noting instantly the concern and care of the seating arrangements. She saw that Vesta knew instantly that she was loved and Vesta was not, and that they, Sallie Gill and Austin, had removed themselves from her just by the very way they seated her at the table.

And it was clear that Vesta had always wanted her to suffer and had never expected to experience any repercussions from her viciousness. But now she did, and as the hatred poured from her eyes and settled over the table like a thick matte blanket, she used the silence to push her case of prising money from Sarianna.

"I must indeed thank you for your hospitality," she said to Sallie Gill. "I sincerely hope that my other relatives will be so kind. Although, it would not be such a bad idea if Sarianna were to provide me with some kind of income. No one wants to be burdensome after so many years of having been independent and wealthy. How awful of Rex," she added, her voice breaking into dry sobs, "to leave me in such circumstances."

She never noticed everyone's acute embarrassment.

And later, she accosted Cade when he returned to the town house.

"I must speak with you."

"I have nothing to say to you, Vesta."

"Then perhaps I should have my say elsewhere," she said slyly.

"As you will," Cade said equably, turning away.

"Damn you," Vesta shrieked, "I *know* Sarianna has been pretending not to be married all these months. How would you like it if I told everybody? *EVERYBODY. And* embarrassed Sallie Gill so she couldn't show her face in Charleston ever again?"

"You're crazy," Cade said calmly, but he felt a fine tremor of fear for Sarianna. Vesta was right on the edge of doing something desperate. She cared nothing about Sallie Gill at all. Her whole force of concentration was bent on somehow hurting Sarianna—as if she could cause more damage than she had already, he thought venomously. He would kill her himself if she went near Sarianna.

He watched her in fascination as she got a grip on her emotions. The last thing she would want anyone to think was that she was crazy. "Nonsense," she said briskly, the maniacal tone gone from her tone. "I'm practical. Rex left me with nothing, and I want to negotiate."

"You have," Cade said brutally, "*nothing* to negotiate."

"I have a scandal," she contradicted, "and I will take it right to Sallie Gill."

Sarianna spent the ensuing days looking for a house. She wondered whether she really expected to find one, or whether it was a way of exercising her monetary muscle, and getting out of the town house and away from the stultifying air that surrounded Vesta.

Whatever it was, she felt a childlike amazement at the feeling of freedom that encompassed her once she stepped foot outside the town house grounds. There was only another week to be gotten through; and then Vesta would be sent packing, and she would have to make a decision.

Her house hunting was no idle chore to while away the hours, but she did have the feeling that perhaps she did not have the gumption to set up a household all by herself. Nonetheless, the moment she laid eyes on the house called Splendid, she knew she had come home. It was a mansion in the midst of the bustle of Charleston, set away from the noise and traffic on sumptuous verdant grounds that were the equal of any plantation home, and gave the impression of limitless space while being enclosed by a half-height, stone fence topped with lacy ironwork.

The house itself was built of mellow brick, two stories, with a hipped roof that supported four brick chimneys and an elaborately detailed center gable. The symmetry of it appealed to her, with its arched shuttered entrance and matching keystone decorated window above, and the two matching wings that hyphenated out from either side that looked as if they were supporting the main building. Each window was surrounded by a pair of matching shutters and topped with a flat white marble lintel. Across the front, beneath the second story windows and over the door, were inset panels of marble with a raised swag detail. Across from the circular drive in the very front of the house was a decorative garden with verdant bushes concealing the surprise within.

She loved the house, and the only drawback was, someone else was interested and had made an extremely tempting offer on it.

"Perhaps I may make an offer as well," Sarianna suggested boldly, and the lawyer who was arranging the sale of the house conceded that perhaps she might. He took it, in writing, and told her he would let her know. What he thought of a single female shopping for a house was not reflected on his face or in his manner, and Sarianna supposed, as she left him, it was really none of his business. But she wasn't averse to appealing to Austin Lundeen for help if there were any problem about it, and she railed in her mind against how constricted she was by these social rules because she was female.

Cade couldn't stop her, and he must know it, she thought. The world was hers now. She had only to reach out and take what she wanted.

Jeralee and Pierce came to dinner that night, and Vesta oozed a kind of mother-proud charm that was a bulwark against her resentment at seeing Cade and Sarianna at the same table, together and separated at the same time. Cade evinced no interest in Sarianna that Vesta could see, and the tenor of the evening was a feeling that it must be gotten through as quickly as possible.

"How nice you have it here," Jeralee said snidely to Lacey as she examined the lower reception rooms in the town house. "I wish I might have thought to come to Cousin Sallie before Sarianna did."

"Oh, but Sarianna needed help," Lacey told her seriously. "And there *you* were getting married all that time. I'm sure Mother would have helped you, too, if you had been in need.'

"Please," Jeralee said, "the only thing Sarianna has ever needed was to spoil things for everyone else. Especially me. She took Cade away from me, you know. She made him marry her."

"Oh, no," Lacey contradicted. "Sarianna isn't married. Everyone's tearing to engage her affections, and she has been so proper all this time. She would never have done anything like that if she were married. Look at how Mr. Rensell followed her here. I think he is dying of love for her. Isn't it romantic?"

Jeralee's eyes lit up as she listened to this artless dissertation of Sarianna's behavior. "Really? I must have misunderstood. Perhaps Mr. Rensell had wanted to marry her and she refused him, and then he came after her anyway."

"They haven't been terribly romantic together though," Lacey added consideringly. "He hasn't much time to win her, you know. We will be leaving in a week or so."

Jeralee knew very well, and she wondered how she could use this information. She, too, had been shocked to find Cade in Charleston, and she wondered why since he hardly seemed interested in Sarianna at all.

But looks could be deceiving, she thought. She wondered if her mother had any inkling of this interesting development about Sarianna. The scandal would be delightful, and Sarianna would be ostracized forever if anyone ever got wind of it.

Even as Lacey was showing her around the house, Vesta was dropping her little bombshell into Sallie Gill's lap. She had wanted to humiliate Sarianna, and here was the very moment: with her own daughter in the house, and Sallie and her husband at the table.

"I wonder if you know what has been going on under your very nose," she started out blandly. She saw Cade move, and then check himself out of the corner of her eye.

Sallie squeezed her husband's hand warningly under the table. "Perhaps you would be good enough to tell me," she suggested, and only Vesta missed the frosty tone of her voice.

"Well, I want you to know it has taken me a good long time and a thorough search of my conscience to even consider coming to you," Vesta said. "But I really feel that Sarianna has been misleading you and acting under improper circumstances and you should know about it."

"And what is it that Sarianna has done that is so improper?" Sallie asked coolly.

"She came to you, pretending that she was not married, and apparently has been flaunting herself all over Charleston as if she were eligible and looking for a husband."

"But my dear Vesta, why else do you think Cade is here? Of course I was aware of the circumstances. I would never have let Sarianna do anything that wasn't proper, even you must know that. And I must say it was hardly her fault that poor Bohan fell in love with her. She did not encourage him or anyone else, Vesta, and if you spread such lies, you will be the one who has much to answer for."

And so, Vesta thought blankly, the family moves together and unites around Sarianna. Of course Cade was here; where else would he be? He would not have let her take a single misstep, and neither would Sallie; she could see that clearly now, but it was only because Sarianna had beat her out again. Everyone loved her and they hated Vesta, and that was how it had always been all her life.

"I should have known Sarianna would have confided in you," she said at last, trying to gather some shreds of dignity around her. "I will say good-night to Jeralee now, and I will make plans to remove in the morning."

Cade found Sarianna in the parlor. "The old bitch," he said succinctly as he entered the room. "Are you all right?"

"I can't take much more," Sarianna said from her place by the piano niche.

She was staring out the window, although all she could see was the darkness of the garden, and hear the noise of the retreat of Jeralee and Pierce. Jeralee and Pierce! She could have sworn Pierce hated her, but she was beginning to feel she existed somewhere outside of reality where nothing made any kind of sense. Truly the only solution was to make her own reality.

"You don't need to," Cade said, coming up behind her. "You broke Vesta, Sarianna, and you did not need to do anything but be yourself. She has no choice but to go away now and leave you alone."

"And you?" she asked point-blank. "What choice do you have?

Will you go away and leave me alone?"

"I think not," he said quietly. "What are you going to do about it? You can let me in, Sarianna, or you can close me out. You never would listen to explanations, and maybe you were right, but it doesn't mitigate my wanting you desperately, or your response to me. You can't negate that no matter what you feel about the past."

Sarianna ran a tired hand through her golden curls. "I suppose not," she admitted at last, "but I'm planning to stay in Charleston, Cade, and I don't see room in my life to try to cope with the mistake that you made."

"And how may I, if you won't give me that room?" he demanded, grasping her shoulders.

"Perhaps I don't want you to."

"Perhaps," he said roughly, "you just love suffering. Maybe I took you away from it all these months. Maybe you lived at Bredwood because that was just what you wanted, and not what you could not escape. Maybe I believed in an illusion of what I thought you were, Sarianna. I'm beginning to think we all have a vision of you, and none of us knows the real Sarianna. I think you're a martyr, Sarianna, and you only believe in mortification of the flesh." He pulled her against him, wanting to shake her, beat her, do anything to move her out of that blankness of feeling that would admit no desire. "And humiliation of the soul," he added in a growl before he crushed his mouth on hers. But this was not the way to win her.

She was passive in his hands and under his onslaught. His fiery emotion and Vesta's fulminating hatred were too much in one night. Nor could she accept that the violence of his assault had anything to do with him loving her. She did not know what love was; she never had known. Only Sallie had given her a faint inkling of what it was to love, and even she was growing weary of Sarianna's vacillation.

Cade forced himself away from her before his senses billowed out of control. "Oh, God, Sarianna," he groaned, "I can't get you out of my blood. How much must I atone for one terrible mistake? Tell me—tell me what I have to do, for love of you, and love of the child we should have had that that miscreant murdered. *Tell me!*"

"Tell *me* who murdered our love," Sarianna whispered, fighting him, almost in tears. "And then maybe I will know what to do."

"If I told you, you wouldn't believe me," he hissed, his body aching with futility. There had never been a chance for them: Vesta—and

Dona—had always stood in the way. His hands left her shoulders, and she slumped against the wall. "The past murdered our love," he told her harshly, "and she's a mistress who will *never* let go."

She knew it, too. She felt no surprise when he left her to her grief.

Deep in the night, Vesta woke from her dreams. She had very few hours before the end finally came. She would leave, and no one would care where she went or what happened to her, not even Jeralee, who would be on her way back to Savannah with the ill-starred failure of all their plans.

Jeralee was practical, Vesta thought. She knew when to stop; she knew when her mother was treading shaky ground. She would never have wealth, she would never have Cade, she could never hope for more than she had attained at that very moment in time, and she was willing to accept it because she also knew how to make do.

Vesta did not know that. But then her daughter had never known Dona, had always felt superior to Sarianna. But Vesta had always had a Dona in her life to overshadow her. Even in the person of Sarianna, Dona had singed the corners of the life she had stolen from her. She was always there, always laughing. She had been laughing when Vesta killed her in the shadowy copse after her rendezvous with all her men, one after the other, so she could tell them all she was finished with them, from Cade right down to Parker and then Rex. She had planned to leave Rex, and Vesta, eavesdropping in the bushes, was absolutely sure there was still another man whom Dona had enslaved. Her fury was boundless that Dona drew men to her with such effortless ease, and she, Vesta, could not have the one man she craved.

She had spied on Dona all the time then, because she was living at Bredwood, but after Dona's body had been discovered, she went to Savannah as soon as she reasonably could in the hopes that someday, sometime Rex would come looking for her. But the whole thing got tangled up, and even though Rex had rescued her, he had never ever cared for her; and the less he cared the more she punished Sarianna. That was the only way it could be.

Even now, she thought foggily, as she roused herself from sleep. Sarianna must be destroyed. If Sarianna were dead, Vesta could sleep and the nightmares would go away. That was the way it had to be, she thought; and Dona would die, too. The laughter would stop, and she might, after all, find some peace.

Under her pillow, she reached for the knife she had secreted from the evening meal and fondled it like the lover she had never had.

Sarianna climbed into her bed, too weary to even pull down the covers, and lay curled up on her side. She felt the room close in on her, as nebulous and encroaching as the past.

"The past murdered our love," he had said, and it was true, she thought in anguish. He had not made a move nor had she that wasn't dogged by a memory of Dona. Dona was at the root of everything, and how did one destroy a ghost? How powerful she was, all these years later, in death. Cade had become wealthy because of her; Sarianna had been immured at Bredwood because of her; Cade had come seeking a wife there because of her; and Cade had married her because of Dona . . . a litany of becauses that she thought might crush her altogether if she thought about them a moment longer. And yet—the past was the reason that Sallie Gill had taken her in, and the past was why Vesta had come running; and all in all there was no escape from the past—ever.

And her baby—the past had murdered her baby. If she were going insane, she might even have said it was Dona who had been in that carriage, and Dona who had spurred on the careless driver. Dona, somewhere in Savannah, wreaked havoc with the tender strands that were beginning to bind her and Cade together.

She *was* going insane. Dona had died—*how* many years ago? And they were all chained to her, imprisoned by her. *That* was the insanity.

Her mother.

Her body began shivering violently.

Her legacy.

Her skin crawled.

Her taint.

She pulled the cover up and around her shaking body like a barrier against something unseen in the darkness.

Her fault. She looked like Dona and she acted like Dona, and for one mad moment in the dead of the night she could almost convince herself she *was* Dona.

She would never be free of Dona, and there was no hope for her and Cade. Dona would always be between them, and Savannah, and

432

whatever had happened there to turn Cade against her.

Shadows moved, and she felt a rising terror. The walls might close in on her and crush her: her agony crushed her, too momentous to bear.

She felt the tears erupt from a place she could not remember, and the burden of her grief suddenly became so real, so heavy.

Someone was on her, out of the shadows and haunted graves, the ghost who would not let her mourn, heavily on her, grabbing at her, scratching her, grunting and cursing all over her, pulling at her arms, her hair, her clothing.

A madness propelled her, and her nemesis. A shriek rent the darkness: "Dona lives!" And with that convocation, her nemesis attacked her. A blade sliced into the cover, and she twisted away. Another thrust into the pillow where her head had just lain. A third caught her dress before she could jerk herself off the bed, and a steely hand enclosed her arm.

"Dona dies," a chilling voice whispered in her ear, and she knew who would kill her and she even knew why. Here was the murderer of her burgeoning love and her life, the one being for whom Dona would always be alive.

She screamed as Vesta leapt on her, and the knife came down once again, and again and again, slashing at her hair, her dress, the cover, the pillow because Vesta could not see; Vesta thrashed as blindly as she in the night, and Vesta fought her with the strength of a man, two men, and her undermining lifelong loathing of Dona.

The blade slicked by her cheek and drew blood. Then she sensed Vesta lifting it again, and she heard the animal growl from the base of the throat that told her Vesta meant to kill her with this stroke. Her body grew taut, and she sought to define the instant when Vesta's arm wrenched downward toward her body.

It came almost instantly, and she rolled her body as hard and as jerkily as she could, throwing Vesta off balance. The blade slashed into her shoulder as she pulled Vesta with her, and Vesta toppled off of the bed.

She shrieked again and lunged at the dark shadow on the bed, the knife swiping Sarianna as she threw herself to one side.

The door burst open, and a long finger of light from a lamp illuminated the wild terror of Vesta's eyes. "*You!*" she screamed, and propelled her body at him, the knife at the ready, as he leapt onto her at the same time.

Sallie Gill, at the door with the lamp, moved slowly into the room as they tussled on the floor and Vesta's curses permeated the air. "You bastard, you son of a bitch, you—you—you didn't take the bait, you bastard, did you; you wouldn't believe that little bitch could betray you, did you, and you didn't . . . you wouldn't believe it of Dona, you stupid louse. They're the same damn piece of garbage . . . one and the same—mother, daughter, the same, the same, the same . . ."

Her voice petered out as Cade pinned her underneath him and the knife clattered to the floor. His eyes shot to Sarianna, who sat curled in a ball, clutching her midriff as if she were in pain, tears streaming down her cheeks unchecked, and he pulled viciously on Vesta's hair. "Tell Sarianna what you did, you old bitch," he hissed. "Tell everyone what you did, you lousy stinking old bitch."

"Nothing, nothing, the same . . ." Vesta muttered.

Austin and Lacey crowded into the room, and Cade looked up at them, his face a blank. "She tried to kill Sarianna." He lifted himself off of her disgustedly and picked up the knife. "She's been trying to kill Sarianna for years." He thrust it beneath Vesta's chin. "I swear, old lady, I'd slit your throat right now, except you need it to tell Sarianna what you did in Savannah. Go *on*, tell her!"

"No," Sarianna whispered, but the tears blinded her eyes and clogged her throat.

"Nothing to tell," Vesta rasped. "You didn't take the bait, the bait, the bait . . ."

"Maybe the hell I did," Cade growled. "*Tell* her."

Vesta looked around her uncertainly, and her eyes lit on the knife not an inch away from her throat. "We made a plan to punish Sarianna. We made Cade believe she was going to have Pierce's child. And it worked, it almost completely worked. . . ."

"And then you murdered the baby you so maliciously maligned," Cade charged harshly. "And I would not have put it past you to have done it deliberately."

There was a deadly silence, and then a long keening cry cut through the air. Sarianna! Cade threw himself on the bed and gathered her shuddering body into his arms. "Take that thing away," he ordered Austin, who marched in and lifted Vesta to her feet and led her into the hallway.

"Cade . . ." Sallie put a hand out to him, and he waved it off.

434

"Leave the lamp," he said, his voice lifeless. "I'll come down soon."

She set the lamp down on a dresser and left the room.

And then it was only the two of them, alone with hopeless sobs and the long repressed tears of a lifetime that could never wash the past away.

28

She cried. She didn't know where the wellspring of all those tears came from, and all those anguished sobs. She felt as if she were standing outside herself, watching. Cade held her and rubbed her back and her hair, touched her face, kissed away her tears, and finally, he let his own mingle with hers.

"I love you, Sarianna," he whispered against the trail of tears on her skin, and she felt his lips and the brush of his wet cheek against hers. "I loved our baby; I wanted it. And then I let her kill our love, and I let her kill our baby. It is my sin, Sarianna, and I'll pay for it the rest of my life. Sarianna . . ."

He murmured her name over and over, and his touch comforted her, as did the sorrow in his voice and the tears in his eyes.

She cried. She heard all that he said, and she remembered all that had happened; and she did not know how they could make it right. She only knew that his arms supported her and that his words were a balm. She understood—a little—now, and for the moment it was enough. There had been a reason, a momentum, an evil that had perpetrated the treachery, and it had not been her.

Soon, soon she could make sense of it, even though it made a convoluted kind of sense now. It was just that her tears would stop and her yearning for the child who had died on such a whim of fate, and by such a sinful design. The monstrosity of it was incalculable, and the reason boiled down to one simple motive: the haunting impetus of Dona.

She could not stop crying. He rocked her against him, murmuring soothing sounds in her ear, swallowing her grief and taking it inside

436

him, drawing it from her like poison from a snake bite.

And he cried with her, mourning his son, reaching for hope, holding her with his strength until the sun flooded through the curtains of the room and Sarianna lay sleeping in his arms.

"She is sleeping," he told Sallie when he joined her at the dining room table. Vida brought him coffee and some hot biscuits in a napkin-lined basket.

Sallie was silent. She didn't know quite what to say. "Austin locked her in an upstairs bedroom," she told him finally. "Jeralee and Pierce have left town. What are you going to do with her?"

"I don't know," Cade said tiredly. "What would you do?"

Sallie shrugged. "This is so unbelievable. I've known Vesta for years with never a hint of any of this."

"I wouldn't think so. As long as Sarianna was confined to Bredwood and Rex was alive and money was pouring in, everything was fine, is my surmise. And I don't think I would be surprised to hear she was wildly jealous of Sarianna because she looked like Dona. My fine hand in this didn't help matters either, I might add. I came roaring back to Sawny on Vesta's invitation—although I was on my way there anyway—with the express intention of confronting Rex and snaring Jeralee away from him because I thought he cared about her. Imagine the shock of seeing Sarianna and finding out what her life there was like."

"So you carried her off," Sallie said. "Yes, I can quite see how you did that. How tragic."

"I blackmailed Rex and bullied Sarianna, and the result was four people died, and Sarianna was almost killed. I would not be surprised to find out that Vesta murdered Rex because she thought she would inherit. What a laugh Rex must have had when he was making out that will. His express intention all Sarianna's life was to keep her by his side, and then he's caught in a position where he has to give her her independence in order to cut out Vesta." He shook his head. "Such hate."

"Well, let me tell you what I am going to do," Sallie said. "I am going to stay in Charleston with Sarianna while Austin and Lacey return to Arboretum. You are going to move back to a hotel. Sarianna may not want to see you at all, I have no idea, but I intend to let her heal at her own time. She's had too many shocks and too much heaped on her all her life, and surely more than a woman should bear in the last six months. You can come to see her, if she wants you, and meanwhile you can decided what you are going to do about Vesta, because I don't want her anywhere near Charleston two days from now."

"That sounds fair," he said tiredly, drinking his coffee, and pushing away the biscuits. He didn't know what hunger was anymore. He only knew the dull ache that had taken the place of his yearning for Sarianna.

"Tell me about the baby," Sallie said suddenly, her sympathy in her eyes and the tone of her voice.

He responded to it, even feeling a pang of gratitude that she divined that he need to talk about it. But then—he didn't know what to say. "Sarianna told me about it before I went up to Savannah with the first baling of the season. I stupidly gave over my town house to Vesta and Jeralee when we went to Haverhill, and just as stupidly, I decided to stay there for the week I would be in town to complete my business and replenish the stores. Vesta didn't come out and say anything about Pierce to me. She knew I would never have believed her. Rather, she threw a little party, and let all the innuendos swirl around until it was impossible not to come to the conclusion that the baby might not be mine. And I foolishly let that, and Sarianna's resemblance to Dona persuade me that it possibly could be true. Shortly thereafter, Vesta and Jeralee *and* Pierce came down for a surprise visit. Their carriage struck Sarianna. To this day, I can't understand how. And I believe the timing and the guest list were calculated and deliberate."

Sallie was silent for a long, long time. "This is insupportable," she said angrily. "I want that woman punished, Cade, and I don't care how you do it."

"Oh, don't worry, Sallie. I'll think of something appropriate, I promise you I will."

A week later, a note came for Sarianna, and she looked up from her pillow with a rare smile of delight. "I own a house, Sallie."

"My dear Sarianna, are you addled?" Sallie sat down at the foot of the bed. "Let me see. Oh, my goodness, Bartlett's. You're not making

438

a joke. When?"

"Two weeks ago. He showed me Splendid, and I made an offer on the spot."

"He must have checked your bank account and your references," Sallie said dryly. "Ladies don't go about buying houses around here just on the whim of the moment."

"But I'm the eccentric Sarianna Broydon, with all that lovely money."

"Are you?" Sallie questioned carefully. Certainly Sarianna looked much, much better, less haunted and far more lively.

"I intend to be," Sarianna retorted spiritedly. "I have to spend this money, certainly. I would love to live there, and I never intend to return to Savannah. At least," she added, her face clouding up, "for any length of time."

Sallie didn't offer any objection. "As long as you're sure, I will have Austin come up and make the arrangements," she offered.

"I would like that," Sarianna said gratefully. She set aside the note. "There was another bidder. I'm glad I won out."

Sallie left her then to write a note to Austin, and Sarianna made herself comfortable in bed, filling herself with comforting thoughts of living at Splendid. That lovely house, those gracious rooms with the shining woodwork and elegant proportions. She would spend a lifetime furnishing it, and she would never leave. Maybe, she thought, someday she might share it with someone.

Share it with Cade.

She supposed, as she lay there, content with the success of the first independent thing she had done for herself, she had to think about Cade. All week long now she had resolutely pushed thoughts of him out of her head, clamping down on anguish that seeped through her at the thought of Vesta's treachery. And he took the whole blame on himself, she thought, her eyes filling with tears, which—nowadays—they did so easily whenever she harkened back to that night, which she tried very hard not to do.

As if she were so innocent, as if she had not given Vesta the fuel with which she could burn them both.

Share it with Cade.

The thought became intrusive now that the house was a reality. Another beginning, with Vesta gone and all her mean tricks accounted for. He hadn't wanted her because he thought she had slept with

Pierce, and Pierce was on his way to her when the carriage knocked her down.

They were puppets, she and Cade. Vesta had pulled the strings, and everything had gone her way . . . almost. But Vesta had not forced her to let Pierce squire her around Savannah once she arrived there. She had planned her own downfall all by herself. Cade could not be allowed to take the blame for the thing that she had instigated by her unconscionable behavior. She *had* been Dona then, toying with fate, and fate had slapped her face.

And Cade had cried because she with her callous carelessness had been the fault and the root of it. He had loved their child; he had wanted it. He wanted her.

She believed it. As long as she understood why, she could believe it. But he wanted her now, after she had seen his tears and realized her own culpability. All that suffering between them, and no one was to blame but Vesta, and her own stupidity.

Not a taint, just a heedless desire to hand her life over to her enemy.

She wondered if Cade could ever forgive *her*. She wondered if he would ever want to see her again.

A week later she signed some papers with Austin by her side, wrote a draft for an enormous amount of money that did not seem real for the paper it was written on, and came away the proud owner of the house called Splendid.

Austin drove her over, and Sallie Gill met them there; then Sarianna took them through her new house. "Yes," Sallie Gill mused as she stepped into the long parlor which stretched from front to back of the house to the right of the entrance hallway. "This was the Crocker house. They had no heirs, and when old Mr. Crocker died last month . . . well—it's a sorry thing when a man dies without heirs." She did not look at Sarianna as she spoke. Rather, she stepped through the connecting door to the library wing and let the words sink in and become meaningful.

The house had five bedrooms, two parlors, a library, a dining room and sitting room to the left of the hallway, and a morning room and the kitchen in the opposite wing.

Sarianna loved the house.

"It's a big house," Sallie said. "A comfortable house."

"There are servants' quarters over the two wings, and that makes everything very tidy," Sarianna said. "I should not need more than a cook and a housekeeper, perhaps a personal maid."

"We'll start looking," Sallie said. "There are free workers in town, or we can arrange something from Arboretum. You can talk finances with Austin." She smiled at Sarianna. "Everything proper, Sarianna."

Sarianna smiled back.

They returned to the town house to find that once more Cade had not called.

When would he come, Sarianna wondered as the days rolled by and she spent healing hours on the verandah staring at the garden. She spent the days purchasing things for her house: a bedstead, sheets, dishes, table linens, but she was curiously reluctant to go on a major shopping spree.

And one afternoon, she understood why: She was waiting for Cade, and Cade obviously was not coming. Maybe he had gone back to Savannah. Maybe he had decided to abandon her altogether.

She couldn't believe the savage turn of her thoughts. She did not want him to go anywhere. She wanted him *there*.

And of course, when he came, she was nowhere around. She was sound asleep in her deep comfortable bed in her room in Sallie's house.

When she awakened, he was sitting at the foot of her bed, and she thought it was a dream, so thoroughly did time tumble backward to those first days in Savannah.

"Hello," she said, and she remembered that she had said just that to him in Savannah, too; if he answered, she thought, she would know he was real.

His expression softened and his eyes glinted. She looked so rested and buoyant even though the sadness still lurked behind her eyes. She had done so very well without him.

But he had known she would. "Hello, Sarianna," he said, and reached his hand out to take hers.

The grasp of his firm hand sent a living feeling spiraling through her. He was real—and the moment his fingers touched her, she came alive, too. But she felt an invasive fear that he had come to tell her something she did not want to hear.

She took a deep breath. "Where have you been?"

He removed his hand, stood up and walked to the window. "I took Vesta back to Savannah."

"Oh, yes? And why?" Had Sallie known, and if she had, why had she not told her? Sarianna wondered peevishly.

He waited a moment before he answered. How, after all, would Sarianna greet the news that Sallie had not wanted to cause a scandal by having Vesta arrested? "Sallie did not want her arrested in Charleston, Sarianna. We both wanted her to suffer much more than she would have in a cell."

"How bloodthirsty of Sallie," Sarianna murmured; even she had not thought so far ahead as what she wanted to happen to Vesta.

"Yes. What we decided to do was reinstate her in the town house with hired attendants who will keep her there, in abject luxury, and strict orders to never let her go out or have company. She may have whatever she wants that money can buy, Sarianna, but she cannot have freedom. She can only have the knowledge that she is living squarely in the middle of a city in the lap of luxury, and she cannot do anything but watch the outside world go by."

She looked at him with luminous eyes. "You did that for me."

"I did that for both of us," he said harshly, relieved that she did not protest his decision.

"And where will you go now?" she asked, a thread of fear running through her question.

"Where shall I go, Sarianna?" But what a burden to place on her— to let her make the decision whether he stayed or went. "I meant to relocate to Charleston," he added suddenly. "I was going to buy a house, Sarianna, and bring our child here. I was going to do a lot of things," he finished bitterly, "and now I can do none."

Tears scorched her eyes. He had been going to do all of that—and without his saying it, she knew it had been for her. She held out her arms to him. "You did one thing," she whispered, as he came slowly to the bed and let her touch him, "one wonderful thing. You held me and you cried for our child, Cade." She leaned forward to pull him down onto the bed. "And I cried for my stupidity in handing my enemy a weapon she could use to harm us both irreparably." The tears started then, again; she could not have stopped them to save her life. "My burden, too, Cade. My fault. My sin. If you hated me for the rest of your life, I could accept it because I was the one who gave them something to talk about. Something to use against you—and our child."

Her body tightened as he did not respond, but she had said too much now to not finish the rest. She sniffed back her sobs and looked away from him for the final confession. "And then—a lot later, I wondered if all my denials that you mocked, all my lies—were the same thing as your rejection. And my worst sin was I cared so much and I still didn't want to find out. It was easier to let you carry the whole thing."

He broke then, pulling her against his chest in an involuntary motion. Her arms wrapped around him awkwardly in that sitting position, but it didn't matter. She buried her face in his chest and cried once again, for her grief over the truths she had told him and the blame that she accepted. She felt his emotion and his relief to the marrow of her bones. This, she thought, was the foundation of the new beginning. In his arms, at last, she felt a dawning hope.

He courted her, with Sallie as their chaperone, and she felt as if she had been born all over again. The pain receded to be replaced by a sharing understanding around which hovered a tentative commitment.

Cade did not want to force her; he wanted her to be sure, and he longed for her with a rare passion that was impossible to keep out of his eyes. He didn't know quite how long she needed to heal and to come to terms with all the betrayals in her life. He was never sure he had not done the most to harm her, even with Sallie's assurances that, to the contrary, he had done the most to help her.

On the other hand, however, Sallie thought Sarianna was being a little too particular with Cade. "He *is* your husband, after all," she told her tartly, "and damn it, Sarianna, *I* miss mine!"

"Well then—*leave*," Sarianna invited her, mindful of the anomaly of her dismissing her hostess from her own home.

"*Have* you told him about Splendid?" Sallie asked.

"Not yet," Sarianna said ruefully. "I haven't figured out how."

"And yet—he had been going to buy a house."

"And it was probably Splendid," Sarianna rejoined ironically. "Would you not trust us here?"

"For how long?" Sallie asked dryly.

"Two weeks?"

"I believe I might, if you'll let me leave Vida and Garnet with you to make sure you behave."

"I do *not* intend to behave," Sarianna said severely. "I *intend* to beg Cade for his favors, because Lord knows otherwise, he will never touch *me*."

"My fragile flower. Come to Arboretum when you settle all that, my dear."

"I will," she promised faithfully, and within two days she and Cade were waving Sallie off in the carriage, without the least thought of the scandal *they* might cause should any of Sallie's friends become aware of their living in the town house together.

Dinner was fraught with tension, and the first time they had really been alone together since she left Haverhill.

Afterward, there was an awkwardness that was almost comical, with Vida hovering around them and not knowing quite what to do with herself. Sarianna sent her out of the room and said, "Join me on the verandah when you're ready." Her nerves were jumping and her fear that he did not want her now, because he was so intensely quiet all through dinner and hardly seemed to know what to say to her after they were done.

He sat alone with a brandy in the dining room, his body tight with unfulfilled desire, and he didn't know how much more he could stand. He had come to find her to make her whole, and now that the pieces had been picked up and sorted, she was again in one piece; but whether she wanted him, or some kind of life together, he did not know.

How much of a chance would he be taking if he made the overture tonight? he wondered. And what would it cost him if he didn't?

He set his goblet aside resolutely. She was his wife, and he wanted her badly; if she did not want him, he would know it soon enough.

He walked out of the dining room and stopped short. There were her shoes and stockings lying in a heap just by the dining room door. Farther on down the hallway lay her simple muslin dress. Beyond that the steel cage of her hoop. Nearby a pile of petticoats. At the door her chemise and drawers. And outside, a shadow in the perfumed darkness, Sarianna in her nakedness, waiting for him, breathless with her overwhelming need for him.

"Cade . . ." her voice pleaded in the deep darkness.

444

"I'm here."

"I'm waiting."

A throat-catching moment passed before he came to her, and she felt the rough material of his clothing against her naked skin. His arms surrounded her and his mouth touched hers. "I need your kisses," she whispered against the curve of his lips. "I need you."

"Are you sure?" he murmured, sliding his hands over the smooth curves of her skin. How perfect she was, firm and soft, and all writhing motion as he touched her here and there, grazing her breasts to awaken their yearning, nipping her lips to beg for her kisses.

He held her so tightly as she gave him her tongue, and she wrapped herself around him, reveling in her nakedness and the feeling of his hard male muscles holding her as if he would never let her go.

"Make love to me in the garden," she whispered, and he carried her off of the verandah and laid her on a soft swath of lawn. The grass felt cool and soft as a feather tickling, and his long clothed body next to her was as natural as the earth. The darkness enfolded them, intimate and caressing.

"How I've missed you," he murmured, as his tongue explored every inch of her skin, from her lips down to her neck, and shoulders and arms, her fingers, one by one, and the lush curve of her breast. "How I want you. Sarianna, can you feel how I want you?"

"I feel you," she whispered, as the thrust of his hips against her thigh expressed his desire in a very satisfying way. "Let me feel you."

His mouth covered hers as her hands worked at his waistband. When he was free, her hands reached for him avidly, and she breathed against his mouth, "I feel you."

Her hands teased him gently, grasping here and sliding there, as his hand found equal fascination in its play with her breast, and in touching the tight hard nipple and teasing it until she almost gave in to the tingling point of pleasure.

Oh, but not yet, not yet. It had been so long since she had held him and kissed him and whispered the entreating words that aroused him as much as her hands and her body.

"Kiss me again," she demanded huskily; and he gave her what she wanted, the whole of his maleness and the crush of his kisses, and he surrendered to her magical hands and lips.

This was the Sarianna he wanted, the Sarianna he needed. His again, as her body heaved against him, demanding his caresses.

"Tell me now," he whispered against her mouth as she ravaged his lips with flicking little kisses that left them both breathless.

"I want you," she breathed, kissing his lips between each word. "I need you."

"I love you," he whispered.

"Come to me now," she begged him, her hands already showing him, pulling him with an urgency that was frantic with need, showing him how much she wanted to feel his living heat within her body.

He poised himself over her and let her love envelop him completely, renewed and reborn, at one with her at last in the dark fragrant garden, as it was in the beginning.

SURRENDER TO THE
PASSION OF RENÉ J. GARROD!

WILD CONQUEST   (2132, $3.75)

Lovely Rausey Bauer never expected her first trip to the big city to include being kidnapped by a handsome stranger claiming to be her husband. But one look at her abductor and Rausey's heart began to beat faster. And soon she found herself desiring nothing more than to feel the touch of his lips on her own.

ECSTASY'S BRIDE   (2082, $3.75)

Irate Elizabeth Dickerson wasn't about to let Seth Branting wriggle out of his promise to marry her. Though she despised the handsome Wyoming rancher, Elizabeth would not go home to St. Louis without teaching Seth a lesson about toying with a young lady's affections — a lesson in love he would never forget!

AND DON'T MISS OUT ON THIS OTHER
HEARTFIRE SIZZLERS FROM ZEBRA BOOKS!

LOVING CHALLENGE   (2243, $3.75)

by Carol King

When the notorious Captain Dominic Warbrooke burst into Laurette's Harker's eighteenth birthday ball, the accomplished beauty challenged the arrogant scoundrel to a duel. But when the captain named her innocence as his stakes, Laurette was terrified she'd not only lose the fight, but her heart as well!

Available wherever paperbacks are sold, or order direct from the Publisher. Send cover price plus 50¢ per copy for mailing and handling to Zebra Books, Dept. 2665, 475 Park Avenue South, New York, N.Y. 10016. Residents of New York, New Jersey and Pennsylvania must include sales tax. DO NOT SEND CASH.

SURRENDER YOUR HEART
TO CONSTANCE O'BANYON!

MOONTIDE EMBRACE (2182, $3.95)

When Liberty Boudreaux's sister framed Judah Slaughter for murder, the notorious privateer swore revenge. But when he abducted the unsuspecting Liberty from a New Orleans masquerade ball, the brazen pirate had no idea he'd kidnapped the wrong Boudreaux — unaware who it really was writhing beneath him, first in protest, then in ecstasy.

GOLDEN PARADISE (2007, $3.95)

Beautiful Valentina Barrett knew she could never trust wealthy Marquis Vincente as a husband. But in the guise of "Jordanna", a veiled dancer at San Francisco's notorious Crystal Palace, Valentina couldn't resist making the handsome Marquis her lover!

SAVAGE SUMMER (1922, $3.95)

When Morgan Prescott saw Sky Dancer standing out on a balcony, his first thought was to climb up and carry the sultry vixen to his bed. But even as her violet eyes flashed defiance, repulsing his every advance, Morgan knew that nothing would stop him from branding the high-spirited beauty as his own!

SEPTEMBER MOON (1838;, $3.95)

Petite Cameron Madrid would never consent to allow arrogant Hunter Kingston to share her ranch's water supply. But the handsome landowner had decided to get his way through Cameron's weakness for romance — winning her with searing kisses and slow caresses, until she willingly gave in to anything Hunter wanted.

SAVAGE SPRING (1715, $3.95)

Being pursued for a murder she did not commit, Alexandria disguised herself as a boy, convincing handsome Taggert James to help her escape to Philadelphia. But even with danger dogging their every step, the young woman could not ignore the raging desire that her virile Indian protector ignited in her blood!

Available wherever paperbacks are sold, or order direct from the Publisher. Send cover price plus 50¢ per copy for mailing and handling to Zebra Books, Dept. 2665, 475 Park Avenue South, New York, N.Y. 10016. Residents of New York, New Jersey and Pennsylvania must include sales tax. DO NOT SEND CASH.